HYPNOTIZING GAME

Who Cross You
It's really not a game

By Earnest Bennett

To buy the book or make comments, please contact:
Earnest Bennett, Jr.
Georgia Gorilla Publishing
1125 Osborne St., SW
Atlanta., GA 30310
Please send $16.95 plus $3.50 delivery charges send cashier
checks of money orders (sorry no C.O.D. or personal checks).
Buy ten or more books and get a 40% discount
ISBN 0-9670248-0-3 (paperback)
Printed in the United States of America
Library of Congress Cataloging-in-publication Data

Because of this book my so called friends really hate me now,
because of this book my family crossed me, because of this
book many lives will be saved if they play the game how it
goes, because of this book many lives will be destroyed if they
take it the wrong way, because of this book some say I am a
philosopher, and because of this book some say I am the
devil's advocate, because of this book the world will now
know the truth, and because of this book I am a self made
millionaire. DONE DEAL!!!!!!!!

99-94309
CIP

HYPNOTIZING GAME

Who Cross You
It's really not a game

By Earnest Bennett
Copyright 1999

DEDICATION

This book is dedicated in the
memories of my gangster
gangster friend Ezee;
my good friend Tunkman;
my cousin Bobby McDonald;
my 'hood thug friend Stink;
and to my little brother Nikia
Bennett.
R.I.P.
I miss y'all.

And all of the rest of the fallen
souljas who lost their lives
 in this dirty world.
The game ain't been the same
without y'all one love.

HYPNOTIZING GAME

Who Cross You
It's really not a game

INTRODUCTION

A Supernatural Playa Pulp Fiction Melodrama

Hello world. I'm going to give you some game, fuck you if you don't use it get ready, get ready, get ready get ready get ready for the truth. What's love? This book gonna shed light on your troubled confused soul and mine. This book is gonna let you know a friend from a foe. The real from the fake, good from evil, rich or poor, bitch or 'ho'. enemy or brother, hustler or buster, lobster or crab, and a rock from a slab. I seen a lotta shit in this crazy world, and I'm not gonna take no shorts tellin' you about it. When I first got off in this poisonous game of jackin', robbin', selling dope and killin' I had to do some crazy shit to see was I made for this game. Yes, I said poisonous. Because this game hold more venom than all the snakes and spiders in the world. So just sit back and listen, because I'm gonna tell it to you raw, uncut, and unedited.

A book like this should have been out about the game. But see, niggas ain't got the time. See, when you're poor you say shit like, "All I want is a million dollars and fuck the game." But that's easier said than done. Niggas make a million and be like gotta get that money, man workin' on some more millions, still in the game cause they fall in love with it. And I'm tellin' you, don't fall in love with a game that has no rules. But we do cars, clothes, money, and 'ho's, material things that comes and goes. Clothes, money, cars, and 'ho's comes with envy, jealousy, greed, and malicious rumors and that shit can kill you.

But really, I'm not tryin' to dogg out my black brothers and sisters, it just we need to wake up 'cause this game is the realest. In this game you got some womens that love to get down and dirty in the street, constantly lying, tricking, and setting up niggas for the kill. And brothers are the same way, running around here with that Chucky love playin' a nigga's home boy trying to assassinate their character. Some niggas fall victim and some don't. The ones that do lay dead in the cemetery over some bullshit and the ones that don't fall for the mess are those you see along with few friends and sometimes none. This goes for the ladies also. This is the only game I know where you get lots and lots of so-called friends just because you're sittin' on stacks. Picture this: just think back, way back, when you had no stacks--niggas stayed far away from your broke ass. A true friend will be there no matter what. Broke, busted, disgusted, down and out, a true friend will be there. But check it out when that down and out turn from rags to riches. They will doggout the one's that stayed true to the game with them.

Look, I wrote this book from the heart. I hope you like it. It's for the ones in the game and the ones who are just thinkin' about getting in the game or would just like to know about it. I hope after you read this book you will say, "Fuck the game!" because the more people that gets into this game the more people will die in this game and that's sad 'cause when you're at the top of the ladder you're the most hated. And believe me, the Devil knows what type of cheese you like on your trap. So don't be fooled.

THE GAME

Get ready for life itself. These ninety-six tricks I'm going to put down for you is like all over the world, but not like in Atlanta!

Calling all freaks, pimps, players, pushers, tricks, lesbians, old and young kids...

Murder, Death, Kill

Peep your game...

...Never let a nigga peep your game; if you do, it will lead to this...

In 1992, (game in progress) seven players just hit a major lick: two hundred fifty birds (keys of cocaine), four million in cash, four pounds of weed. Four supposedly have died in this hit, the other three left town for Atlanta, Georgia, riding into town in a Lexus Coupe looking for some 'ho's so they could put down so they could come up. The first spot they hit was Underground Atlanta, to Fat Tuesday--drinking, drinking, and drinking, thinking about the shit that just went down in New York...

Milk came right out of the blue and asked, "Baller--where the fly honeys at?"

Baller replies, "Man, if you want to find some 'ho's you got to go to Magic City, Dog! That's where the 'ho's at! But, Dog...or you can go to Club Nikki. Yeah, but Magic City got them tightass 'ho's. You got to come on in with them 'ho's.

But Club Nikki is the shit. It's where a player can come up
at, because the tricks' heads ain't that strong...Them niggas
got them tricks' heads fucked up! Some players think they
got them tricks' heads fucked up...some of them do and some
of them don't. Them tricks got each other's heads fucked up
by freakin' each other's pussy cat."

Milk says, "Player! Player! Player!" (all four of them
drunk as hell, laughing at the shit Baller was spittin')
"Player! Tell us how to get to Club Nikki!"

Baller replies, "I can show you better than I can tell you!
And some of them 'ho's are bad as hell...you just got to rep-
resent! And the 'ho's (tricks) will come to you. Yeaaah man!
Shit! What y'all niggas ridin' in?"

Milk replies, "Lexus Coupe, fool! What...you wanna
ride?"

Baller replies, "Hell, yeah--let's get the fuck outta here!"

Milk asks Baller, "Man, what's your hustle? What you
do?"

Baller responding, "Man, I sell dope, weed, pussy, and
info! Shi-id, I just know how to get around! Don't nobody
fuck with me, 'cause I'll kill a nigga! Now, y'all niggas ready
to have a good time? Nigga, here it is--turn right!"

Baller: "Gott damn! This bitch is flooded! Look, Dog,
all kinda outta state tags be off in this bitch! Okay, when we
go in, let's get the VIP! That's where you can get all the 'ho's
at...and then choose! But just represent hard and them 'ho's
will choose hard!"

Baller, thinking to himself, "It's so damn thick in Nikki's
tonight, I got to be tight...I'm dead ass broke, too. These
New York ass niggas smell like flow. And I got to get down
with these niggas, so if I want to be down, I got to represent
super hard!"

Baller talking: "Yeah, Nigga, come on in the VIP."

Fat Albert responding: "Where in the hell y'all fellas think y'all going? The VIP is for boss ballers! Champagne and 'ho's..."

Baller replies, "Big boy, give us all the 'ho's and six bottles of Moet and Dom Perignon and one bottle of Christal. And here's a big face for you!"

Milk replies, "Yeah, boy! I like this shit! Fat Albert walked over to the DJ booth and called all of the ladies to the VIP booth!"

Baller talking: "Yo, Milk! Here them 'ho's comes--let me flex with a couple of hundred!"

Milk: "Nigga, you ain't gotta flex--you with us! We some true hoggs, Playboy. Just be yourself. We got the rest, you showing me love! And now I got love for you! Here's a 'G'!" (a thousand dollars). "Do yo' thang, Baller!"

Baller stands up in the middle of the VIP doorway. "Yeah, y'all 'ho's bring it on! Come and get this pimp shit!!! I got a whole 'G' right here! What can y'all do for my folks from New York?? Yeah, 'ho, it's real, mmm, hmm, umm, hmm. Come here, li'l mama. What's your name?

The bitch said, "Brown Sugar." She said, "What's your name?"

Baller: Baby.

Brown Sugar speaking: "Damn, y'all gettin' to it!"

Baller replies, "Li'l Mama, show my folks some love, cause it's on. Then later on, let's have a private parties. So get up some 'ho's!"

Brown Sugar: "I don't know!!"

Baller speaking: "Well, Bitch, get the fuck on! Get the fuck on!"

Milk speaks: "What's wrong with that 'ho, man?"

Baller: "That trick bitch? Don't fuck with that 'ho! She got a trick daddy!"

Milk speaks: "Man, I bet I could fuck that 'ho, right now. Man, she out there on the floor by her damn self with a hundred niggas and it's four niggas with a hundred 'ho's in the VIP with

six bottles of Moet, four bottles of Dom Perignon, and one bottle of Christal!..."

Milk: "Man, fuck that 'ho!"

Fat Albert: "Hey, hey, man, these niggas gettin' mad!"

Milk: "Fuck them niggas, Fat Boy!"

Fat Albert, with a smile: "Bruh, we need some dancers on the floor! You can get half of them for the night if the price is right!"

Milk: "They got one more song, Fat Boy, so what if they don't want to leave?"

Fat Boy snapped, "Oh, they gonna come, they gonna come. I don't care how much flow you got, half of the ladies got to get their ass on the floor!"

Baller: "Who mad, Big Boy?"

Fat Albert: "All them niggas, man, no disrespect, but this is my job, Dog!"

Baller: "Milk Man, let's leave Tray and Deuce in the VIP, let's get around, Dog!"

Milk: "Yeah, yo, Tray and Deuce..."

Deuce: "Yeah, boyyyy...this is the life, word to God!"

Tray: "I love this shit. I don't ever want to go home--these Georgia peaches, these Georgia peaches! All these 'ho's want to leave with a nigga!"

Milk spoke in a low voice.

Milk: "Y'all niggas hold it down; me and Baller fixing to check out the club and I will call the Boss and let him know that we're in town."

Baller, thinking to himself: "I knew it was going to be my time to come. These niggas are for real! But I see gravy in these niggas, and everybody in the club jocking all four of us, because they smell the smell of money!"

Baller looks at Milk and says, "Yeah, Nigga, didn't I tell you that this bitch was going to be thick, flooded with come ups!"

Milk: "Hell, yeah, Nigga; why don't you get the word around, that we got them birds for the twenty-five G's but I'm going to give them to you for the eighteen G's. You sell them for the twenty-five for me, that's seven G's for each key you sell! Now, can you handle that, Dog?"

Baller responds, "Hell, yeah, Dog! That ain't shit to me! You work that side and I'll work this side, then meet me at the VIP in one hour, so go, Ball Nigga!"

Baller: "What's up! What up! What up! What up?! What up, folks, what's goin' down on this pool table? I got all bets, let me rack 'em, stack 'em, the way I like 'em. Five hundred a game--I don't give a fuck who plays."

O--lake (coming through the crowd): "I'll play, Dog! What's up--my name's O-lake."

Baller speaks: "My name is Baller! From Smoka Holler, the land of the dollar! (southwest). Nine balls a game, all bets!"

O--lake: "Y'all niggas boss ballin', I saw all the 'ho's over in the VIP except Brown Sugar."

Baller: "Fuck that 'ho! Don't nobody want that 'ho!"

O--lake: "Yeah, no one except your best buddy over there rapping to her right now!"

Baller: "That bitch must have went to him! Yeah, Nigga, I got them bricks for the two-five, pure no cut, so you know if it's pure you can buy one and make two; you know how them niggas do it here--you ain't new to the game!"

O--lake: "Yeah, I know how they do it! Yeah, yo' New York buddy all over that bitch. I just might want to go holler at your boy myself, personally!"

Baller: "Hey, Nigga, you holler at me! Or it ain't shit!"

O--lake: "Fuck you, Nigga!"

Baller: "Fuck you!" (And busts his ass in the head with a bottle of Moet and starts kicking his ass! To the floor!)

('Ho's hollering, glass breaking, people watching...)

Milk and Brown Sugar ran over to the fight and pulled Baller off of O--lake.

Baller: "Fuck that nigga! Fuck that nigga!"

Baller snatched O--lake's ass up off the floor and held him in front of Milk's face and said, "Nigga! You holler at me!"

Milk: "Yeah, y'all niggas, holler at my Dog!"

Baller: "That go for all y'all niggas and 'ho's! Man, let's get back to the VIP."

Brown Sugar: "Milkbone, Baby, is it still on for tomorrow?"

Milk: "Yeah, Boo!" Then he turns and looks at Baller after she walks off. "What was up with that shit, man?"

Baller: "You...man, I told you that bitch ain't shit!"

Milk: "Yeah, Nigga, I told you I could get that bitch. That bitch is a top notch 'ho, and I'm a top notch nigga killer dealer. I can handle that bitch; can you handle the business, Dog?" Walking back into the VIP, "Tray and Deuce, where y'all niggas been?"

Man, these three 'ho's are coming with us! Milk, you can have this one."

Milk: "Get them 'ho's number and let's get the fuck out of here. We got work!"

'Ho's: "We want to go!"

Baller: "Y'all 'ho's come here!" (Come on.)

As they were leaving, Brown Sugar ran over to Milk and said, "I want to leave with you."

Milk: "Tomorrow, Li'l Mama. I got business, Baby."

Brown Sugar: "I want to go tonight. I see them 'ho's you leavin' with! You ain't never comin' back! Them 'ho's are tricks! I need you to take me away, Milk."

Milk: "Tomorrow, like I said. Later!"

✻ ✳ ✤ ✲ ✶ ✱ ✳ ☆ ★ ☆

The next day, Saturday, 3:30 p.m., the phone rings. Baller picks up the phone, "Hello!"

Milk: "Yeah, Dog, I been calling all day! You must have been working already. How you like that shit?!"

Baller: "What shit?"

Milk: "You better go check your trash can!"

Baller: "Hold on!" (Goes to check the trash can.)

Milk: "Yeah, Baby, did you find what you were looking for?"

Brown Sugar: "No, Baby, you will have to pick out something for me."

Baller, back to the phone: "Hello, hello, hello...yeah, man, who that 'ho you got with you?"

Milk: "My bitch, Brown Sugar. Now Nigga, did you get the shit?!"

Baller: "Man, that 'ho ain't shit. But when did you put that shit there?" (in the trash can).

Milk: "Nigga, you fucked up. We stopped at the Waffle House, we put the food in the trunk and I filled your bag up with the shit!

Baller: "Yeah, man, I must have eaten and got full and just didn't realize that the dope was in the bag! And I must have threw it in the trash can! Yeah, so, okay, this is four bricks!"

Milk: "Yeah, that's seventy-two G's. I'll hit you back when I get through shopping. Later!"

Brown Sugar: "Who was that, Boo?"

Milk: "Just one of my folks. You couldn't find me nothing?"

Brown Sugar: "No. Let me pick you something and you pick me something."

Milk: "Yeah, I want you to pick me some fly shit."

Brown Sugar: "Some fly shit."

Milk: "A balling ass outfit."

Brown Sugar: "Okay, and you pick some fly shit, too."

They both walk, laughing, through the mall.

✱ ✱ ✤ ✳ ✳ ✱ ✳ ☆ ★ ☆

Baller looked at them four birds and shook his head. He popped out his pocket knife and busted a bag. Took a big snort straight to the head. Baller fell out and when he woke it was night time. He had blood dried up on his shirt. He touched his nose; it was bleeding. That meant that the dope was pure.

The phone rings. He jumps up and answers the phone.

Baller: "Hello."

Flamingo: "This your nigga four-tre Flamingo."

Baller: "What's up, Nigga? Let's go ball tonight. It's on me...pick a club."

Flamingo: "Let's kick it at Club Nikki."

Baller: "Hell, naw, I was there last night. Man, that shit was packed last night. Fat Boy at the door said it's going to be some new 'ho's coming in next week. So we will kick it next week at Club Nikki. Name another spot."

Flamingo: "I know--let's go to the 731."

Baller: "Hell, naw, we kicking it major tonight so pick a big balling ass club."

Flamingo: "OK 112, Illusion, Blue Flame, Little Nikki...shit, I don't know."

Baller: "Shi-id. Fuck it--we're going to all them, mother fucker."

Flamingo: "You got some clothes on, Nigga?"

Baller: "Hell, naw, but I got some flake. What up!"

Flamingo: "What! I'll be there in five minutes. Later!"

As soon as Baller hung up the phone it rang again.

Baller: "Hello."

Dee Dee: "Hey, Baby. This your girl."

Baller: "Yeah, I know what that flow looking like."

Dee Dee: "It's stacking slowly but surely. I need some more schooling, you know; you are the schoolmaster. I want to work."

Baller: "Don't rush it, Boo. I got something coming up and you in it. So what that flow look like?"

Dee Dee: "I just got seven hundred dollars. That's why I call you."

Baller: "You just put that little bit up. Go to the club tonight and put your tricking on."

Dee Dee: "What club should I go to?"

Baller: "731. It should be some trick ass nigga there and I will see you tomorrow. Later, Boo."

Knock knock knock

Baller: "Who is it?"

Flamingo: "Me, Nigga. Open the door. Yeah, Nigga, we're going to ball tonight. I called from the liquor store but the line was busy."

Baller: "Yeah, I was talking to one of my little mamas, Dee Dee."

Flamingo: "You ain't talking about that li'l sweet sixteen you caught at the Silver Fox that Sunday night. That li'l bitch look 24."

Baller: "Yeah, Dog, if she bleed she get fucked. I'm telling you, Dog, this li'l bitch want to be down. She coming on in all right."

Flamingo: "You spank that ass yet?"

Baller: "Hell, no! I don't hit no 'ho."

Flamingo: "Yeah, right. But like I was saying, I stop at the liquor store and got a fifth of that hen-dog to drain with shit and I got a dub of love it's that's fluffy ass chokeweed.

Baller: "Where did you get this broccoli?"

Flamingo: "From Miss Lilly. And it's smoking, too, Dog. So, Nigga, where's that Eddie Murphy Raw at?"

Baller: "Shi-id, right here, Nigga. Here you go, your personal 8-ball. Hit it light, Dog! Don't hit that shit hard. This shit is pure."

Flamingo: "Damn! Look at all the rocks in this shit! It looks damn good. Where did you get this shit?"

Baller: "From some of my folks out of state. Look here, I got to take a shower and put some rags on."

Flamingo: "Take your time, Player, take your time."

An hour later...

Baller: "Flamingo...Flamingo...Flamingo! Wake up! You hit that shit too hard. I told you not to hit that shit hard!"

Flamingo's nose was bleeding. Baller had to give him another shirt.

Flamingo: "Hey man, hey man...that shit is pure. Where did you say this shit came from?"

Baller: "From my folks. Let's go."

Flamingo: "Yeah, let me wash my face and we can go."

Baller (riding out): "Let's hit that Cambleton Road strip. We're just going to ride and see what's poppin'. Roll one, Nigga. Let's choke. Shi-id...let me turn this music up. We balling tonight. Look there--731 is packed."

Flamingo, still rolling the blunt, says, "Let's ride down to club Illusion." Riding down to the club, same thing. All Atlanta clubs stay packed. Because everyone parties down in Atlanta. And everyone is coming up, just like the city.

✳ ✳ ✤ ❄ ✳ ✴ ✳ ☆ ✴ ☆

Beep beep beep

"Yeah, did someone page Milk?"

Brown Sugar: "This Brown Sugar. Hey, Sweetheart."

Milk: "What's up, Love? I was just thinking about you. I want you to go out on the town with me, you know, show me the town. Let's put down."

Brown Sugar: "Well, I like those three girls we met at the mall."

Milk: "You think they got game?"

Brown Sugar: "Yes, I do."

Milk: "Okay, it's done now. Will you fly with me tonight?"

Brown Sugar: "You're one in a million. So it's on."

Milk: "I'll pick you up at 11:30 p.m."

Brown Sugar: "Okay."

Milk: "Later."

Milk: "Deuce and Tray! What's up tonight?"

Tray: "We're going to kick it back at Nikki and get some more bitches."

Milk: "It's this 'ho named Jade Tuff the Death. Ask Deuce."

Deuce: "She fine as hell. Tray might be whipped."

Tray: "Shi-id. All right, I'm going to let you fuck her tonight. We're going to take about a half a block with us tonight."

Deuce: "We got to it last night..."

Tray: "Hell, yeah, we're going to turn them 'ho's out, man. Them 'ho's smoke the hell outta them woo gangster joints. We let them snort good, I mean real good."

Deuce: "Man, last night was wild as hell. We put raw on our dicks and let them sniff it off."

Tray: "Then after that we fucked a li'l bit. And them 'ho's started eating each other and bumping bushes..."

Deuce: "Man, all these 'ho's in Atlanta love to do a li'l tricking. So long as we are on we can take over this city. Just like in Flint."

Tray: "Hell, yeah...more murder, more murder, more murder. If a nigga get wrong, boo, yaa."

Deuce: "It's do or die."

Milk: "I sometime get them crazy feelings."

Deuce: "We're the real gangsters."

Milk: "We can't be stopped, Baby."

Tray: "We done killed men and women and moved state to state. We're not going nowhere but right here. I am ready to use all the game I got on this city."

Milk: "Okay, I am going to check out some more clubs so you niggas move the shit to the other spot before you go."

Tray: "No problem, Milk. We will do just that."

Milk: "Later."

✱ ✱ ✤ ✤ ✱ ✱ ✱ ☆ ★ ☆

O--lake: "Yeah, bitch. What the bitch nigga talking about?"

Brown Sugar: "You need to chill out with that bitch shit, I mean, for real."

O--lake: "Bitch, who you think you're talking to? I'll kick you ass so you won't be going any damn where."

Brown Sugar: "Yeah, and when you do it will be your money you fucking up."

O--lake jumped up and slapped the shit out of her and stood over her and said, "Bitch, I am the pimp, you the bitch. Do you understand me? I don't play."

Brown Sugar: "Yes, Baby, don't hit me no more, please."

O--lake: "Now get your ass to work."

Brown Sugar: "Okay, Baby."

O--lake: "You got enough money for the room?"

Brown Sugar: "No."

O--lake: "Here's three hundred dollars--let that nigga know you ain't no broke 'ho."

Brown Sugar: "Thank you, Baby. Can I get a kiss where you hit me at?"

O--lake: "Anything for my Boo."

Brown Sugar: "See you. I got to go--I'll keep you informed."

✳ ✳ ✤ ✳ ✳ ✳ ✳ ☆ ✳ ☆

Flamingo: "At Club 112 there's some lady off in here tonight. I got to put my pimping on."

Baller: "See, these 'ho's got class about their self. But all 'ho's the same, they just got different game. All it takes is your game and a li'l coversation. Game is what keep them 'ho's coming. And that money stack."

Flamingo: "Two Stingers, please."

Bartender: "What's a Stinger?"

Flamingo: "A Henessey mixed with peppermint schnapps over rocks."

Bartender: "Coming up...two Stingers."

Flamingo: "Look, Baller, there go Nickel & Dime."

Baller: "What's up, Doggs?"

Nickel: "Shit--what you boys drinking?"

Baller: "A Stinger."

Dime: "A what??"

Flamingo: "A Stinger--Henessey mixed with peppermint schnapps."

Dime: "Hell naw--I got to drive tonight!"

Nickel: "Bartender--three Stingers and one Heineken."

Baller: "I got them birds for the low low."

Nickel: "What it whip like?"

Baller: "You guarantee to bubble off this shit. It's pure. 100% pure. No cut."

Nickel: "You mean to tell me you got some shit that ain't

stepped on?"

Baller: "Nickel, this shit is real. I can get you what you need for the low low."

Nickel: "What's the low low?"

Baller: "For you, my Nigga, 25K a brick. If your cooking skills are good you can get 72 ounces instead of 36 ounces. This shit is real pure, Dog. My folks are for real."

Nickel: "Bet. See you on Monday about that. What's up on that friend to friend you was telling about last week?" (Paramid broad games)

Baller: "Yeah, I'm still working on that--it going to be the thing in the 90's. But right now I'm working on these 96 tricks. Man, these 'ho's want to get out of hand. These nigga lettin' them get away with too much."

Nickel: "These nigga handcuffin' these 'ho's staying in a nigga business trying to see what a nigga got."

Flamingo: "But a real nigga show no love."

Dime: "Hell, yeah, I give a damn about a 'ho."

✱ ✳ ✤ ✻ ✳ ✹ ✳ ☆ ★ ☆

By this time, Brown Sugar got to her room. Ring...ring.

Brown Sugar: "Hello."

Milk: "Hey, Boo. I'm down here in the parking lot."

Brown Sugar: "Do you want to come up? I'm on the second floor, room 164, looking out the window where you are. Blink your lights so I can see you."

Milk: "Come on--let's ride."

Brown Sugar: "Here I come."

Down at the car, Brown Sugar: "Who's car?" as she was getting in.

Milk: "Yours if your head is right. You can get what you want but you gots to be down for me."

Brown Sugar: "Oh, I am, but are you serious about me and this family thing?"

Milk: "Most definitely. You're the one, Boo."

Brown Sugar: "Where your friends? I hear from some of the girls they some fools with it."

Milk: "Hell, yeah--them my dogs and I'll kill for my dogs because they will kill for me. Let's ride."

✳ ✳ ✤ ✼ ✳ ✳ ✳ ☆ ✯ ☆

Back at Nikki.

Fat Albert: "Hey hey hey, man, you can't smoke that shit in here."

Deuce: "Fuck you, Fat Boy. We spending loot and you talking shit! Bitch ass nigga, fuck this shit, you can hate me now."

These niggas started knocking over tables, cussing, slapping 'ho's and walking out the door with three bottles of Moet mean mugging folks going out the door. They both got into their Benz and got straight to it with the raw. Snok, snok, snok, snok, snok, snok.

Tray: "Man (snok), you ready to do this shit (snok)?"

Deuce: "Yeah, let's shoot this shit up (snok, snok, snok)."

Fishtailing out of the parking lot, Tray standing out of the top of the car. Busting shots at the club, yelling "Yeah, bitch! Boom! Boom! Boom!"

Deuce: "Hell, yeah, Dog! Where to next?!"

Tray: "Let's get out of this hot ass shit and get back to the hotel. And get to this raw!"

Deuce: "Snok, snok--Hell, yeah!"

✳ ✳ ✤ ✼ ✳ ✳ ✳ ☆ ✯ ☆

Milk took Brown Sugar where she wanted to go. They both went out to recruit some soldiers for this coming family. They had fun. That whole night Milk spoiled her rotten. They went to Milk's room and did an all-nighter. When she woke up, she went snooping around the room. Milk was gone. By that time, the phone rang.

Brown Sugar: "Hello."

Milk: "Hey girl, you know you got that sunshine and you know what that mean."

Brown Sugar: "No, what do it mean?"

Milk: "That tag ass nigga got to go. Look up under the mattress--I left you a li'l something."

Brown Sugar looked up under the mattress--it was three thousand dollars.

Milk: "Go and get you something nice."

Brown Sugar: "You didn't have to do this. I am down for you."

Milk: "I know. Find a way to get rid of that trick ass nigga you been chose and I get what I want later." And hung up the phone.

THE PLAN

Baller took four chickens and made eight birds--the shit is just that pure. Baller started calling all over the city putting down the plan.

Ringing...ring...ring...

Baller: "Hello."

W. C.: "Yeah, who is this?"

Baller: "This Baller."

W. C. "What's up, Player?"

Baller: "I got them birds for the twenty-five. Straight on cut I got the shit that will put your spot on the map."

W. C.: "If it's like that I'll get two."

Baller: "Bet. See you in Smoka Holler."

Baller made another phone call.

Ring, ring...

Crow: "Hello."

Baller: "What up, my Nigga?"

Crow: "What up what up?"

Baller: "Man, I got them birds for the 25 a key and 28 grams an ounce, all 36 ounces no cut. This shit is real. I got some folks from the Big Apple with the real deal Holyfield. And this shit is fire."

Crow: "Okay, if you got it like that I'll do three. I need something to hold me until next month. My nigga flew to Florida to have fun and taking care of some business at the same time."

Baller: "Who flew with him?"

Crow: "Man, that nigga took all 69 of his 'ho's and 15 of his kids and 9 of the 'ho's is his babies mamas. He told me he flying down and coming back up with 200 birds and dropping them off for the 22 a key."

Baller: "Damn, that nigga paid..."

Crow: "He paying $12G apiece. That's $828,000 and he get back here and sell them bitches for the $22G a key and make $1,756,000 off 200 key and, man, he do that shit every six month. If I was to buy them that's what the price will be. Instead he front them to me so I pay 25 a key three keys every six month. Man, I be through with that shit in three month..."

Baller: "Damn, my nigga, that fuck up and you call that nigga folks."

Crow: "We're going to talk some more, just bring that stuff."

Baller: "Bet. Later."

Knock knock knock

Baller: "Who is it?"

W. C.: "It's me, W. C. Open the door."

Baller: "Man, you dead on time. I want you to take me out to Decatur."

W. C.: "Bet. Let's do this."

Baller had the two keys wrapped tight. Baller don't trust no one--they come straight to the 'hood to get the dope, but if you're real good friends he will bring it. W.C. is a wild ass nigga--he did much dirty back in the days, but now he is a roller. But Baller got a plan and he will not let nothing stand in his way.

W. C.: "Hell, yeah, that's what I'm talking about. You got them bitches wrap tight. I'll just bust one to test one."

Baller: "Hold up, Nigga. I got you a sample right here so when you get where you got to go, then bust them up and cook them there. Here you go--a personal 8-ball."

W. C.: "Damn nice looking flake in this. You 'bout ready to go?"

Baller: "Yeah, let's dip. That shit is the bomb--better not hit it hard.

W. C.: "Nigga, I am the bomb."

Riding out to Decatur...

W. C.: "Yeah, man, with them keys in the trunk I'm going to take this to Alabama, Tennessee--man, I put down 15 ounces in Alabama and 21 ounces in Tennesse. Give it to my folks. I will put this other key in the 'hood and just sell break down dimes. Most niggas sell zips for $900 a ounce and make $32,400 off 36 ounces, but me, I take one brick and break it down into break down dimes and give that shit to my project 'ho's and let them be the ghetto star. I pay my 'ho's thirty dollars off a hundred. But I give them the break down dimes for dubs. It 36 ounces in a key, off each ounce $1,800 and off the key I make $72,800 off that."

Baller: "That's a good ideal."

W. C.: "Ideal nigga, that's real. Nigga, I use to jack for a living until I seen how the real nigga put it down so you know it was on from there. But like back in the days I would wait until a nigga get on his toes and knock them off their feet. Can't no nigga fuck with me because I kill every nigga I jack because a rich nigga can put a hit out on you and will not think nothing about it. I still will jack a nigga ass because you got 'ho's when you got money and power. So, I give a bitch what she want. Because the next nigga got what I want. Niggas is scare of a nigga. I should have laid back and played the 'ho's, but some nigga might have try me. So I teach my 'ho's how to be nasty like me. I give my 'ho's the dick and let them snort all the raw they want and they will do anything I say."

Baller: "Because of the powder."

W. C.: "No, because they know I will kick their ass. Shit, man, where this nigga stay? I can't drive and snork at the same time. Who this nigga you going to see, anyway?"

Baller: "My nigga Crow."

W. C.: "Crow--I know that punk ass nigga. That's the nigga who get front dope and whoever front him dope get to fuck his 'ho's. That nigga scare to flip his boss, King Goldie, shit. Man, the way you and that nigga kick it I would never have knew you were dogs."

While riding on the highway, W. C. tried to take a toot, but the wind blew it out the window.

W. C.: "Damn--shit! Will you look at that shit!"

Baller: "Don't worry about that, I will get you some more from my dog."

Arrive at Crow's house. Knock, knock, knock.

Crow: "Who is it?"

Baller: "It's me, Baby Boy."

Crow: "My nigga, you got my stuff?"

Baller: "Right here, friend."

Crow: "It's on now, this shit look good. Who that in the car with you?"

Baller: "That's W. C."

Crow: "I just know you did not bring that wild ass nigga to my house. I just know you didn't. Man, that nigga have almost invade more folks than..."

Baller: "Hold up, Dog. Just be cool. That nigga ain't shit. We're the niggas. We're the one's who going to have the golds in '96 so just be cool. We got to try new things--everybody got the same ideals but the wrong plan. Busters and Fat 'Ho's got off in this game and got on strong because niggas gave the game away for free. And fucking for free that shit ain't right. Niggas should just school the young kids and each other just like how we do. Niggas must pay the cost to be the boss in the land of the lost. You got to be strong in this game, Crow. The weak get stomped. Now, here go your shit and we're going to rob this nigga and kill his ass. That's what he's been doing all his life."

Crow: "Man, how in the hell are we going to rob that wild ass fool?"

Baller: "Look, he want something to sniff. Take about a 8-ball out. This shit is so pure it will knock his ass out. Now bring the sample."

Riding from Crow's house to W. C.'s house. As soon as Crow entered the car, W. C. was on him.

W. C.: "What's up little nigga? You still letting niggas fuck your 'ho's? Every time you get a 'ho niggas come by and take her--that's 'ho shit, not pimp shit."

Crow: "Why don't you come off that shit."

Baller: "Yeah, W. C., chill out."

W. C.: "Fuck you, Baller, you with this nigga."

Baller: "Hell, yeah, that's my nigga."

W. C. pull out his gun and point it at the both of them. Arrive at W. C.'s house. W. C. still got the gun pointed at the both walking to the house.

W. C.: "You see, Baller, what you get trying to help a nigga who don't want to help theirself. You be fucked every time. Now get your ass in this house."

Baller: "Kill me. Fuck all that trying to school a nigga. If I die, I die."

Crow: "If you going to take our life you might as well take this 8-ball I got in my pocket. This shit came from the nigga who put me on King Goldie. You never try no shit like this before. It's from Cuba."

W. C.: "You two nigga lay it down."

W. C. checked the both of them. He found a gun on Baller and got the dope off Crow.

Crow: "Hey, man, can I get a li'l toot before I die?"

W. C.: "Hell, naw, and you better shut your damn mouth before I kill you first. Let me test this shit. Snok, snok, snok, Shit! Shit! Shit! Snok snok snoksnoksnok." W.C. looked at the both of them and frowned up at them and passed out.

Crow and Baller jumped over on W. C., started kicking his ass to sleep and waking his ass up and kicking him back to sleep. Baller cut the tv cord and tied him to the chair. They went searching the house and came up with guns and weed. Eight pounds of weed, four .38s, two 9mm, a pump shotgun, and two hand grenades.

Crow: "Let's get the fuck out this house."

Baller: "Hold up, nigga. It's got to be more, and anyway, you can't just rob a nigga like this. You got to do his ass. Let's go wake this nigga up."

Crow pissed on W. C. to wake his ass up. When he woke up, Baller had a bat and pointed at W. C.'s head.

Baller: "Wake up. Hey, Fool! I said wake the fuck up and prepare yourself for a Rodney King ass whipping!"

Baller went across his head, legs, arms, back...all over his body. Crow was yelling, "Where the rest of the loot?! Where it at?!" and jumped over on him and started beating him with his gat. "Who the punk now, nigga, who the punk now?!"

W. C.: "Don't kill me, please don't kill me! It inside the couch--just please stop hitting me!"

Baller: "Crow, go check it out." Baller stood over W. C. and said, "Nigga, you should never pull a gun out on a man and just talk. You should have handle your business because if you don't kill him he will someday come kill you."

Crow yelled out, "Got it! $80,000 in cash."

Baller took his bat and beat W. C. to death, packed up the money, guns, weed, and W. C. and put it all in the trunk of the car. They dropped W. C. off in Stone Mountain. When the police found him he was butt-ass naked beaten to death.

THE PUT DOWN

Milk was just riding through downtown. Just got off the phone talking with Brown Sugar. They did a lot of recruiting last night. Milk do feel Brown Sugar is going to be the mother of the family. She did some pretty good recruiting herself through the months they bein' together. She have recruited Sky, Sugar Wolf, MJG, Greed, Precious, Eazy, Pee Wee Loc, Raven, Jim Kelly, and Fly-Mar. And so far, Milk have recruited Chicago, Jade, Mona Lisa, Hezzy, Pete, Tennessee, Big Mike, Jazzy Bell, Diamond, and soon to be Baller.

Milk stopped over at Magic City to check out the afternoon action. Putting on about he got the brick for the low low and he's looking for some folks to be down with him.

Milk: "Hey, Player, let's shoot a game."

Hollywood: "Hollywood's the name. What's yours, Player?"

Milk: "Milk, with the low low price."

Hollywood: "Oh yeah? What's the low low?"

Milk: "What you spending?"

Hollywood: "Since we both player, what's a player price?"

Milk: "What do you want to spend?"

Hollywood: "What can you do for the 50 G?"

Milk: "I can give you three birds for the $16,650 a key which give you $49,950."

Hollywood: "Where do the extra $50 go?"

Milk: "It goes on three table dances, two drinks, and the extra ten goes to the bartender. It's guaranteed to jump for you all 36 ounces, 28 grams in each ounce. Picture this--108 ounces at $900 a ounce. Man, that give you $97,200 when you cook it up. You do know how to whip that shit, don't you? It's good shit. So what I'm saying, if you are a hell of a cook, you can get 216 ounces at $900 a ounce, that $194,400. Man, that kind of money for a young nigga is good. You can start you a small family and in the year to come you can have a big family."

Hollywood: "That sound good, but the shit got to be tight."

Milk: "You see, we're going to be good folks because it's good."

Hollywood: "Where you from, Milk?"

Milk: "New York. Player, where you from?"

Hollywood: "Me, I'm from Tennessee, with fades and gold teeth. Look, Milk, I got a family and it's strong, too. We just here for the the Freaknik and the clubs."

Milk: "You just like me, Player. You sure you don't want to kick it with me in the A town?"

Hollywood: "Man, it too much competition here. In Tennessee, we're coming out hard. Believe me, Player."

Milk: "I can believe you getting it like that and the girls here are sweet like a Georgia peach, right?"

Hollywood: "Everywhere you go in the south all the ladies look good."

Beep...beep...beep. Milk checks his pager. It was Brown Sugar. He told Hollywood what it was on the yeyo. Hollywood told Milk he would call him when he was ready. Milk gave Hollywood a look and said, "Later on, Player. Got to run."

As Milk was coming out of the parking lot, five cars was pulling in with Tennessee tags. 64, Benz, Beamer. Milk saying to himself, "Damn, them boys got paper."

THE LICK

Milk page Brown Sugar. Brown Sugar jump out the shower to check her pager. She grab her cell phone to call back Milk.

Milk: "Hello."

Brown Sugar: "Hey, Boo, I just call you to let you know I'm back at the house."

Milk: "You going to work tonight?"

Brown Sugar: "Yes, Sweetheart. What's up?"

Milk: "I got a li'l trick ass nigga set up. Can you handle that for me?"

Brown Sugar: "Yes. Where and when?"

Milk: "Tonight at the club. This nigga from Tennessee, but his name is Hollywood. He turn down my offer and, like I said, I get what I want. So, have you figure out a way to get away from that trick ass nigga of yours?"

Brown Sugar: "I'm working on it."

Milk: "You must show your loyalty tonight. You and Baller. It's about time to do this family. How did you like that spacey love last night?"

Brown Sugar: "It was sweet; when can we do it again?"

Milk: "After you complete this task."

Brown Sugar: "Okay, it's on."

Milk: "Later," and hung up the phone.

Brown Sugar was oiling down her body in the bathroom

when O-lake knock at the door.

Brown Sugar: "Come on in, Baby."

O-lake: "What's up and why you looking so happy?"

Brown Sugar: "I think he's going to show me the money. He ask to marry me, Boo. He's a sucker for love, Boo, a sucker for love. He's going to show me the world tonight."

O-lake: "What else that nigga say?"

Brown Sugar: "He said he will never hit me, curse me, and he said he's going to give me some spacey love in a way I will never forget."

O-lake: "No way, you're not going no damn where tonight just to make fuck faces."

Brown Sugar: "I know you're not going to back out on this money. I do this shit for you. And a matter of fact, this nigga got way more money than you will ever see at one time."

O-lake: "Fuck you, Bitch. You must want to run off with Nigga. I see all that happiness you got on your face. I got money and dope, too, Bitch."

Brown Sugar: "See what I mean--your money. What about me? It's always your shit. You don't give a damn about me. It's always 'do this for me, do that for me'. I never get a break--but I still give all my love to you. I am tired of this shit; I just want to settle down with you."

O-lake: "I am sorry, Baby. I got a little jealous. What you want to see and know?"

Brown Sugar: "Show me the money."

O-lake: "Push a button in the bathroom wall." The wall moved to the left.

Brown Sugar's eyes got big as Cynthia McKinney's. Nothing but a big stack of cash, 15 keys of cocaine inside the wall. Brown Sugar took O-lake to the bedroom and fuck him good.

O-lake: "Baby, you get to that nigga. Baby, you do good on this one and we can go places."

Brown Sugar: "Okay, Baby. It's getting late--I gots to work."

O-lake: "Call me when you get to work."

Brown Sugar: "I will, Boo. Later." She got all her things and left. Brown Sugar jump in her li'l car and call up her real trick daddy.

Baller: "Hello."

Brown Sugar: "Baby, that nigga had the shit in the bathroom wall. Ten million in cash and 15 keys."

Baller: "Lord, have mercy, Butter Baby."

Brown Sugar: "You need to hit his ass tonight. I just fuck the shit out of his ass, so he all tired out. And Milk said he got a job for me and you."

Baller: "And what else he said?"

Brown Sugar: "He say its about time for the family. He said tonight I must show my loyalty."

Baller: "Okay, Baby, I got it. You be safe. Later."

✳ ✴ ✤ ❈ ✳ ✹ ✺ ☆ ✭ ☆

Ring...ring...ring.

Crow: "Hello."

Baller: "Nigga, it's on tonight. O-lake's house."

Crow: "Bet. Let's do this shit, then. How much flow & dope we talking about?"

Baller: "Ten million in cash and 15 keys."

Crow: "I like how that sound. So what's the plan?"

Baller: "Look, you drive the BMW to the club and I will drive the van. Meet me at the club so it will give us a alibi."

Crow: "That's right."

Meanwhile, snok, snok, snok...

Deuce: "Damn, you cut this just right."

Tray: "Snok, snok, I know, I know, snok, snok, snok, man, snok, that nigga Baller think he's the Big Baller telling Milk how to sell the shit. We should just rob that nigga."

Deuce: "Sho 'nuff."

Tray: "Shit, yeah! Just like in the other states--why not the A town?"

By that time Milk and Brown Sugar walk in the room.

Tray: "Where you been, Dog? We been waitin' on you. It's time to work."

Deuce: "Yeah, you haven't put a lick down yet. I'm ready to work."

Milk: "Okay, okay. I got some work for tonight."

Tray: "Who? Baller?"

Milk: "No. Brown Sugar is going to show us where her nigga stay. I want you two to go in and do that nigga. I want you two to go to the club and wait for my call. I'll be calling from the room. When I call, you two come pick us up. Now, me and Sugar got some business to take care. So you two get to the club and wait on the phone call."

Duece and Tray went to the club while Milk put that spacey love on Brown Sugar.

At the club.

Deuce: "What's up, Baller?"

Baller: "What's up, Playboy?"

Deuce: "Just kicking it."

Baller: "What's up for tonight?"

Tray: "Snok, snok, snok, doing a nigga in tonight."

Baller: "Same here, Bitch Nigga; we can just do it."

Tray: "Damn sho can. Fist to fist. Toe to toe."

Deuce grab Tray and Fat Albert grab Baller.

Fat Albert: "Hey, hey, hey, man--not tonight."

The bartender called Fat Albert to the phone.

Fat Albert: "Hello."

Milk: "Hey, man, this Milk. Is my dogs there?"

Fat Albert: "Hell, yeah. Hold on...hey, Tray...hey, Tray!"

Tray was walking to Fat Albert saying to Baller, "You dead, Nigga, you just be here when I get back."

Baller: "No, you just be here when I get back." Baller went out the front door and Crow went out the back. Both got in the van headed for O-lake's house.

Tray: "Hello."

Milk: "Come to the hotel. It's time to work."

Tray: "We're on the way." Deuce and Tray left the club.

Ring, ring, ring.

Fat Albert: "Hello."

O-lake: "What's up, Big Boy--this O-lake. What's popping tonight?"

Fat Albert: "That nigga Baller in here starting shit again."

O-lake: "I am coming down."

Fat Albert: "Naw, man, it's too wild tonight. You just need to relax."

O-lake: "Yeah, I'll just chill out. I been fucking all day. Have my bitch got to work yet?"

Fat Albert: "Not yet."

O-lake: "Okay, then, my nigga."

Arriving at O-lake's house, Baller and Crow, both dress in black, running up to the house. Crow kick in the door. Baller right behind him.

Baller: "Where you at, Nigga, where you at?!"

O-lake came running down the stairs. Here I go, here I go busting at them with a pump shotgun. Here I go--Boom! Boom! Boom!--on your bitch ass.

Baller and Crow was ducking behind shit. But when O-lake ran out of shells it was all over. They both came up busting shots after shots until O-lake hit the floor. Crow strip him butt naked, duck tape his mouth, hands, and feet. Baller was in the bathroom getting everything that Brown Sugar said was there. Baller bag up the money & dope. Crow bag up O-lake. O-lake start wiggling to get loose, but the duck tape is tough like handcuffs. Baller stood over him and shot him in the heart. They both came out of the house with O-lake, the money, and the dope.

Baller drop Crow off at the club. He enter the back way. Baller drop O-lake off on the side of the highway and put the dope and the cash up, park the van and change cars and burn the black garments they wore.

Baller back at the club, chilling, having fun. Meanwhile, Milk, Tray, Deuce, and Brown Sugar ride out to O-lake's house.

Brown Sugar: "We're almost there."

Tray: "Yo, Milk, I gots to kill that nigga, Baller. He think he's the Big Shit."

Milk: "Baller making things happen for us."

Deuce: "Snok, snok, snok. Here you go, Dog."

Tray: "Snok, snok, snok, snok, snok."

Milk: "Pass the raw to Sugar."

Brown Sugar: "Snok snok, snoksnok, woo shit, woo shit, shit, shit--this the house. No wait--yeah--this it. This some fire shit."

Tray and Deuce jump out the car and ran to the house and saw that the door was cracked. They kick the door open, busting shots all over the house.

Deuce: "Come here. Someone got him before we did."

Tray: "Yeah, let's go and tell Milk it done--he's dead."

Deuce: "Why do that?"

Tray: "So we can move on with the plan."

Deuce: "What if that bitch had something to do with this?"

Tray: "Man, that bitch think she going to meet some rich nigga to bring her ass up and keep her ass looking good. Just like in the other state. Nigga, we got to make a name for ourself. Milk not going to be around all the time. Me and you, bruh, me and you. Now let's get the fuck out of here."

Running out of the house, busting shots in the air. Tray yelling, getting in the car, "Got that bitch ass nigga, let's go!" Milk peeling out.

Milk: "Did you get him?"

Tray: "Hell, fuck yeah! Bust that cabbage wide open."

Milk: "Deuce, did you get that nigga?"

Deuce: "Like Tray said, bust his head to the white meat. Where that raw at?"

Brown Sugar: "Right here."

Deuce got straight to it. "Snok, snok, snok."

Tray: "Pass me some of that shit."

Deuce: "Snok, snok--here you go, Dog."

Tray: "Snok, snok, snok--I need something to drink. Snok, snok. Baller ass is next."

Milk: "What the hell you mean 'Baller next'? Baller is going to show his loyalty tonight. Only me who get to decide who dies. Baller have good game and the family need that. If he can't produce, then we will cut him loose. And I ain't talking about just letting him go."

Tray: "Fuck that nigga, Milk."

Milk: "Deuce, how is he to you?"

Deuce: "He's cool. He don't talk that shit to me. He's pretty cool."

Milk: "Sugar, what's up with Baller?"

Brown Sugar: "The only thing I know is that he make money and he like to be the shit when he's out balling."

Milk: "Sho 'nuff. The nigga got good game to me. If he pull this off tonight I got to keep him, okay."

Tray: "Okay. God."

Pulling up at the club.

Milk: "Deuce and Tray, now, tonight be cool. See can you recruit some folks and at the same time scope some tricks."

Brown Sugar: "What do you want me to do?"

"Just do your thing, Sweetheart."

Brown Sugar: "Where you going, Boo? I want to go."

Milk: "You stay here, I got something I got to take care of. Deuce and Tray, go to work. I'll be back."

Milk left the club. Ride back out to O-lake's house to see if the job was done. But by the time he got there the police were everywhere. So he drove back to the club. When he enter the club, Deuce and Baller was in the VIP chilling. Brown Sugar was doing her thing dancing in the nude. Tray on the floor checking out everyone.

When Milk step in the club, Crow bump him.

Crow: "Excuse me, Player."

LETTING GO

Everyone at the club feeling good all raw up. Glad that O-lake is dead.

Deuce: "What's up, Baller?"

Baller: "You, Baby Boy. Have some Dom on me, Ball Nigga."

Deuce: "It's pack in this bitch tonight. You want to do a one on one?"

Baller: "Hell, yeah! Let's get some 'ho's over here."

By that time Tray walk over.

Tray: "What up, Deuce, Baller?"

Baller: "What up? We're about to flake one. What's up--you want to get down with us?"

Tray: "Let's do it."

Baller: "I got nothing but love for you. Who cut it up."

Deuce: "That nigga Tray, he cut the hell out of it."

Brown Sugar over in the corner hypnotizing one of her tricks.

Brown Sugar: "Where you from? You look new."

Hollywood: "I am new, you sexy black thang. How many dances can I get for a hundred dollars?"

Brown Sugar: "Ten."

Hollywood: "Good as you look it should be just one. Well, what can I get for five hundred?"

Brown Sugar: "What's your name?"

Hollywood: "Hollywood--would you like to go some day? I can take you there. It look like you need to get away for a li'l bit and enjoy life itself."

Brown Sugar: "You got to be rich to do me around the world."

Hollywood: "Girl you don't know nann, nigga that can kick the game like me or keep it fresh like me, girl you don't know nann."

Brown Sugar: "Looks can be deceiving. You might just be another scrub acting like you got it all."

Hollywood: "First of all, I am not a scrub, and I aint gotta lie to kick it. I got money, I got money."

Brown Sugar: "Where you from?"

Hollywood: "I'm from the money spot where niggas come up and plot."

After Milk was through checking out Brown Sugar, he walk to the VIP where his love was.

Milk: "I see you fellows kickin' it like big players."

Deuce: "Yeah, Baby Boy."

Tray: "Oh, Baby, I like it raw."

Baller: "What's up, Dog? We just waiting on orders."

Milk: "Let me talk with you for a minute."

Baller: "I got your money."

Milk: "I am not talking about that. I want you to be down with this family."

Baller: "Nigga, I am down for you."

Milk: "I know that, but will you kill for me?"

Baller, looking into Milk's eyes: "Hell, yeah, Nigga, on my mother's eyes. When and who?"

Milk: "You see that trick over there with Brown Sugar?"

Baller: "Yeah."

Milk: "That nigga right there."

Baller: "Do you think she got heart?"

Milk: "I know she do."

Baller: "Okay. It's on, when?"

Milk: "Tonight--and bring me some of what he have to offer. Give me some of that Dom. After tonight we will start the family. I love you, man--don't let me down.

✳ ✴ ✢ ✳ ✳ ✴ ✳ ☆ ★ ☆

Early in the middle of the night, Deuce and Tray left with some of the girls to have a raw party. Milk was at the bar talking to some fellow about the game. Niggas was all ears.

Milk: "I am telling you boys I got them eagles two for $35,000 hard or soft. Now for one I got to raise the price. Now, you need money to make money. I am giving it away, but it's not free."

Niggas started passing out their number like 'ho's thinking that they got their man for the low low. Baller sitting in the corner peeping at Milk but got his on his eyes on his bitch and the trick lick. Crow sitting at the bar watching everyone chilling with four girls dances around him. By that time, Brown Sugar went to the back getting ready to go. Baller left the club. Milk walk over to the bar to check out Crow style so he watch the girls as they dances for Crow. When the music stop, Milk pull out $1,500 and put it in them 'ho face and said, "You girls coming with me." All four of the 'ho's jump to atttention. Milk then shot Crow his pager number and said, "Call me when you want to come up," and left with the 'ho's.

Crow went to take a toot. Sugar and Hollywood left the club. Crow follow them out riding out on the highway.

Baller: "Crow, where you at?"

"Talking on the cell phone. Where you at?"

Baller: "Over by the gate."

Crow: "Stay where you at. They will be coming your way in five minute."

Riding to the hotel.

Hollywood: "You are a pretty black lacquer. I'm glad I got you."

Brown Sugar: "You don't have me yet."

Arriving at the hotel.

"Let's get to the room. I am ready to get blowed away."

Hollywood: "Don't rush it, Baby. You going to get this dick."

Brown Sugar: "I didn't say nothing about no dick. I said let's get high."

Hollywood: "I got some raw right here."

Brown Sugar grab his dick and squeeze his balls. While she did that he got hot.

Hollywood: "I got 60 pound up in my room that's smokin'. Come, let's get to the room, baby." Walking to the room he gave her the raw in the room.

✱ ✳ ✤ ✥ ✱ ✹ ✺ ☆ ★ ☆

Hollywood sat his gat down on the TV. Brown Sugar got to it on the raw.

Brown Sugar: "Snok, snok, this pretty good, snok, snok."

Hollywood: "Let me get a hit." As soon as he took a hit, Baller kick in the door. Brown Sugar jump up. Baller knock her ass out.

Baller: "Lay it down, Fool!" Hollywood reach for his gat. Baller shot him in the side. He fell to the floor with the powder in hand.

Hollywood: "Wait, man, I don't have nothing."

Baller with a black ski mask on firm, tightly on his face. "Where it at, Nigga?! Where it at?!"

Hollywood: "Look up under the mattress."

Crow was in the hallway looking out. He peep in to see what was going on.

Crow: "Hurry up, Nigga!"

Baller: "Come on in, Nigga, and help me get this shit."

Crow hold up the mattress while Baller got 60 pounds of weed. Baller gave Crow 10 pounds of weed. Crow turn to Hollywood and shot him two times in the chest. He died instantly. Crow left. Baller woke up Brown Sugar and grab the 50 pounds of weed. Brown Sugar half way out her mind because Baller knock the hell out of her and she don't remember a thing. Riding out to Brown Sugar's house.

Brown Sugar: "Damn! You didn't have to hit me so hard! What did we get?"

Baller: "50 pounds of weed."

Brown Sugar: "He said 60 pounds. It suppose to be 60 pounds."

Baller: "It's going to be 40 pounds when Milk get it."

Brown Sugar: "Well, what happened to the other 10 pounds?"

Baller: "It was 50 pound."

Brown Sugar: "I think you're lying to me, Baller."

By that time, Baller slap the shit out of Brown Sugar and said, "You don't get paid to think, you get paid to know." Brown Sugar started crying.

Baller: "Now you tell that nigga it was 40 pounds of weed, okay?"

Brown Sugar: "Okay."

Baller never in his life have curse or hit Brown Sugar. It was the first and last time.

Both riding, saying nothing to each other, three minutes away from Brown Sugar's house in Buckhead.

Brown Sugar: "Wait--take me to my mom's house."

Baller: "What your mother's house?"

Brown Sugar: "I just want to see my mom."

Baller did a U-turn in the middle of the street, taking her to her mom's house in the 17th ward, both still not saying a word.

4:30 a.m. arriving at Sugar's mom's house. Baller sat in the car while Sugar went into the house. As soon as she cut the lights on, roaches ran everywhere. She walk into the living room, stepping over two uncles, three cousins, and her two uncle's wives and their seven kids. She peep in the bathroom and shook her head. Walking through the hallway, clothes all in the way. She peep in her little sister's room. She was hug up with her boyfriend asleep.

She walk into her mom's room. She was getting ready for work.

Mom: "Baby, what you doin' here this time of morning?"

Brown Sugar: "I came to see you, Mom."

Mom: "I miss you, Baby."

Brown Sugar: "I miss you, too, Mom. Mom, do you still have those keys I told you to hold?"

Mom: "Right here, Baby."

She kiss her mom on the cheek and thank her. She told her mom that she will fix the house and ran down the stairs to the car and told Baller it was over.

Baller jump at her and said, "Bitch, it not over until I say it's over!"

Brown Sugar: "You told me you would never curse or hit me. In one day you did both."

Baller: "Bitch, I made you! I gave you more than I given any 'ho."

Brown Sugar: "I can give you back what you ever gave me."

Baller: "Bitch, if you got every thin dime I gave you, you can get the fuck on. And Bitch, I gave you over $250,000. Can you buy that, 'ho?"

Sugar look at Baller for a minute.

Baller: "Can you afford it? If not, get your ass in the car

and stop bullshit."

Brown Sugar: "Here--these are the keys to my place in Buckhead and here are the keys to the safe in the wall. It's over $500,000 in cash. See I got down for mine. And you broke the rules. And I am just going by your rules. I paid my way out. I gots to take care me and my mom. You do not control me. I choose Milk, Baller."

Baller: "Well, let's do it in the car one last time."

Brown Sugar: "Baller, I know you're not pussy crazy. It's over, Baller, let me go. You got everything I work for."

Baller: "The shit better be there. If it not, I am going to kill your ass."

Fishtailing out the parking lot, mad as hell, headed out to Buckhead. Brown Sugar walking into the house happy as hell. 6:41 a.m. in the morning.

Brown Sugar: "Everybody, get up! Get up! It time to clean the house. Get up!"

By that time, Mom was coming downstairs.

Mom: "See you, Baby. I got to get to work. See you. Mutt & Jeff, get up, my baby home. Get up."

Everyone woke up in the living room. Isra got the kids ready for school. Mutt & Jeff was gettting ready for work.

Brown Sugar: "Okay, y'all, let's clean this house." Everyone greeted her with a warm welcome.

Isra: "Sugar, you need to talk to your little sister. She growing up, girl, and you need to be there. Me and Abbie will be moving pretty soon, so we won't be here to watch her. Your mom's working two jobs--she just don't have time. You go talk with her; we will clean the house. Go on."

She walk into her little sister's room. She was acting like she was asleep. Brown Sugar tickle her feet. She woke up laughing.

Brown Sugar: "You're not asleep and where that boy you

had in here. I saw him."

Neva: "What boy?"

Sugar: "Girl, don't play with me. Why don't you clean this house?"

Sugar check up under the bed and in the closet. He was not there.

Sugar: "Neva, where's that boy? I know he's in here."

Neva: "Where you been? We miss you."

Brown Sugar look to the left and saw the clothes move a little bit, so she check the clothes and there was Neva's boyfriend.

Brown Sugar: "Get your ass out of here!"

The young boy took off running out the door.

Brown Sugar: "You said it was nobody here. You need to get it together."

Abbie came upstairs. "Sugar, I didn't know anything about that boy in here. But, girl, you look just like your mother. You going to stay, Sugar?"

Brown Sugar: "I am not going to leave until this house is clean."

Neva: "We will handle it. You look sleepy. Why don't you lay down and get some rest. Come lay down in Mom's room--it clean. Now I am going to help clean the house."

Sugar walk around her mom's room, looking at some pictures, her as a little girl. She crawl on her mom's bed. As soon as she lay down she was asleep.

Little sister peep in the door. And look up at God. And said, "Thank you, Lord. Thanks."

And by that time Baller arrive at the house. The first place he look was in the walls. He bust in the wall in the bedroom. Nothing. He try the bathroom. Nothing. He try the hallway. There it was--the safe, everything was there just like she said, but it was more money. $500,000, gold rings, fur coats--he put everything in the trunk with the 50 pounds of weed.

He went back into the house, look into the refrigerator. He grab the hamburger meat, put it in the microwave to thaw the meat out. He then walk to the bar and grab the Crown Royal, drinking out of the bottle. He went back to the kitchen to cook him two burgers. He fix them up. Ate them and he still was drinking. He been up all night. He went to the car and bust open a pound of weed, grab a hand full of it and went back into the house and roll a fat ass blunt.

Peeping out the window at the car, puffing on the blunt. Baller got the munchies. Back to the kitchen to cook two more burgers. He went back to the living room until the burgers were through cooking. As soon as he sat down, he doze off. He was having a bad dream that he was on the highway riding and a car pulls up with Tray and Deuce inside, Tray hanging out the window with a gas Coke bottle bomb, both shooting it out on the highway. Tray throwed the bomb into the car while Deuce bust shots at Baller.

The back seat burning. Smoke filled the car. The car went out of control. Baller hit a pole and got stuck in the car. The car was under fire. Choking from the smoke, Baller woke up and the house was on fire.

Baller jump up with the Crown Royal still in his hands. He took it and bust the TV set and ran out the side door, choking from all the smoke. He jump in his car and peel out super mad. He drove out to the stash spot to put everything up at except the 40 pounds of weed he's given Milk.

Baller was up, but he was feeling down. But he know he broke one of his rules. But he's a dirty boss, Mack. He will not take "no" for an answer. Baller trained Brown Sugar well. She can trick the best. She told Baller she want nothing but the game he gave her. After Brown Sugar told Baller that, he couldn't do nothing but accept it. Baller know that Brown Sugar is a million dollar 'ho. He was hurt, but he play it off like a player. So he call up Dee Dee.

Ring...ring...ring.

Dee Dee: "Hello."

Baller: "Hey--can I speak to Dee Dee?"

Dee Dee: "This me. Guess what? I went to the bank with my aunt. I saw over two million dollars in cash. Now that a nice lick! I told my cousin, Panama Black, about it. He like the ideal. It's the Nations Bank in Greenbriar Mall. It so simple."

Baller: "Look, I don't want to talk about that shit right now."

Dee Dee: "Damn--what's wrong with your attitude?"

Baller: "Just meet me at the Underground Suite Hotel in one hour on the 17th floor, Room 1708. Later."

Baller, riding out to his room, mad at the world because he lost one of his best 'ho's. But a real player woulda just broke that bitch and just let her go.

THE FAMILY

Back at Brown Sugar's mom's house it was late. She woke up and checked her pager. It was overflowing. It was Milk paging her. She looked at herself in the mirror and took a deep breath and then called Milk.

Ring...ring...ring.

Milk: "Hello."

Brown Sugar: "Hey Boo."

Milk: "What up, Girl? Where you at?"

Brown Sugar: "At my mom's house."

Milk: "Did the score come out all right? I'm ahead by one.or what?"

Brown Sugar: "Yes, it worked out okay. You're the one for me as long as you don't lie, curse, or hit me. Just respect me. I will help you get the world. I am down to zero. I need you in my corner."

Milk: "But did the lick go well?"

Brown Sugar: "Yes. He didn't have any money-just 40 pounds of weed. And Baller killed him. I didn't see him kill him because he knocked me out. And left a big ass knot on my head. I don't feel like working tonight."

Milk: "Okay, Boo. Where is Baller? I've been paging him all day."

Brown Sugar: "I don't know."

Milk: "Well, just be ready at 8 o'clock."

Brown Sugar: "What's up for the night?"

Milk: "The family...the family. I just hope Baller don't let me down. I need a nigga like Baller on the team. He's a true hog to this shit. I can see it in his eyes." Brown Sugar: "I know he don't come before me, do he?"

Milk: "Baby, you are the Mother of the Family. They will be the seeds. And me and you will make them grow. Now, get your act together. At 8 o'clock I will be there to come get you. So be clean or be missed."

Brown Sugar: "So what did you do last night?"

Milk: "I just chilled at the hotel getting my game together so me and you and the family will be on top soon. See you at 8 o'clock. Later."

As soon as Milk got off the phone, he had a room full of 'ho's. Some young fine ass, tender with pecan brown skin. One of the girls handed Milk a key of dope. Milk busted the key open and said, "Y'all 'ho's ain't ready for this Jeffrey Dahmer. It preys on the weak I haven't stepped on this shit and I ain't going to step on it. If you snort it one time, you'll pass out for an hour unless someone wakes you up who don't snort. So...do you still want to hit this shit?"

All fifteen of the girls' eyes were very glassy, looking at Milk, saying, "Hell yeah!!! Pass the snok snok!!!"

Milk, butt ass naked, dick rock hard. He lay back and sprinkled the dope all over his body--even his dick--and said, "Come get it!" They were on his ass like rats on cheese. Each 'ho' might have snorted about 3 grams apiece. After 4 or 5 more snorts they were falling out like flies. Milk ate and fuck the shit out of them. He eats them first to get them hot--the flake keeps the pussy wet. Every time he licks down there they smile, but they don't move. When he puts that dick on them they smile. But when he started strokin' they woke up, putting their legs up, and start strokin' back, loving the dick. Loving the dick, taking the dick all kinds of ways. Milk fucks all fifteen of them 'ho's, and when he gets down to the last one he has the 'ho's to eat each other. They're belly to belly, skin to skin, bumping pussy like hell and ain't no dick going in. Milk goes to the table to cut it just a little bit so it won't be so powerful. Milk does this type of shit every time he has a gang of 'ho's or when a big-time person is present.

✳ ✳ ✤ ✲ ✳ ✳ ✳ ☆ ✯ ☆

Abbie: "Your little sister need you. She will not be listening to me or Isra, an' your mom workin' two jobs, an' she be too tired to do or say anything. You're the mom now. But pretty soon your sorry ass uncle going to get it together an' someone have to be there for Neva. She will be in pretty soon. She at the store--she feel lucky so she play the Cash 3 Lotto. She win sometimes."

Brown Sugar: "This house is clean. What time is it?"

Abbie: "It's 6:41 p.m.--they will be in soon. Sit down, Girl. Have a beer. I got a 12-pack in the refrigerator.

Brown Sugar: "No beer, Girl. I 'm okay. I got to get ready for work. I just need Calgon to 'take me away'." Sugar walked upstairs to run her bath water and came back down to borrow some panties--she gave Baller everything, even down to the panties. Baller put the game in her head and she played by the rules. Baller broke one of his rules. In his head he thought she loved bad ways, and with that attitude he'll go a long way.

Because Brown Sugar is one of the baddest bitches in Atlanta night clubs, every player that's got big money thinks that their money and game can get Brown Sugar. It could, if you got lots of it--I mean you got to have money to burn and so much game that it will make a lame nigga turn player overnight. This bitch got lawyers and polices wanting to leave their wives. But it was Baller's idea to make her a million dollar 'ho'.

Like when she got too close to an Atlanta police named Pacman. He used to hit that pussy once a month, giving her $750 every time they fuck. He sometimes run his mouth too much, like the first time she suck his dick. He went crazy, fucked around and said something about a shipment. That some big time nigga is paying cops good to protect their shipment. She put the lick in Baller's hands. Baller told her when he got to the lick they were already hit by Hommie the Clown and Michael Myers, and when someone say them two say no more so she just fuck him and make sure that none of her and her folks go to jail.

Pacman: "Look, I got much work tonight, Boo, but if you can put me on some money it might just be a short night with some long bread.

Brown Sugar: "I know some folks, but you don't have a spot to put all that cash." Pacman's small eye got big when she said money.

Pacman: "Bitch, you must don't know who I am. This Pacman. They made a movie about me standing in the window in his boxers with a pint of Hennessey, popping shit like a player and not like a cop." And Baller's in the hotel across the street with binoculars, scoping out the prey.

Brown Sugar: "Let's go. I hate dis hotel room."

Pacman: "Look, I got big plans for me an' you."

Brown Sugar: "Well, I just ran out of raw."

Pacman: "Here's two grams. I'm going to have enough to supply the whole Zone 3 and my Zone is the shit. I call the shots but my dogs runs the streets."

Brown Sugar: "Do I know your dogs?"

Pacman: "You might know my crew, the Dirty 3."

She was just thinking about some of the shit she used to do

for Baller. Back downstairs.

Brown Sugar: "Abbie, do you have an extra pair of panties?"

Abbie: "Yeah, Girl, look, in that K-Mart bag. There should be a pair in the bag. You sure you don't want a beer? They're ice cold."

Brown Sugar: "No, thanks, Girl. Thanks for the panties."

Brown Sugar went back upstairs. The bath water was just right--bubbles were everywhere. Brown Sugar took a look in the mirror and reached into her bra and pulled out a personal 8-ball that Milk gave her. Straight--no cut. Brown Sugar got off into the tub, looked around, and snok snok snok snok snok. She stood up and sat back into the tub and passed out wth blood dripping from her nose. The raw fell into the tub. The time: 7:50 p.m.

Isra, Neva and the kids burst through the door.

Neva: "I hit...I hit the Cash 3!"

Abbie jumped up. "What's going on?"

Isra: "She hit Cash 3 for $500. She played 2-8-3 straight. Where's Sugar?"

Abbie: "Upstairs in the bathtub."

Neva walked upstairs, opened the door and started screaming, "Help! Help! My sister!" Brown Sugar jumped up and grabbed her sister.

Brown Sugar: "What's wrong?!"

Neva: "Your nose...I thought you were dead!" Isra and Abbie rushed upstairs. Brown Sugar cleaned herself up.

Isra and Abbie: "What's wrong up here?!"

Brown Sugar: "Girl, I fell asleep in the tub."

Abbie: "Girl, I need beer."

Brown Sugar: "Me too. Let's go get it. My high blood pressure, it got the best of me. My nose bleeds sometimes. What time is it?"

Abbie: "8:00 p.m."

By that time, Milk had pulled up, blowing the horn.

Neva: "Ooh--it's some boy in a pearl white Lexus. He's looking good, too. Mmm-mmm."

Brown Sugar ran down with her beer. Abbie looked at Sugar and gave her a hug and a kiss and said, "You take care, Girl. An'still, for me, talk to your sister. She need you." Brown Sugar left, with tears in her eyes, not knowing where she was headed. She loved her family, but she has advanced in the game where there is no love.

Going out the door, saying, "I'll talk to her." Neva was coming in as Sugar was going out.

Brown Sugar: "We need to talk for about 3 minutes." They stepped back in for a minute, Sugar oiling down her body, talking to her little sister.

Brown Sugar: "Look, I need you to understand me. I'll take care of you and you take care of Mom. Let's not let Mom down. She came a long way by herself. Don't disrespect Mom. She needs us to take care of her when she's not able to help herself. Beep me when you need me and tell Mom I love her." Neva reached for her sister and gave her a big ass hug. Both had tears in their eyes.

Brown Sugar: I love you. I'll send some money when I get right." Sugar, walking to the car in her long black leather coat and the panties Abbie gave her. She gave all she had to Baller just to be next to Milk. She plan this herself, because she knew that Baller would kill Milk or fuck it up.

She got some plans of her own. She see money in Milk. She got licks that Baller did not have the experience to handle.

Brown Sugar: "Hey, Boo, what up?"

Milk: "You. Let's dip." Riding out to the hideout.

Milk: "Damn, you look good, I must say."

Brown Sugar: "I don't have anything on."

Milk: "Let me see." Brown Sugar opened up her coat. Milk looked her up and down and told her to take off the coat. She did.

Brown Sugar: "Do you have any raw?"

Milk: "There may be a half in the dash. It's all chopped up, so you can hit it hard if you want to. So, what you think about Baller?"

Brown Sugar: "I don't think nothin' about him."

Milk: "Would you work with him again?"

Brown Sugar: "If you want me to. Whatever it takes to make the family tight. I like your style. You seem to know how to treat a girl."

Milk: "At first I used to tear a woman apart, but now I just let a 'ho' be a 'ho'. I used to be married. That bitch ran me crazy. I tried to make a 'ho' out of a housewife an' that will never work. You got to let a 'ho' be a 'ho' and that's that. I once was a shorty in the game until they killed my captain. That nigga used to give me much game, an' right to this day I live by the code of the game. Now you can be down or be gone." Looking dead into Sugar's eyes.

Brown Sugar: "I work better with a family, so let's make some money, Boo. I am down for whatever. I have some rules, too. Just don't curse me or put your hands on me or disrespect me in any form or fashion." Sugar reached into the dash and pulled out the Eddie Murphy Raw and got to it. Snok, snok, snok. She yelled out, "I love this! Cut that other shit...knock me the fuck out!" It was just too pure. She took three more--snok, snok, snok--and went down on Milk, giving him good head on the highway.

Milk's pager went off. He checked his pager code--164. It was Baller, the call he was waiting for. Calling back on a burnout--that's a phone with a chip. You can talk all day on a burnout.

Baller: "Hello."

Milk: "Hey, Dog, why you call so late?"

Baller: "Shi-id...burning the candle at both ends. Doing it too hard last night. It went down okay. What's next?"

Milk: "I had a little shoo-be-doo for you. Yeah, did you kill that fool?"

Baller: "An' you know it. He didn't have time to do shit. I got the weed...I didn't see no flow. I went across the bitch's head and knocked her ass out so she won't be in the way."

Milk: "Yeah, I feel that knot on my Boo's head."

Baller: "What do you mean?"

Milk: "She serving me up right now an' I feel that knot on my Boo's head. Look here--meet me at the Nikko with that. We're doing the family tonight. Ooh, Baby...shit! Just meet me in room 606 tonight. Later."

Catching a nut on the highway, riding out. "Oooh, Baby...Baby!" Baller had a rough night--two major licks in one night. That's working.

✳ ✳ ✤ ✻ ✳ ✳ ✳ ☆ ✮ ☆

Milk put in much work the four months he was here. Him and Sugar arrive at the hotel early, at 9:00 p.m. The meeting at 12:00 midnight. Milk and Sugar hit it off. Both clean their self up. Sugar was giving Milk a rub down, chopping up his body with her soft hands. Milk doze off for a minute, thinkin' about when he was in Atlanta 10 years ago, when Milk was a shorty in the game. Rollin' crack rock, runnin' with the Four Assassins, trappin'; just like Baller. Milk jump off in the game with the Miami Boys in '82. The Miami Boys ran the dope in Atlanta. Techwood was one of the worst projects in Atlanta in the middle of '82 and '83. 500 strong with dope and money. The Miami Boys ran the traps, 'hood, clubs, and streets. They were the money makers.

They put big dope in projects like Eagle Homes, Herndon Homes, Grady Homes, Dixie Hill. Each project had its own captain, lieutenant, and some damn good workers.

A worker is a person who make the money in the 'hood-- the one who take the most chances with the cops. (A worker is sometimes called a shorty or a soldier.) Every shorty got to work in the 'hood for some underground experience. From there they become a soldier with heart, and then they move up to become a lieutenant with game. (The lieutenant's the man under the captain.)

A captain is the one who scope the neighborhood to see where the money is, if there's money in the 'hood. He get a bitch from the 'hood, wine and dine her to death, gettin' her on his side, fixin' her up so she look better than most of the girls in the 'hood for the minute. The captain then ask about everybody in the 'hood. She tell everything, down to who gettin' money, who roll rocks, and who he can get to help him move his shit.

And then the captain show the whole 'hood love by takin' them to clubs, frontin' them dope, tellin' them, "I got your back," showin' gats, tellin' them if they need anything, "I got it for you." But the gun is for them if they get out of line. They're so hypnotized that they think it's love, but it's just game. A captain get love from everyone because of the hard time of coming up in the game. From a shorty to a captain, it's hard in this ghetto.

The captain lay out the plan to the lieutenant. They lay out the plan to take over the 'hoods, traps, and the club scene. The lieutenant keep check on everything--he even sometimes break the captain's girls off. But it's the captain's order to please them. The captain stay working; he really don't have time for a girl because money come first. As long as money comin', they're happy.

It was hard for a nigga in Atlanta. The dope game was new. The Miami Boys was ridin' good, givin' girls what they wanted, so they sold their soul to the dealer. The girls wouldn't even go out with you if you didn't sell dope or have big money.

The Miami Boys was all over the city and they couldn't stand each other. When they saw each other it was always some shit. The drug war was bad in '81, '82, '83, '84, '85. '86 it was very B.A.D. in Miami. Niggas was gettin' killed left and right, so they fled from Florida to Atlanta with the game they learned as a shorty in Florida. But when they came to Atlanta, it got even worse. They were made lieutenants and captains, every man that deal drugs in their state, and the money was good. And if he or she leave that state, they're on the run for killin' someone or for a big drug case. It don't matter what state or who you is if the law is on you--gots to flee.

With all the dope and money they had, niggas was gettin' killed day to day. Miami is the cheapest place to get dope; $10G a key, pure, no cut. '82, '83, Miami was on the map.

✱ ✱ ✤ ❄ ✳ ✱ ✳ ☆ ✬ ☆

Baller got off the phone, look over at Dee Dee and said, "It's the family tonight, so my game got to be tight. So pay close attention to me. My game is your game, so if my game is on that mean your game on. But if my game is over, your game over. Understand me."

✱ ✱ ✤ ❄ ✳ ✱ ✳ ☆ ✬ ☆

You just need some soldiers. A soldier put in so much work knowin' that one day he will become a lieutenant or a captain. A shorty is a person that emulates a lieutenant or a captain's style. Just coming up and going down. But still hangin' in there. See, as a shorty, you lose before you gain. That's something that every shorty should know.

A soldier put the work in for the lieutenant; the lieutenant tell the captain. The captain analyze the soldier and give him rank. If the soldier fails within a year, his rank drops back down to a shorty. A real soldier moves on because they love money. The captain has to do this because the dope game is not for everyone. A captain go throughout his crew to see where they fit in this crucial game.

It look and seem good, but it's not.

It's a never ending game if you don't get in and get out. Friends come from all angles actin' like they're your friend to the end. Sayin' shit like, "You're the man! Let me hold somethin'. Big money." Just smilin', showin' you love. But behind that smilin' there's envy and violence, so pay attention to your surroundings.

The person that cross you will be the one who can get closest to you. These are words to live by. If you are involved in some way in this game, you will see pain before you see gain. Always switch up on your foe. The devil works all the time--keep that in mind. And God will let you shine if you believe in Him truthfully. So keep your mind on the game and your heart with the Lord. You will make it when everyone fail you. God will make a way no matter how hard it may seem. He will be there with open arms.

There are no friends in this never ending game. And I do mean no friends. Words to live by.

✳ ✳ ✧ ✵ ✳ ✳ ✳ ☆ ✰ ☆

Milk coming out of his short nap. Milk gave Sugar some info on how to work the family. Sugar using her mind to listen to what Milk had to say. She was glad to take orders. She worship what Milk possess--and that's money, power and death to the very end. Pressure and violence play a big part in this game. Evil has no rules.

12:00 midnight. Sitting around the round table at the

penthouse is everyone Milk show love to in the four months he was here. 9 divas and 15 killers showing their love by giving to the family and wanting nothing back but love from the family. Everyone wants a down ass family, a family that can move mountains...

The table was full with money, dope, champagne, guns, everything you could possibly want was on the table. The money and stuff come from major licks that the street people hit on the street of the ATL. It was all on the round table.

Milk broke the family down into four groups and four parts of Atlanta--College Park, East Point, Fulton County, and Decatur. Milk walk out with Sugar by his side. Every family should have a mother and a father.

Milk: "We shall be the family of all families, but we got to stick together. Small but strong, smart and hard, black and fast. I want each of you to show what type of game you bring to the family to better it and let's take heed to what your brother and sister is saying. I hand picked every one of you. I know soldiers when I see soldiers. See, this is going to be the family that takes chances and sacrifices. We kill us. We sleep together, we creep together, we make money together, we hit lick together, we come together. You see, we kill us. No one else but us, and it better be a damn good excuse. Never cross the code or the code will cross you, so be good. You understand me."

Everyone nodded their head in agreement.

Milk: "Now, who want to jump this family off?"

Diamond: "Shi-id...I'll kick this family off right. My name is Diamond, bitch of all bitches. I'll fuck them but not my crew. My crew Sugar Wolf, the Pimp; MJG, the Drunken Master; Greed, the Shiftier. When I met you we were kickin' it like big players, me and my crew. Until I saw you over there kickin' it the same way. I was like, 'What?!

Crew, spread out--let's work!'

We were at Club 112--I thought you was a trick ass, and then that's when you lay game on me just a little bit. As we were kickin' it, the later it got. See, I wanted a li'l something and I wanted it to be some new meat with that money taste. I did a sign to call off my crew. They broke off with doubt in their mind like, this nigga got loot, big loot! What's up? That when I throw another sign sayin' I'll keep him.

I sometime need a dick with game in my corner. I can't stand a broke dick that, shit, leave a bitch pussy swollen and I can't have that. The bitch can't go for that. So we hit it off o-tay. You put us up on a nice something something. Sugar Wolf had the scope on tight at the club.

MJG had the parking lot; MJG check outside, actin' like he lost his keys, dead ass drunk playin'. MJG is a pro safe cracker. This nigga use the drunk technique on his victims. He catch customers outside the club, follow them to their cars, rob them at gun point (rings, watches, ropes, and cash). But if he catch you right like when you open your car door, that's where the grave is--in the car (drugs, money, and weapons).

"Greed the one who kept Tray and Deuce tied down with that real talk. You hear me? Our shit was tight!!! Sh...I ain't lyin'."

The crew (Sugar Wolf, Greed, and MJG) was shorties on the streets and clubs and it was hard for them to hit a nice lick. They were shorties, not soldiers. They will easy drop window shop all over but couldn't put shit together. Diamond make things happen. When she got with them boys they made big bank. Money out the ass.

Diamond use her own lick with the money put in the family. Milk had another lick set up. Diamond is a go getter and get the job done. Bad ass bitch. She like being in control.

She got her own way of stingin'. She love the family. She a workin' bitch and she always say, "I am my own boss." The lick that Milk set up was for 7 keys. Diamond and the crew kick in ten keys with ease and they all said there more where that came from!

Everyone stood up and saluted very expensive wine, top quality coke, and some of the best weed on this God given earth. Four or more keys was busted open. They were havin' a good time, all gettin' to know their true self, gettin' to know each other. Like brother and sister, makin' a true family.

✳ ✳ ✤ ✳ ✳ ✳ ✳ ☆ ✭ ☆

This next family has been doin' good in the past years gettin' it. But they also have seen pain and bad things in life. "My name is Sky, a place of freedom."

And, "My name is Mona Lisa, Black Like My Sister."

"And me, I am Chicago."

Tray: "Damn, Baby, is you colder than the Windy City?" Chicago colder.

These ladies are some of the most treacherous bitches on the street, always ready to work.

Chicago: "Well, we were just comin' out of a small family and it was not tight like how we are now. A family bring strength and love. We met Milk out at the Lenox Mall. He had Brown Sugar walkin' with him throughout the mall, shopping. It look as if they were havin' the time of their lives. But we were workin'. Brown Sugar step into the Victoria's Secret. I sent Sky in behind her to see what type of money this bitch was spendin'. Excuse me, Sugar; I didn't know you at the time."

Sugar: "Go ahead--tell your story. We're all bitches, but some bad ass bitches."

Diamond: "That's right, Girl."

Chicago: "I talk with Milk outside the store. We talk while Sky went to work on Sugar."

Sky: "She look around for a minute. She pick up somethin' for herself. By that time she look up into my eyes, and that was it. She saw freedom. As she look into my laid back baby blue eyes she was hook, so I lure her into the fittin' room. I kiss her slowly, place my hands on her cookie, and softly rubbed across her nipple."

Sky is a six foot tall Cuban girl with pretty skin. And hair like silk--and have eyes to die for. Many tried her because she so pretty. But she quick to snap and beat a bitch ass. And she works out to keep her body tone.

She's been hittin' licks for a living. Her mom left. At age nine she was turnin' tricks. Her mom left out of town with her dope man boyfriend, heading for Hollywood. She came back at age 18 in a body bag. Her and her boyfriend was found beat to death in their hotel room. Because of the way they die, from the police report they say it was drug related and it was two or more killers with baseball bats with ten or more nails stickin' out the end of the bat. Body fill up with hundreds of small holes.

Sky left Cuba at age 21 and came to Atlanta and got her a girlfriend to make it with. She doesn't want to follow in her mother steps.

She got down with Chicago, a dark girl with school sense. She got degrees at Spellman, but she got turn out by a smooth talkin' player who is well feared and barely seen. And the most serious about the mighty dollar. Her school and street smarts put her at the top of her game. Sḷ   ᴺ this clique. Chicago got more game than the averaꝑ this game. Her mind and attitude is perfect fᴵ today.

She knew with Sky she have something goᴵ

tiful chick has wit, charm, and style. They both use to hit licks for big time dope boys gettin' 15%. The dope boys wasn't givin' up shit. 15% wasn't shit. They gots to split that down the middle. But the more big licks they hit, the players tighten up on their game. So many have died in '91, '92, and even more in the year to come in '93.

The girls got down with Frank the Bank, a old retired pimp with some of the baddest bitches by his side. Frank came out of retirement when he got a call from some of his Jamaican customers from out of town. They were here on some big business.

Frank: "Hello."

King Willie: "Hello, Frank, my American friend."

Frank: "Who this? My Jamaican buddy King Willie??"

King Willie: "Why, yes it is, man. How do you do, man?"

Frank: "Just kickin' it like a big ol' pimp. How you Baby?"

King Willie: "I be in town for a couple of days. Me need some girl to rock me world. Can you still hook me up, man?"

Frank: "I ain't never let you down, have I? I am the king of bang, bang, bang. I get everybody some bang, bang. Hell, I even got Bill Clinton a li'l something something when he was here on business. Look here, my new 'ho's don't come cheap. You got to pay the cost to be the boss. Now, King Willie, where you at? I'll send you over a limo."

King Willie: "Yeah, man, that will be nice."

Frank: "You got anything for me?"

King Willie: "Do you like diamonds? I got diamonds. Tell me, do you like diamonds? I get two million in cash for the diamond. Can you buy that, Frank?"

Frank: "I got three bad ass bitches for you. $20G apiece. That's $60G. Can you buy that, Mr. King Willie?"

King Willie: "Frank, I was just kidding."

Frank: "I wasn't."

King Willie: "The Atlanta airport, that's where I'm at. The Airport."

Frank set it up when the Jamaican got from the airport to the hotel safe. This lick is very important to Frank. He sent his baddest bitches on this one--Sky, Chicago, and Frank's prize 'ho', a snow white bunny, Mona Lisa. His main girl. He don't trust Sky and Chicago on this one--too much involved because these 'ho's can steal their ass off.

Frank and the girls dress real nice. Frank, Versace and Armani; the girls sometime wear Cynthia Rowley to show most of their breast. Breasts are in. Everyone showing them to turn heads. It don't matter what these girls wear. Heads are going to turn. Silk, furs, diamonds. Natural born foxes. With the face of an angel and the heart of a lion. Every man must have a fox in his lifetime. If you have had a bad experience with a bitch and she got you down, a fox can come in your life, pick you up and let you go and you will feel no pain because a fox is a real woman. She understand a man better than a bitch or a 'ho'. Frank got the foxes. And they stay ready for work. I mean, love to work!

Frank put a master plan together. Frank told the Girls about the lick and said, "This is how I want to go out--with a big bang! You 'ho's seen that movie Scarface? See, I am not that Frank on the movie--that guy was soft. He didn't take care of his destiny. He let his boys up under him get bigger than him. You got to listen to your soldiers. And respond big and quick. And it will work out okay. Rank him or her. And if he or she fails, set them back and school them more. That's how you make soldiers. After this last one I want you two to run the stable. You got good potential. I got a million dollar spot on Grab Avenue. Good money spot. You just got to keep the damn cops right."

"Now, my main girl is going to tag along to keep you 'ho's in check so that way she'll let Daddy know what's goin' on."

Chicago: "What you mean, 'in check'? We can handle this ourself."

Sky: "We don't know nothin' bout this 'ho'. She might be Five-O."

Frank: "Shut your damn mouth, just shut it up. This is my bitch what you talkin' 'bout." Frank call Mona Lisa out. She step out.

Frank: "Come on, Baby. Show 'em what you got. Ladies, meet my honey money bunny Mona Lisa."

Sky was movin' her legs like a cricket. Chicago lick her lips and rubbin' her tongue across her teeth with a small smile. They both like what they saw.

Chicago: "Why they call you Mona Lisa, Black Like My Sister?"

Mona Lisa: "See, back in the days there was a woman raped and killed because of her skin color."

Chicago: "There were a whole lotta black womens being killed, taken away from their families and was rape and slave for all their lives."

Mona Lisa: "True, but the white man was doin' so much fuckin' the black woman that his wife wasn't no more good. And the white woman know it. So the white woman went sneakin' around with the black man.

One of the white women got pregnant by a black man and had twins. One was black, one was white. The slave master kill the black one and spare the white one. Even if the black woman has a child by a white man and the baby come out black the slave master will kill the child. And if the white woman get pregnant by the black and the baby look white, the slave master will be satisfied. But the baby will still be black.

"So I am one of those kids with a white mom and a black father. So that's why I say I am Black Like My Sister. Mona Lisa was a black woman; that's why her painting was so important--not because of her smile. She was the one who had the twins, so she's the first white woman to have had a baby by a black man and live to tell white woman about how the black man is in bed. You have lots of people walkin' around lookin' white, but they're really black."

Sky: "So what all that mean?"

Frank: "That mean she a bad ass bitch who can work on both sides, black and white. Just like Moses do good on both sides; it don't matter who you are if you got the skills to do the job.

Chicago: "She can kick it, but why now and not when it was all bad?"

Frank: "This is what she want. We're gettin' married after this one, and anyway, she need this experience. We're going to be in Honolulu, Hawaii on the beach, butt ass naked, smilin' ear to ear. And when I get back it's work, work, work.

"Them young cats buyin' pussy like crazy, so you girls keep it clean. Bang, bang, bang. Now get to it."

Frank kissin' all over Mona Lisa sayin' "we're going to be rich." She slowly move him off.

Mona Lisa: "Baby, let me chill with the girls tonight."

Frank: "Look at my li'l mama, smart like a fox. Baby, you watch them for Daddy now." Frank walkin' around the house, poppin' his fingers, sayin' "Just like Daddy, just like Daddy."

Mona Lisa, Sky, and Chicago left Frank castle and headed to their condo. On the way, Chicago was droppin' all kinds of things on Mona Lisa's head, tryin' to get her to leave

Frank and tag with them.

Chicago: "Girl, you need freedom. I can see you're not happy with that ol' ass pimp nigga."

Mona Lisa: "I love Frank. You don't understand."

Chicago: "No, you don't understand. You're in your twenties; you don't have time for sucker love. You need family love. I'm not the one to sit on my ass and wait on a nigga. My mom was like that, waitin' on a man. A man is going to do what they wanna do. So that's what we got to do is move on. My mom work day and night to put me in school. By herself, without a man. Come join us--we don't need a man, we got each other."

Sky: "You are a beautiful person and he just with you because you look white. He want to get back at white folks. But, Girl, you're black and he want to be your slave master. I won't go for that."

They got to the condo and snort coke all night. They both subdue her. Chicago first did her thang. Whipper pill to whipper pill. Chicago got up and left but told her to get ready for Freedom. Sky freak her all night, Cuba style. When Chicago return that morning, the day of the lick, Lisa was sittin' on the couch talkin' about the lick.

Lisa: "After this lick we go right to Frank and kill his ass." Silently crying, "He's not right, he's not. He treat me like a slave, not family. You two treat me like a sister. Now I see family. I love you two; just love me for me and not what you can use me for."

Chicago look up at Sky and smile. Sky is the best when it come down to takin' a woman from a man. And Chicago is the best at takin' a man from a woman.

Chicago: "Let's eat. It's on me, Girls. I got a taste for some pancakes and sausage with maple syrup."

Sky: "Me too, Girl, me too. How about them ten silver

dollar pancakes? Or some blueberry and pecan pancakes?"

Lisa: "Oooh--let's go!"

Before they could leave, Frank called.

Chicago: "Hello."

Frank was talkin' all loud, "You 'ho's ready to work?"

Chicago: "Yes, Frank, but we're going to step out and get something to eat."

Frank: "Eat, my ass! They're on the way. They're going to feed you. So put some bad shit on... Let's do this, Chicago. Work it for me, Baby. The Jamaican have cash and dope-- they sold the diamonds. And it's five Jamaican, not three. Go with the same plan, just blast fast. I want you to make them to hang back about two hours. They're going to want to go back to the hotel to bang, bang, bang. So when they start to take off their clothes I'm going to bust in the door and catch them with their pants down. I want you girls to pack that steel, scope that room. Blast when I blast or soon-er. Now let me talk to my boo."

Chicago: "Lisa, telephone. It's Frank."

Lisa: "Hey, Boo."

Frank: "Hey, look. Them 'ho's ain't fuck with you, are they?"

Lisa: "No, Boo. I got these 'ho's in check."

Frank: "That's good to hear. They're street smart, but I know you headstrong. I want you to stay back on this one. This is a bad one--hang back."

Lisa was listenin' with tears in her eyes. Knowin' that Frank was saving her from something bad and Chicago and Sky was showing her freedom and new ways to be a fox 'ho'.

Frank: "It's going to be blood, Boo, so hang back. If you don't you might get killed."

Lisa: "Okay. We'll be ready," and hung up the phone.

Frank, yelling: "Lisa, Lisa--don't hang up!!"

Sky: "Lisa, what's wrong with you?"

Lisa wipes away the tears from her eyes. The telephone rings.

Sky: "Hello."

Frank: "You stupid white bitch! When I tell you something I'm going to kick!!"

Sky: "Frank!! Wooo, wooo--what's wrong?"

Frank: "Who this?!"

Sky: "This Sky, Frank. What's wrong?"

Frank: "Nothing. The little bitch just out her body, she going to act right. I see you girls later on. Now put that white bitch on the phone."

Sky: "Now, Girl, he just want to say something sweet to his Boo here."

Frank: "Bitch! I got you out the gutter and you want to turn your back on me! If you fuck this up I'll kill your ass, Bitch, just like the last 'ho'! Bitch! Don't test me. Now you do what Chicago tell you. Now let's get this money honey. I don't want no shit out of you. This is the big one."

Lisa, shaking her head, smiling: "Okay, Boo. It will be all right. Love you."

Chicago: "What's up? What did he say?"

Lisa: "Nothing. He just don't trust me with you two."

Chicago look up at Sky and shook her head as if she didn't do her job. An hour later the white limo pulls up. The girls step out of the condo and into the limo. There they were, lookin' and smellin' good. The Jamaicans couldn't believe their eyes. As they entered the limo, their hands was all over the girls' ass."

King Willie: "You girls is as lovely as Frank explained to me. My name is King Willie, God of gods. My friend's King Rasa. I got what you girls need--puffin' a fat ass blunt."

Chicago sat next to King Rasa.

Rasa: "Here, smoke this. It will blow you away." Chicago hit the weed and started choking. Everyone laughed.

King Willie: "This is my magic friend, Lock Face. He can't talk or be killed. He's been shot over a thousand times in war... They say when a man face is lock he already dead and his soul is trap outside heaven and hell. So to kill him you got to cut his head off to free his soul for the Devil. And the Devil wants his soul but can't get it until his flesh is destroyed."

Sky: "I just love a man in war."

Lisa curl up with King Willie.

King Willie: "Let's get back to the hotel to do some major things like let's get butt naked and fuck."

Chicago: "I got to get something to eat before I do anything. And when I eat it's all good then."

King Rasa: "What would you like?"

Chicago: "Some International House of Pancakes."

Rasa: "Tell the driver." She did.

Riding out to the IHOP. By the time they got to the restaurant, Lock Face pull out a ounce of raw powder. The girls' eyes stuck to the bag.

King Willie: "Now, do you ladies want something to eat or do dis coke? It's been stepped on a li'l bit. It's the best in the west."

Chicago grab the cell phone and call in to place the order while they got coked up in the limo. The cell phone rings; it's one of the dreads back at the hotel.

Rasa: "Hello. Who this calling at a time like this?"

"It's Reggie, man. Where are you? Me and Jungle were worried, man."

Rasa: "We're getting something to eat. We cool, man. Be there when the food get ready."

Reggie: "Bring me somethin' too, man."

Rasa: "Order room service, man. We're on the way."

Chicago: "Is it going to be a switcharoo? 'Cause I can't do you and you and him at the same time in the same room. And I will still do my girls in front of you."

Rasa: "You like it freaky, don't you? You are a nasty girl. And I am a nasty boy. We're going to do it in the same room, but we have two rooms. Right, King Willie?"

King Willie: "Yeah, man. Two--212 and 214. Which room do you want, nasty boy?"

Rasa: "It don't matter to me, man."

Sky: "Chicago, what time is it?"

Chicago: "Wait, let me check my pager. Wait...hold up. Lisa, you seen my pager?"

Sky: "Why don't you beep it. It's bound to be here some-where--just beep it."

King Rasa handed Chicago the cell phone to beep her pager. She page her trick Daddy and put the room number, 212-214. He beep her pager to let her know that he got the room number. The pager went off. King Willie was sittin' on it.

King Willie: "Here it is, Girl, but let me see if you know the number you put in.

Chicago: "555-5555."

King Willie: "Here."

Riding to the hotel. Frank was at the hotel an hour early. He knew which hotel, but he didn't know the room number until he got the page he was looking for. Frank walk up to Room 213 and had to figure out which room has the money and dope. One room is where they party and the other room is where they chop up the money and dope. He step to Room 214. It was quiet, but he can slightly smell weed coming from under the door. He reach in his jacket and pull out his 44 mag, thought about it for a second, and walk to room 212 and put his ear to the door. Listening, he can hear Reggae playing. He ease back, ready to kick the door in.

The elevator door started to open. Someone was coming up. Frank walk off from the door. It was room service. Frank walk around the corner to see what room he was going to. The service went right to Room 212. Frank walk pass the door. He could hear the Jamaican guy tell the server, "Bring me my bread stick then I tip you. Now go get my bread stick!"

The room server came out of the room and in the hallway, cursing, saying, "Fuck them damn bread sticks! I ain't gettin' that shit. Get them your damn self, Lenny Kravitz."

Frank walked back to Room 212. He pulled out his 44 mag, knocked on the door.

Reggie: "Who there?"

Frank: "Room service."

The dread came to the door without checking the peep hole. When Reggie open up the door, Frank put his 44 mag to his forehead and led him to the middle of the room, where the other dread was. Frank got one to tie the other. Then Frank tie him up, tape up their mouth. Frank knock Reggie out. There was a knock at the door.

Frank: "Who is it?"

"Room Service. I got your bread stick."

Frank: "I've finished my food, but here's a tip." Frank slid $20 under the door. "And don't come back no more." He left.

Frank pick up Jungle, put the pistol to his head.

Frank: "You goin' to show me where the shit is or you a dead dread."

Jungle look at Frank eye to eye with his hands, feet and mouth tape up. Eyes blood shot red, breathin' hard, shootin' mucus out his nose into Frank's face. Frank jump back cursing.

Frank: "You dead, now, Nigga."

The dread was hoppin' around, breathin' hard, still shootin' mucus from his nose. Knocking over the lamp, TV, and the food he'd just ordered. If Frank hadn't knock Reggie out, they might have lived. The dread was tryin' his best to get loose. Frank got the mucus from his face and jump over on him and was beatin' him with his gat. Frank's pager was going off. Frank grab Jungle by the neck and was chokin' the shit out his ass.

They fell to the bed. Frank started back hittin' Jungle with the gat. The more Frank beat Jungle with that gat, he got stronger and stronger and his hand broke free. He grab Frank by his neck; his eyes even more fire red. Frank grab Jungle back around the neck with one hand and he was slowly puttin' that 44 to his head. Pop! Pop! Blew his ass to the floor.

The gunshot woke the other dread. He started shakin', bumpin' the floor. Frank jump at his ass right quick, hittin' him with that 44 in the head. He pick him up and show him his partner, and then lay him on his belly with his knee in his back. And with a low voice, "Now you know what it is, so when I let you up you will show me where's the shit."

Beep. Frank hear the beep. Frank felt for his pager--it was gone. He look around the room, broken bloody glass everywhere. Frank pick up his pager. It was all bloodied up. He wipe the blood from the pager. It was the killer code. Breathin' hard, lookin' around. Gettin' ready for round two. He posted up by the door with his 44. He knew that the beep meant they're on their way up. He almost didn't have time to check his pager because of the struggle.

Reggie didn't even talk. He knew it would be his soul. Lock Face will kill him then his entire family. He could only hope that his brother can save him from this horror scene.

Frank put his ear to the door. He can hear his girls coming through the hallway. The girls got louder and louder. Reggie had eased off the bed and hopped over to the window. Frank look back at the dread. Reggie look back and jump out the window. He felt that a evil spirit approaching his soul. Something way more powerful than Lock Face.

Frank kept his ears to the door and act as if he didn't see shit. It was the girls and King Willie, King Rasa, and Lock Face. Walking into their room. King Rasa put on some music--it was a cut on there by (Grace Jones' Island Life, "I've Seen That Face Before".) The girls lookin' around, smilin', nasty dancin', feelin' each other.

Chicago: "Where the raw?"

Sky: "Where the raw?"

Chicago: "I'm ready to go."

Lisa: "Girls, be cool. I'm sure they're going to let us powder our noses. And give us the world. Just relax. I'm going to have my way with Shaka Zulu right here."

Chicago: "You meant Mandingo."

Sky: "Okay, let's just chill. It look okay."

King Willie came out into the living room where the girls were with a suitcase. From the way he was holdin' the suitcase, It look as if it was heavy as hell. People love to come to Atlanta for some peaches & cream. There ain't nothin' like some peaches & cream. Atlanta is a place where the girls are sweet like a Georgia peach. Atlanta is a place where the money is fast, but the tag on your toe is faster. Peaches & cream turn into ditches & scheme.

King Willie set the suitcase down. He open it up. Everybody's eyes got big--50 keys of raw, uncut dope. He look up and around the room at everybody and said, "All eyes on me." Everyone burst out laughing, but their eyes was still on the suitcase. King Willie took a key and bust it on the table.

King Willie: "You, you, and you come help yourself."

The girls ran-walked to the table and got blown away. King Willie took Lock Face to the room with the money to talk about the girls.

King Willie: "Lock Face, listen to me. They're just what we need, some snake ass 'ho's. We can teach them the ways of the scale."

By that time King Rasa walk in on the conversation.

King Rasa: "Man, they're buck ass naked, throwing powder on each other, laughing Geek up, man. Let's keep them.King Willie, they are the ones we're looking for to help move the coke."

King Willie: "It sounds good, Rasa."

Lock Face nodded his head and agreed with King Willie and King Rasa.

While they were talking in the next room, the girls were getting coked up and checking their purse for their guns. Lock Face walk out of the room and stare at them for a minute then walk out the door. King Rasa was naked, ready to fuck. Lock Face look left and right and walk to Room 212. He had a key to the room. As soon as he open the door, Frank put that 44 to his head and said, "Come on in, Friend."

Lock Face look around the room and saw his dead friend bloodied all up, broken glass, signs of a struggle. He yell out, "IIIIIIIiiiii!!!!!!" and grab Frank. Frank shot Lock Face in the face. He fell to the floor.

Frank step over Lock Face and ran to Room 214 with gun in hand and kick in the door, holding the 44. Rasa and King Willie ran for their guns. Chicago, Sky, and Lisa reach for their guns when the door blew open. The girls open fire on

King Rasa and King Willie, hitting them in the back of the head and back. And aim the guns at Frank, shaking but not scared.

Frank yelling: "Lisa, come on! Sky, get the yayo! Chicago, get the cash! Let's get the fuck out here!"

Frank grab Lisa by the hand. As they headed out the door to get away, Room 213 opened up. A nigga with a Michael Myers "Halloween" mask on with a Mac 10 45cap tellin' Frank to drop it like it's hot. Frank stop and look at this horror figure that's fuckin' up his well put together plan. He couldn't tell who was behind the mask. Too much weed smoke comin' from the room.

Frank shook his head and look again--it was another nigga comin' from the midst of the smoke with a Hommie the Clown mask on. He fire a shot and hit Frank in the leg and said, "You heard my Nigga! Drop it like it's hot!"

Frank fell to the floor in the hallway. The water sprinkler came on. People was comin' from their rooms but couldn't see much because of the smoke-filled hallway.

Michael Myers and Hommie the Clown got off with $2 million in cash and 49 bird. Sky look at the cash and dope and just shook her head. Chicago grab Frank by the arm. "Let's go, let's go. The cops is comin'. Frank, let's get home."

Back at the house. Everyone got a little blood on their hands that day. Frank lay back in his chair, mad at the world. Thinking "who cross him?" Frank went for all his weapons. Limping to the bar and got a fifth of Hennessy. As soon as he got it he poured it on his leg. Yelling "IIIIIIIIII-II!!!!" Limping to his pool table; reaching under it and pulling out a personal key of cocaine. The girls was in the kitchen looking confused.

Sniffing raw powder, sipping on a martini, looking all glassy-eyed. Frank sat back down in his chair with a key of coke in his right hand and his 44 in his left hand. Frank then grab the phone and sat it in his lap. Took the coke, bust the bag open, the flake jumping out the bag. Frank had that Scarface look in his eyes. Looking around the room at all his weapons. Getting ready for war. Drinking, snorting, laying back, talking in a low voice. "Me and my girlfriend, me and my girlfriend" and kiss his 44 and said "I love you, don't let me down."

He held the key of coke to his nose. Snok, snok, slowly snok, snok. He drop the key of dope in his lap on the top of the phone. Moving in slow motion, he took his 44, dip the tip of the barrel into the key. There was about 3 grams on the tip of the barrel. He grab the Hennessy, taking a big gulp. Putting the barrel to his nose and took a big snort. The whole 3 grams was gone into his right nostril. Took another big gulp of Hennessy. Dip his gun back into the dope. Three more grams, and again one big snort in the left nostril. Frank's head fell back, hands still on his gat.

The phone was ringing. Frank so high, mumbling, "Bring it on, bring it on. If it's going down, let's get it over with." The phone still ringing.

Frank was out. The girls were worried about two things. And that was Michael Myers and Hommie the Clown, the diabolical born killers, the most feared, a dope dealer's worst nightmare. They rob, cross, and kill more dope dealers than the police, F.B.I., C.I.A., D.E.A, G.B.I., A.T.F., and S.I.D. If they would have been back in the days with Robin Hood they would have rob his ass. Touching fools who thought they were never going to get touched; snapping on snapper touching the toucher, killing the killer. Everyone talk about the two but know nothin', just the things they do. The girls rush into the living room to see why Frank haven't answer the telephone. It's gettin' on their nerves. Raw powder all in his lap and his hand still on his 44 mag.

The girls had thought it out. It was time to leave Frank. He was out, looking bad. Somewhere in the house Frank have a big stash of money and big dope. The girls went looking, tearing up the house. The phone still ringing. Lisa walk over to Frank crying, sniffing powder off Frank, while Chicago and Sky was tearing up the house for the cash. Lisa's makeup was running down her face, mixing with her tears. She pick up the phone.

Lisa: "Hello."

The Voice: "Drop it like it's hot, Bitch!"

Lisa threw down the phone in Frank's lap screaming, "No! No! Leave us alone!"

Frank jump up and fired a shot. Look around his house and seen it was mess up like someone was looking for something important. Frank look up at Lisa and spit in her face and slap the shit out of her. She fell to the floor. He aim that 44 mag at her head. Sky and Chicago ran in the room.

Sky: "No, Frank, no!"

Frank turn around and bust a shot at Sky.

Frank: "Fuck you, Bitch! I trust you 'ho's and you turn your back on me." Frank fired another shot.

Chicago yell out, "Please, no, Frank! We're saving you. Lock Face is on his way to get his money and dope. He just call you. You were out, Frank. We was just looking for your stuff so we can get the fuck out of here!"

Frank, shaking his head: "No, no, you're a smart ass little bitch! You 'ho's tryin' to rob me." Frank grab Lisa off the floor and put that 44 to her potato.

Frank: "So long, Pretty Lady."

Sky jump up. "No, Frank! Don't do it!"

Frank: "Why not?"

Chicago knew if Frank kill Lisa he got to kill Sky. And if

he kill Sky he gots to kill her. So she jump up and when she did she look Frank dead into his blood shot eyes, looking crazier than ever.

Chicago: "Frank, we don't have no money or dope. Look, we're your bitches, Frank. You made us, Baby. We can't cross you, Baby. No money, no dope. You need us, Frank."

Frank look at Lisa and said, "Go get my stash so we can get the fuck out of here." Lisa walk into Frank's game room wiping the tears away from her face. Next to the pool table is a big polar bear rug. She unplug the juke box and pull the back off. 7 keys of uncut cocaine inside a Glad Bag. She then walk back to the polar bear, reach inside the mouth, and pull out a sharp razor blade. Then move the rug out of the way, cutting the plush rug and the 5-inch thick insulation and 1 inch thick of plywood. Down below was a safe. Safe number 8 right, 14 left, 29 right, 7 left, 5 right, 25 left.

You wouldn't believe it--$6 million in cash. Frank was a '60s-'70s-'80s pimp, player, hustler, who had it all. Frank mess up his friendship and connection for something he already had. Greed play a big part in Frank's life.

Lisa brought out the money and drugs to Frank. Sky looking disappointed and was mad at the same time. Chicago got her eyes on Frank.

Frank: "My Boo, she down to the end with me."

Chicago: "Frank, we need to get the fuck out of here."

Frank cut the TV on and there it was--five Jamaicans found dead at the Hilton. Found with gun wounds and chopped up body parts.

Lock Face head was chop off. King Rasa right shoulder and left hand was gone. Someone from the police depart-ment said that someone used a small, sharp knife to cut his nuts and penis off. King Willie was chop in half and both eyeballs was gone. And for that dread that jump out the window, he was not long. Reggie was on top of him...

The police have no suspects in this unusually sick killing. All they know is that the suspects were fast and black. Frank and the girls' heads was fuck up after hearing that the bodies was chop up--that's Black Magic. They were bumping into each other, feeling uncomfortable. But knowing what's going on. Death wanted to pay its respect.

Chicago grab Frank; Lisa grab the money; Sky got the yayo. Frank holding onto Chicago while they headed out the door of freedom, ready to leave Atlanta. Too much crime in '92-'93, the tenth year anniversary for crack cocaine. So many people invest in Atlanta in '92 while it was the murder capitol. Everyone running to the door.

As they were running out the door, they saw the white limo pull up--the same one Frank sent to King Willie. They saw that and ran back in the house. Frank look out the door to see what they were running from. Stepping out the limo was Hommie the Clown, coming in slow motion. Running with a pump shotgun. Michael Myers right behind him with a MAC 10 45cap.

Frank push Chicago into the house, turn around and fired a shot and fell to the floor into the house. Everyone ran to different rooms except Frank. Frank went for his guns and to the raw flake that was in the chair. Frank half killed his self. He sniffin' 14 grams of raw powder in 5 seconds. Turn around with his 44 mag and pump shotgun. By that time the door blew open.

Frank bustin' shots after shots, yelling, "I've been waitin' on you two bad mother fuckers!" Bustin', yelling, "You ain't shit to me." Bustin' shots. "Fuck, nigga, die! die!! Die!!!" Bustin' rounds after rounds.

The girls had drop everything in the living room. They were in the next room, head down, eyes closed. The clown enter the house, bustin' a shot, hittin' Frank in the arm. He drop the shotgun and fell to the floor. Reloading his 44, his life saver. Raisin' up, bustin' at the clown, the clown bustin' back. Shots after shots. Slowly but surely, Michael Myers was coming in the door with that MAC 10 hittin' Frank 46 times, tearing chunks off Frank's body. The bullets was hittin' Frank so fast he couldn't fall. When the shootin' stopped, Frank was still standing.

Michael Myers and Hommie the Clown walk up to Frank. Frank was still talkin' shit, "Fuck you, Nigga," with his 44 in his hand, high out of his mind, bloodied all up, yelling, "You can't kill me!" Heart pumping fast, "Fuck you! Fuck you! You can't kill Big Bank Frank! I take you all to fucking hell!"

Michael Myers reach for his baby ax. Hommie the Clown with a smile on his face. Michael Myers chop Frank's head off. Frank's pistol went off--two shots. Fire, fire. Frank die talkin' shit. But was too high to win the fight. The girls had stop screaming. They heard Frank's death, knowing that Frank was no punk. And they heard footsteps over broken glass and a car leaving.

Lisa walk out into the living room and saw Frank's body. Smoke was coming from his body. Lisa broke down crying, but when they saw that Frank had no head it was time to go.

Chicago: "So here we are and all we got is game experience and $75,000 apiece. For the family, from three the hard way. Mona Lisa Black Like My Sister, Sky, and Me, Chicago."

✳ ✳ ✤ ✳ ✳ ✳ ✳ ☆ ✲ ☆

For a family in this game it get better then worse then better. Ears for eyes, love for life, drugs for pain, death for glory. This next clique run the trap world with years of experience.

Jazzy Bell a heavyset female, been in the game since crack hit the street in '82-'83. She was a roller in Techwood big time for the Miami Boys. Hezzy got in the game in '86, a jet set player who keep his grind on, day to night, rollin' 10, 20 dub sack. And when the weekend came, shoppin' for new gear and Rap CDs. This nigga is a master chef. For six years he been whippin' and dippin'. He keep his game on the down low from crooks and police. If someone put salt in his game, he can feel it. Or if someone try to cross him, he can feel that, too. Some people say that he has powers by working Black Magic. Just last year, in '91, he made over $75,000 in cash from rollin' and $50,000 just for cookin' up dope for other dope boys. Everyone love his recipe.

This next hustler is Ezekiel, a.k.a. Eazy. He grew up in the 'hood, but had good skills. A straight gangster in the club, he get much love. He was one of the first niggas to use retaliation on the Miami Boys to get them the fuck out of Atlanta. He was more feared than loved. But everyone show him love. Back in the days, he stuck up the Miami Boys for two birds and $40G, and killed three of them. After that he got respect. No one never see him enter a club because the guys at the front take a small break and go to the back door to let Eazy in. He always slip them a big face bill and tell them to be good and point his finger.

He keep his gat with him everywhere he go. When he enter the club, he always slip the bar tender $200 and get the info on who spendin' the money. Then he walk the club. Everyone who speak he hug and kiss, showin' them love. But was pattin' them down at the same time. And they felt his gat on him. And they can see that wild, crazy, gangster look in his eyes. And for the ones who did speak, he show out on them. But after he do his thang, first with the 'ho' in the club. If he got a crew he will spend about $5,000 in one night on drinks and food. All the 'ho's would dance for free because he spend money while he get coke up and he get his dick suck. He sometime get about ten 'ho's in the club on his dick. He treat people like how he wants to be treated. In the club he show love. But on the street he known to be a jack-er.

These next two guys Strength and Mind. Strength a.k.a. Tennessee, a trigg happy nigga. It's blast on sight with him. He did three year down the road for shootin' five people. Another drug dealer sold him a car and stole it back the next day. The dealer put a extra set of keys up under the hood somewhere. So he can sell the car again. When Ten confront the dealer he was havin' a baruce. Ten jump out his car with it still runnin'.

Tennessee: "Hey, man, I want my damn money."

The Dealer: "Man, what the fuck you talkin' about, give your money back? A deal is a deal."

His boys gather around Tennessee and said, "What's wrong, li'l nigga?" and "You better lower your damn voice."

Tennessee: "This nigga sold me a car and stole it back. I just want my damn money."

The Dealer: "Look here, Player. I'm not that type of nigga to do some 'ho' shit like that. What you need to do is check your niggas because real niggas don't steal cars, they steal money. Now, I can't help you if you can't help your-self."

Tennessee look down because that's true and walk back to his car.

The Dealer: "Next time, Player, don't come around with that shit or it's going to be fireworks."

By that time the person he sold the car to was ridin' past the house and he stop in front of Tennessee, rolled down the window, and told the dealer, "Hey, man, this mother fucker ride good as hell, that's all," and he hit the horn and left.

Tennessee look back and went to his trunk saying, "Fireworks? I'll show you some damn fireworks!"

He grab his AK-47 and bustin' shots after shots, hittin' five people, but no fatality. He got three year for that. And that's where he met Mind, a.k.a. Big Mike, a six foot, nine inch, 316 pound crazy bank robber. This nigga love to gamble. In 1991 in a card game Big Mike kill a man with his bare hands--he say that the guy was cheatin'. But people who gamble with him say that he hate to lose. He did seven year in prison for a bank job in '85. He hook up with Tennessee. They both got out in '91 and hit over eleven banks in one year. Tennessee swore that his next new ride would be a motorcycle because cars seems to be jainky to him.

Jezebel, a.k.a. Jazzy Bell the money maker, stood up and said, "I got a story to tell. Yeah, I was a roller, but then I became a smoker. I met Milk in '81-'82. Back then he was a shorty with that player gangster look in his eyes. He was lookin' as if he was free, so I rollin' with him. He turn me on to this game. Money was coming from the left and right. After we made money we smoke a couple woo joints. See, a woo joint is when we take a li'l crack rock or a li'l powder and put it in with our weed. Roll it up and smoke it.

"Milk told me not to fall in love with the taste, because cocaine is the most unpredictable drug on the street, beside heroine. Milk use to come by and kick it with me. Sometimes he bring his boys with him and we all just chill and smoke woo joints. Milk told us to stack our money and slack up on the clubs. I use to ask him why he tell me these things. He would just look at me and say, 'You're going to make it' and kiss me on my forehead. He say that Cat Daddy use to tell him and show him good things. Like the Four Assassins was Cat Daddy's backbone, his killin' team.

It was like in '82, we had hundreds of people in line wantin' to buy some break down dimes. Sometime people get 500 break down dimes at one time. No change, no ones, just five, ten, twenty, fifty, hundred dollar bills. We made $30,000 in one day (from 7 a.m. to 3 p.m.). The next crew (3 p.m. to 11 p.m.) pull in $40,000 to $50,000 a day. Just in that whole day, Cat Daddy was pullin' in $100,000 a day. Just from break down dimes. The other crews was bringin' in $25,000 in a day by just movin' raw powder. Raw powder was the shit in the '70s, but in the '80s everyone was rockin' it up. Bass was the thing back then. Snortin' got old. Now into the '90s, snortin' dope and woo joints is king.

See, we had things lock down in Techwood. Two of the Assassins stood on each corner with Uzis & Techs. Another Assassin walkin' around passin' out 3 sack to each geek monster that stayed in the 'hood lookin' out for Cat Daddy's operations. They were call 'Lookouts'. They tell us when Five-O show or when some more Miami Boys try to move in and make a quick $100,000 and dip to another million dollar spot. And that's how wars break out. Just the Miami Boys had big dope. The Miami Boys will follow them to see where these fools is trappin', not to jack them but to take their trap then trick them into a drug war. And kill them. The Miami Boys came with some artillery, and everyone knew it. Every 'hood will see some type of killing. If drugs are there, then death is there, no matter how you dress it up.

Jazzy Bell look over at Milk and said, "What are you going to do when things get hot? Leave, just like last time?"

Milk just look Jazzy Bell eye to eye. She couldn't look him down. She turn back to the family. "Well, Milk, when you left town it was drug wars like crazy. I caught hell when you left town. I had game. I got so into woo joints, smokin' back to back. Part time rollin'. Yeah, I stop clubbin'. And that damn weed just wasn't gettin' me high no more. I want more. I mess around and took a hit; from then on my world turn.

I had a fat stash, $40,000, but I fell in love with the taste. I had a pimp daddy. He work the shit out of me. He never fuck me. He just front me some work. Even though I was hustlin', I was hustlin' backward. Smokin' all the dope. And payin' him with money from my stash. He broke me and left me with $300 left in my stash.

I use to get other smokers to make love to me and after we do it, we both get our blast on. The first blast is the best. I've hit the pipe over a thousand times, and not one time was like the first time. I lost my house. I was in the street and I was out there bad. Going to a dealer to suck their dick just for a blast. I'm not scared to say it, a woman on dope will just throw herself on any old man that even glances her way. They would lick their lips and twist their hips. Some men know they're on dope, but some can't tell. But any man will get his dick suck for $10.

"On the down low. But any ol' way, I finally got off the dope in '91."

Chicago: "O-oh, Girl, that's sad."

Jazzy Bell: "But, Girl, I got with God, my Saviour. He change my life and strengthen my heart. So I change my ways of thinking. Sometimes I've wish Milk will come save me from the pain I seen. How did you find me, anyway?"

Milk: "I have my ways. You look good and you pick up weight. So you can see, I got you a family. Now you can pick your own crew. Hezzy is a master chef and he's down for his crown--love to work. He's a fool in the trap, quick to snap. Eazy will love to stand next to the lady who hold the dope. Eazy float like a butterfly, hold game like the sea. Tennessee and Big Mike is you backbone. They got skills to open and close a trap. If there's trouble, they will shoot for you. Hezzy can roll like no other. Eazy will be on you like a bulletproof vest. Tennessee and Big Mike is your shooters. They stay ready for the funk. So will you join us?"

She look around the room at the family. And look at the stuff that was on the table and said, "I have nothin' but my game."

Hezzy reach in his bag and pull out $50,000 and said to Jazzy Bell, "$25,000 for you and $25,000 for me" and kiss her on the forehead. You can see the tears in her eyes. She rub on her cross around her neck and said, "Thank you, Lord."

Eazy reach in his black duffle bag, pull out $50,000 and gave her half. Tennessee and Big Mike pull out a bigger black duffle bag and set it on the table. Pull out $100,000. They both showed her love, giving her $50,000, and gave the other half to the family.

Eazy: "Here $200,000 from Tennessee and Big Mike, and me and Hezzy. The Village People the king of the traps."

Milk look over at Jazzy Bell and ask her if she down. Jazzy Bell look at the family with tears in her eyes and said, "Yes, I am down for whatever." She walk to the corner and got down on her knees and gave a blessing on the family.

✳ ✳ ✛ ✳ ✳ ✳ ✳ ☆ ☆ ☆

This next crew is in a category all by theirselves. Precious, a nice pretty lady, your best friend. This bitch will fuck your man and steal anything you lay down--money, checkbook-- and then come back in your face to help you find what you lost. A snake ass 'ho'.

Her comrade is Pete, the mailman. A short, fat, 23 year old having the best of things. This nigga works at the Post Office, stealing everything in sight that's worth something on the street--credit cards, travelers' checks, money orders, info, "Most Wanted" paper, and food stamps. He's been workin' at the Post Office for six years on the job and never call in. It's always, "Pete, you're a nice guy." Pete was well love on the job. But on the street he dress like a goodfellow.

Together on the streets, him and Precious use their charm to get you hook. If you're down, their skills will pick you up. Pete give Precious clean credit cards. She take the cards to her friends that's down to earth. She get her friends to go to the stores and get her what she need and then she let them have the credit cards. But if her friends have money she will sell them for $500. Sometimes she go through fifteen credit cards a day.

Her life is what most girls want to do. She a strong woman. She has the power to talk for others. With her comrade Pete the mailman, she split everything down the middle. Because without Pete she will be just another scandalous 'ho', schemin' and creamin', tryin' to stay alive.

Pete love expensive restaurants. He go to the restaurant and get in good with the waiter or waitress, give them the credit card to see if it clean, and they check the cash limit. Some credit cards had $10,000 limits. See, in restaurants it's just like the malls--if you dress to the T, no questions ask. The credit cards that have big limits, they keep them. Pete kept it lookin' good, all the time. But he crave that gangster shit.

He sometime have a problem with true gangster. He eat where they eat. The goodfellows look at him because he look like a goodfellow. So they sometime test him by bumping him. Sometime they talk, but when they do they put their hands on you by talking with their finger, and in the mob world, if I can touch you, I can kill you. Blood for glory. Pete was no punk. He just was checking out their style so when he become a gangster he will already know how to handle it.

Pete pull off his money belt. Inside was $75,000. Precious open up her pocket book and pull out 100 credit cards, all with $10,000 limit. They lay it all on the table and said "Here," to the family. "May our lives change and our enemies die."

✱ ✳ ✦ ✾ ✳ ✱ ✺ ☆ ★ ☆

This next trick is name Raven. Don't no girl have to be like this comin' up. Because you will regret it in the end. We know there are lots of deadbeat daddies, but Raven is a deadbeat bitch. She was 13 when she got turn out by a wild young dealer name Fly-Mar who is three years older. He was turn out at age 16. He was rollin', gettin' paid. And also gettin' rob, bustin' at folks, kickin' ass, and also gettin' his ass kick. He started robbin' folks just because he got rob. And right to this day he still have Raven lock down. He keep his game tight with the ladies. But now he's a 26 year old jacker with a strong game. He's a heavy snorter.

Raven, she got four kids with ten different baby's daddies. Four of her so-called baby's daddies was killed. Some people say she got the bomb pussy, but those who know her will say she got that killer pussy. This bitch can lay on you for two or three years. When she get you where she want you, Fly-Mar step in and jack your ass.

Fly-Mar sat a set of keys on the table.

Milk: "What is this?"

Fly-Mar: "I have a van downstairs, full of fur coats, TVs, name brand clothes. And I got $50,000 right here from me and Raven." Raven set the money on the table.

Milk sent Deuce and Tray to go check it out. Everyone sat and waited until they came back. Deuce and Tray is Milk's right and left hands. And also his killers. They ran with Milk in cities like Birmingham, Flint (Michigan), Washington, Baltimore, Newark, St. Louis, New Orleans,

Detroit, Miami, and in '92 it's back in Atlanta. Milk go city to city with his game; every city he's entered, the crime grew high.

People was lovin' and hatin' this game at the same time. The ones that hated it was the ones not gettin' paid. Some people kill to get in this game. Some people snitch to get out. Some do time to stay in; some run to get out. You can run, but you can't hide. This game don't give a fuck--if you get in it you will never forget it. Ever since '82-'83, this world has just been about money, dope, and guns. And when a man uses his mind just on money, dope, and guns, you become a master of the game. And that's just how Milk is. He was born in the game, so he will die in the game.

By this time, Deuce and Tray walk in with everything Fly-Mar said was in the van. It was there, just like he said.

✳ ✳ ✦ ✳ ✳ ✳ ✳ ☆ ✩ ✩

This next bitch got the best pussy in the family. Jade, the lady with that whip-a-pill. She got a fat monkey on her. She have to wash it two times a day. That fat rabbit of hers always ready to jump out her pants and whip-a-dick. So she play with it herself to cool it down. When you see her, your dick automatically jump on hard. It take a hell of a dick to whip that pussy because she packin' a powerful cookie. Men leave their wife, and when that happen she break them and leave them. She know not to be tied down.

She love married men. She use her whip-a-pill to get what she want. She love to shake and break men with money. She the best at what she do. Start shit between friends, wreckin' a happy home. It's always conflict and confusion. All pussy ain't good pussy. Even though she have a fat rabbit on her-- let someone else pull that rabbit out the hat. See, most people don't know about that savage pussy; it will fuck your head up every time. She have four houses in Atlanta. And land out of town. She got by from selling that whip-a-pill.

She gave the family $45,000 in cash. Deuce and Tray try her out to see if she do got that whip-a-pill. So Deuce and Tray told Milk about her. Milk like her style. She also have skills cashing and forging checks.

✱ ✳ ✥ ✲ ✳ ✱ ✳ ☆ ★ ☆

The next two players in the family is a tool. Jim Kelly, the bondsman and a professional pickpocketer and Pee Wee Loc, the burglar. Every family need this in their organization. These two players work like this: Jim Kelly get dope boys out of jail quick, fast, in a hurry. He call Pee Wee Loc to come down to the job to scope out the trick. So when the dope boys go to the bond company, Pee Wee Loc act like he just got out jail, too. Or sometime he act like he's down there to get someone out of jail. Jim Kelly get in good with the dope boys. When the cops take the dope boys' money, they will call Jim Kelly, dead ass broke. He gets them out of jail for free. But when he get off work, he go to the dealer's house and get choke on weed, snort lines, and then get paid for his services. All the time he's there, his eyes are on everything.

Pee Wee Loc is a burglar by nature. Jim Kelly give him info on all the rooms in the dealer's house. Pee Wee Loc break into the house. Two licks a week. Pee Wee come out with big dope and big cash. Jim Kelly keep up with the doper's name and address. Some nigga get out of jail flexin' and poppin' like he can do this and he can do that. Jim Kelly and Pee Wee Loc can't stand flexin' ass niggas. Kelly give some of his good friends a get out of jail free card. He treat the popper and flexer like family, and they fall victim to his kindness. And their whole stash will be gone with the blink of an eye. See, when you get a dealer's car tag, get someone to run it in--it will show the address. And you better believe that where he lay his head, that's where the stash at. If nothing is in his name, you got to follow his ass, study his ass, and then take it to his ass.

Many die over that "he say-she say" shit. Sometime it be animosity that kill a person. Anyone can say, "Hey, that nigga got money." The ears and eyes will follow. The person who spread the word wants something bad to happen to that person. Word of mouth is bad business in this game. Because when someone say you got money and you got dope, the street people listen. The street people crave money and drugs. That's their power. They will take you off the map. So for you people with money, watch your mouth and protect your ass on the street. Because the street people are lookin' and listenin'.

Jim Kelly and Pee Wee Loc gave the family $75,000 in cash and 20 names of big time dope boys. So many blacks were going to jail in '92, Atlanta was in for a drug crisis. With Milk game and skills, Atlanta will never be the same. The dope will make the city grow. But at the same time, it will bring us down. Atlanta is a city of sacrifice--they will kill their own to move on. But they will not take a risk and that will be the downfall of the city itself. And that's the bottom line. Believe that, 'cause Earnest Bennett said so, ya know.

THIS THING OF OUR

Milk ask everyone to rise and bow their head to thank God for the blessing.

Milk: "God gave us the power and the skills to make this happen. We were once outcast, now we're all the same family who has seen pain to gain. So, family, no more pain. So by us knowing each other ways on the street, we're going to have more money than we can count. Money will be no problem. We gots to stick together as a family. That's why it's Blood in, Blood out. Our family will be the last one standing. Because it's love right here, real love. Fools are dying for all this game. Everyone in this room can retire right now and can still live like folks. But you rather go out with a family, someone who got your back, so when you do retire in this game your family will be the backbone. See, we have family, the other guys are the gristle. So when the enemy eat that rib sandwich, that animosity send your way. They will easy eat the meat and when the meat gone, then they will eat the gristle. But they know they can't do nothing with that bone, so they leave it alone. See, the enemy think they got backbone, but we'll know they are meat and gristle. We're going to grow with this city. We're going to take traps, run 'hoods, get big respect from the other families. By scaring up the competition to see if they can stand the heat. It's a lot of crews out there popping that shit like they're all that. We're going to put them on, make them bigger, and take them out. We're going to twist the game, make our own rules. Now hear this: each key will go for the $16,500 a key. The only way you can get this price, you got to be on this 4444 plan. And to be in this 4444 plan, you got to be in this family. Sugar will explain it to the lady. And I would explain it to the Good Fellow. But first it's Blood in. No one shall know this code but us. This is for us. You can recruit some of your folks, but if it's a problem, you got to take them out. It don't matter who it is--Mom, Dad, Sister, Brother, Aunts, Uncles. This family and the game it holds is going to be bigger than Godzilla. We going worldwide. But we must have passion for the game.

Milk pull out a small knife that he got from the table between the pounds of weed Baller brought for the family. Milk cut a small "C" in his left hand. Deuce got up and cut a "C" in his hand. Him and Milk touch bloody hands and Milk kiss Deuce on both of his cheek and said, "May nothing in this world and in this room separate us from what we have right here." He was looking Deuce in his eyes and said, "Your love."

And then Tray got up. Milk did the same thing. Then everyone got the deal. Everyone got their hand wrapped with a cloth rag. Everyone had the small "C" cut in their hand. But Tray and Deuce have been with Milk in eight different cities. Milk got family all over the world. And where you got family, you got enemy. But if the family is strong, you will always move on.

Milk: "The name of the family is called Corporation Bigger and Better. We can't be stopped. This 4444 plan is bigger and better than the 401(k) plan. Now that the family is family we have power sulu. Everyone sulu. Everyone kiss each other, showing love. Nothing but love."

Drinking good, smoking good, snorting damn good. Brown Sugar put on some music. Everyone laughing, having a good time balling. Waiting to here this 4444 plan half through the night. Milk got all the fellows up, took 'em to the next room. Sugar took the girls on a li'l school trip with this new game, this 4444 plan is something new.

Milk: "Fellows, were gather here tonight to make absolute power. To better yourself, be more ready for the future. See, when it's drama, you use fire. But when it's money, you use your mind. Trust no one. Now, 4 number one: every four days we will do a David Copperfield, a Master of Illusions, to shake the cops, DEA, Feds, CIA, GBI, Jacker, ATF, SID, and the fake jacker who poses as a junkie to scope out your trap. Even the cops acts like your friend or a junkie to give you a sell case.

4 number two: in four weeks we make money, scope, and collect money.

4 number three: every four months we hit a major licks and get a new shipment. We're going to make this family happen. It's too much power in this. Let no man in this room have in their heart of failing, and the family will meet to discuss business. No one must never see us all together. If you can be seen, you can be scope, and if you can be scope, you can be kill. So build your game so you can move up in position.

4 number four: in four year it will be 1996, the year of the Cracker. You see, every four year the Cracker have this big party to see who going to be President and where they going to have this Olympic game. The Cracker prepare for this. So let's prepare ourself to achieve the gold. In '96 we will keep everything on the down low; the first three years belong to us, but the fourth year the year of the Cracker. So we change our game, just like they change President, and move

to a city that on the rise to work this dope game just like the Olympic game. The game go where the money is. Believe that. The white man time is running out. In eight year it will be the year 2000--the year of the black man. We will have freedom. That's why it's 4 days, 4 weeks, 4 months, and 4 years work out by the Corporation 4444.

"When Brown Sugar finish up with the girls, we will pass out the rank. So far I see good soldiers. You soldiers will have to put in much work to become a lieutenant, and you lieutenants will have to put in much work to become a captain. And that goes same for you captain if you want to be a major factor in this game. Before it's all over you will all be captain running your own shit."

The lady talk was way different from the men. Ladies bond more better than men--they're more sensitive.

Brown Sugar: "Ladies, let's get dis on an off to bigger and better things and I do mean better things. First of all, you're sisters now, true life. I will be here as a mother figure giving you the outlook on life. Now, I know you girls have been through much shit. Because if you didn't, you would not have been here tonight. Now the way dis 4444 plan work-- all this mean is that you bitches got to work! I mean, work, work, work, work, work, work, work, work!! Now, 4 number 1: you got 4 day to snatch a trick, make a trick, break a trick, and shake a trick. See, trick are the good guys mama boys. Trick pay for the pussy. They love for a real woman to lay next to them giving them the big head making them flash more. Ever player in this game want a foxy brown bitch on his arm.

Mona Lisa: "You forgot about the white one."

Brown Sugar: "I haven't forgot about you, Bitch. You just ain't no fox yet. You're a snow bitch. Now tell me what nigga never play in the snow before. You white bitch, you got black sisters and brothers and don't you ever let them down. Or it will be your life. This is a family--we got to stick together.

"Snatch a trick, make a trick, break a trick, shake a trick. That's our steelo. If we go by all these rules, we really can't be stop. Always look your trick eye to eye. Steer him the wrong way. And when he come back he will be paying the right way. And he will continue paying. Any question?"

Raven: "What if you snatch him, make him, break him, and shake him in two days and he come back paying twice the amount. How do you get rid of him?"

Brown Sugar: "Good question. Okay--if he's rich and got no wife and making legit money, I want you to marry the mother fucker and that's that. But if he's a drug dealer I want you to lie, steal, cheat, set his ass up. Break him. So he can go to his major stash. Any question?"

Jade: "What if he's married and will still pay the cost, no matter what?"

Brown Sugar: "See, with a marry man he will do anything for some better pussy than his wife--that's why you control the fuck. Don't let that nigga knock your pussy all out of place. Just ask him how he like it. And fuck him another way he will like it. But stay in control. Go through his pocket, paper, files, safe, because if he's rich he want that rich looking bitch on his arm. We are the women of the '90s, do you hear me? A marry man keep money--that's why he's married. So check everything so we can blackmail his ass if he get out of line."

4 number two: ever four week I want you to have set up people with money. Put your tricks to the test to see how much he care about you. Let him know you're the reason he is on top. Keep checking his pocket. Tell him ways to better his game. Just have him thinking you're guiding him

right. Break him away from his friends. I want you ladies to switch up on your tricks. Let your sister break your trick if he's that easy. Play with his head. Lie constantly and lay low. Have him thinking he's the Mack daddy doing shit behind your back. But you will know his every move. Because your sister will inform you. See, tricks love the honey. But the real love is the money. And money is power. Don't let no one tell you different.

"4 number three: we meet up every four months with new moves. And that's when rank is given so we move up in position if your game has advanced. It's a lots of fools out there who has not learn the ways of the street people. If he or she got money and playing in the street, the street people will watch and scope and will kill. Just to move up while another nigga goes down. The ways of the street. The street people rule the street. We are the street people. We dream, we scheme for the cream. So we can get off the street. It's not always good on the street--it's so much pain. But we do what we got to do to make it on the street. Do you bitches hear me?!!"

"Every four months I want you bitches to bring in 7 licks, 7 customers, 7 boyfriends, and 7 marry men. In one year, that's a 211 combo. Any question?"

Precious: "So you saying at the end of the year there will be two hundred eleven men in our present?"

Brown Sugar: "No, no."

Diamond: "Sugar, can I explain?"

Brown Sugar: "Go ahead..."

Diamond: "It is our duty to leave all trick broke, longly leaking dick, rob, or kill. It's a job to keep a trick up. But it is easy to bring him down. So we keep them happy a whole year and, at the right time, bring him down and leave his ass. And bring what he got to the family. And that's money, loyalty, and respect."

Diamond couldn't stop talking. Everyone listen to her because Diamond speak from the heart. She love the work and the rules that come with it. She very aggressive, love to take charge. A 211 is easy to her because everyone love her personal. She a go getter.

Brown Sugar: "Ladies, no crime family never had womens in their organization. We got to make the best of this. This is the first real family in Atlanta, Georgia. Chicago have it's Al Capone, New York have John Gotti, and Las Vegas have Lucky Luciano. And we have the Corporation. Ladies, we got to make the best of this so our name will go worldwide. We're at that big time stage now.

"4 number four: in four years we do a Tina Turner."

Sky: "What's a Tina Turner?"

Jazzy Bell: "Sugar, I can answer that. Could I?"

Brown Sugar: "Go ahead..."

Jazzy Bell: "See, after four years we will leave the street of Atlanta, Georgia just like Tina Turner left Ike Turner. And the only thing she had was her name and her game--the pain made her stronger than most women. It's funny how pain makes us stronger. Just when you think you're at the end of the road, reality kick in and then we realize who we are and what we want out of life. This is a four year trail. Just like four for the President, a four year trail. When his four years is up it's time for some new game. If his game is good, he get re-elect."

Brown Sugar: "Dat's right. See, the whole family had some downfall in life. But Jazzy Bell has been up and down, drag through the mud. Now she 99% with God. But she got more game than most. She has already did a Tina Turner in this game. Now she in it for the money. And with the game she got, she will make lots of it.

The ladies talk for about ten more minutes until they were all in the same room.

STREET GAMES

Milk put the family in fours and each crew had a captain, lieutenant , and two soldiers. Milk pick three captain, Sugar pick two. Milk pick Baller, Diamond, Jazzy Bell. Brown Sugar pick Chicago and Sky to be her captain. Milk ask his captain to pick their lieutenant. Baller pick Hezzy, Diamond pick Jade, and Jazzy Bell pick Big Mike. Brown Sugar's captain did the same. Sky pick Sugar Wolf. Chicago pick Pee Wee Loc. Milk ask his lieutenant to pick their soldier. Hezzy pick Pete, Jade pick Raven, Big Mike pick Jim Kelly. Brown Sugar's lieutenant did the same. Sugar Wolf pick MJG, Pee Wee Loc pick Eazy. Milk ask his soldier to pick their other soldier. Pete pick Tennessee, Raven pick Mona Lisa, and Jim Kelly pick Fly-Mar. Brown Sugar's soldier did the same. MJG pick Greed, and Eazy pick Precious. It was everyone's job to move ten keys apiece every four month. So each crew got 40 keys every four month at a price of $16,500 a key. Each crew brought in $660,000 every four months. With five crews, that's $3,300,000. In one year, that's $9,900,000. Each crew did their own thang and set their own prices.

First crew was Baller. Baller was a good weight man now he's with the Big Boys. Milk made Baller captain because he like him. He had that look in his eyes. And plus, he got a million dollar spot. Hezzy is the Steven Segal in the kitchen.

He can make it butter and he can keep it white, and for the soft he cut it just right. The dope is 100% pure, no cut. Hezzy broke the dope all the way down. All 40 keys. 40 keys every four months was simple with this crew. In '92 on the street the keys went for $25,000 a key. When Hezzy broke the dope all the way down, he got 80 keys. If you got lower than $25,000 a key in '92, that meant you're a under-cover cop, or a jacker. But it's fools on the streets. When the drought season hit, niggas get out on the street, take their last little money and put their game on. Telling niggas he got the low low and give you a good price. When niggas find out you got it for the low low they get their last and borrow some more thinking they're going to be the only nigga on the street with some dope. Some niggas get up to $100,000. And when it time to take care business, you might get shot if you don't lay it down. You don't get shit for the low low when it's drought season. You will be walking around looking sick with a "For Sale" sign on all that shit that made you famous.

Pete never roll rock before but it's a first time for everything. Hezzy will show him the ropes. Pete was a ready made person--if you mole him right he will be tight. His skill was good outside the 'hood. But no respect in the 'hood. He needs this experience. Baller showed him part of the weight game. He had to teach Tennessee the whole weight game. Tennessee was mostly a bank robber that needed more 'hood experience. The crew call him "Ten" -- short for Tennessee.

Since Tennessee have a appetite to kill and to see big money, him and Baller can get much shit done. Someone just as trigger happy than him. Baller uses his mind most of the time when money involve. Jealous fools player hate for no reason at all. Baller sell half in weight and Hezzy cook the shit so good he bubble a key up and get 72 ounces out one key when you suppose to get 36 ounces. But when you are a good cook, that's how you get 72 ounces. Hezzy's job was to sell ounces, halves, quarters, and break down dimes.

Ounces go for $1,200 for 28 grams; half go for $600 for 14 grams; quarter go for $300 for 7 grams. Hezzy sold half in weight and broke down the other half in 5, 10, 20, 50, 100 pieces. Pete learn how to roll rocks in the 'hood, him and Tennessee. Pete was a mailman by day and a roller at night. Baller and Tennessee got the day shift. Hezzy and Pete got the night shift.

Pete know this is his big break for some of that gangster shit. That's what he wants to be. Pete come from a good family, but for every good family there a bad seed. But for every kid that's born in a bad family will live to be good. And for every kid that's born in a good family will just die to be bad. Living good all your life is something you must keep up if respect is involved.

Baller lock down the whole Zone 3. Milk never showed his face in the 'hood.

✱ ✳ ✤ ✽ ✳ ✱ ✳ ☆ ★ ☆

Brown Sugar put the next crew to work the club scene. Brown Sugar is one of the most baddest foxes in the clubs. She was one of the first 'ho's to put work in the clubs with the raw. She can easily move club to club. Because, like I said, she a fox. Sky is the same way, she's just light skin. Body tone to the tee; she's mean, love to fight. She get down & dirty. She go both ways like Brown Sugar, but the person she choose have to be top notch and hard to touch.

Greed kick it in the clubs. Puttin' on saying his crew got the goods at a good price. When someone need something, Greed call up Sugar Wolf. Sugar Wolf and MJG, the safe-cracker, bring whatever to the club. MJG is Sugar Wolf bullet proof vest. Wherever Sky put Greed he bring in money.

Sugar Wolf and MJG are the ones who push the weight. They drive club to club. Greed is the watchman for Sky. Sky, like I said, is a bad ass bitch. Niggas get mad at her because she can take a bitch from any man. If she got a problem, she give Greed the eye. He then follow the trick and call up Sugar Wolf and MJG. If he got money, they scope him to rob him. But if he's a loudmouth, they beat his ass good and tell him to leave the girls alone.

Brown Sugar was stuck on this crew. She couldn't believe her eyes--Sugar Wolf and Sky was bringing in girls that was sexes bad. Sugar Wolf a true player with the ladies. And Sky is good at taking a woman from a man. Her eyes have a story to tell. If it's a trick in the club spending big, Greed scope him out. He all the time slipping the bartender a big face fifty to see how much a trick really spending. If it's major flow, he will follow him to check his location. He then go back and tell Sugar Wolf.

Sugar Wolf keep his 'ho's working in the trap. So he tell Sky about Greed lick. She put some of her girls she got working for her to hang in the trick location. Because if he's a dope boy, he going to feel like he's the shit. So, in his mind, a new bitch in the area, he got to hit that. All be because he getting the dollar, he think every girl want him. Real nigga don't give a fuck about a bitch or a 'ho. A real nigga will give his bitch away before he give you a dollar. That's game that every player should know. The girl you might be fucking can be your girl or wife and someone else's bitch or trick. Breaking you in for the kill. It don't matter how long you been fucking her--you can have a baby by this bitch. She can still be other nigga bitch breaking the fuck out your ass. It's in a woman nature. She was the first to sin, so everything that come out a woman is born into sin. It's a man job to work his way out of sin. That's what make him a man when you choose the right path.

But on the real shit, that go both ways. It's like Sugar Wolf, he go out and get 'ho's that roll rocks for their boyfriend. Most girls that roll for her man and make lots of money and really don't have shit to show. They have low self esteem. She just can't leave her drug dealing boyfriend. Because a drug dealer put in a woman head, "If you get out of line, I'm going to kick your ass. If you don't have my money, I'm going to kick your ass, now roll my shit. I'll be back."

When Sugar Wolf see something like that, he move in smooth. He make his 'ho's feel like somebody. He treat them different. He know all they want is a name and a li'l fame. He got 'ho's to roll for him. And he paid them real good. He don't fuck them. He just might come by and get his money and a quick dick suck. 'Ho's love him.

Sugar Wolf have 36 customers which are all ladies. Half on coke, the other half roll weight, rocks, and powder for Sugar Wolf. In a slick way, he make them and break them and they still love him.

This crew makes money, too. And that make Brown Sugar a major bitch in this game. The dancers at the club is loving the stuff Sky is bringing in the club. Some girls just can't wait to get off work so they can do their thang. Some of the girls' pimp take all their money and just give them what they want them to have. Since Sky on at the club, most 'ho's break theirself and then can't face their pimp. The money they make, Sky gets it. Because she got the good stuff. I mean good, good stuff--pure magic. Most 'ho's just come to work to see Sky. So in the clubs, Sky is the Red Queen Bitch at all the clubs. Now its some more girls in the club doing their thang. But it just be too much cut on it. When it's way too much cut and not enough dope, it will turn people the other way.

Milk put this crew down with just big-time major players. Diamond is at the top of her game. She has a eye for big-timer players. She did her own choosing. Diamond is working on this big-time dealer name Big Six the Untouchable. She have already hit him up for ten keys, but this nigga is smart. Ten keys ain't shit to him. This nigga move forty keys a week and no one knows where he put his money at. And that's what Diamond is working on. The Feds, 'ho's, the robbers follow him, but can't pin shit on him. This nigga got money out the ass. Every week he visit different graveyards to see his dead Hommies, mom and dad, brothers and sisters, friends and family. He's a true drug dealer, but he have a li'l love in his heart. But will kill in a heartbeat for that dollar.

He love people who he can't figure out. That's his way of getting by. If you are a person on drugs, he will be your friend. If you are a drunk that hang around the liquor store, he will be your friend. If you are about to die with AIDS, he will be there to help you. Every dealer has a dark side, so when a drug dealer come to help you it may look like he's helping you but it really help him more than help you. Drugs are the work of the Devil.

Big Six own five liquor stores and two homeless shelters. He take care everyone in his shelter and all the drunks that hang around his liquor store and, when someone dies, he have a big funeral and he's in a white suit with black locs on at every funeral. Sometime he have to go out of town. He ship people to their homeland so they can rest in peace. The funeral home love him.

Diamond put her sister on some of the other big-time dealers that had made a name for theirself. Jade was working on this big-timer lawyer name Bread Bout It. He's a white boy who love black woman. Raven was the 'ho who mess around with all the dope boys' heads. If one of the girls have to get away for a few days, Raven step in for her sister and make the dealer happy so he will not be love sick. All the girls in this family has some good pussy.

Mona Lisa is working with this Jew. Him and his family got stores all over the city. His name is Fidel Cartel. On the down low he's a drug dealer. Diamond heard through the grapevine he love rich white woman. All these big-time dealers have one thing in common--they all got money. Big money.

✳ ✳ ✤ ✼ ✳ ✳ ✳ ☆ ★ ☆

The next crew had the Decatur on lock down with big rocks & dope and good game. Jazzy Bell ran a crack house--all she do is count money and give orders. Big Mike guard the door. Jim Kelly put the stretch on the dope. The shit he use to stretch the dope is call B-12. This stuff look just like dope--most dealers use it to cut their dope up with. But if you got good dope, this shit whip better than Arm & Hammer Baking Soda. This crack house move nothing but keys. Jim Kelly break down 20 keys for him and Fly-Mar. This nigga just sell break down dimes big as your thumb in the house next door. The house next door is a ran down vacant house. Jim Kelly go out the back door of the crack house and enter the back way in the vacant house. He also guard the back door of the crack house. Fly-Mar stand out in front of both houses. He stop people on the front lawn and ask them "what will it be?" If it's a key, they go to the house where Jazzy Bell and Big Mike are. But if they want break down dimes, Fly-Mar show them in the vacant house where Jim Kelly chills. Fly-Mar chills outside with a bullet-proof on and strap with two nines. If his kangol come off his head, Big Mike, Jim Kelly, and Jazzy Bell will open fire, blasting on any fool that come through and try to take theirs. It all about the money. This crew love money more than life, so they will die trying to make it. For the break down dimes, $500 or better. Niggas was coming, spending $2,500 at one time just for some of them big ass dimes rocks. You just couldn't come and buy one or two rock. Off one break down dime you can make forty dollars. And the dope be tight, too. The middleman buys break down dimes so they can get on their feet and stop working for other nigga. Everyone in Decatur had dope. The big boys broke their keys down and sold their own shit and made their rock big so they can get in. But them break down was taking over the streets. Now the whole Decatur, Georgia is looking good and riding good. This is one of the biggest dope traps and the most serious. Jazzy Bell, Big Mike, Jim Kelly, and Fly-Mar ran the trap world. No one duz it greater than Decatur.

✳ ✳ ✣ ✲ ✳ ✹ ✳ ☆ ★ ☆

But this is the outcast clique. They go to each crew and give them info on what's going on around them and in the street. Chicago work the club scene. If Sky crew run out of dope, Chicago make sure they get what they need, and if Chicago need some girls she get them from Sky crew. Chicago throw big coke party for rich black and white business people who get coke up just around people of their kind. She throw party like get together on 4th of July, Labor Day, Halloween, Christmas--but she really make money off big boxing fights. For some of the events she makes $50-G a party--she charge $5-G a head. When you enter the party, everything is free except the pussy. You got to pay for the pussy. Coke, weed, wine, and fine food is on the house, but the pussy cost money. Chicago get big respect in Atlanta from business men and women. They both just love to take her to bed. She mostly make out with womens because they spend the big bucks. She charge the women $15-G a fuck and the men $10-G a head and, believe me, she get paid for her service. And the girls Sky send over get paid $7,500 and give Chicago half of that, and when they get back to Sky she get half of that, so the girls only get $1,750, but they like it and they don't complain.

Chicago crew also be at her side watching her back, but at the same time learning how to stick up the rich for what they got. Pee Wee Loc stand out in the front of the house and get the car keys and park the cars. He then search the cars looking for the insurance card so he could get the address, make copies of the house keys. Pee Wee Loc go to Jazzy Bell crew to help them out on work and info and what's going on around them. Fly-Mar go with Pee Wee Loc when he break in people's houses. They mostly get jewels, paintings, and most rich people who do dirt have a safe in their house and sometimes Pee Wee Loc and Fly-Mar get lucky and find a personal stash of coke. Pee Wee Loc and Fly-Mar got some good experience in Decatur with Jazzy Bell crew. He also scope out some of the dealers that come to buy dope. When Jim Kelly goes off to work, Pee Wee Loc, Fly-Mar, Big Mike, and Jazzy Bell run just one of the crack houses part time. And when he don't go to work, he stay down and put in work while Pee Wee Loc and Fly-Mar turn into the dope man burglar. Everyone help everyone.

✳ ✳ ✤ ✼ ✳ ✳ ✳ ☆ ✭ ✩

Eazy and Precious walk the floors getting to know the ones who love to snort big and who's spending the money on the pussy. Eazy and Precious stay up in the mix of everything. Some niggas act gangster, but this nigga Eazy don't act he is gangster. And some bitches act like they all that. Well this bitch is all that. She is the nasty bitch; when she fuck you she fuck you and fuck your head up at the same time. If you are hurting on the inside she will make it all better. Eazy and Precious make house calls.

Eazy put the "G" in gangster. He bring out the life to the parties and clubs--he is just so gangster. If you see him in the club and you don't speak to him or show him love and you acting like you put Atlanta on the map with this gangster shit. The Miami boys ran all the clubs in Atlanta back in the days when a nigga from Atlanta didn't know about being a gangster player or shit. Until Eazy buck on them fuck niggas sending their ass back home or somewhere else. Eazy will show out on your ass big time. He just don't give a fuck. He will just come over and take your li'l glory and respect. And o' course he will buy a drink for the ones who show him love and after that they buy him rounds all night because the Atlanta dope boys wouldn't have it like how they got it now all good. Now if niggas come down trying to run shit, every nigga in Atlanta will show their ass just like Eazy. He get his 10 keys and roll that shit where he fuck his 'ho's. He hung with Baller clique, so it was mo' money, mo' money, mo' money. Baller love that nigga because he was a livin' legend. He come through the 'hood and let them know what's going on in the clubs and what's going on in the street, like who to fuck with and who not to fuck with.

Precious' work was to satisfy the tricks' emotions. She always peep in the rooms at the parties. Some respectable like to have a little privacy when they get to it. See, the keys she work with go fast because this bitch work, she get in the head of her opponent. She make them feel just like the real thing. Mens, womens, if your husbands, wives, boyfriends, girlfriends, tricks, bitches walk out on you, Precious make it all better having you thinking she the real thing. It's just she deal with your emotions. So, if you have a flashback about the good high or a good fuck, men and womens, pull out your black book and give Precious a call--she will make your day.

Precious work with Raven in Diamond crew. She's stomping with the big boys. Her and Raven plays with all their sisters for big time boyfriends' emotions. Diamond clique hang in there for the money--these womens hang in there for about 2 or 3 years acting as your wife or girlfriend it don't matter because at the end she is going to sting your ass good. Diamond clique entraps their victims. Precious and Raven do the dirty work. Precious move her coke with ease--she do men and women daily who love to get coked up. (You know, Sky-High.)

✽ ✳ ✤ ✲ ✳ ✱ ✳ ☆ ✶ ✫

Milk put the family down with some of the best shit money can buy in the days of now. It's nothing a drug dealer can't afford. Dealer uses cell phones with the chip. But real player change up their style and direction every four months. Staying in style, moving with time, Milk family got cell phones that transform into walkie-talkie and uses them on the down low so that no other family will copy their style. The Feds are in town and they're cracking down on cell phones--young teens and crack smokers breaking into people's cars for cell phones and taking them to the drug dealers for cash or dope. In '92, beepers was the shit. But in '93, '94, '95, '96 cell phones, crooked cops, prisons, pay phones, gold teeth, gold rings and chains, the clubs, automatic weapons, 5- and 10-dollar blow jobs, fly rides like Benzes, BMWs, Jeeps, Low Riders, 64 Impalas, Lexus Coupes, illegal searches and seizures, triple beam scales, Nikes, Fila, Polo, Tommy Hilfiger, Versace, Timberland, crocodile shoes, Nautica, Gucci, Rims, Atlanta, B-12, Arm & Hammer Baking Soda, crime, police brutality, funeral homes, all this shit just blew up because of cocaine. And believe me, dope boys get some of the best toys and fly 'ho's to play with just like James Bond.

The Corporation--Atlanta, Georgia's first real family. This is the family of the 90's. Tray and Deuce stay at Milk's side when there's work to do. Milk kick it by himself when he's with his bitch, Brown Sugar, or when he talk with his supplier. And his supplier supply the world. See, Milk is connective and well protective. He often call himself "GC". Brown Sugar asked him what did it mean. The only thing he said was, "Well, I was born a God child, raised off the government, so that make me a government child. But when I die I will be back a God child." GC the Hustler.

Brown Sugar gave up everything on Pacman and his squad, the Dirty 3.

THE LAW

Pacman is one of the most coldest cops on the street. He may not have pull a cat out of a tree or help young kids across the street during school hours, but he stay on the bad guy's ass.

He stay on the dealers' ass by taking their money. But when he hook up with Milk he became crooked cop burglar. And his squad was having the time of their lives. Getting paid off small time dealers. Some dealers pay off the cops to keep the cops off their ass. Pacman squad have so much rank in Zone 3 and lock up so many people that they move all over Atlanta doing the same old shit. By that time they were unstoppable and, on top of that, they became famous by using every artifice to catch a crook.

Everyone knows Pacman and Reebok. Pacman rough up the big boys and Reebok handle the up and coming dealers. Niggas made a song about the two cops. Good cop, bad cop. Pacman the black cop and Reebok the white cop, but they both were bad cops.

Reebok squad didn't give a fuck--they just wanted to get paid. Dope boys had it pretty good until the Red Dog Squad jump out on scene, kicking ass, taking names, and locking your ass up. You be in your cell fuck all up with a drug case and they come to court so that they can send your ass down the road. Red Dog means running every drug dealer out of

Geogia. These cops was tough. We needed cops like that because the city was under siege. Crack cocaine has got out of hand--the Chief of Police order the special unit and it work. Niggas was more caution on the street when they roll their dope. When the Red Dogs roll through, something got to give. You can just chill out when they roll through or you can take off running if you are dirty, but when they catch you, that's your ass. When they ride through the 'hoods, all four of the doors be crack open ready to jump out and do damage.

If you move or flinch, they at you. See, the Dirty 3 was ran by Pacman and Reebok. It's one cop that everyone trust and that's happy. A fat cop with gray eyes and has lots of small bumps on the back of his neck just like Forrest Whitaker. He don't work with Pacman team. He only lock up drunks, prostitutes, and patrol the school area. Every time you see him he's drinking a coke and having a smile. One of his eyes is halfway close. He was shot by a drug dealer in '86. The dealer was arrested and got out on bond six months later, but he never made it back to court. He was found in the trunk of his car, dead, with bullet holes in the head. Five shots was fired into the trunk of his car.

The city grew and so did crime. The cops have their hands full with drug dealers, robbers, killers, thieves, burglars, men who rape women, and child molesters. But the saddest thing on the street is that blacks are killing blacks over turf and cocaine. Everybody want to make a name off cocaine. You can't make a name off cocaine..cocaine makes a name off you. It bring the best out of you so that it can do the worst thing that could ever happen to you. And that's raping you for your life! If you don't believe me, check your local jail house or grave yard. It won't be hard to find a black drug dealer. Ya heard me!

A WORD TO THE WISE

Niggas getting niggas, niggas getting 'ho's to get niggas 'ho's, even getting 'ho's to get niggas and other 'ho's. See, some people play your friends but are really your secret enemies and you got some people that were your friend but are now your enemy.

Because of your cash or that good things are happening in your life, everybody is just getting everybody. It seem as if everyones wants to do the Devil's work. But there still people on the face of the earth who do work for the Lord. But we need more to fight the battle when dealing with the work of the Devil. It's Hell or jail in this dope game. The Devil use you for a minute and then he destroy you. Sometime people die for no reason at all. Kids and old folks get struck by stray bullets all over the world by people who deal in drugs. It's a dirty game. God is getting up good strong soldiers to carry out his duty. People who use to steal, use dope, or sell dope. God use these people because the Devil don't have a hold on you if you're strong, but if you let your flesh run you then the Devil got you. God don't go out looking for perfect people; He look for the ones he can make a example out of. God love all of us, but He need good soldiers to fight with Him. The Devil works all the time because he know his time is running out. God is about to do something big for the ones who believe in His words. The Devil makes the flesh happy and the soul weary. God made flesh and he knows that the flesh is weak for the Devil tricks. So let God control your soul because God give eternal life and the Devil give you heat and flames. These are some of the tricks that the Devil play on the Mother Earth. So every day you wake up say Fuck the Devil! And praise the Lord, He so real. You heard me.

THE DEVIL TRICKS

Milk got straight to work with Diamond clique, stomping with the big boys. These boys was buying more than keys. These was the big boys on the block and Milk had a plan that made history in Atlanta, Georgia. Milk started fucking Jade first and she was juicing Bread, this rich ass white boy love the shit out of Jade. He give her big bucks for sex. They get fuck up something awful. He would tell her things that was personal-like. He was buying keys with no problem. Milk got with this white boy. This honky ran three clubs that his wife didn't know about. Everyone knew everything except her. He kept everything on the DL from his wife real good.

He own three clubs. The first club was name Club Dominique. The shit was jumping off good, and then he had a club call Club Dion. Now that shit was off the hook. That shit stayed pack with bitches. And his last club, Diamond & Pearls. This club was the bomb--it did it all.

Bread Bout It love himself a black woman. Jade will get her sister Raven to fuck with his head, have him crazy. One night, he had ask her did she know any dealer that would kill his wife. She said yeah and turn him on to Milk. Milk didn't come by his self; he brought along Jade and Raven. They met up at his house on Friday and they left on Monday morning.

Milk: "So Mr. Bout It, how do you maintain three black clubs and keep your white business owned and operated?"

Bread Bout It: "Well, I have a underboss that's real good and I trust him with my life."

Milk laugh and said: "Underboss, I am here to be your boss and to help you run your business. I am your problem solver. You like my girls, right?"

Bread Bout It: "Just wait a minute, Bucko. Jade is my girl--you better back off."

Milk: "Look here, Bread, I got what you need. I know what you want. I am your man, so let's just have a good time."

Jade got close to Bread, rubbing him down, getting him to relax. They had it good with some of the best step-on coke in the street and was drinking some good liquor. They got him fuck up--he was talking out the side of his neck. By this time it was Sunday. The girls had done work him overtime. He really overdid it this time. Both of the girls had just come out of the room. Milk told the girls to start cleaning up the house before his wife get home. Milk went into the room with Bread Bout It. Bread was halfway out his mind with a fifth of Jack Dan in his hand, cursing and acting bad. Milk walk over to Bread and pull out a personal ounce of uncut dope and hand it to Bread. Bread look at it and lean back, nodding his head. Milk look at Bread with a evil eye. Bread sniff the dope and pass out. Milk pull down his pants and stuck it in his ass. Milk came out the room zipping his pants, telling the girls, "Let's go."

Bread Bout It told Milk everything he needed to know. He told Milk that the clubs he got was ran by a black man name Billy Lawrence and he's a car salesman with skills to kill.

It was Monday morning. Bread was still in the bed butt

ass naked. His wife walk in with the kids. His wife cover him up with a blanket and woke him up.

Ms. Bout It: "Bread, Bread, get up."

Bread got up slow, holding his head, trying to get right. His head was spinning.

Bread: "Hi Honey. I got a bad headache. Could you get me something for it?"

Her and the kids left the room. Bread laid back trying to recall what happen this past weekend. He could not remember shit. He said to himself, "Damn I had a good ass time!" until he felt his behind and he went crazy when he felt like he had been violated. He yelled out, "Damn! Damn! Damn! I am going to kill him!"

His wife ran back to the room with his Alka Seltzer. "What you say, Dear?"

Bread: "I said I love you, Dear. And thank you for the Alka Seltzer. I feel better already. Honey, can I be alone for a minute?"

She left the room again without saying a word. He sat down and thought about it.

He call Jade all week and did not get a answer. He was going crazy. Milk watch his wife for about two weeks, then made his move on Bread Bout It's wife. Three weeks later he was fucking her and getting what he wanted out of her and putting shit in her head. The fourth week, Bread met a young lady by the name Precious and--guess what?--he was in love all over again. But Milk and Jade stayed on his mind.

Milk got off Bread Bout It and jump right on Fidel Cartel, the rich Jew who love white women. Milk started digging on Mona Lisa, the snow white bitch of the family. Lisa had a plan from Diamond to break this Jew who live the good life. Fidel's wife stayed on his ass because he was a horny son-of-a-bitch who love to flirt with classy broads. Him and his wife goes out to some of the best restaurants, his eyes be everywhere. She constantly would kick his foot everytime he wink at a other woman. He don't give a fuck, he's rich. But when he gets home he kick her ass. She take that ass whippin' and then let her get coke out by herself. She sit back and act as shit never happen. He leave her alone at the house while he goes clubbin'. This shit goes on all the time. Every time he act she act and then she get what she want and he get what he want and then he go club hopping. Fidel went to Club Dion to get his fuck on and that's where he met Mona Lisa. She was kickin' it with Precious.

Diamond gave order for Mona Lisa to be at the club that night because Fidel Cartel was headed there. Diamond stay on top of hers. Fidel walk over to the ladies, offer to buy drinks. He order the drinks, they switch names. She ran game and he was in love. They kick it all night, but he did not get no ass. Not that night, anyway.

Every time Fidel's wife, Angela, wants to get blow away, she show her ass, he give her coke and then dip. Fidel and Lisa kick it a few more weeks. He told her about his business; he also told her he was marry. She just act as if she was hurt and she was ready to leave. He ask her not to go and he explain that him and his wife fight like hell and she talk about leaving him all the time. Three weeks has gone by-- he still haven't touch her. Fidel was open about everything. He really wanted Lisa. He always send his wife out of town for different trips while he take care of his business and business can be fucking some new chick or receiving his shipment of dope. He give his bitch about $15-G every time she leaves and this bitch come back broke every time ready to start shit. On the fourth week, he took Mona Lisa to his big ass house in Roswell and yes, he fuck her, and then his love grew stronger for Lisa and through the whole fuck she control it. And he went wild giving her anything she'd ask for. He started trying her by asking her if she get high. She said, "No, do you?" He said, "Yeah, this the 90's. Everybody doing it."

Lisa: "Why, Fidel?"

Fidel: "It make the pain go away."

Lisa: "Well, what do you have?"

Fidel breathing fast, pulling keys of cocaine from under the sofa and chairs. He had about 20 keys laying around the house. His wife will be out of town just a few more days, and then she will be back. Lisa then gave him that happy ass hell look. He said, "Lisa, you don't have to want for nothing. I got whatever you need right here for you and me."

Lisa: "But you suppose to make money off this stuff, not to constantly use it. Haven't you seen the movie Scarface? Don't get high off you own supply--that goes for all coke dealers. You think that I want to be like Michelle Pfeiffer? She couldn't have kids she would get so coke out. She should have slow down. She was with the best. Every time you see her she's getting high. She should have took him out to ball games or to the movies or something. You know, family things. They were marry; she really didn't give a fuck about him. It was always the high."

"We will just do a li'l bit."

He like Lisa, but he felt like if he flash a li'l bit she could be just like Angela.

But Lisa was smarter than what people think. And anyway, she didn't give a fuck about what people thought. She did it her way.

They snort half the night and made fuck faces the rest of the night. When morning came, Lisa ask Fidel would he like to go to a fight party where the coke is free but the cat cost money and it $5-G a head. It's for major players. He look at her and said, "Where? Let's go." And that's where he met Milk, at Chicago's fight party.

Mike Tyson was just release from prison and he was fighting Bruce Seldon. Fidel took Lisa out at the Phipps Plaza to shop for something nice for tonight. Fidel pick him up something also for the night. They went back to the house and hit it off once again.

Lisa ask Fidel if she can wear some of Angela's nice jewelry. He said no, that bitch love her precious stones. "But you will have your own, just you wait. You'll see." Lisa told him, "I ain't mad at you. I just ask. She have nice taste."

Fidel: "I know. That shit cost me a fortune. I use to love that woman."

Fidel took a sip of his drink, and when he brought his glass down he had tears in his eyes. Lisa ran to him and ask what's wrong. He act as if he didn't want to talk about it. They both got dress. Looking good for the fight. All over the world people wear nice things on a fight night. Black and white males flash big time, hollering about bet, bet, bet, nigga, bet. Woman love that type of shit. It just like li'l Las Vegas when you got lots of beautiful women, coke, and cash everywhere in each room. All Chicago's parties be on fire burning up with surprise.

Everyone was at the party. Lisa & Fidel arrive early so Fly-Mar and Pee Wee Loc can go to work. Mr. Loc and Fly-Mar had their hands full. The house was pack. Precious was with Bread on fight night. Break 'em off with that good stuff so she can leave him soon Raven took her spot at the party. Diamond was at the party with Big Six and all eyes was on them. Everyone was dress nice but Diamond and Big Six was looking like movie stars. Gold sparks fill the room. (Bling Bling)

These two got big props. Big Six was so cool he gave

Diamond a kiss and got in front of the tv screaming "Bet!"
Somebody yelling across the room "Bet, Nigga, bet!" It was
Eazy. Everyone was having a good time. Jade was there
also, putting in work hunting for a quick rich dick so she can
break 'em and shake 'em. These 'ho's work this game in the
street better than Eve work it in the Garden of Eden. They
really don't need a snake ass nigga to show them the evil
ways to get a man. Their mothers taught them the ways of
bein' a real bitch of a woman.

Fidel couldn't believe his eyes. Rich people just like himself, men and women of color. He started thinking to his
self, "This party is the shit." Everybody was getting coke out
and the smell of money and sex was in the air. He took a
double look and saw that the black woman had it going on.
Chicago walk over and gave Fidel a drink and rub him
under his chin and told him he was cute and walk right off.
He lick his lips and kept his eyes on Chicago's ass. Jade walk
to the left of him and she had powder cocaine sprinkle on her
breast. She ask Fidel would he get it off. He put his nose in
between her breast. When he came back up he was spinning.
With powder on his nose he look around, and everyone had
powder on their nose, laughing, have a good time. He step
back and took a sip of his drink and saw that Lisa was having a conversation with a black cat. He frown up and realize that he couldn't go off. By that time he open up his eyes
to take another look and Raven grab him by his hands and
said, "Come on, Baby, I know what you need here." She was
feeding him raw 'cain that was better than the 'cain he have
at his house. He told Raven that his whole fucking body was
numb. Raven took him to Room #T, which means Trick
Room. She play with him, got him hard. She call for more
'cain and something to drink. Just for the moment he forgot
all about Lisa. Raven had him so hot he came out his pock-

et and pay for the pussy. Lisa was out on the floor having a good time. Chicago pull her to the side and gave her advice on Fidel. She told her to keep him paying. He love this type of life. Anyone who can keep his dick hard the longest got him. Chicago took Lisa to the Camera Room. Raven was fucking the shit out of Fidel, had him talking Chinese. Fidel was turn out by some good black pussy while everybody was balling watching the fights.

❉ ✳ ✧ ❋ ✳ ✳ ✳ ☆ ✭ ☆

Pee Wee Loc and Fly-Mar was dress like souljas ready to do work. Chicago went back to Pee Wee Loc and gave him order just to video record the house inside and out and do not touch nothing, so Pee Wee Loc and Fly-Mar hit Fidel's house first and did just what Chicago said. That night they hit up about 11 houses and they came right back out, all right. All together, 9 keys and $27,000 in cash and a video tape of Fidel's house.

Pee Wee Loc brought the tape back to Chicago and she gave the tape to Diamond so that Raven, Pee Wee Loc, Fly-Mar, and Lisa can learn the house so that they can be in and out in minute. You got to be quick in the white folks neighborhood in Roswell. The cops don't play with a nigga.

An hour later, Raven was back out in the crowd doing her thang. Fidel came out the room in a daze. Milk jump right on his ass, asking him do he like the taste of the raw coke he had tonight. Fidel was shaking his head in slow motion. He was worn out.

Milk took advantage of that and walk him to Room D. Fidel was like, "Wait--I got to get my girl!" Milk was like, "Man, she having a good time. Be cool, friend, relax. Look what I got for you."

Fidel's eyes got big.

Milk: "This is a key. You do know what a key is, right?

I step on it about four time. It's the same dope you try tonight. Go ahead and take a hit--it's yours. I am going to front it to you; I am your friend. You just give me your business card so I can stay in contact with you. And here's mine--call me when you need me."

Milk put his key in a green polo bag, smile, and left the room. Fidel bust open the bag, rubbing down his gums, and took a li'l toot toot before he walk back out in the crowd. Chicago and Lisa was back in the Camera Room watching Fidel, studying his moves and at the same time learning how Milk play the game.

By that time it was time for Tyson to fight. Everyone was coming out all the rooms from A to Z. The house was pack. By the time everyone came out the fight was over--just that quick. Every fight Tyson have be over quick because nigga was scare of Tyson. Everybody be like, "damn, is there anyone in this world that's not scare to fight this Tyson?"

Eazy was talking big shit because he won $50-G off of Big Six. Big Six always bet or go with the underdog. His boys brought the money. Chicago was standing by the door while everyone was leaving, giving her hugs and kisses. Fidel was jumping up and down, looking for his baby Lisa, calling out her name. While he was jumping he notice that there were 19 more people carrying green polo bags; some with one key, some with three or five keys in their bag. And when Fidel saw that, he knew then he was with the big-timers. He found Lisa, they both saying to each other, "Baby, I had a nice time." Lisa wink her eye at Chicago as they walk out the door.

A month later, Fidel sent his wife on a trip so he could handle his business. He did his business with Milk--20 keys. And then he call up his private pussy, Mona Lisa. Lisa told him she had to go out of town to see her sick mom and he respect that, so he call up Raven, someone who can ease the pain. Raven stay two hour away, but he didn't give a fuck; he went to get that pussy. They hit it off all that weekend and then it was time for his wife to come back home and time for Lisa to come back from out of town. While he was taking Raven back to where he pick her up at, on the way there they both was getting mellow. Fidel always ridin' dirty because he got customer all over town who buy ounces for the $1,500 in soft in the powder form. He stop and sell to anybody that look cool and that's a no-no. In this game everything that sound good ain't always good for you. Pee Wee Loc and Fly-Mar was trying to break his ass for all he got. They got the 19 keys that Milk gave him and $40,000 in jewels and four abstract paintings. The painting was Pee Wee Loc's ideal. He got them for Jazzy Bell. She love stuff like that. It was no cash. Well, they couldn't find it.

When Fidel got back he was like, "Oh shit." He was trying to make a U-turn, but the police was everywhere. At his house he saw his wife was coming out the house crying, so he drove up to the house. His wife ran up to he car yelling, "Someone broke in the house". Fidel was like, "What did they take?"

She was still crying. "They took all my jewelry and the painting." Fidel ran into the house to see what was really going on. When he got in the house, he got dizzy and fell to the floor. The house was tore up bad. The police made its report and left. It's good that that Ms. Cartel had insurance on the painting and the jewelry so they will get a fat ass check for that. Ms. Cartel was acting a donkey all night. She wanted to get high. Fidel was silenced by greed--he just jump up and beat his wife ass. She was getting on his nerves about she wanted to get high. After he beat that ass he went to his car and got the key he was ridin' with. They both were sitting on the floor crying, getting fuck up. An hour later he jump up and ran to his secret spot, the family picture of him and her. He got lucky. He move the painting--there it was, a safe full of cash. He paid Milk.

THE LIGHT RULES LIFE

Hustling is a way of life; I can't stop even if I had to.
But if I did, people will try to hustle me.
I look right, but I go left so no one will see me.
But I want to be seen so they will know.
But my name will shame me.
It wouldn't if my people back me.
Maybe we need a wake up call.
You know, Mike Tyson just got out of jail.
Yea, yea, yea I want to fight Mike Tyson
Because everyone I fight I knock out.
It's fame, but not respect
Because of the name I was labled.
But if I lose to Mike Tyson
My name will not be in the light no more.
I guess that's why I keep my hustle on
And my name goin' Nigga.

- By Earnest Bennett

PLAYER NIGHT OUT

And ask him for a other front. And Milk gave it to him.
These niggas was true players hard-core money-makers
back-breakers, jack your ass for the loot if you got it they
want it . All in one house--40 keys in powder and 40 keys in
rock hard. Cook up how any dealer would like it. And it all
be broke down just right with a 4 plus cut on it. Baller,
Hezzy, Pete, Tennessee, always did it the player way. In the
'hood, they're call 'hood stars, ghetto players. These niggas
was living ghetto fabulous. Everytime you see these type of
niggas in the 'hood they always putting in work, kicking it,
talking good game about 'ho's and making money and how
to get their hands on some more money.

Eazy come by and see these black cats because they always
ready to put in work, you know, get their hands dirty and
Eazy was the nigga to get with because he know right off
hand who real and who not but in this 'hood money come
from the left and right. Baller crew wasn't the only dealers
on the block. There was the Powder Rangers thug niggas
that snort dope and still do business. They sniff powder
more than they smoke blunt. They also steal cars, sell dope,
hook up niggas music in niggas cars and then steal their shit
and put it in their car. If it's not the best they sell it. And they
also is fucking young 'ho's and jackin' and they make big
money in the trap. But in this trap there was a lesson to be

learn. If you don't keep up you will get squash and left behind. These niggas don't play. See, the nigga who ran the Powder Rangers use to be real good friends with Baller. Until Baller crazy cousin, Razor, got drunk back in the days 1990. Razor got mad over a customer who wanted ten bake beans and Razor, Baller, Cuddie and a few of Cuddie's Rangers was all fighting over the customer. Razor couldn't get in. Cuddie got in , so Razor threw his whole cup of Hennessey into the junkie face and drink got all over Cuddie face because he was bend over into the car window. Cuddie put his rocks and money in his pocket, reach into his trousers, and pull out his gat busting caps everywhere. Razor was busting back, and then the whole 'hood was busting caps. Shots after shots no one was hit. The trap was rolling but the streets was clear. The dope fiends was in the streets selling flex dope, fucking the trap up. Niggas was just laying back, holding on, their pistol ready for whatever. But it cool off because niggas money was getting low and you know how that go--niggas got to eat. Everybody was coming out slow, trying to build the trap back up. The fiends had it fuck up; pretty soon the street was back rolling. Niggas still strap instinct in high, but the trap was rolling like a mother fucker.

Baller on the left side of the street and Cuddie on the right. They knew that if they wanted to make money that they all got to get along. Now, right to this day, they roll together in the street, making cabbage and cornbread. Hezzy and Pete be out in the street talking about here I go, here I go, nigga, getting paid running up to cars. Cuddie crew do the same shit, be out there actin' bad, talking 'bout how many buddy right here. I am your friend, right here.

Hezzy showed Pete everything on getting paid on these rough street. He show him how to use his elbows when he's at a car serving bake bean. Baller & Tennessee show each other the ropes. Ten learn Baller the ways to rob a bank. He said, "If you gone do it, nigga, do it. Don't bullshit with it. It's money to get, you just got to have heart to go and get it. Baller showed him how to move big dope.

Baller let him know the dope game is the same way and he said the only difference is that you be dealing with more demons and once you touch this cocaine you are a different person. It don't matter if you sell one rock a day, man, this is the only game the white man left for us to play. You got to be made for this shit--it's not for everybody. And always remember this--you lose before you gain. But with my teaching you're gonna make money and if you fall don't look back because I'll be there to pick you up. You understand, Ten?

"I understand, but Baller, man, when I be off in them banks my adrenaline be pumping and then I see all that money and that's when I cool down because if you get out of control, man, you might fuck up and kill someone, and that's the wrong way, you dig?"

Baller: "Yeah, man, I understand."

Baller's million dollar spot was jumping off just like he expected. Baller also showed the clique how to play them 'ho's. Baller also had Dee Dee in his corner, his ace in the hole. And this li'l chick was down for her crown. Baller put her in all the spot where niggas got money. She been putting in work for Baller and she never fail him, not once. She also have some girlfriends her age who look up to her and Baller is fucking them and Dee Dee knows that. Shit--she don't care. She said it's the game she love.

She said she love what Baller do to her because she know it going to pay off in the end. One of her friends told Baller that she said she will walk to the edge of the earth and jump

off if he ask her to and she only sixteen. Anything to satisfy
Baller. Half of Dee Dee's friends was fucking the Powder
Rangers, the other half was fucking the Jury. The girls play
it off good in the 'hood. The Rangers made their money in
front of their girls and that's a no-no. Keep your girl or your
wife far away from how you make your money. She know
all she got to do is just stay sweet and sometime raise a li'l hell
with you in the trap and act like she going to fuck some other
nigga that sell dope and that shit will throw a nigga off his
game if he care for his girl. See, in the traps anywhere you
got to be hard as steel. And in this game, your girl or wife
can be working for a other nigga real close to you and that
nigga will find out you're weakness and will do his best to
destroy you. It's a dirty game, never let them see you sweat.
Even if things get hot, keep it going. Never give up on life,
let life give up on you. God put us all here for a reason.

   Every week they all sometime get together and go out to
the club with Eazy and plot on some bootsee ass nigga who
don't have no reason for having a fat pocket actin' like a
buster ass fag. Eazy get with Baller and point out who got
loot. It was this one nigga name Dawg. Nigga had big
bank--no lie--but he run his mouth and flash too damn
much and he love to shine. He met up with Eazy and Baller
in the club talking about he's going to buy him a fly ride.
This nigga was just flexing his ass off when Eazy and Baller
act like they were not listening. This fool pull out a big knot
of money and bought rounds of drinks all night. From hour
to hour Baller had a ideal. He whisper a li'l something in
Eazy ear. Now, the music was loud and Eazy didn't quite
hear Baller. But these COBRA thugs put in so much work
that they know how the game goes. Baller told Dawg he had
a friend who had a Lexus Coupe that he don't drive no more
and he will sell it if the price is right. Dawg was like, "Oh,

yeah, I'll buy it. Where he at?" and he pull his money out again and said "See, I got money." Eazy walk off. The club was pack. Sky, Greed, Pete, Hezzy, and Ten was at the club kicking it.

Baller: "There--that nigga is right there." Acting like the drinks had him drunk, Eazy had put ten on what were going on and he walk off. Dawg feeling good; he walk over to Ten. Ten and Pete was having a conversation.

Dawg: "Yo. Say, Bro. Yo! Yo!"

Ten still talking with Pete. Eye to eye. Ten stop and said, "Can't you see we're talking business" and started back talk to Pete.

Dawg was like, "Damn--this nigga don't want no money! He went into his pocket once again and put it between their face. They both look at Dawg. Dawg said, "This is business. Now, I hear you got a Lexus Coupe for sale. Now what's up, Nigga?" and he spread out the money. All big bills.

Ten was like, "Yeah, we can do business. But you're going to need more than that."

Dawg: "Well, how much will I need, Player?"

Ten: "About $28-G."

Dawg was like, "Bet, Nigga. That's no problem. When can I come pick it up?"

Ten: "Give me four days."

They switch numbers.

Dawg: "Okay, I don't want no shit. This big bread, you know."

He walk off and pull him a li'l lady off the floor, drop her a few bucks, and they left. He pick up Mia, one of Sugar Wolf's girls. MJG and Sugar Wolf was tailing him, getting the location of his stash. Everyone at the club was having a good time drinking and snorting coke and peeping game.

Next day Baller went to Milk to buy his Lexus Coupe for

$20-G. Milk sold it. Three days later, Dawg call Ten ready to do business. Ten told him to meet him at the Tune-Up Clinic. Ten told him he want to make sure it's run okay and he also told him to bring an extra $1,500 because that what it cost to get it tune. Dawg was like, "Okay."

Dawg left his Buckhead home with a brief case full of cash. MJG and Sugar Wolf had the location on where he have his stash, so they stay on him until he met up with Ten at the car shop. Ten paid for the tune up with a credit card that Pete gave him. See, you got to put a bootsee ass nigga on charge. The credit cards came in handy. This whole family spend about $250G a month just on clothes and $175 thousand on food, plus $250G on jewels. This family live life to the fullest.

Baller had an extra set of keys made that sat under the hood of the car. Dawg pull up with two high-powered gangster strap ready to blast if anything go wrong. He gave Ten the cash. Ten peep it. Ten gave him all the paper on the ride. They shook hands and left the scene. He broke up with his crew and went to go get his pussy, Mia.

He ate that pussy and she fuck him good that day. She started crying, saying she wanted her own place and that her mom was tired of her shit and she told Dawg that they were fucking in her mom's room. He ask to see her room and she did. Her room was fix up like a li'l girl room. Dawg said, "Fuck it. What you want to do."

She said, "I want my own place so we can be doing things wilder in our own shit. I can cook for you." He got Mia, his new girlfriend, an apartment in College Park. They went to go get some furniture and when they came out the store his car was gone. He broke down. She look him in his eyes and broke down with him. He went to go call the police to make a report. He then call his thugs to come pick him and his girl up. They came. He went and took Mia to his house where his stash sit. She went to work with her eyes and her hands. He took her to the garage where he have five more car. She stay the night.

The next day she was back at her mom's until the apartment came through. She gave Sugar Wolf all info he need. Also gave him the alarm code on the house, which was 1876. Mia beep Dawg. He call back. She told him that the apartment came through and the furniture people was on their way and they needed to be there. He said, "Okay. I am on my way."

An hour later they were pull up in the apartment. He look to the left and saw his Lexus Coupe . He drove to his ride, got out the car. It was in perfect condition. Mia was talking to him. He threw his hands up telling her to go on. She got to the apartment. A minute later he drove to the apartment. He walk in happy as hell.

He yell out Mia name; he only hear his voice. The long hallway echoed. He ran to bedroom and when he got there he was rush by three Cobra thugs, Hezzy, Pete, and Greed. Dawg was fighting for his life. Pete step back off him and shot him in the back of the head. Dawg fell to the floor. Greed turn him over. Pete shot him five more times in the chest. Mia got the cash from his pocket--$3,500 her cut. Hezzy roll him up in the
rug. They walk him to the truck. Mia got in the truck with Hezzy to go dump the body. Greed got in the Lexus, strip the tag and the number from the dash and burn the car. Pete did the same with the Cadillac Dawg came in. Hezzy call Baller and told him it done and it's cool to go 'head.

Sugar Wolf, MJG, and Baller walk up to the house, punch in the code, and kick in the door. They went to work on the house. Baller got all the paper on the cars. Sugar Wolf and

MJG had a problem with the safe. It was a big ass safe weld in the floor so MJG had to crack that bitch right there. It was a new type of safe. It took him 46 minutes and when the safe pop MJG pull it open and that put a smile on their face. Baller ran to the kitchen, turn the trash can upside down to dump out the trash. They fill the bag up with big knots of cash, $200,000 in cash. Nothing but big bills while riding to the hideout. Baller peep the cash and saw that there was some thousand dollar bills in the bag and he went to thinking where in the hell did he get some big bills like that from. He just thought about it for a minute and that was that. They got to spot to break bread. Sky clique got $80-G. Baller crew got the same. They gave Eazy the $20-G, so they all got $20-G who all had put in work.

Eazy didn't have to do work because he point the trick. It was Pete first killing. Now the family call him Pete the Killer. That shit only hype him up. Him and Hezzy love the malls, clubs, and the fly ass restaurant, and when these two player hit mall they get the newest shit then eat and then it's club hoppin' and from there Eazy show them how to kick it. See, you can't be in the club looking like you don't know what's going on. See, it two type of people that be in the clubs, and that's the creamer and schemer. See, the creamer come to find some sex to ease the pain and the schemer move in on you, man or woman, and hear what you got to say and just that fast you become a victim. So watch how you be clubbin'.

Now in the shake joint, Atlanta got some of the baddest bitches. We got this new shit off in the clubs--'ho's boxing and shit and, wouldn't you know, Sky is a boxer, too, and she be kicking ass, too. She win all her fights. Greed bet all his money on Sky and he win. When he win, niggas get mad, but they pose no threat. Greed is a true patron in the clubs in all the spot where Sky work. This nigga got eyes like a eagle. Sky bring his gat to work with her. She give the bartender the gat and then the bartender give the gat to Greed and Greed give her medicine, which is a 8-ball of raw powder. In these days and time, cocaine can get you what you want or whatever you need and the white man know it, man. Shit, this shit is killing black people. Cocaine harmful effects, dependence, depression, appetite loss, irritability, insomnia, exhaustion, nervousness, brain seizures, heart attacks and strokes, respiratory failure, loss of teeth, dramatic weight loss, lack of personal hygiene, self respect, an empty pocket, violent, erratic and paranoid behavior, diarrhea, miscarriages, stillbirths and premature births. And its a guarantee that your offspring will be crazed sociopaths on a funky ass high that last for 7 to 10 minutes.

Ten sometimes kick it with Greed when he feel like club hoppin', learning how to play them club 'ho's. Greed showed him how to be and while they were at the club they watch each other back. Ten told Greed if he wanted to know how to rob banks that he will show him. Greed was like "okay". Ten knew that this nigga Greed had good eyes to scope out a bank and armored cars. Ten and Greed sometime kick it with Jazzy Bell gang when they're just chilling.

STRICTLY BUSINESS

Jazzy Bell's clique had money. She was strictly about money. They worked and also jacked. Because they had the most customers. I'm talkin' about sellin' out fast. If things be slow for Greed on a Sunday in the daytime, he go and hang out with Jazzy Bell's crew. Now, don't get me wrong. All the clubs be packed on Sunday nights--Club Flava, Club 559, Frozen Paradise, and Club Escape, just to name a few. Some of the crews outside the family fronted out their dope, you know, but not this clique. It's "show me the money".

Fly-Mar will sometimes be with Chicago's crew, puttin' in work helpin' Pee Wee Loc. Chicago had some good ass ideas. She knew that Milk had good connections with the Po Po's, so she told Milk when the customer don't want to spend no money or take the fronts no more that mean that they have found some other nigga with a better price. See, in the '90s, everybody had dope. Everywhere you look, there's somebody sellin' some dope or tryin' to purchase some weight. The city was growing and if you out there bad and you don't have a family to back you, you better roll with God because He's the only one who can save you from these demons in this dirty game. It's a quick come-up, but it's hell or jail--that's the price you pay if you don't get in and get out and that's real.

Chicago will sometimes get her own parties busted if the

cops raid the house and bust the big-time rollers at the party because the customers just started comin' to get high, turnin' into a junkie, and stopped buyin' pussy. Chicago's pussy was still snappin'--bitches was breakin' their self.

Most of the customers started ridin' with their keys & gees. They just got tired of people breakin' in their house and takin' their shit. But the dope Chicago had was way better than the dope they had, so you know niggas be tryin' to sneak out with a 8-ball of that fire raw power. And guess what--Boom! "Everybody on the damn floor right now! We're not bullshittin' you! Better freeze, nigga!" And they all froze, just like Jim Carrey in the movie "The Mask".

The police got money and dope off some of the customers, right in front of Chicago. They just dropped their heads. The cops then took them to their rides and guess what--most of the cars had big dope like four or five keys. The cops played games with them by asking them "what shall we do?" The customers be so nervous they fuck around and say silly shit like, "Let me go." And they got two or three keys in their ride. See, these are the important people and they can't afford to get busted. So the cops just keeps everything, giving them a break, telling them to get the hell on before they bust their ass.

The cops pull off at the same time except one car and that was Pacman's crew. The party was packed. Chicago made good money; $5G a head, and there were 39 heads off in the party. The cops got about $117,000 and 123 keys. And the ones who had dope at home and didn't get busted at the party. Pee Wee Loc and Fly-Mar tore that ass up good. They came out with 13 keys and $96,000. Chicago gave the cops their cut, which was $48,000 in cash. Pacman got out his cut and split the rest out with the other 23 cops.

So when the cops left, Jazzy Bell's whole clique came over

to watch the fights. Chicago and Jazzy's crews counted up the riches--they made about $165,000 and got off with 136 keys, altogether. The customers were scared to death, so they stayed home and started back makin' house calls and started back takin' fronts. Chicago and Jazzy Bell's crews split up all what was made and then they sat back and kicked it like big players.

✳ ✳ ✤ ✳ ✳ ✳ ✳ ☆ ☆ ☆

After the fight was over, Jazzy Bell got back on her block. But her crew wasn't the only ballers on the block. There was a clique down the street--the Killahoe Posse. These baller blocking niggas was on the wild and dirty side. The way they're living they're going to get took out of the game. When they can't have things their way they do stupid shit like put their jack on hittin' up Jazzy Bell's customers sometimes with big money or, after they leave Jazzy Bell's house, with their big dope. But most of the time when they try that shit they get jack by no other than the awesome twosome, Hommie the Clown and Michael Myers. It was good and in some ways bad, because they scare the Killahoe Posse away, but it scare the shit out of the customers, too.

Jazzy Bell wanted to see where the Killahoe Posse's heart was, so she did a Chicago. She staged a fake bust. She planted 19 synthetic keys and $60-G of fake money. When the cops busted the house, the Killahoe Posse was all eyes tryin' to see what was comin' out of the million dollar spot, but they couldn't see shit. The cops came in and they were all in the house settin' up small video cameras and they got to steppin'. The cops dropped off Jazzy Bell's crew where they wanted to be. They stayed away four days, and when they got back the house was ransacked. The fake money and dope was gone--they took the bait, and Jazzy Bell had it all on video tape. The Killahoe Posse was lyin' back, chillin', sellin' cocaine as usual. Jazzy Bell played it off real cool, too, until it was time to get them. They went back to work--she used Greed's eyes part time and Big Mike and Ten for retaliation and had Jim Kelly down at the office gettin' a background check on them fools. Jazzy Bell called up Baller and asked him can she rent Hezzy because her chef is so busy. She like Hezzy's recipe.

Baller was like, "For how long, Jazzy? I need Hezzy also." She said, "I just need him to cook up 20 keys and I need to make it bubble.

Baller: "So you really need him to cook up 40 keys, right?" Jazzy Bell: "Yeah," in a soft tone.

Baller: "Yeah, okay. And when he get through tell him I said come on back home. Take it easy, Jazzy." Jazzy gave Baller a blessing and then hung up the phone.

✳ ✳ ❖ ❊ ✳ ✳ ✳ ☆ ★ ☆

Brown Sugar was havin' the time of her life livin' it up on the million she had made, even though she had lost it all. But she had no problem gettin' it back. She got it back and four times the amount. This bitch dresses in some of the best shit. Whenever she walk into a club, people freeze up, scared to speak. Everybody want to know what she drove up in. She tell them to go look and see, and they do, and she ride better than most big-timers.

She use to pay for lick. Now 'ho's want to fuck her and put her up on lick for free. Rich, black and beautiful is a wonderful thing to see when you're in control of your own destiny. Brown Sugar is the Mother of Pearls and Sky is her most valuable. Sky is the shit. She keeps Brown Sugar on charge. She worked Brown Sugar like no other the first time they hit it off. Sky was in control of the fuck, makin' her sweat and call out her name. Sugar loved the way Sky made her cream so she paid whatever Sky charged and Sky don't come cheap. Sky learned from the best--Chicago, a school smart schemer.

Brown Sugar then visited Diamond, an agressive leader. Diamond gives Brown Sugar respect, but she mostly laughs in her face because she's strictly dickle. Diamond, Jade and Raven was chillin' out at one of Jade's phat farms. She's got houses all over the world. Jade is Miss Real Estate. When she came over, the house was full of weed smoke. Diamond was puffin' on a fat blunt. Sugar just stopped by to see how the girls was doin'. By the looks of it, they was doin' real good--plush carpet wall-to-wall. The house inside and out looked like a movie star's house.

Brown Sugar asked, "Where's Mona Lisa?"

Diamond: "She's with her trick. You know, I think she really loves that fool Fidel."

Raven: "Shi-id. He's givin' her the world. That night at the fight party he was callin' out her name and I put this snappin' cat on him, Girl."

Jade: "For real, Girl," laughin', sniffin' on a line of raw powder.

Raven: "I mean, Girls, this Mona Lisa is somethin' else. She takes him out to ball games, movies, and even the zoo."

Diamond: "Shi-id! She's almost as bad as me, sippin' on a glass of lemonade, blowin' big smoke. See, when Mona Lisa get a trick, she go all the way to break him. And that's one to grow on."

Brown Sugar dropped some big-timers' names who need-ed to be worked on and she knew that Diamond's crew was the one to get with it when it come time for the top notch players. Diamond was still gettin' money off of Big Six. Jade was still on Bread Bout It. Right now Precious got his head fucked up with emotion. Jade knows its now time to break his ass. Precious goin' to get him high on coke next week;

Jade goin' to show him some love. Raven got traps to set and kids to raise.

Brown Sugar was high as hell; when she left there she went to visit Jazzy Bell and high was not the way to be around Jazzy Bell. Gettin' high was not her thang no more. God was in her life so she speak from the heart. Jazzy Bell, Big Mike, Greed and Ten was playin' a friendly game of cards when Brown Sugar came over.

Big Mike, Greed, and Ten was thinkin' of a master plan while Brown Sugar and Jazzy Bell was in the next room having a sister to sister conversation. Jazzy Bell's crew already had hit up about nine banks and eighteen other jacks they made in the street in two and a half years. Brown Sugar was so high she couldn't stand up right. She was also dozing off. But while she was there, Jazzy Bell gave her spiritual advice because Brown Sugar was talkin' out of the side of her neck.

Jazzy Bell: "Sugar, you are a beautiful girl. You need to slow yourself down--you're killin' yourself."

Brown Sugar: "Look, Jazzy, I understand what you mean. I'm just spreadin' my hustles, Sweetheart. I'm goin' to put this family on the map, Baby. Gettin' high is just a part of the game, Baby. Look, the family is doin' real good right now. We're goin' to the top of the world, Baby, so be cool. You're my pearl, my sunshine, my boo--I love you," and she dozed off.

Jazzy Bell was listening with tears in her eyes. Jazzy Bell called Sugar's name--she barely moved her head. Jazzy Bell held Brown Sugar close to her and rocked her to sleep. She lifted her up and put her to bed and then she got down on her knees and prayed all night for Sugar to change her ways because she was movin' up too fast. The next day Fly-Mar came back to the house and he'd had a long night. It was fight night. The Golden Boy Oscar de la Hoya was fightin' last night, buildin' up his game. He won the fight.

Fly-Mar had a good night--he had made over $65-G and 18 keys, so he went to the IHOP before coming home. He brought breakfast for the whole crew--hot pancakes and sausage, cheese and eggs, and some OJ. Fly-Mar woke up the whole house. Brown Sugar woke up and saw that Jazzy Bell was down on her knees. She prayed all night for Brown Sugar and the family. Sugar was still feeling a little down high, but she was better.

There was a knock at the door.

Jazzy Bell: "Come in."

It was Fly-Mar with he breakfast. He saw that Sugar was there and he apologized for not having gotten her anything to eat. Jazzy Bell told Fly-Mar to give her food to Sugar and he did and walked out of the room. Sugar saw that Jazzy Bell was serious. Jazzy Bell left the room so she could eat and get herself together. She walked in the room with all the boys and they showed her love by sharing their food. They all loved the shit out of Jazzy Bell, more than they loved their selves.

They all ate together and also checked out their plans on the next bank job and the move on the Killahoe Posse. By that time, Brown Sugar had gotten up, ready to go. She spoke to everybody. Jazzy Bell walked her to the open door. Outside was Fly-May and Jim Kelly, next door, ready to put in work on the 15th of March check day for some major crack heads.

They hugged and kissed and both took a deep breath and that's when the tears started coming. Brown Sugar could barely get it out. She told Jazzy Bell that she loved her and that the new shipment was coming in two weeks on April Fools' Day. Jazzy Bell told her that she wouldn't forget and to go see her little sister--it will do some good. And she left.

She hadn't seen her sister since the last time she visited home. As she was ridin' out she knew she had one more fox to see and that was Chicago the Deffa Heffa.

Brown Sugar went out to Chicago's big ass house in Alpharetta. When she got there, there was a big argument. Chicago went straight for the throat. Chicago called Sugar a traitor and all hell broke loose.

Sugar: "Bitch, you just don't know."

Chicago: "Bitch, I do know."

Sugar: "He went against his rules. He put his hand on me and cursed me. I was hurt."

Chicago: "Bitch, that wasn't the real reason. Bitch, I know you. If it wasn't for him, you wouldn't be here now."

Sugar: "I needed my space."

Chicago: "Girl, your space is killin' you. You shouldn't cross your real family."

Sugar: "We don't need that family. We got a new family and I am runnin' shit."

Chicago: "You ain't runnin' nothin'. If you couldn't run the first family, what makes you think you can run this family? Milk don't give a damn about you--he wants to break us and make us. You know the game."

Sugar: "Chicago, I love you."

Chicago: "You don't love me; you love that shit you're puttin' in your nose more and more each day. That's what you love, Bitch. Get your shit together!"

Brown Sugar, crying to Chicago: "What shall I do?"

Chicago: "Get back with us. It ain't that hard. You the only one who can get close enough to Milk. Girl, we still love you."

Brown Sugar: "How is Baller?" wiping the tears away from her eyes.

Chicago: "Girl, he's okay, he's okay." Chicago, with a

smile on her face, gives her sister a great big hug and kisses.

Brown Sugar: "So what's really goin' on?"

They both talk for hours until it is time to go see her little sister. But when she got there, the house was the same mess, but this time it was worse than before and the same old crew was still there--uncles, aunts, and little cousins.

Brown Sugar didn't like it at all that the house was always a mess. And when she saw that her little sister was one month pregnant, she almost had a fucking fit. She checked the whole house and the place was messed up except for her mom's room. It was clean. Brown Sugar took he sister away from there and took her to the hotel. She told Neva to call home to see if anyone has gotten there yet. The phone just rang and rang. The room had two beds. Sugar had a lot to say to her little sister, and she knew she hadn't been there for her, so she just sat back and let her sister talk her to sleep. When Neva saw that Sugar was asleep, she got on the phone and called her boyfriend. She talked all night with him, until morning finally came.

When Sugar woke, Neva was sound asleep. Sugar got in the bed with her little sister and kissed her on the head and she woke up. Sugar told her to call home and let Mom know where she was. She called and there was no answer. They come and go, day and night. Sugar was like, "Fuck it. Let's go."

She took her little sister to the Mall and told her to get whatever she wanted and then told her to get a few baby clothes. She also said when she found out if it was going to be a girl or boy, she was going to take care of it like her own. Sugar was just braggin' on the baby. She just got happy all of a sudden. And from the Mall they went to the furniture store and bought furniture for the whole damned apartment.

Sugar paid the furniture mover to haul the old out and put

the new in. It was done. The whole apartment was fur-
nished. It was the nicest apartment in the project. Aunts
and uncles and the kids came home and were in shock.
Sugar laid down more rules this time; she even put food in
the new refrigerator. Li'l sister was so happy of her big sister she had tears of joy. Sugar just started to realize that she
was someone important, so she knew it was time to take care
of her responsibility. The talk with Jazzy Bell put a little
love in her heart, but it will take more prayer to turn a heart
of stone into a heart of flesh. God works in mysterious ways.

Mom was still at work and it was gettin' late and Sugar
had to serve Milk. She gave her little sister a few clean credit cards and told her to page her if she needed anything more.
Brown Sugar gave a blessing and left.

✸ ✳ ✤ ✳ ✳ ✸ ✳ ☆ ★ ☆

Tray and Deuce were puttin' in much work servin' the
streets of Atlanta with 50 keys and 500 pounds of weed.
Money, money, money. Milk's family was the most powerful, influential, and richest family in the state of Georgia.
Tray and Deuce are Milk's mechanics--if Milk say kill, they
kill. These niggas watch the family with an evil eye.

When these niggas are at the clubs, there's always a fight,
everywhere they ball, and if they don't win the fight there's
going to be a shootout at the club and it always be over stupid shit like some nigga in the club might step on their gator
shoes or bump them. They're not havin' that shit! Or it
might be some nigga in the club louder and got a gang of
'ho's and makin' their shit look weak and soft. These niggas
just get 'ho's who just love the taste of coke, you know--a
bitch who sniff a line or who smoke coke joints.

A bitch like Diamond or Chicago--they can't get no bitch
like that. Bitches like Chicago or Diamond is headstrong.
Cocaine only weakens you, but some think sniffin' dope

makes their nuts bigger. On the real, they both still come out of the pocket when fucking with Jade. Anytime she want something, she get it--and she don't have to give up no pussy because she got it like that.

But these two niggas made a li'l name for theirselves over the two and a half years they been here. When it come to jacking and killing, they rank fifth now. In the two and a half years, Atlanta has had over 842 jacks and over 483 killings.

From Ten to Number One; Atlanta's most feared crews:

Number 10 - The Killahoe Posse (15 jacks and 2 kills).

Number 9 - Big Six (15 jacks and 112 kills).

Number 8 - The Jury (23 jacks and 8 kills). These niggas own a burglar bar door company and a rim shop. These niggas put your door on and take it off without you askin' and then go in your house and get you for what you got. You will always notice these niggas because they got a rim shop. Everything they ride on be the shit rims dipped in gold. They got the best gold rims you ever want to come get.

Number 7 -Dee Dee and her young friends (29 jacks and 0 kills).

Number 6 -The Powder Rangers (32 jacks and 23 kills)

Number 5 -Milk, Brown Sugar, Tray, and Deuce (34 jack and 50 kills; Milk thinks it's 34 jacks and 51 kills).

Number 4 -The cops (41 jacks and 87 kills). The cops started goin' crazy, beatin' niggas, takin' money from dealers and takin' payoff from bigger drug dealers and givin' them protection. Right now Atlanta is the Murder Capital of the world until the mayor heard that the Olympic Committee is comin' to town and that's when all the checkin' began. The Internal Affairs was checkin' the police and the police was checkin' the police and the big timers was checkin' their own boys. Friends was checkin' friends and everybody who had dope and money was paranoid like Jerry Fletcher and Truman Burbank.

Number 3 -The Corporation All Together (188 jacks and 87 kills).

    Diamond's Crew -22 jacks and 7 kills

    Jazzy Bell's Crew -27 jacks and 6 kills

    Chicago's Crew -33 jacks and 13 kills

    Sky's Crew -40 jacks and 18 kills

    Baller's Crew -66 jacks and 43 kills

Number 2 -Baller and Crow (190 jacks and 100 kills)

And the Number One jacker and the most feared on the street is:

Michael Myers and Hommie the Clown (275 jacks and 14 kills).

69 FREAK SCENE

It was April and the family has done well, so Milk decided to start giving each crew 50 keys. He figure if Deuce and Tray can move 50 keys every four months and sell ounces for the 600, then his family can do the same. The family can, but they're not going to change their prices. It's Spring Break. Niggas roll hard as hell the first three months of the year, so when Spring Break roll around, the big dogs chill out the middle man and the man under him always get caught up in the drought season because the big-timers want to get their freak on, so they don't sell shit until May kick around and then they still might hold back because the street be hot and 'round this time the cops start trying to get a nigga.

But when it hot, the south be jumping off the hook. On Spring Break every year it seem like the whole world be down in the south the first three week of April. People be down in Florida kicking it like big players talking about what they going to do next week in Atlanta on Freaknik. See, down in Florida they just be getting their self ready for the Freaknik which be crunk! First of all, every lady in Atlanta be out looking good as hell, even the ugly ones. Niggas be horny, ready to just stick something. The whole Atlanta be crunk. All the li'l spot--the Westend, Downtown, Underground, Greenbriar Mall, Ashby Street, Lenox Mall, the Pimp Strip (Stewart Avenue). Every 'ho's hair be fix up and clothes nice and tight and that pussy cat be fat. Some 'ho's will show you that fat rabbit if you got a video camera. No lie--bitches be dancing all on top of cars and check it. The highway even be pack--I mean pack. Niggas be all on the Highway Bankhead bouncing and running up to car, fucking with 'ho's. It be a car full girls howling freak something and it be a car full of niggas doing the same shit but sometime it be funk but most of the time it all good. For the niggas who love to be grindin' in the traps, sell out of dope and from there on he catch hell the trap be booming! But it be hard to find dope. Niggas leave their trap and go to other niggas trap and get flex or rob--no lie. Niggas come from everywhere just to get their freak on in Atlanta Freaknik. It's the biggest event in the world, I don't care what you think I know. Fly cars, fly 'ho's, all the stores sell out of shit, like beer and liquor stores, shoe stores, gas stations, and all the malls sell out of clothes. The T-shirt maker make a killing. You might hear some niggas say "I am not freaking this year", but you can't help it. Soon as you step out the door you will see niggas who never put on clean clothes or comb his hair. He be like, "I'm Freaknik," smiling, happy as hell, because he know everybody freakin' and every nigga in the 'hood be washing their rides, getting ready to ride all night hopin' to catch. The girls who got mens don't say a word on Friday. She let her man do his thing and when he come home he lie to her, but she know. She put his ass out and then on Saturday she go out and do the same shit you did. So if you got a girl you better go out together, because if you don't you might go out and don't fuck, but she will if she get hot enough because it be real pimps out there ready to put a bitch on, if you know what I mean.

'94 Freaknik. It was the biggest black college Spring Break ever. It estimated over 300,000 black college students and over 200,000 other blacks from out of town. Atlanta was like a big ass block party from April 17 to 19. All you seen was fly ass cars, blunts, alcohol, and smiles. All you heard was loud music and a few gun shots. It might be in the 96 degree heat, but other than that everyone was friendly and flirtatious. Snoop Doggy Dogg and the Dogg Pound, Too Short, Luke, Nino, and the Wu Tang Clan came down and did their thang and all the shows was on and popping.

THE CRUCIAL GAME

Twenty months later; December, 1995--a week from Christmas and the players in the 'hood was puttin' in a li'l work to have some extra money in their pockets. Baller's crew just got their shipment. Hezzy and Pete are in the back cookin' up 50 keys. It took them all day. Hezzy cooks it and Pete weighs it and bags it and Ten and Baller are puttin' in work by rollin' $10, $20, $50, and $100 slabs while the big dope is gettin' cooked up and ready to serve in quarters, halves, and ounces.

Hezzy was listenin' to one of his mixed tapes he made and tellin' Pete that they need to open up a record store sellin' Rap and R&B CDs and tapes. "That way we can put a studio in the back so when the rappers come to the store to thank us for sellin' their shit we can take them in the back, let them do their thang, and then they do one for us. Man, we can get all the baddest underground Rappers up and have a mean ass compilation album."

Pete: "Who we going to get?"

Hezzy: "Man, we can get C-Loc, Juvenile, BG, The Hot Boys, Dog House Posse, Bust Down, Ruthless Juveniles, Sporty T, PNC, Prime Time..."

Pete: "Okay, okay!" laughin', sittin' 36 zips to the side, askin' Hezzy where the Rappers was from.

Hezzy: "The Big Easy dope man graveyard."

Pete saw that Hezzy was dead serious so he told Hezzy to name some more Rappers and he did and "Then we can get some of them niggas from Texas, like The Convicts, Black Monks, UGK, Crime Boss, CC Water Bound, Wreckless Clan, ran by that nigga point blank but that nigga point blank got a big ass clique. He can run his own shit like Master P, he got another hard ass crew called the SPC, South Park Coalition, with K-Rino, The Terrorists, Klondike Kat, and that crazy ass nigga Gangsta, Nip the Hardest Nigga alive on wax. Nino, Kotton Mouth, PSK13, the whole Fifth Ward circle and ESG." Hezzy was gettin' hyped because the Rap game is his hobby. "And then we can get some of them Tennessee Niggas, Skinny Pimp, Three 6 Mafia, Gangsta Blac, Playa Fly, Playa G, Slicc, DJ Squeeky & The Family, and I can't forget about Pistol. You can learn something off that nigga. Well, really, you can learn off all these niggas. I am going to turn you onto it. There's some niggas from Flint who be on that real with that dope game Rap and that's Top Authority, The Dayton Family, and my nigga Jake the Flake."

Pete: "Well, what's up with some of them niggas from the West Coast?"

Hezzy: "Just wait, nigga, it's these three groups from Chicago that's on fire."

Pete: "Who you talkin' 'bout?"

Hezzy: "Man, I'm talkin' 'bout Crucial Conflict, Do or Die, and that nigga Twista. Man, them players in the mid-west got a nice style. And hell yeah, I got some West Coast thugs--we can get Messy Marv, Mafiosos, Young Celski, Young Rich, 115, C-Bo, Imp, Dru Down, AMW on D-Shot Record, Above-the-Law, Dangerous Dame, Dre Dog, B-Legit, King George. Li'l Rick, Totally Insane, RBL, the Whoridas, and I can't forget Young Soldierz. We can sell all that shit. That's makin' much money. Groups like Puff Daddy, E-40 & the Click, Hard Boys, Busta Rhymes, Jay Z, Ray Luv, The Luniz, Mac Mall, Tru, Mystikal, DMX, Westside Connection, Mase, Wyclef Jean, L L Cool J, Kool G Rap, Outkast, Goodie Mobb, The Suave House Camp, JT the Bigger Figger, The Geto Boys, Too Short, and man that shit will sell good in the 'hood. Just think of all them mixed tapes I be makin' and sellin'."

Pete: "What we going to call it?"

Hezzy: "We call it 'Cry Now Laugh Later Record Shop'."

Pete: "Man, you think we can really do that there?"

Hezzy: "Hell yeah, man--I got the hook-up."

By that time Baller came in the back where Hezzy and Pete were. Baller turned the radio down so they could hear him clearly. He told Hezzy that he needed 25 keys right now. Pete was like, "Who that there want to buy 25 brick??"

Baller: "It's that nigga Oz Escobar from the Jury."

Hezzy: "What? His folks don't have anything??"

Baller: "I don't know."

Pete: "You think that nigga cool?"

Baller: "I don't know."

Hezzy: "I want you to watch his eyes when I turn my back and Pete, you watch our back. Okay, let's go."

They came out the back. Oz grabbed at his gat. Baller was like, "Hold on, Nigga. They just want to ask you about some rims." Oz said, "Big business first." Baller handed Oz his package of 25 keys. Oz popped the case open and looked at the boys and said, "It looks good."

Hezzy was like, "Test it...I chop it up. It got a four plus cut on and with that type cut you can do your thang."

Oz Escobar gave Pete the suitcase with the money in it--625 Gee's. Hezzy and Pete counted up the money while Baller and Oz Escobar were havin' a drink. Baller stepped outside to throw away the bottle. Ten was outside with two of Escobar's boys, Cotton and Blood, chopping'up game to see where these niggas comin' from. While Baller was going out the door, Oz Escobar's eyes was all over when he peeped at Hezzy and Pete. Pete took his eyes off him and acted like he was still countin' the money when Baller came back in.

Hezzy: "It all here."

Baller and Oz Escobar shook hands. Oz was like, "I can put a good strong burglar bar door up for you for a small nice price. I bet it's a lot of niggas that want to get off in here, say Bro?"

Baller was like, "That's okay--I got much heat for that ass if they try anything, you hear me, Bro?"

Oz turned his back, ready to walk out the door. Pete tapped him on his shoulder. Oz turned around. Him and Pete was eye to eye.

Pete said, "Hey, what do you think about some niggas like us openin' up a record shop sellin' Rap and R&B CDs and tapes?"

Oz stepped back and gave Pete his earnestly opinion. He said, "Openin' up a business is a good move because legal money lasts longer than drug money. See, when you make it fast it goes fast," and Oz walked out the door and got in the car with his crew and left.

Baller asked Hezzy, "What's up with dat there?"

Hezzy said, "Me and Pete thinkin' 'bout doin' dat there, makin' that move."

Baller: "Yeah, that's a smooth move. If you do it, cut me in on it. What we got left back there?"

Hezzy: "We got 50 keys of hard and 25 keys of soft. But, Baller, do you trust that nigga Escobar?"

Baller: "Hell naw...But that nigga show us respect, so let's show him some."

Pete: "But do you think that we're going to jack that ass?"
Baller: "I don't know, we might. But is you two niggas going to work tonight or you going club hoppin'?"

Hezzy: "We're going to stay down tonight and make a li'l Christmas money."

Baller: "Well, I need you two to go to the liquor store for me and get some Cognac and snacks."

So Hezzy and Pete drove to the store. Hezzy slap one of his tapes in the deck. The tape he put in was Pistol's Money and the Power album; the song "Rags to Riches". Hezzy was rappin' with the song while ridin' out. The song went like this: "Rags to riches, ugh, spend your money on your folks and mother fuck these bitches. Rags to riches, ugh, stay low key up in this game and watch out for these snitches" until after Hezzy played the song five times they were pullin' back up at the house and Pete was rappin' the song, tellin' Hezzy: "Hell, yeah, I like that mother fucker! Let's do that shit." He was convinced that pushin' underground rap was a good idea.

See, underground rap is played a lot in the 'hoods but gets no air play over the radio. But with good street promotions, niggas be buyin' CD's and tapes like a mother fucker, so I say to all the underground rappers, "Keep keepin' that shit real and fuck what people say. Because your music reach lots of people in the 'hood who go through that shit they spit." Now white folks listen to rap and they like it. But if they heard some real underground rap they would be scared of a nigga. Imagine that if every black rapper went multi-platinum and was black owned it would be worse than it is now. Rest in peace to all the Rap Soldiers: 38, Rapping Ron, Eazy-E, Kilo-G, Pimp Daddy, G-Slimm, Seagram, Mr. Cee, Big Popa, 2Pac. Believe me, you helped lots of people make it in this cruel world with your voice. We will miss it. May God bless and rest your soul.

Baller and Ten was inside takin' orders in code over the phone. Pete and Hezzy was outside smokin' and rollin' and sippin' on Cognac, havin' a good time makin' money. All of a sudden a geek monster yelled out "5-0, 5-0!" and the cops, two cars from the right and two cars from the left, all four cars slammed on their brakes right in from of them. All of the cops was lookin' crazy. One cop yelled out the window while the other cop jumped out at the other people in the street. The one cop say, "Get your black ass in the house. I don't want to see nobody on this street when I leave and come back."

Pete stepped out his blunt and poured out his liquor and asked the cop, "What's wrong with you, man? Cool down."

The cop then ran up on Pete and grabbed him by his shirt and said, "Look here, you li'l fat nigga! A cop has been killed by a drug dealer and that dealer look just like you! The cop then pulled out his gun and put it in Pete's face. When Hezzy was lookin' at Pete he thought Pete was cryin' so he looked harder and it was just that the cop was spittin' and yellin' at the same time while the gun was in Pete's face. Pete was eyein' the cop down with a mean mug. The cop was talkin' shit and spittin' but Pete didn't blink. The cop eased off. Pete still had his eyes on the cop who pulled that fuckin' shit. All the cops pulled off with their lights and sirens on and doin' about 60 in a 25 zone.

Everybody went into the house. The street was clear. Pete went in the house mad, tellin' Baller: "Man, I'm going to kill me a cop. Them dirty ass mother fuckers."

Baller was like, "What happened?"

Hezzy said, "Man, the cops are out there bad-actin' a donkey." Baller turned on the TV set an it was all over the news. A cop was killed. Yes, we get cops killed in the streets of the

A-town. The reason and who the cop was: The cop was a big ass Russian named Ivan Danko; a nasty cop. He don't take payoff, he just take your shit. When he's pullin' up and you take off runnin' this fool bust at your ass tryin' his best to kill your ass.

He stayed on this one drug dealer's ass named Cougnut, a buck wild dealer who just got tired of his shit. So, Cougnut came up with a provocative plan. A week before Christmas, Danko was rollin' through to collect a little Christmas money. Everybody looked up to Cougnut, so they did what he did. Danko jumped out of his car with his hands out-- Cougnut pulled out about $4G. The next dealer did the same thing, and so on. Danko was smilin' when he got to the last dealer. Cougnut tapped Danko on his shoulder; when Danko turned around--Pop! Pop!--dead in his face.

All the dealers took off runnin'. The big Russian cop was still standing. Cougnut popped him two more times in the face. He hit the ground. Cougnut then went in his pocket and got about $12G. Then Cougnut got in his car and ran his ass over. Took his pump shotgun out of his car and shot up his car while the car was on top of his ass. And then got in his own GTO and fled the scene, mad at the world.

So that's really why the cops are pissed off. Even if the cops take a payoff they will still turn against you if one of the boys in blue gets killed. That night, Zone 1 cops switched with Zone 2, Zone 3 switched with Zone 4. Each cop was in a new zone takin' no shit. If you were J-walking after they warned you to get your ass off the street they'd lock your ass up.

Hezzy went back outside to get his gat he had hidden in the bushes. He look left and right. It was quiet outside. Before he could get to his gat, two dirty ass cops jumped out of the woods. No Neck Jeff and Officer Bacon grabbed

Hezzy and told him he smelled like weed and planted an ounce on him and told him, "You're going down, Buster!" One minute later, a car came by and swooped them up, just that fast.

They took Hezzy to jail. Baller, Ten and Pete was worried. They didn't know what had happened until Jim Kelly called and said, "Man, won't y'all come down here and pick Hezzy up. Man, I been callin' all night. Man, the cops goin' crazy lockin' folks up tonight, so drive safe."

A week later it was Christmas. Cougnut was arrested. He was at a hotel with his family; celebrating Christmas with his girl and two kids when the cops busted in the door. Cougnut and his family was all prayin', asking God forgiveness of his sin. He kissed his kids and they took him away.

Cameras was everywhere. He came out the door like a man with his head up, with a mean mug on his face. It was a black cop that took him to the jailhouse. He told Cougnut that he should have ran because Danko was a dirty ass cop who had no respect for the law. Christmas is a good day for giving, and it is the day that Jesus Christ was born.

✳ ✱ ✤ ✲ ✳ ✱ ✳ ☆ ✴ ☆

All last week Milk had been tryin' his best to set up his family, just like how he did the other crews on the street. But every time he tried, Michael Myers and Hommie the Clown showed up and messed up his plans so he could never put his rob on his family. So he thought that someone in his family was Michael Myers and Hommie the Clown, but he just couldn't put his finger on it.

Last week he gave each of his crews 50 keys to work with, and later they picked up their keys. Milk had them followed. He put Deuce on Chicago's crew and Tray on Sky's crew and himself on Baller's clique. He told Brown Sugar to watch Jazzy Bell's crew. He said there was no reason to watch Diamond's crew because it is an all girl clique.

Sugar called back first and told Milk that Michael Myers and Hommie the Clown was watchin' her big time. Deuce and Tray called back sayin' the same thing. While Milk followed Baller he looked in his rearview mirror and saw that the two were following him also, and that right there shook Milk. He'd heard so much about these two, and it wasn't good things; he got the hell on and just made it his business to just make lots of money and find out on the down low who the two were behind the two masks.

Brown Sugar stayed close to Milk, learning his slick moves and at the same time giving the family info on his next move. Milk got more into the police than his Family. Michael Myers and Hommie the Clown spooked the shit out of Milk and in his mind he thought that Michael Myers and Hommie the Clown were trying to bring him and his family down so he was making the cops a full member of his organization. Milk was getting a big, big shipment in--six tons of raw uncut cocaine--and he needed the cops to guard it.

Right then and there Milk lost trust in his family. Milk guaranteed Pacman and the other 23 cops $50G each for the safety of his shipment. Milk was with Brown Sugar, Deuce and Tray, and Pacman and three of his Dogs, Reebok, No Neck Jeff, and Officer Bacon, they all chopped up game over drinks and coke. Milk saw that Pacman had an eye for Sugar, so Milk put Sugar to work on Pacman, not knowing that they used to hit it off.

✱ ✳ ✦ ✵ ✶ ✲ ✳ ☆ ★ ☆

Well, it's said and done that the Olympics is coming to town. So Mayor Bill Campbell put the new Chief of Police, Beverly Harvard (yes--a lady), in charge of the safety of the Star Olympian gods and the other thousands of important people that will come to the city. She made it her business to clean up the city and when a woman cleans up, she cleans up. She started with her own house; she hired 100 more new cops and 50 of the cops worked for the Internal Affairs here to investigate the dirty cops situation. The dirty cops didn't know a damn thing--they just did their jobs, collected money, and stayed low.

Since the new cops got on the force, they also got a new police dog. Since the old one died, the Fulton County Commission voted unanimously last week to give honor to the pooch. The drug sniffin' dog was a Golden Retriever who was killed in the line of duty. The police busted a house where some drug dealers trained Pit Bulls to kill. The Atlanta police kicked in the door and let the dog go and when they did that, four Pit Bulls jumped on him and tore him apart. When a few of the officers went for the dealer, the Pit Bulls got off the pooch, Butch, and headed for the officers and it turned it into a shoot-out. The dealers got away, but there were four wounded officers and five dead dogs.

Butch helped the police seize 876 pounds of marijuana, 44 ounces of cocaine, $164,000 in cash and 25 vehicles. Commissioner Duncan Lowe gave honor on December 18, 1995 with Butch Day in Fulton County. The state now has a new dog and it's a girl dog named Cheatha. And this time it's a Pit Bull with a good nose and a vicious bite.

✳ ✳ ✤ ✳ ✳ ✱ ✳ ☆ ✫ ☆

It was Christmas and each crew was celebrating in its own li'l way. Chicago threw a party on a big ass boat and this was one time they didn't jack nobody; they just partied the whole weekend. But she had something cookin'. She wanted all her customers to build up their money and then strike. She knew that her crew had to pull off a big job in '96 then relax until the Olympic blows over. Everyone who got dope from her picked up their package after the weekend. The party was nice out there in the middle of the ocean, snortin' and drinkin'. The party was packed.

Chicago's whole crew was there, Jazzy Bell and Fly-Mar was there, Big Mike and Jim Kelly stayed behind. Hezzy and Pete was there with two foxy brown li'l mamas, Jewel and FeFe. They met in '93 comin' from the Soul Train awards, two airline flight attendants who had seen the world. And they know real Gs when they see them. Diamond and Big Six was there. Diamond left behind the crew so they could handle their personal business.

Raven went to see her four kids and her six babies' daddies--three boys, ages 12, 10, and 7, and one little girl, age 6. She had gifts for all of them. She stayed lookin' sexy--her babies' daddies just shook their heads and wished they could get some more of dat there. She took all the kids to see each of the Daddies and told them all, "This your boy right here, too. Look at him." The baby's daddy be like, "No way--this my boy right here." She have all of their heads fucked up thinkin' they got more than one kid and the baby's daddy who do the most for their kid, she put the little girl on them. They really don't know how many kids they have. Two of the kids' real fathers was robbed and killed. She set them up and she set up two more who thought they were a baby's daddy. The little girl belong to Fly-Mar. Raven's grandmother keep her. But she still got all the boy's daddies thinkin' they got a little girl, too.

She took the kids out to one of Jade's houses. Jade and Lisa gave the kids a good Christmas and when the night fell in, Jade left to go get her gift from Bread Bout It. She have Bread payin' out the ass and, believe me, he don't mind. He still been tryin' to get someone to kill his wife for him.

Ms. Bout It spent over $20,000 this Christmas on gifts and the only thing she got him was a $20 tie. She got gifts for the kids and friends and bought Milk a gold and diamond filled Rolex watch. She even gave Milk info on when Bread visited the bank. She gave him the safe deposit box number, 1637, and told him there was over $18 million in cash in the box. When she said that, Milk gave her some spacey love.

✳ ✳ ✣ ✣ ✳ ✳ ✳ ☆ ★ ☆

Mona Lisa was still with Fidel Cartel. He often thought about Raven--he sometimes caught himself thinkin' about Raven and playin' with himself. Raven got some good pussy, but he thinks she's a jinx. Right now Fidel Cartel have a big problem. He sent his wife on a trip and she never came back. He made a police report three months ago. He hasn't heard a word, so on Christmas Fidel asked Lisa to marry him.

Lisa: "But what about your wife?"

Fidel: "Lisa, look at me. I love you. She's gone and she's not comin' back."

Lisa saw that Fidel had tears in his eyes. She held him tight and said, "Yes, yes, I will marry you." Fidel went into his pocket and pulled out a 14 carat diamond ring with a price tag on it sayin' $38,000. They got married in a small church in Atlanta on Christmas night, but there is still an ongoing investigation into the disappearance of Ms. Cartel, his use to be wife.

✳ ✳ ✣ ✣ ✳ ✳ ✳ ☆ ★ ☆

Greed and Sky was also on the big ass boat gettin' all the attention. She also brought along some of the li'l foxes from the club. The boat party was a good idea for Chicago. The customers love it. They was also gettin' suspicious but they didn't really know what was takin' place with all of the fun-lovin' things all up in their face. When on drugs and havin' a good time spendin' money to get sex and more high they're confused.

✱ ✳ ✢ ✶ ✳ ✱ ✳ ☆ ✯ ☆

Pimpin' you saw the mack. A bitch will break herself if the words are right. And a pimp will love her to death if her stroll is tight. Sugar Wolf and MJG been pimpin' 'ho's and sellin' dope over the years, but a pimp's pimpin' get better when they find a spot or a strip to dip. See, if a mack's got a track, the bitches will lay on their back, get the cash then dash with the cash. Take it to Daddy then wash that crack and get right back on track. Pimpin' was the first hustle on the street. Sugar Wolf get his 'ho's to get other 'ho's. MJG then get the 'ho's to turn a trick or two. The main thang about these two--they keep a bitch broke and happy at the same time. Everytime I see a bitch and she happy, I think she happy because she got lucky, but I never seen a bitch so happy to be broke until I seen niggas like these two. Break yo'self, Bitch. Big pimpin' ain't never goin' to die if the words stay fly. Sugar Wolf and MJG spent their Christmas wrappin' up bitches all day, gettin' them ready for the world of big pimpin'.

✱ ✳ ✢ ✶ ✳ ✱ ✳ ☆ ✯ ☆

Brown Sugar spent Christmas with her family, where they love her for bein' her. And yes, Neva had her baby. It's a girl and her name is Sweet Sable. She weighed in at 9 pounds 7 ounces. She is the most cutest brown baby you ever want to see--thick, black, curly hair, Chinese eyes just like Foxy Brown, and two dimples with some fat cheeks. Brown Sugar spoils the baby rotten when she comes around. She always holdin' the baby, tellin' Neva, "get me this, get me that, so I can feed the baby, so I can change the baby, so I can bathe the baby and put her to sleep..." The house stayed clean while Sugar was there. She puts her foot down. Sugar visits her mom's house every month since the last time she visit. She also give her li'l sister food stamps and credit cards to help out the family. The baby was six months old and had more clothes than everyone else who lived in the apartments put together. She had the greatest aunt on earth.

❋ ❋ ❖ ❊ ❋ ❋ ❋ ☆ ☆ ☆

They all had a good Christmas. Milk and Deuce and Tray was kickin' it at Milk's Al Capone suite with a key apiece and with 97 more keys sittin' to the side. They was thinking of a way to bring the family down just like they did in the other states. See, a person like Milk is a monster. He builds and then he destroys. Coke out, coke out, coke out on Christmas with just evil on their minds. They plotted all the way into the year 1996, the year of relaxation. Milk knew that each crew had to pull off a big lick before relaxation.

It's going to get hot in '96 with the Olympics coming. Freaknik almost didn't make it in '96 and, you know what? Black people was talkin' crazy, sayin' what happened in '95 was nothin' compared to what we will do to them honkies if they don't get freakin' down here in '96. Some said that New Orleans and Jamaica wanted to sponsor the event. The people in Atlanta was like, "Hell no! It started here and it will die here." The mayor got threats from people's parents sayin', "We will not vote for your ass if you don't get your shit together." So it was written--Freaknik every year in Atlanta.

Milk had him a big ass house with 50 rooms built from the ground up. He called it the Al Capone Suite. Milk, Deuce and Tray was also thinkin' what state they were going to hit next after they left Atlanta, Georgia in '96. Tray was like, "Let's hit Texas. We can put big dope in Port Arthur, South Park, 5th Ward."

Deuce was like, "No, bro. They got gangs down there and gangs draw heat and we don't need heat. Let's hit the twin cities, Kansas City, Kansas and Missouri."

Tray sniffed off his key and said, "Fool--they got bigger gangs up there. You think them gang fools don't be thinkin' money? They sell dope too. There were some gangs in St. Louis, but we made it all right, big knots of cash. There's money to be made all over this crazy world and we got to go out and get it. No matter what."

Milk: "Yeah, right. We got to move to a state where the state itself is on the rise."

Tray: "So, where you think we need to be, Yo?"

Deuce: "Yeah, where you think?"

Milk: "I say we shall take this game to Memphis."

Tray and Deuce said it at the same time, "...Memphis."

Deuce: "What's down in Memphis, Yo?"

Milk: "Good pimpin'. We need to get our pimpin' on a li'l more, you know. Twist the game a li'l and maybe we can get some real ass pimp niggas to invest in the dope game. We'll teach them the mean ass dope game and they give us a few moves on the pimp game. Now, I know you niggas can handle some 'ho's I know. See, a Memphis nigga love to dress nice and ride nice and listen to good smooth music like Willie Hutch, Al Green, Sam & Dave, Otis Redding, Marvin Gaye, the Staple Singers, Isaac Hayes, and the Infamous Curtis Mayfield."

Tray: "Hell, yeah, that shit sound good to me, Yo."

Milk: "How 'bout you, Deuce?"

Deuce: "It's a brilliant plan. Yo, let's do it."

Milk: "Let's bring big pimpin' back to life in '97. We're going to invest in things black people love. I gotta go see Boss next year you heard."

Tray and Deuce was so high they just nod their head.

There was about an ounce left from the key they started on Christmas. They toasted, "Happy New Year!"

THE EVIL MEN DO

Baller work them 'ho's the way they need to be work. He advise Dee Dee last year to find a young boyfriend and to get a job to keep her mom from askin' so many questions that question every mother ask their little girl when their body starts to fully develop. A real player keep his face and shit clean.

Dee Dee got a job workin' for the IRS in the mail room-- that's where everybody start at. She give Baller the info he need. Now 'days, niggas got money in the bank it's either in their mother's name or someone they trust a lot. Someone like a wife or a parent. And with Dee Dee workin' for the IRS, she can give Baller info on how much money a nigga really have comin' in. She just got to find out whose name the money's in and it's Baller's job to follow the trick and see who's he very close with. This job is good for 'ho's who just want to fuck a nigga with major figures.

A player like Baller mostly work like this, you know, when you see a fine ass girl and a fat ass girl with her, she there for the inference. For whoever choose the fine chick see a player set it up like this; he put a fat girl with his fine girl. The trick choose the fine girl, she act like she want to do it on the first day but she can't because she have her fat ass friend with her and besides, the fat girl got a ride and a phone and a place to go lay her head. It's set up where the fat girl will have it goin' on and sometimes the fine girl will stay at her fat friend's house until she get her shit together, so she use her fat friend's phone to stay in touch with the trick.

Now, a nigga who think he's got it goin' on will think that he can fuck the both of them and get away with that. But what he really don't know is that he really gettin' played. See, fat 'ho's have gotten smart--they been gettin' played for so long they just pick up the game and hook it. Not proficient yet, but hook it.

See, when that trick ass nigga got a taste of that fine pussy, he wanted some more, so he call over the fat girl's house.

Fat Girl: "Hello."

Trick: "Hello. Is Dee Dee there?"

Fat Girl: "No I haven't seen or heard from her all day." But all the time she right next to the fat girl listenin' in on the call.

The fat girl hit on the trick to see will he fuck; niggas stay ready to fuck. The fat girl just kickin' game over the phone lyin' about she got this, she got that, she used to pay her boyfriend, she got a big check comin' in from a car wreck she had five months ago. The trick love that shit he hearin', so he go to see that fat pussy. He get there and he start frontin' like he got this and that until he get that pussy.

All the while he in that pussy he killin' it and the fat girl is just lovin' it. She let him dogg that pussy out until he was satisfied with the four nut she gave him. She do just like the other girls sayin' she didn't come but she got herself ten nuts. She suck him every time he ask and shit like that will hook a nigga.

A real player really don't love them 'ho's but he don't want another nigga doggin' out his best bitch pussy. Because she got much work to do. The pussy got to be tight and right to get a nigga hook, cause if a nigga get some big ruined pussy he can dogg it out, and he will not pay for it. After the trick have dogg out the fat pussy, he then would like to get some good tight pussy from a pyt. I'm not sayin' that fat girls have ruined pussy--they have some good pussy, too, now don't get me wrong. They can take dick better than most women.

Dee Dee hook up with the trick; Dee Dee told the trick that her fat friend stole her bank card out of her purse after they went shopping and got all of her money out of her account.

Trick: "How much did she get?"

Dee Dee: "All my li'l money. It was about $1300."

Trick: "How did she get the code?"

Dee Dee: "Well, I needed some money so she took me to the bank and we went to the drive-through. She was drivin', so I pass her my card and I told her to press in the code and get me $200 out."

Trick: "Why didn't you do it yourself?"

Dee Dee: "There's so much crime I didn't want to get out the car and I didn't want to reach over her. With her bein' fat, reachin' over her would have been a problem. I trust her--she was my fat best friend. I made her fat ass my friend when no one else would be her friend," cryin' to the trick.

The trick happy on the inside because he think that the fat girl is goin' to pay him because he's fuckin' her good. He felt sorry for her, so they drove from Dee Dee's mother's house and went right to the bank drive-through and the trick got out $1300. She peep his bank code. He gave her the money and she stop fake cryin'.

They went to the hotel to make fuck faces. She fuck him real good. He then took her back to her mom's house so he can go and check on Big Mama. So as he left, Dee Dee called her cousin, Panama Black, to follow him. She told him what type of ride he was in and where he would be in the next thirty minutes. The trick goes to the fat girl's apartment. She's nowhere to be found, so the trick beep the fat girl. She call back and told him to meet her at her apartment and wait on her.

The trick ask her, "Boo, did you break that 'ho'?"

Big Mama said, "I will tell you all about it when I see you, Boo. Later."

He got to the apartment. He saw a car that look just like Big Mama's car, so he got out of his car and when his back was turned he grabbed by Panama Black and Flamingo. They kidnap him and took him right back to the bank drive-through. At gunpoint they force him to break himself. $18G. This nigga was flexin'. He had money. They took him from there and beat him with bats until he told them where the stash was at. $89G. After they got the cash, they shot him and left him for dead. He died with a gunshot wound to the head. Altogether, $107G. Baller got $50G because he call the shots. Dee Dee got $15G, Big Mama got $14G, Flamingo and Panama Black also got $14G apiece.

✳ ✸ ✛ ✳ ✳ ✻ ✳ ☆ ★ ☆

January 3, 1996. The Family was workin' real hard and plannin' big licks for the '96. Milk had plans also to make more money this year than he did the last three years. He took his money and Tray's and Deuce's money to buy six tons of cocaine. And he had the cops to guard his investment. Early in the year, Milk told the Family that to get ready ready. In the month of April each crew will receive a ton of coke. The Family was happy to hear the news. A ton of coke split four ways. It was more than just enough to last each crew the rest of the year, but in this last year they have to pull off a big lick in '96 and then just chill out. Elevate their game and jump to the next city and exercise the game.

At the end of the year Milk, Tray, and Deuce will collect big if Milk's plan go through.

The family knew once the dope get here it going to be on. But what they didn't know is that the dope was already here. The cops had their hands full; the city was full of dirty cops. But there's something about dirty cops--as long as they got money they feel like they can't be stopped. They have that shield and that shield take them a long way and they use it to the fullest. You can be the baddest, coldest brother on the street, knowin' it in your heart that you can't be fucked with, and then all of a sudden you see these blue and red fucking lights and worse, some ass loud ass siren and that shit scare the shit out of you. But if you are bad, you got to handle dat shit an' go out blastin'. Now, that's bad. I guess people just be actin' to impress each other. Cops are just human, but dat shield got so much respect. Sometimes the shield will save you and most of the time it will destroy you for the money and the power. Cops don't get paid much, so it's easy for them to turn dirty in crime-filled streets.

But here's somethin' I can't understand--a cop goes throughout high school and graduates with honors and most drug dealers drop out of high school. A cop rides around all day in his car lookin' to save people, while a drug dealer rides around all day killin' people. A cop tells good hearted people, "We're going to clean the streets. Don't worry." And a drug dealer tells a cold hearted person, "I hate fuckin' cops; they always fuckin' with a nigga." But in reality they both need each other, you know, just like positive and negative and you can't have one without the other.

Milk had some dirty ass cops watchin' over six tons of coke when he should have his Family to hold it down until the time come. It's funny--drug dealers be workin' together but they don't trust each other. Cops don't trust drug dealers but they trust each other. And cops love to live the drug dealer life. All of the cops was plottin' of a way to kill Milk and keep all of the drugs for their self and put their snitch crew on with dope and to make their self Kingpin cops. If you are sellin' dope and a cop is your supplier, you can bet you got some good ass protection.

But Chief Beverly Harvard had a hell of a plan. In the year of '96 it was a cop watch--it was just too many complaints. We had niggas snitchin', women bitchin', and cops wantin' to be drug dealers and true hogs was layin' low because they know with all the important people comin' down to visit it's time to chill out for a li'l bit until things blow over. Milk gave Brown sugar a new job. Her duty was to stay close to Pacman. Milk is a man who looks everyone eye to eye. He saw a look in Pacman's eyes that he like Brown Sugar. But Brown Sugar knew that from all the money and dope. It was turnin' Pacman into a monster.

Pacman knew where the stash was at and Brown Sugar knew this so she had to come up with a plan. So she got back with Baller. He put her down with a plan, one that will work this year. All the captains got up their crews and called a meeting. So they all met up at one of Jade's safe houses to discuss business. And while they were discussin' business, Milk and Pacman was havin' a discussion on the place where the coke was stashed. They were both worried about the coke, but Brown Sugar was on Pacman's mind and Milk knew it so he never ask Pacman nothin' about his girl because he knew that he would lie because he is fuckin' her and he's tryin his best to keep it away from Milk.

Milk had an Ace in the Hole, so Milk came up with a plan. He can see it in Pacman's eyes that the power in the pussy of Brown Sugar. She can get this fool to do anything, so he school the cop on a little somethin'. The Family had a plan from the start.   See the Family stay waitin' on big timers to come to Atlanta from other states thinkin' that they can come to Atlanta because they got big money and dope and run shit.   But the Miami boys fuck that up for all states. Atlanta is for Atlanta.   When they all got together there were tears of happiness in their eyes.   They all haven't got together like this, just them, in three full years.   They just been plannin' and plannin, waitin' on a day like this to happen.   It was hugs and kisses--it was like a family reunion.

When all the girls saw each other, they all got in a circle and put their arms around each other and said "AAAAAAaaaaaaaright!" and bust out laughin', just that happy to see each other.   The fellow was like in a crowd poppin' the tops off all ten bottles, off the fifth of Hennessy, and start yellin' "Who you with?   Who you with?   Stack your money!   Kill your enemy!   Who you with?   Who you with? Stack your money!   Kill your enemy!   Who you with?"

They were all just havin' a good ass time.   See, this family got love and attitude, and that's what makes a strong heart and in this game you got to have a heart of steel.   They have the weed, coke, and the plans all down on the table.   They were all gettin' high and havin' a great big fuck fest. Pete got with his girl Precious, Fly-Mar got with his baby Raven, Sky got with Brown Sugar and some of the boys, Baller got with Chicago, and everybody else was just doing it wild and gettin' high from morning till night, then it was time to plan. They was all half naked, plannin' out the plan to be.   Eight long hours till morning came.   Everybody pack up and start passin' out hugs and kisses and "see you soon!"   Sky's, Brown Sugar's and Diamond's crews stay back to help Jade clean the house.

As they were cleaning the house, Sky went to the back and pull out the boxing gloves.   Brown Sugar was a little exhausted, but she knew she had work to do. All the girls was sittin' around sippin' on brews. Raven ask Sky have she ever lost a fight at the club?

Sky: "Hell, naw. I been fightin' all my life. I'm not tryin' to lose. You got to fight hard in this dirty world if you expect to make it. After this year--fuck it. I got enough money. Fuck goin' out of town. It's rough all over, if not rougher. When this year blow over, I'm goin' to just live like folks. I'm tired of fightin', trickin' the killin'. It's time for some positive to come of me.

"I been feelin' God talkin' with me on and off. No lie. You know, I sometime feel like goin' to school and gettin' some kind of business license to run my own business and I am not talkin' about some damn beauty shop. See, my mother left me at a very young age, and when I have some kids I'm goin' to look them in their eyes and tell them I love them every day."

Jade: "You would like to have some kids some day, Girl."

Sky: "I do, Girl. I just want to love somebody that goin' to love me for me. I love y'all, but this life we're livin' ain't no joke. I don't want to lose y'all like I did my mother to this dirty game we play."

Diamond: "Girl, I didn't know you had it in you. This is my last year doin' this shit, too, but we got to finish what we started. If not, that shit will come back to haunt us, you bitches agree?"

They all agreed. Sky got up and put on her boxing gloves and told Brown Sugar, "It's time, Baby Girl."

Diamond and the girls cheered Brown Sugar on while she put on her gloves so she and Sky can box it out. The plan was to make as if a man beat her up for sex. As they started boxing, Sky put it on that ass left, right, left, right. Sky knock Sugar to the floor. Sky bouncin' up and down tellin'

Sugar to get up, had enough? Raven pick Sugar up off the floor. Mona Lisa went to go get some ice cubes. Diamond was like, "Damn, Sky, you got some power behind your punch--you don't play, do you?"

Sky: "Not even a li'l bit."

Mona Lisa came in with the ice cubes. Sugar was kind of dizzy and a li'l swollen, but she'll live. It was just minor.

Brown Sugar: "How do I look, Girls? Be real."

Jade: "You look good, Girl, they will fall for it. Now it's all on you to do your job. You can handle this, right?"

Sugar: "Bitch, I am the best."

Diamond: "No, Girl, I am the best."

They all bust out laughing.

Diamond: "You just do your thang, Girl."

Raven: "Sugar, you got to keep them both deep thinkin' so it will be hard for them both to get their mind right."

They talk a few more hours and then went to work. They look left and right and left the safe house. Sugar beep Pacman to let him know that she would like to see him. He told her when he's off duty he'd meet her somewhere downtown.

✳ ✳ ✜ ✴ ✳ ✳ ✳ ☆ ✯ ☆

Just as planned, she went to see Milk and Milk saw her face.

Milk: "Who did this shit?"

Sugar: "It was that dirty ass cop you put me with. I fake like I wasn't goin' to fuck him just like you told me to and he just went wild on me. I told him I was goin' to tell you."

Milk: "What he say?"

Sugar: "He said he don't give a fuck--he's the man, and he got you in his back pocket."

Milk: "Dat nigga said that shit?"

Sugar: "Yeah, and he beat me some more until I gave it

up.

Milk: "Damn dat dirty ass!!! Okay, okay...look, I want you to act like you didn't tell me shit. Tell this."

Sugar took the words that Milk told her to say. And she told the family and they all got on the phone on the three-way; all 21 of them was on the phone at the same time giving Sugar words to give Pacman. This family had their shit right.

Brown Sugar got with Pacman. He was like, "Damn-- who did this shit? I'll kill the mother fucker."

Sugar: "It was Milk."

Pacman: "Why did he do this to you?"

Sugar put on her unhappy face, with a tear rolling down her face. "He said I stay out in the street fuckin' around on him and not takin' care of business just like a dirty ass cop I know."

Pacman: "That nigga said that shit?"

Sugar: "Yeah. I believe he know about us. As soon as I got to him after I left you his eyes was blood shot red like he been up all night sniffin' coke. He then grab me and started sniffin' on me, tellin' me I smell like fuck. He slap me to the floor, rip off my clothes, and panty sniffin' on my panties and checkin' my pussy and that's when he kick my ass."

Sugar then fell on Pacman's shoulder, cryin' her heart out to him. He was like, "Okay, Boo, I'll fix his ass. Why you with a nigga like that anyway, who do those things to you? I can help you but you got to help me help you.

Sugar: "What you mean?"

Pacman: "Let's set his ass up. Rape that nigga for his dope. Then, Boo, it will be me and you."

Sugar: "But what about Milk?"

Pacman: "Fuck that nigga. We will kill him. I got some of the best killers on my team who will kill a punk ass drug dealer in a heartbeat."

Sugar: "You know, Boo, my period is late so I just might be pregnant. Boo, what we goin' to do?"

Pacman: "See, Boo, that a sign we got to set that ass up now. More money for the kid. Look, I know where the dope is stashed. Six tons, Boo. My dogs are watchin' it right now."

Sugar: "What you mean, six tons? He told me it was only one ton. Six tons is a lot."

Pacman: "Yeah, I know. See, this nigga lyin' to you. That mean he didn't trust you from the start. Come on--let's ride."

Sugar: "Where?"

Pacman: "Out to this warehouse where the coke is stashed. While ridin' out, Sugar was all eyes gettin' the whereabouts on the location. Thirty minutes later, arriving at the warehouse; two blue jeaned cops was outside of the door guardin' the six tons of coke while on duty, when they supposed to be out on the street going after the bad guys. Pacman and Brown Sugar enter the front door. Pacman let Sugar see all the dope. She stay natural.

Pacman look her in her eyes and ask her, "Is you down with me?"

Sugar: "I am."

Pacman: "Okay, let's do it."

Sugar: "Do what?"

Pacman: "Unload. Reload. Let's get this shit out the back door."

Sugar: "You mean right now?"

Pacman: "Hell yeah, right now!"

Sugar: "What about Milk?"

Pacman: "What about him? Look, he don't give a fuck about you. Feel your damn face. That's Milk."

Sugar: "He say he love me--that's why he do the things he do to me. He do a lot for me."

Pacman: "Boo, I am going to do a lot for you. Just help me load this shit in the trunk of my car."

Sugar: "Okay."

Pacman: "That's my boo. Now come on--we takin' it out the back door."

Sugar: "But the car is at the front."

Pacman: "Just come on."

They walk out the back door. Reebok had already parked the car out back. The cops had their shit together, also.

Sugar: "What if Milk find out?"

Pacman: "He's not. We're going to put the word out on the street that the Jury is tryin' to take over the up and coming spot. Right now the Jury is clockin' big bank and right now the word is on the street that they are lookin' for big dope. Them fools are trying to come up with the city. Their rim shop is doing well and everywhere you look people are putting up burglar bar doors. They are makin' money and once Milk hears that there's a family out on the street tryin' to take over he will focus on them. Now, let's get this dope to my house."

And when he said his house, Sugar knew that she had his ass then. That's what she been waitin' to hear the last five years is to go to his house. Pacman threw up a cop sign which was a "C" tellin' the on duty cops to be safe. And they left with a trunk full of dope headed out to Norcross, Georgia.

While driving out to his house, he switched cars. Now Sugar knew why it was hard the first time to hit his ass up for what he got. Load, unload, load, unload. This dog ass cop know how to shake off the ticks and fleas. Fourteen minutes they arrive at the house. He drove up to the garage door. The door open up, they drove in.

Pacman hand Sugar the 9mm; he got the pump shotgun from the back seat and they walk through the whole house, gun first. They check everything. A cop don't miss shit. They expect things to be the same, even the temperature. The house was safe and sound. They walk back to the garage.

Pacman set his keys down and Sugar saw that. She eased over to the keys while Pacman was moving all the excess junk out of the way. While he was doing that she went to the bathroom to make a wax impression of all the keys. She came back out to the garage and she slowly put the keys back in the same place.

Pacman: "Good--you're back. I need you to help me with the chain horse." A chain horse is used to pull motors out of cars. Pacman hooked the chain to the floor hook and they both had to pull the 5 inch thick concrete, 4 feet in length and 4 feet wide, six feet deep. It was big knots of money and now on top of that went six tons of coke. Load, unload, load, unload the dope into the concrete floor and cover it back up with all of the excess junk.

Pacman look up at Brown Sugar and ask her how did she feel. She said, "I feel sexually active."

Pacman walked up to her and they started to kiss. Things was getting steamy, so the took it to the bedroom and started doing the nasty. The next day, Sugar reported back to the family where the family gave her more info to push in Milk's ear. She got back to Milk and told him that Pacman was actin' real funny

Milk: "Did you tell him what I told you to say to him?"

Sugar: "Yes, I did. I think he's going to try something."

Milk: "Why you say that?"

Sugar: "He was sayin' the word on the street is that there's a family out on the street that makin' lots of noise buyin' high and sellin' low, trying to build clientele, and they always in power with dope."

Milk: "Who is this family?"

Sugar: "I think he said the Jury."

Milk: "The Jury. Do you know anything about this family?"

Sugar: "No, not really, but there's a girl in the family name Dove who work at the club with Sky. She dance and hustle and I can get our family to run a check on the Jury for you, Boo."

Milk: "Bet. You do dat there for me."

While all that was goin' on, the Corporation was sitting back, plotting another lick, also, so when Milk's stash get gone he will think the Jury hit 'em up and not the Corporation. See, in this game you got to keep your adversary off balance.

✳ ✳ ✧ ✳ ✳ ✳ ✳ ☆ ★ ☆

February 27, 1996. It was Hezzy's birthday and he was gettin' fucked up big time but still gettin' ready for the big lick his crew got comin' up. And once they make this lick, it's all gravy the rest of the year. Over at the house was Eazy, Baller, Pete, and Ten and soon as night hit Hezzy came out with the plans that will put them more in power so that they can all go ahead with their dreams.

Hezzy wants to open up a record store for his crew. He told Eazy about it to see if it was a cool idea. He wanted to do it but he wasn't sure so he asked him.

Hezzy: "Yo, Eazy."

Eazy: "Yeah."

Hezzy: "I been thinkin', man."

Eazy: "What you been thinkin' 'bout, Nigga?" Eazy with

a smile on his face, sniffin' on some raw flake. His eyes was so glassy that Hezzy could see his reflection in them.

Hezzy: "I was thinkin' 'bout openin' up a record store sellin' gangster CDs and tapes. Me, Pete, Baller. You think that's a good move?"

Eazy: "Look here, Young Blood. Hell, yeah, that's a good move. The game only last for so long."

Eazy staggered back a li'l bit and took a sip of his Hennessy and told Hezzy "Happy Birthday" and gave him a big ass hug and kissed him on both sides of his cheeks and told Hezzy "I love Baby Boy Mafia-style like". Eazy always kept it gangster. You make him happy, he's happy; make him mad, he's ready to kill somebody--he don't give a fuck.

But tonight they were all happy. Pete came over with the blueprints on the lick and, with a fifth of Hennessy in his hand, he put his arms around the both of them and kissed both of them on their cheeks and said, "Let's get to work."

Eazy grab the plans from Pete's hand. Pete pass the bottle to Hezzy. Hezzy turn the bottle straight up.

Pete: "There you go, Baby Boy!!!"

Baller and Ten was cheering him on. "That's right, Boy!!" When Hezzy came down with the bottle he went "Ugh!!!" Just like Master P. The crew bust out laughin'.

Pete gave him a big hug and said, "That's my Ninja! This my Ninja, y'all" and went into his pocket and pulled out a fat ass gold rope bigger than 4tay Herringbone and with a charm big as Slick Rick. It was a charm shaped like the state of Georgia filled with diamonds.

Hezzy was in shock. He sat down at the table. Baller went into his pocket and pulled out a fat knot of money which was $5G and slid it across the table to Hezzy and said "Happy Birthday, Baby Boy" and they both stood up. Baller kiss him on both cheeks.

Hezzy look over at Ten. Ten gave Hezzy a big hug and kiss him on both sides of his cheeks and pull out two fat knots of money, about $10G, and said "Happy Birthday, Baby Boy. Get your dream together. Do that rap thang. Baller told me about it. Just do it."

They all sat down around the table. Eazy was like, "Man, this here is a bank job."

Baller: "That right; what wrong, Play?"

Eazy: "Man, this is a bank in the Atlanta airport. How in the hell are we going to pull that off?"

Hezzy: "Okay, check it out. It's so simple. This bank take over five million in cash. Every Friday at noon the bank be pack with all type of people who work there in the airport getting their check cashed. And a armored car arrive at 12:30 p.m. Always two guards get out and come get the money made through the week. While the first three bank tellers are cashing checks, the guards go to the fourth bank teller, on the end.

The guard smash a button and the bank teller come out from the back. She then see the guards; then she go back in the room and come right back out with a tray full of money in big stacks. Five million in cash. The guard then slide the two money bags under the bullet-proof glass. If you're not payin' attention on the line waitin' to cash you check, then you will be lookin' at the teller on the end grabbin' big knots of cash money, puttin' it in the money bags.

Pete: "See, we're going to be in line, dress just like airport security guards, actin' as if we're there to cash a check, standin' at the end line by the door to avoid the camera."

Eazy: "I understand that, but how in the hell are we going to get the gun past the airport detectors?"

Hezzy: "Look, to get to the bank we don't have to go past the detectors."

Pete: "We're going to catch the MARTA train, leave the train with all the other security guards. You know, blend in."

Baller was sitting back rollin' up some blunts for the boys to choke on after they got through planning.

Hezzy: "When the armored car guards get the money and start to leave the bank, Baller and Ten, they will come past you two. Hit them from the back and draw down on them, givin' them a warning. Tell them to get their hands up so the camera will not have a clear view. Baller and Ten, you then tell them to drop the cash and guns. I will get the cash and guns. Pete and Eazy, you two watch our back as we come out of the bank."

Ten: "How in the hell we going to get away? No, wait-- don't tell me. We're going to shoot it out with the whole damn airport."

Hezzy: "Hell, naw, Nigga. We run about twenty yards and make a right and there will be a 1991 Lincoln Town Car, dark blue, with the keys already to go."

Eazy: "Can you trust the person who leavin' the ride?"

Pete: "Hell, yeah. It's me and Hezzy's two faithful lams. These girls know the airport in and out."

Baller: "How do you know that the lick is cool?"

Hezzy: Shit--the girls are the ones who set it up. Look, these are real women. Me and Pete got them on lock. And there will be another getaway car on down on I-85. We take the homemade cocktails and blow that bitch up on the highway. Leave no evidence. And then we get to our third ride, and we then wipe that second ride down and head on back home to chop up the scrilla. Now, if something goes wrong, we keep our mouth shut. But we Gs, we plan to win and we going to win, now you niggas all in?"

They stack their hands on top of each other and said,

"Hell yeah. Nigga blood in, blood out."

All night they plan and plan and plan, over and over, gettin' high and watchin' bank robbin' flicks from "Set it Off", Point Break", "Heat", "Dead Presidents", and "Dillinger". They had their shit tight.

Eazy call Hezzy to the side. They both lookin' eye to eye.

Eazy: "Hey, it a brilliant plan, Baby Boy. I like that in you. You talkin' like a general in this game. You're going to make it. Just keep on keepin' on. Look, I got a li'l somethin' for you." Eazy went into his pocket and pulled out a diamond filled day and date President in platinum with diamond dial Rolex. Eazy kiss Hezzy on both cheeks and said, "See you in two days. I got business. Tell the Ninjas I see them later. Take care, Baby Boy."

Hezzy: "All right, Dog."

Eazy left. Hezzy walk back in the room with the Ninjas.

Baller: "Where dat nigga, Eazy?"

Hezzy: "He had to dip, hey, but check it out. Each crew take care of their comrades on their birthday. This family is so true."

✳ ✳ ✢ ✵ ✳ ✳ ✳ ☆ ✭ ✩

Two days later Baller's crew was ready to go to work. It was six in the morning. They all were in deep meditation for four hours. There was no type of drug in sight. Some people think that drugs make them ruthless before they do some type of lick. Drugs only make you more dumber. Yes, it's true powder get you hyper, but when you're hyper you can overreact and when you overreact you lose control. And messing with that weed doing a job--that weed make things look the way that things are not.

Baller know all you need is brains and guns, and this crew got both of what they need to make it. This the only crew that have four guns apiece for the whole family. Ten went in the back room and came back with the artillery. He came back out and told the boys to get what they like. It was everything from Uzi 9mm, Cobray M-11, MAC-10, AK-47, M-16, 380, 12-gauge pump shotgun, 357, Glock 9mm, 22, 25, Intratec 9mm. Pete grab the MAC-10. Eazy pick up the Uzi 9mm, Ten got the Cobray M-11, Hezzy pick the Intratec 9mm, and Baller pick the Glock 9mm with the 30 round clip. Eazy had parked the gray van out back.

Hezzy: "Yo--we're goin' to go to the Oakland City train station even though Lakewood train station is up the street. But we don't want to be seen, so that's why we'll drive up to the next station, into the parking lot, and change in the parking lot. And then we get out one at a time. We walk in the station with our heads down to avoid the camera. Stay alert, stay alive. How dat sounds, everybody?"

They were all with it. The phone rings. Baller picks up the phone.

Baller: "Hello."

FeFe (Hezzy's girlfriend): "Hello. May I speak with Hezzy?"

Baller: "Yeah, hold on. Hezzy, telephone."

Hezzy ran to the phone. "Hello."

FeFe: "Hey, Baby. It's still on, right?"

Hezzy: "Yeah. The car is going to be there, right?"

FeFe: "Yes it is. I was just callin' to see was it still on. It's going to be more money than I expect it to be. The airport is pack with people. There's a convention in town."

Hezzy: "So that means there going to be more cops at the airport, right?"

FeFe: "Right. There going to be more cops at the baggage claim area. You think you and your crew can still pull it off?"

Hezzy: "It's on."

FeFe: "Tell Pete Jewel ask about him. See you soon, Baby."

Hezzy hung up the phone. Eazy walk over to Hezzy and ask him what's wrong.

Hezzy: "Nothin'. It's just going to be more cash because of a convention in town."

Eazy call everyone to the room. They came in saying the same thing--"What's wrong?"

Hezzy: "It's going to be more money."

Ten: "Shit--that good!"

Hezzy: "But more money mean more cops. There's a convention going on in town. It's up to you, Ninjas, if you still want to go through with it."

They all look at each other and say, "Let's get this money, man!"

Baller: "It's about that time."

Ten: "Let's pack this shit up and dip. Have heart have money."

They got packed and turned on the inside video camera in case some fool get a dumb ass idea to break in their house while they're gone.

Leaving behind 50 keys and a half million dollars in cash, Hezzy popped in the video tape and they left. While ridin' out they were listenin' to Master P West Coast Bad Boys Volume I, Headed for the Jack by C Bo and Master P, and changin' clothes. In the back of the van, these Ninjas look just like the real thing. They also wore bullet proof vests under their "ARC Security Guard" uniforms. From the hats, shoes, and jackets they had it on.

They arrive at the train station. They miss one train because they left the van one minute apart. It was 11:45 a.m. It's a ten minute ride from the Oakland City train station to the Airport station. When they enter the train, it's pack with

ARC Security Guards and they were havin' conversation, happy about gettin' their checks today.

One of the ARC Security Guards ask Pete what concourse does he work on.

Pete: "I work on Concourse B."

ARC Security Guard: "Naw--I work on Concourse B."

Pete: "Ssshi-id. Me too."

ARC Security Guard: "Man, you must be new."

Pete: "Hell naw--I just got transferred to Concourse B. I was on Concourse C, third shift."

ARC Security Guard: "O-oh. Okay. You going to pick up your check, too?"

Pete: "Ain't we all?"

ARC Security Guard: "Hell, yeah, man. You be cool. By the way--what's your name? I go by the name Kilo; you know, like the Atlanta Rapper?"

Pete: "My name is Sammy Sam; you know, the Atlanta Rapper who be dissin' Kilo?"

Pete was lookin' Kilo eye to eye. Kilo walk off and went to go mess with someone else. Kilo walk all over the train. The rest of the boys put their mean mug on their face, letting him know, "I ain't the one to be fuckin' with." Kilo went to go talk with some of the girls on the train.

Pete play it off cool. Pete look around the train at everyone. Baller threw up a "You did okay" sign.

Oakland City. Lakewood. East Point. College Park. And the next stop and the last stop, the Airport station. Everybody left the train. Time: 11:55 a.m.

Baller's crew was headed to the bank. The armored car guards was early. As soon as Baller's crew was settin' up, the armored car guards was on the way out of the bank. Baller's crew reached for their gats. It was set up just like they plan. As soon as the two guards walk past Baller and Ten, they took their gats and hit them over the head, knockin' them down.

Ten yellin' "Get back into the bank!"

Baller ran into the bank and told everybody to get 'em up and then stuck the gun up under the bullet-proof glass and said, "If you want to live, put them on the glass and get them hands up."

Eazy and Pete had the gun drawn down on everybody, lookin' around, just ready to blast if things go wrong. Hezzy got the gun and money from the guards. It was two bags, four million in one bag and five in the other. Hezzy yellin' "Come on!" while leaving out of the bank.

The ARC Security Guard Kilo and some of his work buddies was comin' to cash their checks.

Kilo: "Hey, Sammy Sam! What the hell is you doin'?"

Pete just started bustin' open fire on the crowd of people. Women yelling and screaming. They all quickly hit the floor for safety. The police heard the gun shots and they came in packs, guns first. When they came around the corner, Baller's whole crew let their guns do the talking, bustin' shots after shots. The cops was bustin' back, but it did no good because of the body armor. The two armored car guards both had backup guns in their ankle holsters. They came out blastin', yellin' "Freeze!"

Baller and Ten turned around, still bustin' shots. Baller was hit in both legs. He fell to the floor. Pete turned around and grabbed Baller off the floor, back and forth bustin' shots. Ten was unloading and reloading clip after clip and went crazy, killin' both of the guards and then turned back around bustin' back at the cops. Baller, limping, still bustin' shots, headin' for the door. Nothin' but gun fire as they were headin' out the door.

The car was running. Hezzy threw the money in the car

and got in the driver's seat. Ten jumped in, then Eazy and Pete got by the car door and turn around bustin' shots back into the airport, breakin' glass. Baller was limping to the car. A cop came out with a pump shotgun and shot Baller in the back. Baller fell to the ground. Eazy was hangin' one arm out the window lettin' loose shots. Pete was goin' off, yellin' "Baller!!" while he was bustin' caps into the cop and killing him. But more cops was comin' out.

Hezzy yelling, "Pete! Come on!"

Pete got halfway into the car, still bustin' shots, and Hezzy pulled off. They were all pissed off because of what happened to Baller.

Hezzy: "Damn, damn, damn! Did you see all those fuckin' cops??"

Eazy: "Drive, Nigga, drive! Put your weight on it! Drive, Nigga, drive!"

Pete: "Damn! Did you see the look in Baller's eyes? He look as if things were all right."

Eazy: "That nigga was real. He didn't give a fuck. You niggas couldn't see that shit in his eyes? He wanted us to go, get away, didn't you see it?"

Hezzy's doing 120 on the highway. They made it to the second ride, jump out of the first car, got the cocktail out and blew up the ride. They then got to the third ride, which was the van. They got out of the car. Ten wipe the car down; they got in the van and started changing back into their clothes. They then drove out of the train station, drop the clothes off in a nearby dumpster, and headed back to the house.

They then got to the house and turn on the TV set to hear the news. Hezzy set the money on the table and then sat in front of the TV with the rest of the Ninjas. And there it was on the News: Five armed men dressed as airport security guards rob the Airport Bank. It's the first time in history to have that to happen. The bank teller said that the men seem to know what they were doing. She also said that they made off with $9 million in cash. One of the gunmen was captured; the police thought the gunman was dead, but with the protection of body armor...

That's when Eazy, Ten, Pete, and Hezzy jump up saying, "He's alive! He's alive!" They were all glad to hear that Baller was alive.

Hezzy: "Yo, yo. Wait...the news..."

"...The police do not have a name of the suspect. He had no type of ID. He was shot in both legs. The police have the man in custody at Grady Memorial Hospital."

That's when the phone went ringing off the hook. Ten pick it up.

Ten: "Hello."

Big Mike: "Yeah, what's up Nigga? We all seen the news, Yo. Me, Jim Kelly and Fly-Mar goin' to help you niggas go down there and get our nigga."

Ten: "Nigga, what?!"

Hezzy: "Who in the hell is that?"

Ten: "It's Big Mike. He said he saw the news and he would like to know if we're goin' down to the hospital to break out Baller."

Hezzy: "Man, tell that fool that it too early. They got guards all around. Maybe later."

Big Mike: "Nigga, Nigga, we know that. Y'all niggas just call us when it's time to be down."

Ten: "Okay, man. Later."

As soon as they hung up the phone it rang again. Hezzy told Ten to unplug the phone because it was just too hot to speak on the phone right now. Ten sat back around the table with the Ninjas.

Pete: "Man, we thought the worst and got the best."

Hezzy: "Yeah, man, God work in mysterious ways."

An hour later they went back to sellin' cocaine, playin' it off until things cool down.

✻ ✳ ✜ ✼ ✳ ✺ ✳ ☆ ✭ ☆

A week later, Mona Lisa from Diamond's clique was ready to pull off a fat lick, so she pick Sugar Wolf, MJG, Greed, and Raven--and the trick was her new husband, Fidel Cartel, who made good money workin' with Milk buyin' and sellin' dope. He love Mona Lisa's company and he love her as a wife, but he still have jungle fever for some good black pussy. Black pussy is the best in the world and he know it. Him and Raven still bump from time to time. Mona Lisa had him sized up--she knew when he was low on cocaine he like to get with Raven and show her what a big man he is. Mona Lisa keep her shit tight to be a white woman. She told Fidel that her mother was sick and she had to go to her aid.

Fidel: "For how long, Dear?"

Mona Lisa: "Just for a few days, I hope." Lisa packed her things, gave him kisses, and left.

He wasted no time gettin' on the phone callin' Raven. Mona Lisa was on her way to Chicago's house--it was fight night. It was Oscar de la Hoya versus Pernell Whitaker. Chicago had licks set up also--big licks. Her crew stay busy. She also had to get help from the other crews to help her pull off so many licks.

Fidel pick Raven up at the same spot like always. He was so happy to see her, as soon as Raven got into the car his nature rose.

Fidel: "Look up under your seat, Boo. I got a li'l somethin' for us."Raven reach up under the seat and pull out a key of uncut cocaine.

Raven: "Shall I bust it open now?"

Fidel: "Do what you like."

Raven bust the bag open and took a li'l sniff and turn to Fidel and said, "Lookin' good."

Fidel, feelin' good also: "I miss you, Boo."

Raven: "How much?"

Fidel: "Look here, Boo. You got my dick harder than ten pounds of frozen neck bones."

Raven look down at his dick and started to laugh.

Raven: "What's up for the weekend?"

Fidel: "It's all on you."

Raven: "Well, I just want to relax and sniff a li'l coke and then handle some thangs; that's what I want to do."

Fidel: "It sounds good to me." Fidel then stuck his nose down between Raven's legs, sniffing out of the key of coke. Raven took another sniff and they both got mellow.

They arrive at the house. When entering the house, Raven said, "Damn--I love what your wife have did to your house. It's beautiful. She have good taste."

Fidel: "Yeah, I know it."

Fidel went down to the wine cellar to get a bottle of wine; he also put some fire wood into the fireplace. He cook a li'l something for her, a small appetizer to get the romance going. He was giving her a nice time and then Raven sex him up and that drove him wild. Raven work herself. The hard sex gave her a strong appetite.

Fidel wasn't thinking about food; he was thinking about getting Raven her own place so he could have a spot where he could just lay up, get good sex, and hide his coke. Because he wanted the right life for Mona Lisa, he love her so, he did-n't want her around the fast life.

Raven: "Boo, it's fight night. Let's order it. And Boo, I'm hungry--let's order some pizza."

Fidel: "Sure, Boo. Do what you like." Fidel lying on his back with his face to the ceiling, sniffing on coke, high as fuck.

Raven: "What's the number, Boo?"

Fidel: "I don't know--check with information, 411."

Raven pick up the phone actin' like she was calling for information when she really call her crew. She was sittin' right next to him playin' it off. Raven dialing the phone. Sugar Wolf picks up on the other end.

Sugar Wolf: "What city?"

Raven: "Roswell."

Sugar Wolf: "What location?"

Raven: "Pizza Hut."

Sugar Wolf: "We will be there in 30 minutes" and hung up the phone.

Raven: "Ooh, Boo, hand me a pen. Boo, just remember the first three numbers and I'll remember the last four. 555-4080. You got it Boo?"

Fidel: "Yeah, 555."

Raven: "Okay, now let me call Pizza Hut. What's the first three numbers now, Boo?"

Fidel: "555."

Raven: "It's ringin', Boo. Hello, Pizza Hut? I would like to order two large The Edge pizzas. My phone number is...hold on... wait--Boo, what's your phone number?"

Fidel: "555-6177."

Raven: "It's 555-6177."

Pizza Hut: "Okay, we got the address Ms. Cartel. Yes, two large The Edge pizzas.

Raven: "What I want on it? Just make them two supreme pizzas, okay? Thank you. Okay. Boo, they said in thirty minutes." And she hung up the phone. "They said, Boo, it's thirty minutes or it's free."

Raven took a sniff of the coke and gave him some head and jump on top of his dick and rode it like a pogo stick and in a minute he was bustin' a nut.

Raven: "Was it good for you, Baby, like it was for me?"

Fidel couldn't talk--he was speechless.

Raven: "Boo, I got to take a shower and come back fresh later for round two.

Fidel: "I'll be waiting."

Raven taking a shower, the doorbell rang. Fidel stagger to the door.

Fidel: "Who is it?"

MJG: "It's the pizza man. I have your pizzas, sir."

As soon as Fidel open the door, MJG bust him on the head with the pizza boxes and they all push him into the house. Greed and Sugar Wolf had their guns drawn on Fidel, asking him where the safe at. "We know you're a big-timer. Where dem dollas at?" Then Greed hit him over the head with his gun. Fidel fell to the floor, still butt ass naked. Greed grab him by the back of the neck, liftin' him off the floor.

Raven heard all the noise and confusion. She came out of the bathroom and saw that Greed had Fidel by the neck with Sugar Wolf with his gun drawn on him and she went screaming. MJG ran up on her, slappin' her to quiet her. They took both of them to the bedroom. Raven hug all up under Fidel, cryin'-acting as she was fearing for her life.

Sugar Wolf: "Shut up, Bitch, 'fore I give you somethin' to cry 'bout. Now, where's the safe with the money?"

Raven: "I don't know nothin' about a safe with money."

Greed: "But your man do."

MJG went searching the house; he came back into the room and said, "I can't find it. Kill the bitch." Raven, hiding behind Fidel, crying louder for help.

Fidel thought about it. He had one murder case hangin' over his head and the FBI is watchin' closely for his wife's murder. So he just gave it up to be on the safe side.

Fidel: "Okay, wait--don't kill her. I'll show you where my coke is." Fidel walk slowly to the closet, Sugar Wolf right behind him with his shotgun drawn on him. Fidel got to the closet and pulled out three keys and said, "Here, take it. This is what you came for."

Sugar Wolf pump his shotgun and put it to Fidel's head and said, "This is nice, but show me the money and quit fuckin' around."

Fidel: "There is no money."

Sugar Wolf hit Fidel over the head, put one foot on his chest, and aimed the gun at his face. "You wanna die, nigga?!" Greed then hit Raven over the head with his gun, threw her to the floor and put his gun in her face. Raven crying, telling Fidel, "Boo, please. It's not worth it. Please, Boo, it's not worth dyin' for."

Fidel look around at the three ski masked men's guns. He slowly got up off the floor and moved the family picture off the wall and then he went to playing dumb.

Fidel: "I can't think of the number right off hand. I'm scared and nervous with all these guns pointed in my face." Sugar Wolf hit him in the back of the neck. He fell right in Raven's arms.

Sugar Wolf look at MJG and said, "Go to work." He did. It was a complicated safe, but MJG is an expert on safe crackin'. He brought along his tools. Fidel was in shock--it took MJG only four minutes to crack the safe. $875,645 in cash. They fill the bags cleanin' out the safe.

Fidel is a rich man--he got money in the bank. $10 million. And if anything was to happen to him, his wife, Mona Lisa, gets all of the money in the bank.

Greed took ropes and tied the both of them up tight but not tight enough. It held them for a minute, but by that time they were gone. Fidel wiggle his self out of the ropes and untie Raven. She was pissed off. Fidel was thinkin' to himself, "How in the hell did they know??" Fidel look at Raven and said, "You're a jinx."

And when he said that, Raven went off on him. "Let me tell you somethin', you mother fucker. You call me. You want it to see me. Now you talkin' shit 'cause you got rob. Hell, naw, mother fucker. Blame your damn self. Them fools draw down on me, too, and put a knot on my head and you don't have no knot on yours. Hell, naw, mother fucker, you might have set me up. You just take me back where you got me, because I don't need this shit. Fuck this!"

Fidel: "Baby, I'm sorry. It's just...."

Raven: "'It just' my ass! I'm ready to go--you can't explain shit to me, man! Take me back where you got me. I ain't playin' with you!"

Fidel drop his head, sad that now he lost his dope, money, and his side girl Raven all in one night. Raven was mad at him. She said nothin' else to him ridin' back to the spot. He offered her some coke. She didn't care.

Fidel: "Boo, I am so sorry. You're not a jinx."

They arrive at the spot. Raven got out and slam the door. Fidel couldn't get her to say nothin' until after she slam his door and he call her a black bitch. Raven turn around and said, "What you call me??" Fidel pulled off laughin', sniffin' on coke, lookin' out his rearview mirror. Raven was givin' him the finger.

Fidel had a lot on his mind; like, he was still tryin' to figure out who set him up. His pager goes off; he checks. It's a customer. Fidel got on his cellular phone to call the customer.

Customer: "Hello."

Fidel: "Yeah. This Fidel. Who page me?"

Customer: "Yo. This Vanilla Ice. Hey--I need a key. You got one for me--I got money."

Fidel: "You got it right now?"

Vanilla: "Yeah, I got it right now. Where you at?"

Fidel: "No, no. Where you at?"

Vanilla: "I'm at the Amoco gas station in Roswell."

Fidel: "I'm on my way. Be there in ten minutes."

Fidel arrive at the gas station. Vanilla Ice jump out of a parked car flaggin' Fidel down. Fidel became conscious when he jump out a car with another person in the car. Fidel fix the dope up, you know, gettin' it to look tight. It was about 2.2 pounds of coke, worth about $21G, and his prices was $30G. He needed the street money. But before he wrap it up, he took another sniff, clean his nose, and pull his car over to Vanilla Ice's ride. Vanilla Ice jump in Fidel's ride.

Vanilla Ice: "What's up, Dude? Got the coke?"

Fidel: "Right here. Now show me the money."

Vanilla Ice flag his friend over to the car. He got in the back seat. As soon as he got in the car, Fidel asked, "Who's this?"

Vanilla Ice: "This my neighbor, Rebel. He's cool."

Rebel: "Yeah, man, I'm cool. Can I taste it?"

Fidel: "Yeah. Where's the money?"

Rebel: "Right here."

Fidel: "That's $30G, right?"

Rebel: "$30G."

Fidel: "Yeah, $30G. Hey, man, I don't know you. Now is that a problem?"

Rebel: "Hey--that's cool, Dude. My man Vanilla Ice said it will be $35G. $30G no problem. Now let me taste it. Here's your money."

Fidel hand him the key. He took a sniff and said, "IIIIiiii like it!"

Fidel look down at his money and when he look back up he heard "FREEZE!" It's the police. "You're under arrest for selling a key of coke to an undercover officer."

Fidel dropped his head. He couldn't believe it--ever since he allegedly killed his wife things was goin' downhill for him. His bond was set for $250,000. He couldn't get to his money because his wife was out of town. He sat in jail until Lisa came to his aid.

✳ ✳ ✛ ✳ ✳ ✳ ✳ ☆ ★ ☆

Jim Kelly called at Chicago's fight party to give Mona Lisa the info on Fidel. At the fight party was Jazzy Bell, Big Mike and Raven. The party was packed. Chicago's customers had built up much money, so things were lookin' good for Chicago's crew. Pee Wee Loc and Fly-Mar knew the party was filled with big timers. Diamond was there with Big Six He was placin' big bets all over the party, but Eazy was there to cover all bets. Eazy was bettin' on Pernell Whitaker and Big Six was with Oscar de la Hoya. No matter what, Big Six always bet with the underdog.

Pee Wee Loc and Fly-Mar hit over 20 houses, but came back with nothing. The customers had made so much money that they bought the best and biggest safes on the market. The safes were too complicated for Pee Wee Loc and Fly-Mar. Every house had state of the art equipment to guard their house--electric eyes everywhere. They came back to the party and whisper sweet nothings in her ear. She look at the boys with a happy face and said it will be another time, and then it will be even more money.

Chicago walk back into the room. The fight party was ending and the winner is Oscar de la Hoya. The whole house was in shock. They all thought he had lost that fight-

-he couldn't even put his hands on Whitaker. Whitaker threw his hand up anyway and said, "Hey, I'm used to it. They always rob me of a win." And everyone left the party then.

Chicago and the crew talk about what had happened tonight. Chicago made good money off the party. She said all they have to do now is come up with a plan to knock out all 50 of the customers in one night.

Chicago: "Just don't worry. There's a big fight comin'--Mike Tyson and the Real Deal Holyfield. So let's get back to work."

✱ ✷ ✣ ✼ ✶ ✹ ✵ ☆ ✯ ✰

In late March, Milk had tight surveillance on the boys and they knew it, so they just did their thang, making it look normal. So Sugar got with a couple of the girls to help her pull off the lick with the cops and blow. It was Brown Sugar, Sky, Jazzy Bell and Big Mike. Big Mike always stay close to Jazzy Bell. All of the girls are great, but Jazzy Bell is somethin' special. We all are children of God, but you can feel a movement when she's present.

So they all slip out of sight to pull off their biggest lick ever. Sugar had the whereabouts on Milk and Pacman. They got to Pacman's house. Sugar took the wax impression of the keys she had made to the house. They all creep into the house and head for the garage. I must say this is their most easiest lick ever. For every lick that is easy, the consequence can sometimes be great or painful. They all wore rubber gloves for fingerprints. As Sugar move the excess junk out of the way, she tell everybody to get ready, get ready. She told Big Mike to bring the chain horse over; she then hook the chain hook and hook it to the concrete floor hook and told Big Mike to pull the chain.

Up came the concrete floor. It will take the strength of

two men to lift the floor, but Big Mike has the strength of three men as he pull the chain. Sky and Jazzy Bell was bringin' out the duffel bags. Sugar's eyes glued to the floor. Big Mike breathin' hard. When the floor was lifted, the girls went to work to unload and load six tons of coke and Pacman had a fat stash--$3 million in cash. They got it all-- a 25 minute job. They fled and got back on their post. Each crew had a ton to work with, but whoever had Brown Sugar on-lock had a extra ton to work with. But workin' wasn't on their minds...

✳ ✳ ✣ ✳ ✳ ✳ ✳ ☆ ★ ☆

Sugar got with Milk and gave him the info on Pacman.

Sugar: "All he think about is sex. I think he's plottin' something."

Milk: "You said he might be plottin' something."

Sugar: "Yeah, he was talkin' some shit about going big time this year."

Milk: "You think that nigga will try me?"

Sugar: "I don't know. He got much backup."

Milk: "I do, too. He don't want to fuck with me like that. Anyway, I pay that fool good money and he know I got posse."

Sugar: "Yeah, and he also know that you don't trust your posse, and from that he know you don't trust him. Cops always thinkin' of a way to better their days of bein' a cop. They try their hardest to beat the dope man at his game, but they can't so they join them and you know and I know never trust a dirty cop. They'll flip on you and if he will flip he will flop."

Milk: "That's right. Okay, look, Boo, I will deal with him on the slick side. I want you to tell the family to get ready. Next week I got a ton of fun for them."

Sugar: "When, Boo? April the 4th?"

Milk: "That right. The 4th all the time."

✱ ✷ ✥ ✼ ✶ ✸ ✳ ☆ ✯ ✰

At Fidel's house, Mona Lisa went and got Fidel out of jail and the boy was glad to see her.

Fidel: "I am so glad to see you! Did you have any trouble gettin' the money out of the bank?"

Mona Lisa: "Yes, I did. They ask for ID. I showed them my ID and my marriage license, but they still have your ex-wife name on the joint account. For hours I try to convince them that I was your new wife. The money is still in your dead wife's name, so I didn't get the money from your account. I got it from a friend; so when are you going to the bank and straighten out this matter?"

Fidel: "Soon, Dear, because I need some street money. So how is your mother?"

Mona Lisa: "She wasn't really sick; she just wanted to see her li'l girl. We sat down and talk. She just needed my love. What happen?"

Fidel: "It's a long story. I was so stupid. I was ridin' dirty and the cops pull me over and start askin' me questions about my ex-wife and my dumb ass had the coke on the passenger seat layin' next to my heat and when he saw that he grab me out the car, slam me to the ground, put his knee in my back and ask me where the rest of the dope at. I was so high I can't lie. They question me all night. My eye was hurtin' from the one big light. I stay down, but they still lock me down. My body and eye was weak and I refuse to eat, so the days I was there I would just sleep and dream and hope. I didn't want to hear shit because I was in a jam. I couldn't even hear the cell door slam. But when I heard my name call for my bail, I knew it was my Boo savin' me from hell. So, Baby, here I am."

Fidel was out, but it wasn't over. He still had to go to

court. Fidel took a good hot bath and when he came out
Mona Lisa put some 'always think about some of this pussy'
on him. And when she was done he was sound asleep. Mona
Lisa put out some clothes for tomorrow. It was time for the
meeting and she didn't know what to expect, but on the real,
no one knew. They just know that Milk promise them each
crew a ton of coke. But with the coke gone, they knew it was
going to be some shit. So everybody had to play it cool. But
with six tons of coke gone, they knew that somebody was
going to act a donkey.

✳ ✳ ✤ ✱ ✳ ✳ ✳ ☆ ★ ☆

Winter, Spring, Summer, Fall. Still they meet up every
four months at Milk's Al Capone Suite to discuss business,
licks, and new things to improve the family. Everybody was
there sittin' around the round table with the money they
made off the 50 keys Milk fronted them. Milk was in the
back room with Brown Sugar gettin' a back rub and he was
thinkin' of a way to break the news to the family that all of
the dope was gone.

Tray and Deuce was out in the room with the family
countin' the money. Each crew brought in a nice stack.
Money fill the table. Raven was dancin' on top of the table.
They all were havin' a good time--the day was suppose to be
a ton of fun day. The family was playin' it off because they
knew that the six tons was gone. For each stack Tray and
Deuce counted, they took it back to Milk. Milk came out of
his thoughts. He ask Tray & Deuce how are they acting?

Deuce: "The same, no expression."

Tray: "Let me give them the evil eye. They'll break, I
know."

Milk: "Naw--just stay cool. But play them close, check
for sweat."

As Sugar was rubbin' Milk down she could feel the tension in his body so she lie him back and give him some head. The kind of head that make your toes curl up. She took it down the throat and came back up lookin' Milk in his eyes. He showed no emotion. When a man lose six tons of coke and get some good head and still show no expression, he really holdin' something back inside that's going to hurt him or someone else.

Brown Sugar clean herself up, took a deep breath and told Milk to come. "Let's get the rest of our money. Let's make it happen, Boo." Milk and Brown Sugar walk out into the room. Everybody got quiet to let Milk speak.

Milk: "Well, family, I got some bad news and I got some good news. But before I get started, Hezzy, how is Baller?"

Hezzy: "He's doin' better. Me and the family is thinkin' of a way to break him out."

Milk: "Well, how's the plan comin'?"

Hezzy: "It's lookin' good."

Milk: "That's good to hear. And everybody else is doin' okay, right?"

They all said yes.

Big Mike: "Yeah, but it could be better." Everybody bust out laughin'.

Milk: "I know that's right. But back to the news. The bad news first. The tons of coke I had for the each of your crews is gone. I had the cops guardin' it and someone creep it right from under their nose."

When Milk said that they drop the smiles on their faces and they all started actin' as though they were upset.

Chicago: "Who do you think could have did this to us?"

Milk: "I don't know."

Jim Kelly: "You don't think those dirty ass cops cross us, do you?"

Sky: "What are we going to do about this? I got people at

the club dependin' on me to have coke this Spring. That bitch Dove from the Jury clique, she'll try to take over my clientele if I don't get some product."

Jazzy Bell: "Yeah, this suppose to be a good money year. Atlanta is going to be fill with people who want to get high for this coming Freaknik and for the Olympics."

Hezzy: "Milk, we can make it through this month because this is the party month. But after this month it's back to business. Whoever have dope will have money, big time. This is the money year for this city. If my crew can't get dope, we'll just double up on our jacks."

Chicago: "And my crew will do the same."

MJG: "Word on the street that the Jury is scoping."

Pete: "Yeah, those fools came to us and brought big weight."

Sugar Wolf: "They got dope."

Ten: "We need to jack dat ass."

Milk: "That sound like a good idea, but let's watch them first to see where they get their stuff from then jack dat ass."

Eazy: "If these fools got big money and movin' big weight, then they gots to have a big man that runnin' shit right to this day. Them fools came in Atlanta the same year you did, Milk. Four months after you got here."

Milk: "So what you gettin' at, boy?" Everybody saw a little sweat on Milk's forehead.

Eazy: "I'm just sayin', you know and we know there ain't no family out there that will try to go against us."

Milk: "Get to your point."

Eazy: "I think that the Jury is your crew. The last state you left was New York and the Jury crew is from New York. You got them to steal the coke and now you are tryin' to figure out a way to get us to buy from them."

Milk snap. He jump toward Eazy and try to pull that

Nino Brown & G-money shit on Eazy. When he jump over at Eazy, Eazy jump up and grab Milk in a head lock and pull out his butterfly knife and started stickin' him in the side of his rib cage. He stuck Milk over 13 times--it would have been more, but at that moment the Deuce and the Tray was bustin' shot at Eazy. Bullets flyin' everywhere. Eazy got off one round and ran out the door. Milk fell on the table on top of some of the money. Everybody was gettin' up off the floor. Blood, money, blood money everywhere. Milk was in pain.

The family didn't give Milk time to explain the good news. Somehow evil just took over. The good news was that Milk had Bread Bout It's safe deposit key and he had a plan to get all of the money out of the bank without him even knowin' with the help of his wife. Milk had shit luck, and when Eazy was stickin' Milk the key fell from his shirt pocket and when it did, Precious pick it up.

Jazzy Bell yell out "Get an Ambulance!"

Brown Sugar was in a corner cryin'.

Milk: "No hospital...no hospital..."

Big Mike yank Milk off the table. Tray and Deuce was aimin' their guns at everyone. "Get some fucking help!!"

Chicago got on her cellular phone calling one of her doctor friends.

Chicago: "Come on--let's go!"

Chicago, Tray and Deuce, Jazzy Bell and Big Mike all left Milk's Al Capone Suite. Blood was all over Big Mike.

"Eazy fuck him up."

Jazzy Bell was drivin'; Deuce yelling "Drive! Drive!"

Sniffin' on the coke, Tray was talking with Milk. "You going to be fine. You going to make it, Baby."

Deuce: "Drive! Drive you fat bitch!!"

Big Mike grab at Deuce. Tray put his gun to Big Mike's head. "Don't make it two, mother fucker, in here bleedin', so back off, Big Baby, right now. I don't give a fuck."

Jazzy Bell: "No, Big Mike!" Big Mike slowly ease off.

Chicago: "Turn right here--this the house."

Chicago's doctor friend was at the door when they arrived. Tray and Deuce grab Milk and enter him into the house yelling, "Save my Dog, Doc, save him!" The doctor wasn't ready for this--guns aimed at him, Deuce and Tray yelling and making threats.

Chicago: "Do it for me, Doc."

Jazzy Bell and Big Mike was still in the van. Big Mike was mad with tears in his eyes saying to Jazzy Bell, "I'll kill him, I'll kill him, I'll kill that mother fucker if you just say so." Jazzy Bell put her arms around Big Mike, telling him "everything going to be all right, Baby, it's going to be all right. Don't worry, Mama will be all right. He's going to get what's coming to him, don't worry."

Chicago came back out to the van and put her hand on Big Mike's shoulder and said, "There will be a next time."

NO TRICKS

Sometime what you know can hurt you
And what you don't know can save you.
But in this game it is best to know
All you know to make it happen. Get in
And get out because if you don't you'll never
Know until you are looking out of a
Coffin in spirit or 20 years in prison
On down the road feeling sorry for yourself
And others who dare to get in this game
Thinking that because they're young that make them
Tough. Sharp strong smart slicker and full of vigor
Just because they are in a game where you
Makes a lot of money but all that don't matter
If you're playing a game that has no rules and after
You find this out you will look back and see
How close you were to death and that's when you will
Seek God and find out he is the answer to our prayer.

- By Earnest Bennett

WHO CROSS YOU

Brown Sugar stayed close to Milk until his wounds healed up. For the last two weeks, Sugar was all hands and feet helping Milk. It's said, but now it's written, when a person is going through something that's bad, like getting shot, stabbed, or depression, and that person heals mentally and physically, it's time to handle business. A priest will say "chill" and a gangster will say "kill". And Milk sho' ain't no priest. Ever since Milk was stabbed he stayed in deep thought.

While just about the whole Atlanta was down in Florida having a good time at Spring Break, Tray and Deuce, all they did was sniff coke and pace the floor waiting on orders to do whatever. A week later it was the Freaknik weekend. Brown Sugar, Milk, Tray, and Deuce was just chilling on that Friday. Milk was doing better. There was a knock at the door. Tray went to the door to answer it.

Tray: "Who is it?"

Pacman: "It's Pacman."

Brown Sugar's heart was pounding at a fast rate. Milk then put his eyes on her to read her. When Tray opened the door, Pacman walked in. Milk stood up to greet him with a handshake. Milk was happy to see Pacman.

Pacman: "What up, Baby? How you feeling?"

Milk: "It's getting better. Look, here's your girl."

Pacman: "Hey, Boo."

Brown Sugar: "I ain't your Boo, mother fucker. Milk, why you being friends with him? He set us up. He got our six tons of coke."

Milk: "No, Boo. We set you up and you got my coke."

Brown Sugar: "What you mean?"

Milk: "You're so predictable. I put a li'l bug in my cops friends ear. I knew you would try some shit. Now, who put you on me and whoever did that, that's who you workin' for. Now, you take me to my coke and I promise you I will not kill you."

Brown Sugar: "I don't know what you're talking about. I work for you, Boo."

Milk: "You can kill that 'Boo' shit. That's when I know you're lying."

Tray and Deuce each cocked a bullet in the chamber of their guns. When Brown Sugar saw that, she headed out the door. Deuce fired a shot to put more fear in her heart. She ran out the door fearing for her life. Pacman got on his walkie-talkie radio telling his dogs to be on a lookout for Brown Sugar. It was the Freaknik weekend, so the street was packed with police. So all the police saw was beautiful faces dressed in a sexy fashion, so it wasn't going to be easy to pick her out on the crowded street of beautiful girls. Brown Sugar knew what Pacman's crew looked like, so she stayed on the low because there was cops everywhere. Milk wanted her followed to see who's got her under control so he could then find his dope. But if Brown Sugar just would have stayed cool Milk was just testing her to see if she would break, and she broke. And now she's on the run.

Brown Sugar knew she couldn't go straight to the Family at the time because she was being followed. So she stayed in and out of public places. She then walked into a public library. There she got a pencil and paper to write two letters. She wrote one to Hezzy to give Baller and one to Chief Beverly Harvard. She was giving up info on the dirty cops, salutation cash, cops, and cover ups.

She then finished the letters. She walked out of the library. She got into her car and looked around and saw Tray and Deuce. They were coming her way. She pulled off in fear. Losing them in traffic, she pulled up to a mailbox and dropped the letters off. She knew she was safe as long as she stayed in public places, so she rode around all afternoon. The more she rode around, the more the streets got packed with Freaknikers.

An hour later she was stuck right in the middle of traffic. People were in and out of their cars, walking around, flirting car to car, mens and womens. You got some girls in their cars who show their body from inside their car. The mens will then crowd around the car jumpin' on it and rocking it and showing their body parts, trying to get chosen. Everybody was having a good time except Brown Sugar. She was running for her life.

She was in her car looking around. All of a sudden - Boom! - the crowd rushed her car yelling, "Take it off! Take it off!" It startled her for the moment, but then she saw that it was just mens who wanted to see her naked body parts. So she got with the program. She opened up her legs and showed some breast. The mens around the car went crazy. Just for that second she was a li'l happy knowing she still had it. But there was one man around the car who glanced out a gun and when Sugar saw that she went out the opposite door into the crowded streets.

Everywhere she turned there were strange faces and dirty cops that was on Pacman's team. She was so paranoid--she turned right, she turned left, she ran, she walked, she laughed, she cried. She ran by a nearby school and at that time school was letting out and there was Happy Officer Friendly who was directing traffic for the school kids. She ran to Happy for help.

Brown Sugar: "Help me, Happy, please! There are some bad people out to kill me along with some dirty cops."

Happy: "Calm down, it's going to be okay. Just be cool. Look, go over and sit in the back seat of my car and get down so you won't be seen. I'll be off in a few minutes and then I will take you where you got to be."

Brown Sugar: "Thank you, Happy, thank you. Anything you want, you got it."

Sugar got into the car just like Happy told her. Thirty minutes later Happy entered the car.

Happy: "Where to?"

Sugar: "Take me to 405 Lake Front Drive. Oh, Happy, I am so glad to see you."

Happy: "Now who you say was trying to kill you?"

She took a deep breath and said, "My crazy boyfriend thinks I stole from him and now he's got Pacman and his whole squad after me. You're not a part of his crew, are you, Happy?"

Happy: "Naw, Sugar, I am solo. Besides, I'm the good cop."

Sugar: "Yeah, I know. It's just my head is just messed all up right now. You know, I left my car in the middle of traffic. I was scared to death."

Happy: "You're going to be fine. I am going to put you in a better place."

Sugar: "I truly believe you, too, Happy. I thank you from the bottom of my heart."

Sugar was still down on her knees. Happy then turned into a dead end street where her car was parked.

Sugar: "Happy, is there anything that I could do for you right this moment to show my thanks?"

Happy: "Well, since you're down on your knees already, could I get a li'l head? I don't get it on the regular."

Sugar: "I understand you. Come on back here, you big sugar bear."

Happy got in the back seat. He left the back door cracked just a little. Sugar unzipped his pants and pulled out his snake and then she went to work on him. All head is good head as long as she don't bite it. Happy was loving the feeling and when he started coming his eyes rolled into the back of his head. He then grabbed Sugar around the neck, slowly choking the air out of her. She then went fighting for her life. She hit him in the balls. He let her go. She then attacked his face and the back of his neck with her claw like nails. Blood poured out of the bumps in the back of his neck and face. Happy then fell out of the car.

As soon as Sugar could step out of the car, the man who showed her the gun at her car was stepping toward the back door with gun in hand. He grabbed Sugar by the hair and put the gun to her head. Sugar was breathing hard; her hands were bloody; sweat, tears, and sperm was all running down her face. Happy was getting off the ground.

Happy: "Bring her."

The hit man dirty walked Sugar to her car. Happy then reached into the car and got out the keys to open the trunk. Happy unlocked the trunk and told the hit man, Dirty, to put her into the trunk. That's when Sugar started fighting for her life. Dirty struggled four minutes, and then he slammed her into the trunk. He also fell off into the trunk with her. Happy then closed the trunk with the both of them in it. Sugar was screaming and still fighting for her life, even though Dirty had a gun to shoot his way out of the trunk.

But he couldn't even get in position Because Sugar was all over him with her claw nails making him scream and bleed.

Dirty was yelling, "Happy! Let me out of this fucking trunk! This bitch is going crazy on me!"

Then the yelling went to crying. See, Happy was Milk's ace in the hole. And what had happened to Happy today, he don't want it to get out. And besides, he don't like punk ass drug dealers, so he pulled out his gun and shot holes into the trunk. He unloaded his clip until everything was silent. He pulled out his handkerchief from his pocket to stop his face and neck from bleeding. He then got into the car and put it in gear. He took the bloody handkerchief to wipe down the steering wheel and he got out of the car to check the kills.

As soon as he opened the trunk, Sugar jumped out at him. Again and again, she was still fighting for her life. But that's when Happy put his hands around her neck once again and choked the life out of her and that's when he closed the trunk and pushed the car off into the ditch.

A few days later some kids was playing and spotted the car in the ditch. They noticed blood dripping from the bottom of the trunk and that's when it was all on the News.

"Live from Channel 2 Action News, I'm Mase Gumbo. Here on this dead end street, a young dancer stripper and a hit man drug dealer were found slain over the Freaknik weekend. The dancer was choked to death and her alleged boyfriend was shot seventeen times. Right now the police are doing a heavy investigation, but there are no leads. The law enforcement community is calling this killer 'Mr. Unknown'. This is the second time a killing like this has happened and it is similar to the killing that took place way back when a drug dealer was found slain in the trunk of his car. I'm Mase Gumbo from Channel 2 Action News. Back to you, Monica."

Monica: "Mase, this had nothing to do with Freaknik, did it?"

Mase: "No, Monica, the students all had a great time and now they're heading back out of town. But there were a few incidents where some womens were pulled from their cars and almost raped. And there was one young lady who had her clothes ripped off of her and her sister was hit in the head with a beer bottle."

✳ ✳ ✧ ✳ ✳ ✳ ✳ ☆ ✰ ☆

When the family heard the news they were all in shock. Chicago, Pee Wee Loc, Fly-Mar, Sky, Sugar Wolf, MJG were all working on the big 50 licks coming this next big fight between Iron Mike Tyson vs The Real Deal Holyfield. Jade, Raven, Mona Lisa, Precious, Big Mike and Jim Kelly got plans to break Bread Bout It for his bank. Jazzy Bell, Greed, Pete, Ten kept a sharp eye on the Killahoe Posse, waiting on them to make one false move with the 19 synthetic keys and the fake $60G they been sitting on all this time. And still haven't made a move with it yet. That's what I call keeping it on the down low. The Killahoe Posse have been putting in much work since Jazzy Bell's crew been putting in work jackin' and stackin'.

She still got love for the dope game. It's just that evil is watching. There's one thing Jazzy Bell teaches her crew every day, and that is to have patience. She says that she learned that from the Holy Bible and that is, if you're going through something and you see no way out, get on your knees and ask God for help. He hears you. He might not come when you call Him sometimes because it is a test and when He thinks you have had enough He's coming to save you with open arms. When Jazzy Bell and the crew heard the news, they broke out in prayer. As they all held hands to pray, Jazzy Bell fell to the floor and fainted. Greed got down on his knees to wake her. Ten went to the bathroom to get a cold rag to wipe her face and neck. With that cold rag on her face she woke and came to herself.

Jazzy Bell: "I see more death in the family. We need to be more careful. Milk and the cops are working together to destroy us. Come, let us pray."

They all prayed. Diamond was out of town with Big Six in Cancun, Mexico having a good time. See, in the game, people with money, first they go to Florida to have fun for the Spring Break and then from there it's Atlanta to party for the Freaknik and then it's back to wherever you make your money. But people with big bank do all that shit and then there are some who like to party. After Freaknik it's balling in New Mexico with a loved one. And, believe me, Big Six got big bank and Diamond is using the long term technique on Big Six because a person like this can lose big money over a year's time and won't miss it.

Diamond is going to keep him. He already asked her to marry him. She's playing him close. She told him "let's wait awhile," but she did move in with him a couple of months ago. And while she was there, her eyes, hands, mouth, and pussy was working. She told the girls she's going to hit him up for about $50 million and give each crew $10 million apiece and then she out the game this year.

✺ ✳ ✜ ✳ ✳ ✺ ✳ ☆ ✭ ☆

Eazy steady moving from girl to girl, house to house, friend to friend, with people who just wanted to be down with a real nigga, so they kept him safe. He went to the family from time to time. He knew that it was tight surveillance on them, so he stay low. Hezzy was working on plans to keep his nigga Eazy safe and his nigga Baller free. Day and night he kept his hustle on.

Baller was in his cell doing push up the time he heard the

news about Sugar. You can tell when there's a lot on a man's mind when he does a thousand push ups a day, stayin' to his self, reading books to better his education. Behind death, pain, and pressure, some fold, but the Real focus. So Baller called Hezzy.

"This is the operator. I have a collect call from Baller who is an inmate in the Atlanta Fulton County State Prison. To deny charges, hang up now. To accept charges, press 4 now."

Hezzy: "Hello."

Baller: "Hey, what's up, Baby Boy?"

Hezzy: "You, Ninja."

Baller: "What cha doin'?"

Hezzy: "Thinking of a master plan to free my ninja and trying to free Eazy from this day by day madness and I got to get you out from behind them gangster walls because that ain't no place for a player."

Baller: "Yeah, I know."

Hezzy: "You heard the news on your girl?"

Baller: "Yeah, man, I peep that shit on the News. It's about time to kill that nigga Milk."

Hezzy: "Yeah, but we got to get you out that hell hole first."

Baller: "Don't worry, I got a plan. You just make sure you keep Eazy safe. Now, how is everybody holding up?"

Hezzy: "They doing all right. But Jazzy Bell had a fit. She fell out over there. She told Ten, Pete, and Greed that there was going to be more death in the family and hey, man, I feel her."

Baller: "And I feel you, Baby Boy, I feel you."

Hezzy: "Everybody miss you, man."

Baller: "Yeah, man, it will get better, Baby Boy, you just hang on. What dat nigga Eazy doing to keep his head above water?"

Hezzy: "Shit. Staying out of sight until this shit blow over. Milk got Tray and Deuce on the hunt, but when you get out I know for a fact things are going to get better, so we can plan out a way to do that nigga Milk and his li'l clique. I wish Eazy would have finished that nigga off."

Baller: "In due time, Baby Boy, in due time. We going to give that nigga a military funeral."

Hezzy: "I feel you. I like dat there."

Baller: "But look here, Baby Boy. You just keep keepin' on. I'll see you in a month's time."

Hezzy: "Sho' 'nuff."

Baller: "Sho' 'nuff. Now you take care. Later."

Hezzy hung up the phone, wrapped up his plans, and took a deep breath. He picked up the box of Swisher Sweets blunts and busted open a blunt. And busted open, stuffed it with weed. He also poured up a glass of Hennessy. He took a sip and walked out to the mailbox. As he was going to the mailbox, Cuddie and his crew was out in the street, makin' money. The trap was booming. They had a line of cars waiting to buy rocks, quarters, halves, and ounces. Hezzy puffed on his blunt, smiling at the traffic. He loved to see his 'hood booming with money because when a nigga making money they ain't got time to hate on the next man. But if a nigga is broke, somebody's ass is in trouble because broke niggas make the best crooks. Anyway, Smoka Holler is the block that stay crunk at all times. Right then and there Hezzy had an idea. He reached into his mailbox, pulling out the light & gas bill and the letter from Brown Sugar to Baller. He looked at the letter for a minute and went back to puffing on his choke and sipping on his drink. While doing that he called Cuddie over to speak with him about business. Cuddie and his crew was going from car to car telling the customer to get it and go. Get it and go! There was so much traffic it had to be a fast transaction, because if the cops ride through and see all this traffic they would set up a road block trying the catch the buyer and seller. Sometimes the cops pose as drug dealers to catch the buyer, and in the ghetto we call that right there entrapment. Man, you can just be swooping through the 'hood just to buy you a bag of weed or a few rocks so you can go chill with a bitch or someone you get high with. It's like this--you see your dealer who you buy from but he don't say shit, so you buy from the cop. And once you purchase the drug and start to walk toward your ride, they jump out at you and take your ass to jail. Like I said, it's a dirty game.

Hezzy: "Yo, Cuddie. Yo."

Cuddie: "Yeah."

Hezzy: "Let me holler at you for a minute."

Cuddie told his BGs to hold it down and keep their eyes open. Cuddie walked over to Hezzy. It's been a long time since these niggas really spoke to one another. They just made money on the street and attended to their business.

Cuddie: "What's up?"

Hezzy: "What's up? You want to choke with me?"

Cuddie: "Why not?"

They gave each other dap. Cuddie puffing on the choke, talking at the same time with smoke coming from his nose and mouth, saying, "What's really going on, Baby Boy? It's been a long time." Before Cuddie could say anything else he was coughing--choking and coughing up phlegm.

Cuddie: "Damn! That's dat fire!"

Hezzy: "Yeah, I know. I got a plan for the 'hood to make more money for us if you are interested."

Cuddie, still choking, telling Hezzy to keep talking.

Hezzy: "Come. Let's talk in the house." They walk into the house.

Hezzy: "Now look here, my nigga. Me and my crew is on vacation and we going to try some new shit. Now, I got good shit, fire shit, and the best shit. Now, the good shit got a 4 cut on it and the price of a ounce in '96 go for the $800. Try it."

Cuddie pulled out a half of a straw. Hezzy knocked off a gram from the good key of coke. Cuddie took a sniff and was like, "Damn, that's good." Then Hezzy pulled out the fire key of coke and knocked off a gram from it. Cuddie took a sniff. Cuddie stood up and peeped out the door and sat back down and laid back and asked Hezzy, "What's the price and cut on it?"

Hezzy: "Okay, an ounce of this goes for $1,000 and the cut on it is a 2. "

Cuddie: "I like dat there. That shit got me tweeting. You hear me, bruh'? Damn--I might not have to try that other shit you call the best."

Hezzy: "Oh no. But I want you to know there's no cut on this here shit and it's $1,200 and ounce. Now, don't hit this like you hit the others."

Hezzy knocked off half of a gram.

Cuddie: "Man, don't be like that. Knock off that other half--make it a gram."

Hezzy: "Man, I am telling you, this shit is the best on the street."

Cuddie: "Yeah, I know it's the best." Cuddie took his straw and sniffed the whole gram off the table. He turned his head left and right and made a few funny faces and fell out. Then blood started pouring from his nose. Hezzy just shook his head and went to wake Cuddie. When Cuddie woke up he was like, "Damn!"

Cuddie: "Hey, man, I'll just take the good shit for the $800. That other shit you got right there--Damn!--that shit will kill a nigga the way I sniff, too. It will bust a nigga's heart. When you want to get started?"

Hezzy: "Whenever you are ready. Now, you got to keep this shit on the low low and look, I'm going to put you on some nice licks. I know some niggas who be kickin' at the hotel with them li'l 'ho's and be leaving their dope and money in the car and on the licks we split out 50-50. Is that cool with you?"

Cuddie: "Hell, yeah. Anything else?"

Hezzy: "Yeah, we will watch the hood together and we watch each other's back."

Cuddie: "So no more animosity between us, right?"

Hezzy: "Right."

Cuddie: "Hey, that was some fire ass chokeweed. You got any more? If you do I would like to buy an ounce of that shit so me and the boys can choke on weed and lay off that dope. It's time to make some big paper."

Hezzy reached into a trash bag and pulled out a big handful of choke and told Cuddie, "Here you go, Friend."

Cuddie: "Damn! Thank you, Friend. See you later." Cuddie went back to work.

Hezzy opened up the light & gas bill and just stared at the letter that Brown Sugar wrote to Baller.

✳ ✳ ✢ ✳ ✳ ✳ ✳ ☆ ★ ☆

A couple days later, Diamond was back from out of town. Her crew broke the news to her and, like everybody else, she was in shock. Brown Sugar's death saddened everyone. Retaliation was all they could think about at the time. But they know business first and business is money.

Chief Beverly Harvard received the letter Brown Sugar wrote to her. She read it and right then she started two secretive operations. One is called Operation Deep Pocket for the small and big time dealers on the street and operation two was Operation Street Sweep. It was a deep undercover

operation for the dirty cops who deal with any types of nar-
cotics. With the Olympics only two months away, the Chief
did everything in her power to clean the streets of Atlanta.
To avoid getting locked up you had to be slick and cunning.

Chief Beverly Harvard and Mayor Bill Campbell wanted
Atlanta to be the safest city in the world, so they sent out a
message--"If you do the crime, you do the time. There is no
getting out right away if we catch you out there acting bad.
There is no bond until the Olympics are over." So before the
judge could even look at your ass, you had to stay locked up
for at least four months.

There were over 1,000 drug cases and 500 other arrests
made and, believe me, the street got the point. And a month
later, June 1, Chief Beverly Harvard turned right around
and arrested 18 crooked ass cops on the force and a week
later 6 more cops, all from Zone 3. Cops from other zones
acted as if they were in shock, but they knew what it was.
Beverly Harvard got on TV and told the City of Atlanta that
she wasn't having it. She also said as long as she is the Chief
of Police, there will be justice for all. As time passed, more
cops were arrested. It was all over the News. Just to name a
few whose faces was all on the news: Down & Out, Monk
Man, Robocop, Deputy Dog, Pat the Cat, Action Jackson,
No Neck Jeff & Bacon, Narco, Big Boy, Smith & Wesson,
Pacman & Reebok, and when niggas in the 'hood saw it on
TV they all threw parties in the 'hood. Some of the cops was
arrested on police brutality, fatal killing, rape, ass kicking,
false arrest. Officers Down & Out, these two cops always
come around asking drug dealers, "Let me hold something
'cause I'm Down & Out in Atlanta, Georgia." They take all
of the drug dealers money and just leave them with a few
rocks so they can come back up and then take the rocks they
got from one dealer and give it to another dealer to work off

for them and they stay off their ass.

People was all down at the Internal Affairs trying to get money back. Some people came in talkin' about Monk Man and Deputy Dog beat the death out of their cousin, but the cops said in their report they went to bust a crack house and the suspect fled the house so they gave chase. As the suspect fled, he had swallowed 28 grams of cocaine and when we caught up with the suspect he then was having a heart attack. But that was a lie. The cops beat his ass while he was in handcuffs and there was nothing said about it. The cops went to court. At the time they said there was no excessive force. The two officers were acquitted. Now the State will have to reopen all of the dirty officers' cases and look into them.

✱ ✷ ✥ ✼ ✶ ✸ ✺ ☆ ✯ ✰

Raven, Mona Lisa, and Precious was kickin' it at one of Bread Bout It's popular clubs, Diamonds & Pearls, putting the scope on Bread and his business partner, Billy Lawrence. They were discussing plans about his wife. Bread offered Billy $55G to take his wife's life. Raven, Mona Lisa, and Precious was having a good time on a dull Monday night, but the club was jumpin'.

Bread: "Billy, I want you to do the job this weekend and I want you to make it look like a non-premeditated murder."

Billy: "Okay. I understand. Is there anything else? You should have been got me for this job."

Bread: "Naw, I didn't want no connection between me and you on this one. I could lose everything on this if something goes wrong." Bread pulled out some pictures of his wife with Milk.

Bread: "Here are some pictures of my wife."

Billy: "Who this nigga she with?"

Bread: "That's some nigga she's fuckin'. Kill him, too, if

they're together."

Billy: "Look here, now, that's going to be an extra $55G. And watch that nigga shit, you know what I'm sayin'?"

Bread: "I know."

Billy: "That's $110G."

Bread: "Hey, I know!"

Billy: "Ha, ha. It looks like your wife's having a good old time with this black brother. What--that li'l old dick of yours done play out or your tongue ain't cuttin' it no more. Ha, ha!"

Bread: "Look, I'm serious about this. Kill the both of them."

Billy: "Okay. I got you, man. You need to lay off that black pussy for the moment--ha, ha--it's got you wantin' to kill your wife. I'm telling you, that savage pussy have you crazy all the time. Ha, ha."

They talked a few more minutes before wrapping things up. They separated in the club. Precious was on this, so she put Mona Lisa in his direction. Mona Lisa was looking so good that night Billy Lawrence had to strike a conversation. Lisa had much time to flirt because Fidel pled guilty Monday to selling cocaine and was sentenced to six years in prison. The drug case is not related to his wife's murder charge, but there still is an ongoing investigation of Fidel concerning the death of his wife. Fulton County Superior Court Judge Wendy E. Shoob sentenced Fidel to 10 years in prison with 6 to be served and the rest on probation, as the State asked.

To Billy Lawrence, this was the baddest white girl he ever laid eyes on. He used all the game he had trying to get Mona Lisa to fuck. She laughed, talk, drank, but yet and still, she never talked about sex until Billy pulled out that bankroll and then asked her had she ever humped for money.

Mona Lisa: "All the time and every time. Ohhh--you want some of this."

Mona Lisa then opened up her legs and stuck her finger down into her Victoria's Secret and tasted her pussy, eye to eye with Billy.

Billy: "Damn, Mama, what's it going to cost me to have some of you?"

Mona Lisa: "$2,500."

Billy: "Damn, you're a high-priced 'ho'."

Mona Lisa: "Bitch, maybe, but not 'ho'. Anyway, you get what you pay for. See, in this game bitches pimp niggas, too."

It was Mona Lisa's job to fuck Billy Lawrence's head up with sex games because time is gettin' short. Bread needed someone to kill his wife because she started gettin' too damn nosy about his business. But what really burned him up was that his wife was fuckin' a nigga. See, when you got a nigga with a big dick fuckin' a white woman, or it could be a black woman getting that big dick, it don't matter if she's married or her family don't want her to fuck with that nigga no more, that dick be callin' them 'ho's keepin' them in line. She not going to listen to no one but the person who's throwing that dat dick. And Bread knew this, too, because it's the same with black pussy or just some good pussy. A white man can love the shit out of his wife, but once he hit that good black pussy can't nobody tell him shit. And white boys love to eat the pussy, and those fat pussy lips be talkin' to them white boys. See, a black man take that dick and talk back to that pussy. If it's a big fat pussy, you got to work that pussy to whip it or it will take that dick and whip it. But if it's a small pussy, take your time with it and when she start lovin' that dick, ram it in one or two good times. Let her know who's the man and then take it back slow. Bitches love a man who know how to throw that dick. And ladies, mens the same way. If your man got a big old dick, work all the muscle in your pussy. Work that dick. Don't let him kill your pussy because pussy is money and you don't let other people handle your money. Ladies, you got to wear that dick out. Feel his nuts. If they draw up, you just about got him. Four good nuts. His nut will draw up and that dick will be wore out. In other words, whipped. Now ladies, if your man got a li'l dick, you sho' 'nuff gots to work. First of all you gots to keep that dick up. Stick your finger in your pussy and rub it across his nose and when that dick get hard make that motherfucker work and when he feel like he's ready to nut, take that dick out that pussy. Kiss on his body to keep him hot, but if you get off that dick and he's nutting, suck that dick. Get all that nut from that dick. Do that three or four times and you got yourself a pay master and if the motherfucker don't want to pay for a good fuck like that take your business elsewhere.

So Mona Lisa left the club with Billy Lawrence. Raven watched Precious' back as she moved in on Bread Bout It. When Bread saw Precious in the club, he stepped to her with a warm smile offering to buy her a drink. That night Bread was in a talkin' mood. He asked Precious did she know anyone who can pull off a murder job. She said, "Naw."

Bread: "Hey--where is your friend Milk?"

Precious: "I haven't seen him in awhile, but the last I seen him he was with some white chick talkin' about big pimpin'. He showed me a safe deposit key he had got from her saying that she going to get him some money out the bank to help him fix up his Al Capone Suite.

Bread: "Al Capone Suite?"

Precious: "Yeah, a big ass house he built from the ground up. I been in it. It's going to be nice when he finish putting the finishing touch on it. With the money he talkin' about getting from her, he should be finished in no time. He was so happy--I never seen him that happy before. She had his nose wide open."

Bread: "In bed she must be good--what you think?"

Precious: "Naw, I just think she pay good. And why you askin' me about Milk? He's not my man."

Bread: "I just like the taste of his coke and I wanted to see him about some."

Precious: "Ohh--I might can help up on that. I love what you have did to this club. It's nice."

Bread got close to Precious, nibbling on her ear, telling her how nice she looked. They talked for a few more minutes an left the club to just talk some more, not to have sex. The words Precious throwed into Bread's ear had him on high. He took her to a nearby caffe to talk and eat a li'l something--T-Bone steaks and baked potatoes.

Small Problem Precious got just that deep into his head, dealin' with his emotions on a pro level. She reached down into his soul and straightened out all the small problems he had floatin' around in his head. They ate and, before walking out the door, Precious grabbed hold of Bread's hand as they walked out the door. A man likes it when a woman just take charge.

Meanwhile, Billy Lawrence was having some unbelievable sex with Mona Lisa. As they hump all night making fuck faces, morning came. Mona Lisa got up and left Billy asleep when she left. But when he woke up his dick was still hard so he got up ready to go to the bathroom. As he walked past the mirror he noticed some writing on the glass as he walked past that read, "Welcome to the disease where there is no cure for." Billy Lawrence grabbed his nappy head of hair and yelled out, "Oh, Shit! I'm going to kill that bitch!!! "

That shit drove him crazy, catching the AIDS virus and he's not even gay. That shit will run a person crazy. The disease is known to be caused by homosexuals and drug needles that is used to do heroin. Billy's mind was off track. He wasn't thinking. He got a boy to do a man's job.

He went to College Park and got a heroin crack smoker hustler who hustled for drugs and sometimes cash. Name Corn Bread. This nigga be off in the trap yelling 'bout "I got that hard, hard, flexin' sometime." And if you ask him what's he doing in the trap, he will tell you tryin' to get this Corn Bread, man. These niggas don't want no money, they in love. Let me have $20, I'll pay you back. And everybody tells him the same thing, "I ain't got it right now." But this fool make money because he will do anything for money. Billy Lawrence went to him and told him he had a job for him and it was to kill this bitch and maybe a nigga and I'll give you $10G.

Billy's hate grew for women since he was told he have AIDS.

Corn Bread: "You want me to do a job for you, right?"

Billy: "Right."

Corn Bread: "When?"

Billy: "This weekend."

Corn Bread: "Bet. I'll bet you ready Just come pick me up. And, yo...let me have $20."

Billy reached into his pocket and gave Corn Bread $20 and told him that's $9,980 and walked off. Corn Bread looked at him and shook his head and said to himself, "Cheap mother fucker."

✳ ✳ ✤ ✲ ✳ ✳ ✳ ☆ ★ ☆

Jade called up Bread Bout It and told him she would like to see him and without a doubt he was on his way to meet her at one of her estates. She had the house set up lovely--

rose petals, and candles burning in every room, along with coke, good liquor, and the sounds of some smooth nut-bustin' music playing. Isaac Hayes Black Moses (They Long To Be) Close To You. Bread laid back into the sofa with his drink in one hand and with some coke in the other. Jade danced around the room naked giving Bread eye to eye contact. Bread got a li'l hot and came out of his clothes and his glasses got steamed. Jade had him going. She played with his sexual body parts; she kissed him on his ears, neck, and shoulders, and feeding him coke. Bread loved this type of life, but what really drove him crazy was that Jade have shave all the hairs off her pussy and that made her cock look even fatter. A fine light brown woman with a pussy that looks bigger than a tennis shoe. She stuck one of her breasts in her mouth, sucking them herself and playing with her crevasse, taking her feet to play with Bread's penis. She then got on top of him. Putting his penis inside her, she took his drink from his hand and took a sip and grabbed the coke and took a li'l toot toot. They both sat there getting coked up. Jade wrapped her arms around Bread's neck, giving him eye to eye contact all the time, and she rode that dick. Sweat and veins is all you can see in Bread's face. Before Bread could bust a nut, Jade got off that dick and they took it to the bedroom. For 19 hours they both passing energy back and forth between their bodies by kissing each other's private parts. It was more love making than sex. They drove each other crazy off makin' love. When the sex was over, they just laid in bed, holdin' each other, talkin' about a better life.

Jade: "What's up with your wife? Have you found anyone yet to kill her?"

Bread: "Something like that. After this weekend, Honey, I will be free."

Jade reached over and got the coke and sprinkled coke all

over Bread's body, lickin' and sniffin' coke from his body.

Jade: "What did your wife do so bad for you to kill her?"

Bread: "Let's just say she's just not my type anymore. And I must say it is true, once you go black you don't want to go back."

Jade: "Ha, ha, ha. No doubt."

Bread: "I'm going out of town this weekend to clear my story. You want to go?"

Jade: "Where to?"

Bread: "Western Europe."

Jade: "Why go to Europe. Why not to the Bay--San Francisco?"

Bread: "See, Honey, I'm taking money out one bank and putting into another. I have friends that told me the First National Bank of Switzerland is a good bank to put away money."

Jade: "How much money we talkin' about?"

Bread: "$18 million."

Jade yelled out, "$18 million! Boo, are you crazy?!! You mean to tell me you will leave your hard earned money across seas with some fool you don't even know shit about?!

Bread: "Well, what do you suggest?"

Jade: "Take it to another state. But God knows, not across seas! Look, you told you wife that you're going out of town on business. Okay, first you get your money out the bank. Then we fly out of town Friday with the money. Get to the airport, get a locker to put the money in. You keep your own key. We check into a hotel. From there we do some shopping, get some sights of downtown, get back to our room and do what we do."

Bread: "And what's that?"

Jade: "Enjoying each other's company. You do enjoy my

company?"

Bread: "Of course, my dear."

Jade: "So pick a city, Boo."

Bread: "That sounds good. Maybe a li'l too good. How long you had that dancing around in your head? It sounds like a plan."

Jade: "I just thought of it and it is a plan for you, Boo. Look, you are moving your money because you think your wife is tryin' to break you, right?"

Bread: "Right."

Jade: "Now, if you some kind of way have your wife killed, they're going to freeze you and her account. Now, if you go out of state and use your middle and last name, you could then put your money in a safe deposit box and we come on back home, hear me? Now you got an alibi and your money is safe out of town. And after things calm down, it's me and you, Boo."

Bread: "Okay, but where should we go?"

Jade: "Look, Boo, that's all on you. Your money, your state."

Bread: "Yeah, how 'bout Chicago? The airport, O'Hare, it is ranked number one in the world on safety."

They hump 3 more hours and it was time for the both of them to handle their business. Bread got to it workin' on plans for the weekend. Bread got with his wife and told her that he have business out of town this weekend. She told him, well, she's going to stay the weekend over her sister's house and she will be back home Sunday night. Jade went to the mall to get her a nice outfit to wear this weekend and out at the mall she ran into Milk. He was with Dove, the chick from the Jury clique. When they spoke to each other, Jade gave Milk the natural look as if she didn't know that he had something to do with Brown Sugar's death.

Jade: "Hey, Milk. What cha doin' out here--spyin' on me?"

Milk: "Naw, I'm just kickin' it with my new friend."

Jade: "Isn't she with the Jury?"

Milk: "Dove, would you excuse me for just a minute?"

Jade and Milk stepped out of sound.

Milk: "I'm just kickin' with her tryin' to pick her to see if she knows anything about my six tons of cocaine."

Jade: "You heard what happened to our sister Brown Sugar?"

Milk: "Yeah, what a loss. Good girl. So when is it going to be me and you together running shit?"

Jade: "Well, I got business and you know just like I know business is money. When are we going to get our pay cut from the investment from that 4444 plan?"

Milk: "Ohh, I'm working on that right now. See, I got this li'l white chick and she's worth millions, so tell the family not to worry."

Jade: "Okay, Milk. Oh--I think Precious wants to see you about a key. It's no one in the family's, so it must be yours or Tray's or Deuce's. It looks like a safe deposit box key."

Milk: "Sho' 'nuff, yeah. Yeah, I did lose a key. Thank you. Okay, Boo. Where could I find Precious?"

Jade: "Don't come at me with that 'Boo' mess. She's going to be at Club 112 Saturday night. Just look at that bitch all in our mouth."

Milk: "Don't worry about her. But it is good to see you."

Jade: "You too."

Milk was at the mall to spy on her and she knew it, but that was the general idea. Jade knew if Milk got his hands on that key any sooner he would rush Miss Bout It down to the bank so she can break herself.

Bread Bout It got back with Billy Lawrence on Thursday

Night. Bread tellin' him that he will leave the back window to the bathroom unlocked and that she will enter the house through the garage side door, so are you ready this weekend?

Billy: "Yeah, man. You going to have my money when the job is complete, right?"

Bread: "Right."

Billy: "Now look, I don't want no shit about my money, you hear me? 'Cause if there is some kind of problem I'm going to clown on your ass and you don't want to see me clown."

Bread: "I'm going to have your money. You just do your end. Now, you got a good man to help you on this?"

Billy: "Hell, yeah. He's a friend of mine. He call his self Corn Bread. He say when he was a baby his mama used to feed him breast milk and cornbread and right to this day the mother fucker still drink milk and eat the hell out some cornbread."

Bread Bout It: "You mean to tell me he still suckin' on his mama's titty and eatin' cornbread? How old is this Corn Bread?"

Billy: "Hell, naw. He don't suck his mama's titties no more."

Bread Bout It: "But you said he sucks his mama's titties."

Billy: "I said when he was a li'l boy. Now the mother fucker drink butter or sweet milk when eatin' cornbread. Shit, I don't know. And he's about 21 years old."

Bread: "How much is you going to pay him?"

Billy: "Now, look--you gettin' too damn nosey. You don't worry about that. You just have mine so I can pay him. Now I can't pay him until you have me 'cause my money is my money and I don't pay no mother fucker out my stash."

Milk got in touch with Ms. Bout It and told her he would like to see her and she agreed to see him. Friday morning,

Bread and his wife hump a li'l bit, both for the last time. They both got up and cleaned their self up. Bread went to get dressed. Ms. Bout It got ready and cook the family some breakfast. They all ate together for the last time. Bread kissed his wife, rubbed his kids' heads. When he finished his breakfast he told them he loved them and headed out the door to meet up with Billy Lawrence givin' him more instructions.

Jade had tight surveillance on Bread Bout It. Jade then put Raven on Billy. She wanted Raven to keep his head fucked up with feeling, so Raven step into his direction. Bread and Billy split up and so did Jade and Raven. Bread went to the bank to withdraw out the $18 million in his safe deposit box. Jade was right on him. As soon as Bread came out with the money, he beeped Jade from his cellular phone. Jade got the page and called him back from her cellular phone.

Bread: "Hello."

Jade: "Hey, Boo."

Bread: "Where you at?"

Jade: "I'm down here at the Ramada Hotel."

Bread: "I'll see you in 15 minutes."

Jade was only five cars away from him. Bread was driving down the street, going to get his Boo. Jade was right behind him watchin' her money. Bread pulled up to the front of the hotel. Jade pulled to the back. She entered in the back and came out the front, greetin' Bread with open arms. They kissed. As she entered the car, Bread asked her have she ever seen $18 million before. She said no, so he showed her. They then headed for the airport.

They arrived at the airport checking in the little luggage they had, but Bread kept his money at his side. Bread had his mind on his money and his money on his mind. They entered the airplane which is a two hour flight. They are both used to flying. Bread back and forth doing business and Jade will go cross country to break a trick. She bring so much lust to the bedroom, there's nothing that her client wouldn't do just to get next to her. This bitch is bad.

FeFe and Jewel was the flight attendants. They made their trip so comfortable it made Bread and Jade feel like they were in heaven.

FeFe: "Welcome to Delta Airlines, Mr. and Ms. Bout It. Could I get you anything to drink, or maybe some peanuts?"

Jade: "Yes, I would like..."

Bread: "Wait...wait. How did you know our names?"

FeFe: "Oh, I'm sorry. As you two entered the plane your wife said that you two were on your honeymoon and I was just here to make it all good for you. We treat our customers with pride."

Bread looked at Jade and kissed her and said that he was sorry and ordered a few drinks.

Jade: "It's okay, Boo. I got to go to the rest room."

FeFe came back with the drinks, putting a pillow behind his head and giving him that soft soft touch with a medieval look. Jewel walked back an forth with a nasty twist. Jade came back to her seat.

Jade: "Oh, I'm so excited and I just can't hide it. Have you ever had sex on a plane before?"

Bread: "No, but it sound good."

Bread's sex nature was up from just eyeing FeFe and Jewel, so him and Jade went to the rest room to have sex and right then and there Bread's mind was off his money and sex was on his mind. In the rest room it was only five minutes of funk. Jade and Bread went back to their seat laughing. They cuddled up and enjoyed the rest of the flight and an hour later they touched ground.

They got off the plane with smiles on their faces. Bread didn't want to be walkin' around in Chicago with all that money, so he got right to it. He got his locker key, put the money into the locker, locked it, put his key into his left pocket, and they walked away from the locker. Bread then turned his attention to the two flight attendants from the plane and they both had that nasty walk going on and Bread wasn't looking where he was going and--Boom!--he bumped into Jim Kelly and Big Mike.

There was a small confrontation. Bread jumped up off the floor and got eye to eye with Jim Kelly and said, "Hey buddy, watch where you're going."

Jim Kelly: "Yeah, Fool, you lookin' all over there at them ladies when you got a nice li'l lady right here. Damn, Mama, you look good. You better hold on to her 'fore someone steal her from you buddy."

Bread: "Hey, mind your business, bucko, and I'm not your buddy."

Big Mike: "But yet and still, watch where you're going, buddy." And they walked off.

Jade: "Baby, are you all right?"

Bread: "Yeah, them punks don't scare me."

Jade: "I know, that's my Boo. Now let's get to our room and have some fun."

They got to the room. Jade pulled an ounce of powder cocaine from her crevasse. She gave it to Bread and she went to the restroom to take a shower. Bread was in the room hiding the locker key.

Back in Atlanta, Raven had met up with Billy Lawrence. Billy, he was still upset with what Mona Lisa did to him, so he wanted to take it out on any fine ass woman he could get. Billy wanted some payback. Billy felt that someone gave it to him, so he wanted to give it to someone else. It's a dirty world we livin' in. Raven set up a date with Billy for Saturday night.

Friday night Ms. Bout it got to her sister's house. She stayed for a little bit, called Milk, and she left her kids with her sister. She told her sister she would see her in the morning. That night, her and Milk spent the night in a fancy hotel having some spacey love. Half of the night Milk broke her off some dick and the other half was strictly conversation about the money in the bank and when is she going to leave her husband. She told Milk first thing Monday she would go down to the bank and get out the money and as the days go by she would file for a divorce. Milk had her dick whip in the pussy and head. It was once said, but now it is written, fuck the head and the body will follow. Ms. Bout It asked Milk did he still have the key she gave him?

Milk: "Yeah, Boo, but not with me. I will have it for you tomorrow."

Ms. Bout It: "Now if you don't have the key it will be a big problem. Without my key they will ask me about my husband's key, then I will have to say he lost his key, too, and then we'll both have to be there when they open up the safe deposit box with a drill gun."

Milk: "Don't worry, Boo. I will get you the key."

Night to day. Saturday morning, Ms. Bout It went back to her sister's before the kids woke up. Her and her sister made breakfast for the kids. Her sister had two kids herself, a boy and a girl. Nile saw that happy as hell look in her sister's eyes.

Nile: "Girl, what got you all perked up this morning? You look great."

Ms. Bout It: "Girl, just think black."

✱ ✳ ✠ ✼ ✳ ✺ ✳ ☆ ★ ☆

From Chicago to Atlanta, Big Mike and Jim Kelly came

home paid in full. And the funny thing about it, Bread didn't even check his key. Jade and Bread was having a good time shopping, eating, drinking, sex and drugs. Later on that day, back in Atlanta, Billy Lawrence couldn't wait to get Raven in the sack. They kicked it all day and half of the night, having a good time. He did some of the nicest things you could do for a woman in one day that will make her happy to give up a li'l something something. But, see, Raven is a professional bitch. She stood her post. So Billy did what he always did, and that was pulling out the bank roll. Raven jumped to attention. Billy thinking to his self, "Yeah, I got this bitch." See, in this game money have a strange effect on women. Some keep it, some give it away, but the bottom line is money is the root of all evil. Raven told Billy that she hated hotels.

Billy: "No problem, baby. We're going to my house."

They partied a li'l bit, but quickly Billy came out of his clothes and was pulling on Raven's clothes.

Raven: "Show me the money."

Billy reached into his pocket and spread out $25 hundred and said, "Get naked, bitch. You on the clock now."

That's one thing that a woman can't stand is for a man to be rude when it's time to have sex. That's why most girls yell out "Rape!"--they feel cheap and disrespected.

Billy: "Come on, 'ho', let's get busy."

He jumped on top of Raven, all wild-like, trying to rip off her clothes and take the pussy. Raven fought him off and headed for the door.

Billy: "Bitch, where's my money?"

Raven turned around and walked up to Billy, spit on him, and threw his money in his face and told him, "Fuck your money!" and headed back toward the door. Billy grabbed onto Raven's arm, jerking on her. She picked up the telephone and busted Billy in the head with it. Billy fell to the floor. Raven headed out the door. Billy got up and headed for the door. There he was, standing in the door, butt ass naked, cursing and looking crazy with blood running from his head. Now Billy Lawrence's head is fucked up not only on the outside but on the inside, fo' sho'.

✱ ✻ ✛ ✽ ✳ ✺ ✴ ☆ ★ ☆

Cokeout, Locout, with a mind full of game, Milk went to Club 112 to see Precious about a key. The club was packed with big ballers. Precious was inside the club lookin' damn good. Ten and Pee Wee Loc was on the outside watchin' what goes in and what comes out. They kept their eyes on Milk. Precious was doing her thing keepin' all eyes on her. There was a lot of fine ass women in the club, but Precious had mens all over her like a tattoo. She had it like that so Milk couldn't act a fool on her about a key. Milk saw Precious surrounded by mens; now he had to find a way to step to her.

Milk got about 13 girls in the club on his dick to dance for him. He gave the DJ $100 to play two songs for him--Drop It Off Your Ass by INDO-G and Li'l Blunt and Sho Nuff by TELA. Milk then pulled out $500 to give to the winners, and what Milk was lookin' for is the best dancer, the most flyest, and the most creative style on the dance floor. All the girls got in the dancers' circle and did their thang. When the DJ played the music the club jump on crunk. Everyone wanted to see what was going on, so the circle got thicker.

Milk slipped over behind Precious and tapped her on the shoulder. Precious turned away from the crowd and saw Milk and gave him a kiss with a big hug. Precious saw that Milk's eyes was all glassy and on his face he had a devilish smile.

Precious: "Hey, Milk, what you been doing these days?"

Milk: "Just kickin' it."

Precious: "What brings you to the club?"

Milk: "Well, I ran into Jade at the mall and she said you might have a key for me."

Precious: "Ohh--I got it right here. I picked it up off the floor at your Al Capone Suite. You lookin' good."

Milk: "Thank you."

Milk put his arms around Precious and they stepped into the circle watchin' the others do dat dances. When it was over, Milk picked three winners and told the girls that they are going with him. He then went to the bar and bought drinks for everybody. Milk gave Precious a kiss and thanked her once more and he left with the three girls. The three girls belong to MJG and Sugar Wolf. Milk got busy all through the night. See, Milk was supposed to have been with Ms. Bout It for the whole weekend. Ms. Bout It wanted to be with him, too. Instead, she sat with her sister and the kids watchin' TV videos all night by the phone. Sunday morning came. Ms. Bout It got a page from Milk. She called him. He asked her, will she meet him at the City Zoo. She thought about it for a minute and said yes.

Ms. Bout It: "Where was you last night?"

Milk: "Boo, I was so high last night that it slipped my mind and when I came to myself I got right up to call you."

Ms. Bout It: "I miss you."

Milk: "I miss you too, Boo."

✽ ✻ ✣ ✽ ✳ ✳ ✳ ☆ ★ ☆

They met up at the Atlanta Zoo and viewed a few animals like the birds, lions, bears, monkeys, apes and zebras, and after that they talked about the bank. It was off to the hotel Milk had before he met up with Ms. Bout It and at the hotel they were doing the nasty and Ms. Bout It love to do the nasty with the opposite color of her skin. It was getting late after ten long hours of hard sex. Ms. Bout It had to get her kids home and play wife and get up and go to the bank to break her husband and pay her man, so she think.

Sunday night Billy Lawrence and Corn Bread was getting in position. Corn Bread was inside the house getting high, shooting up heroin in the vein and smokin' rocks at the same time. He was out of his mind. Billy was trailing Ms. Bout It from her sister's house to home. Corn Bread and Billy communicated by walkie talkie, Corn Bread singing to his self, "I got five on it," loading up his shotgun. Billy come in. Corn Bread come in. Corn Bread: "Who's this? You got five on it, too?"

Billy: "This me, Fool. She's on her way in, so get ready."

Corn Bread: "I'm ready." Corn Bread put away his drugs and cocked a shell into his shotgun and went into the garage and unscrewed the light bulb and got behind some junk in the garage.

Ms. Bout It and the kids was feeling great. They were singing happy songs. She clicked the key chain to open the garage and drove in. She cut off the car, unlocked her seatbelt and turned and said, "Wait here until Mommie checks the lights." She then got out of the car, clicked the lights and seen that they didn't work, so she clicked them two or three more times. Nothing happened, so she went to check the bulb and felt that it was unscrewed.

As soon as she screwed in the bulb, Corn Bread jumped up at her and drew down on her, scaring the hell out of her, ordering her to get into her green '96 Volvo station wagon. She got in on the driver's side and he entered the passenger side, still with the pump shotgun aimed at her. The kids was in the back seat crying, "Please don't kill our Mommie."

Corn Bread: "Shut up and set your little ass down 'for' I give you something to cry about."

Ms. Bout It cursing and crying, yelling, "Don't you curse my kids, you bastard!"

Corn Bread slapped the shit out of Ms. Bout It and told her to open up the garage door so they could get the fuck out of sight. She opened and closed the garage door. She drove away from the house. Billy Lawrence right behind them, watchin' and waitin' for Corn Bread to do his thing so they can get paid. Corn Bread's job is to drive her four miles away from the house then kill her by driving the car off a bridge. But they could only get 100 yards away from the house. The kids and Ms. Bout It and the drugs was all on Corn Bread's brain at the same time. He was getting frantic, sweat drippin' from his face, the kids cryin' in one ear and Ms. Bout It yellin' in the other.

Corn Bread: "If y'all don't shut the fuck up right now I'm going to kill your ass right here and I mean it, Gott damn it!"

Ms. Bout It crying to Corn Bread, "What do you want from us?"

Corn Bread: "Bitch! I want your life! And if these li'l fuckers don't shut up I'm going to kill them, too."

Ms. Bout It slapped Corn Bread and said, "I told you don't curse my kids."

Corn Bread just went wild and started slapping the shit out of Ms. Bout It non-stop. One of the kids jumped up and grabbed Corn Bread by the face and scratched blood from his face. Corn Bread shook the kid off him and hit him in the face with the butt of the shotgun. Ms Bout It turned toward her kids and that's when the pump shotgun went off and blew Ms. Bout It's head clean off her body. Blood covered everyone in the car. The kids got down and curled up under each other, silent. The sat covered in blood. Billy Lawrence pulled on the side of the station wagon and blew the horn. Corn Bread got out of the station wagon covered in blood and hopped into the car with Billy and they drove off. The kids sat on the side of the road all night until day-break. When morning came they was found by a passing motorist.

Billy Lawrence was taking Corn Bread back to College Park in the dope trap.

Billy: "You okay?"

Corn Bread: "Yeah, I'm cool."

Billy: "Did you kill the kids?"

Corn Bread: "Hell, naw, Nigga. Corn Bread don't kill kids. That shit is for busters who tryin' to prove a point. Corn Bread ain't got to prove shit to nobody!"

Billy: "I was just askin'. Damn."

Corn Bread: "Don't ask me no shit like that. Corn Bread real. So can I get paid?"

Billy: "Yeah, you'll get your money. You did good. Just calm down."

Corn Bread: "Calm down, my ass. If I don't get my money I know something."

Billy: "What you know, Nigga?"

Corn Bread: "Don't play with me, man."

Billy: "Don't worry, I got you."

Corn Bread: "Yeah, right, well let me have $20."

Billy: "I ain't got it right now."

Corn Bread got out of the car sayin' to Billy as he was pullin' off, "Cheap mother fucker." Corn Bread pulled out his straight shooter to get him a blast. He took a hit and noticed that the trap was dead. There was no one in sight; it was like a ghost town. It was because the cops had been through there and made a few arrests. So Corn Bread was just walkin' down the street, smokin' on a rock on his way home. Then a car pulls up wanting to buy some crack. A clean cut white male. "Hey, hey, buddy."

Corn Bread turned around and leaned into the car.

Corn Bread: "Yeah, what's up, buddy?"

White Male: "You know where I can score?"

Corn Bread: "Score some what, Honkey?"

White Male: "Some crack, buddy, rock. Come on, I got money."

Corn Bread all geek up.

Corn Bread: "How much money?"

White Male: "I got $100 right here and I want to get five twentys."

Corn Bread reached into his pocket and gave the white male five dimes for twentys.

White Male: "Hey, how do I know if this here is real? I been shitted on this street thousands of times."

Corn Bread got into the car and pulled out his straight shooter once again and took one of the white male's rocks, busted it open, and put the whole rock on his straight shooter and got a free blast. He passed the shooter to the white male. He took a hit and blew that shit out. Corn Bread got out of the car and the white man asked, "Hey, buddy, what's your name? So if I come back I could just ask for you."

Corn Bread: "I'm Corn Bread. I be out here all the time. But hey buddy, since I help you, can you help me?"

White Male: "Sure, buddy. What is it?"

Corn Bread: "Let me have $20."

White Male: "I ain't got it right now." And the white male drove off around the corner and called it in. The white male is an undercover blue jean cop.

The cop noticed the car had a foul smell to it. He cut his inside car lights on and saw blood all over his seats. See, the cops will bust a trap or raid a drug house and then they will leave and send an undercover cop back to see if there is anyone back out there dealin'. When the cop saw the blood he drove back to the trap to find Corn Bread, but he was gone. The cop left but he stayed suspicious about Corn Bread.

✳ ✳ ✤ ✼ ✳ ✳ ✳ ☆ ✭ ☆

When morning came, the kids was found in the car shaking and covered in blood. It was all on the news. Some figured it was foul play, but to make it look good Bread Bout It was out of town, nowhere near the murder. Jade and Bread was getting ready to go back to the airport to get the money and then head for the bank and shoot back home to play off the upcoming situation in Atlanta. They knew back in Atlanta they would have to separate to avoid anything that would make it seem as if he had anything to do with his wife's murder. Bread got the key from his secret little hiding place while Jade wasn't looking.

They checked out of the hotel and headed to the airport. Bread told Jade to check in the luggage while he go and get the money. Bread went to go get the money from the locker. On his way there he ran into FeFe and Jewel. They both gave him a big hug and asked him about his stay in Chicago.

Bread: "Ohh, it was great, and I'm looking to come back."

FeFe: "I hope I see you again also."

Bread: "Well, if you really mean it, here is my card. I'm a lawyer. Call me if you need me."

FeFe kissed him on the cheek and said, "I will, big boy." Right then and there Bread's mind was off his money until he saw Jade coming his way. FeFe and Jewel shied off when they saw that Jade was coming. Before leaving, FeFe winked her eye at Bread and slipped a number into Bread's top suit pocket. Jade came over.

Jade: "What are you doing?"

Bread: "Who, me?"

Jade: "Yeah, you. We got business. Have you forgotten that? Where is the money?"

262   HYPNOTIZING GAME

Bread: "Oh, yeah--the money. It's in the locker, Boo. Let's go together and get it."

They walked to the locker. Bread reached into his left pocket where he put the key. It wasn't there.

Jade: "What's wrong?"

Bread: "Nothing."

He then reached into his right pocket and there it was. Bread opened up the locker, grabbed the black bag, opened it and saw that the money was gone but the bag was filled with Holy Bibles. Bread fell to the floor saying, "Oohh, my God."

Jade: "Boo, is everything all right?"

The bag fell loose from Bread's hands. Jade picked up the bag and got down on the floor with Bread to help him up. They slowly walked to their concourse where they sat feeling doleful.

Jade: "Boo, who could have did this to us?"

Bread just sat in silence with his head down until it was time for their flight. Jade saw that Bread had no words, so she just sat in silence with him. They almost missed their plane, but they made it on the plane. Bread talking to Jade in a low voice.

Bread: "Boo, Boo."

Jade: "What, Boo?"

Bread: "You think those guys who bumped me could have switched keys with me?"

Jade: "But, Boo, if they switched keys with you how did you open up the locker? Now, don't tell me they got the money out then broke into our room and switched keys back. You want to know what--I think it was those flight attendants."

Bread: "Naw, Boo, that's where you're wrong."

Jade: "No, no. Look, Boo, you remember on the flight

where we left our seat to go do the nasty? Those flight attendants could have switched bags. You know, we didn't check the bag before puttin' it into the locker."

Bread: "But if they did that, why would they still be workin' and coming around for? Not just to see us go back home, I know."

Jade: "Look, I know how a bitch work. They just were playin' it off and they probably switched keys with you back at the airport for the second time.

Bread: "Naw, Boo. I had the key in my left pocket at all times."

Jade: "But, Boo, the key was in your right pocket, you remember?"

Bread: "I guess I don't know, Boo. Help me, please. I'm so confused."

Jade: "I will help you and we're going to get your money back."

Bread: "You sure?"

Jade: "I'm positive. Just watch--things are going to get better."

But Jade was wrong. Things got worse. They arrived at the Atlanta airport and that's when they both split up. Jade got off the plane two passengers behind Bread Bout It. But when Bread got off the plane, he rushed by news cameras and reporters askin' him questions about his wife's murder. He was already hurt from the money that was stolen from him, so when he heard the news his face was set for saddest already. They were all over him, left and right. A Detective Ren Shockley came out of the crowd tellin' Bread that he was not arrested but they would like to ask him a few questions about his wife's murder.

Bread: "Are my kids okay?"

Detective Ren Shockley: "Yes, your kids are fine. They're

with their grandparents. You know, I think they seen the killer's face. They're not talking right now. Come, let's get down to headquarters."

They got down to headquarters and put Bread in the room with one light, one chair, and five detectives who were workin' on the case. They were coming from all angles, putting pressure on him, but Bread didn't break. He came out of the room with flying colors. They had nothing on him.

When Bread came out of the room, there was Ms. Bout It's parents with the kids. Right then the kids jumped from their grandparents arms and into their father's arms. He gave them both a great big hug and a kiss. They all shed tears. They let Bread Bout It leave, but it wasn't over. Detective Ren Shockley, he always gets his man, no matter what.

Meanwhile, the Corporation all got together and chopped up the $18 million. Each team got their money and put it in their own little stash spot. Chicago took Eazy's share and put it up until she see him. Hezzy got Baller's share and did the same, while all the time Baller was in jail he was plannin' his escape.

Baller had it all figured out. He called up his under-ground unseen clique, Dee Dee and Flamingo that morning. At Atlanta-Fulton County State Prison it was breakfast time. Baller sat at the table and didn't eat a thing. He traded his food for two cigarettes. He then took the plastic sandwich bag that came around the sandwich and poured his warm cup of coffee into the bag. See, you can't smoke in Georgia prison, but if you got some guards on your side, anything is possible. Baller got back to his room and took the cup that holds his toothbrush. He washed out the cup, then took the coffee that was tied in the sandwich bag and put the bag over into the sink and ran warm water over the bag to pre-warm the coffee. Once the coffee warmed up, he poured it into the cup and lit a cigarette. From every puff he took on the cigarette, he dipped the ashes into the coffee. After smoking the first cigarette, he lit up the other one and did the same thing. And after the cigarette he drank the coffee and that shit had him throwin' up and lookin' sick and he came down with a small fever. He called for the guards. The guards came down and saw the mess in the jail cell. They checked him out, so they called up the hospital, askin' them to send over an ambulance. "We got a sick one." And in a minute the ambulance arrived at the state prison. Out jumped two paramedics to come handle the matter. Two went in and five came out.

Baller, the two paramedics, and two prison guards leaving the state prison and heading to Piedmont Hospital, where he was sent to Dr. Fox, the same doctor who patched up Milk. See, Crow turned Balled on to Dr. Fox, and Baller turned Chicago on to Dr. Fox also, in case of a family emergency. The paramedic rushed Baller to Room 4-E on the fifth floor. The paramedic put Baller on the operating table and left the room and the two prison guards guarded the door. And, wouldn't you know it, down the hallway, dressed up like a doctor, holding a black doctor's bag, walks Flamingo. The guards stop him at the door.

Flamingo: "I have to give the doctor his tools."

The Guards: Okay, you're straight. Go on in."

Flamingo gave Dr. Fox the black bag which had in it $60G and a change of clothes for Baller. Flamingo then gave Baller some love, a big ass hug and a kiss on both cheeks.

Flamingo: "Damn, it's good to see you, Nigga. Lookin' good, boy. Look at you, done growed some muscles and shit."

Baller: "Yeah, yeah, you lookin' good, too, folks. But, yo, Dr. Fox, this is Flamingo. Flamingo, this is Dr. Fox."

They both spoke.

Baller: "Now, Flamingo, this man can help you out on a face off or patchin' up gunshot wounds, and he got a asylum if you want to lay low for about five or six years from the law or from whatever."

Flamingo: "Okay, that is good to know man. The streets have been fucked up without you being on the street. For the last few weeks it just been cop land because of that funky ass Olympic that's coming, you dig?"

Baller: "Yeah, I know, we just got to get around that shit. They're going to be worried about the folks that's coming to town, so the cops are going to have their hands full. And guess what--the streets belong to us."

Dr. Fox: "That's right."

Flamingo: "Ha, ha, man, this is a cool ass doctor. But yo, I got to go get in position."

Baller: "Okay."

Flamingo: "Yo, it's going to be on at Club Nikki tonight. See you there."

Baller: "Bet. Yo--and give me four minutes before you do your thing."

As Flamingo was walkin' out the door, he said, "Bet." Flamingo left the room and went down to the first floor and was waiting four minutes before pulling the fire alarm. Baller was changing his clothes.

Dr. Fox: "Hey, what's the extra $10G for?"

Baller: "Ohh. See, okay, $10G go to each of the guards and the same goes for the paramedic. But you see, the family got bodies to stack we don't want to half kill 'em, we want to kill 'em. So if our enemy come in this hospital half dead I want you to add the finishing touch. For every body we send in half dead there's a $10G spot for you."

Dr. Fox: "So why the ten spot now? You're good for it later."

Baller: "Yeah, I just feel like soon as I hit the street it going to be some shit like murdering a fool over some stupid shit."

By that time, Flamingo hit the alarm. Baller asking the doctor do everyone have their story straight?

Dr.: "Yes."

Baller: "How about the guards?"

Dr.: "They're going to be just fine, and the paramedic, too. Now, go. Go and be safe."

Baller walked straight out the door, past the guards. In the hallway, people are yelling and running through the hospital trying to escape as if there were a fire. Baller took the stairs. Baller got down to the first floor and walked right out the front door. And guess who was parked out front in her '96 candy red convertible Mustang with her top up and her window tinted but rolled down. Yes, Dee Dee.

Baller walked to the driver's side where she was sitting. He gave her a kiss and she moved over to the passenger seat and Baller got in the car and rolled up the window. And they drove off.

The escape was on the news, but the news didn't make a big deal of it because of the Olympic Games was only a few weeks away. Now, over the last four years there's been over 52 jail breaks. Now believe me, the state do care about convicts running loose in the city. It's just right now they're trying to keep things on the hush hush. But what was said on the news was that an inmate shook loose from a guard when he was brought in from prison from having a high fever. While being transported to his room, someone accidentally pulled the fire alarm and then the inmate hit both guards over the head and dipped through the crowded hallway.

Baller: "So what's been up, Li'l Mama?"

Dee Dee: "Waitin' on you. "

She then pop the dash and pull out $85G in cash. She put the money in between her legs and started coming out of her clothes. Now, it's been four years, 349 days, two hours and twenty minutes since they first met and Baller still haven't laid a hand on her and she brought in over $1.2 million in cash. She was sweet sixteen when Baller first started schooling her about the game and today was her birthday. Now she 20 years old. Baller had this day planned very well. Some niggas break out of jail and then want some pussy then they think about going out and getting that money, but not Baller. Baller grabbed the money from in between Dee Dee's legs and sat it on the floor in front of him. Dee Dee was butt ass naked in the car. Baller played with her breast and pussy. Dee Dee then pushed a few buttons on her CD changer, playing a song which was "Mahogany" by Eric B & Rakin off "Let the Rhythm" CD. She started rubbing on his chest and unzipping his pants. Baller was getting hot. Dee Dee went down on Baller, givin' him head while he was drivin' to check his crack house down in Smoka Holler where his crew was.

Baller drove past the 'hood and took Dee Dee up to the Lakewood train station. They pulled into the station, got into the back seat, and that's when Baller got in dat ass. He was hittin' dat pussy until she said she had enough. Baller just sticking that pussy. He shot about four good long nuts in that pussy and Dee Dee got some good tight pussy, but when Baller was hittin' that pussy it stayed slightly loose and wet. For Dee Dee to be so young she sure knows how to throw that pussy. Baller knew if he hadn't fucked her brain first he would have been in trouble, but he's a soldier boy so he know how the game goes.

But after all that bumpin' and grindin' it was time to talk about bank. She was still tryin' to tell him about the bank job from way back. She blew the bank plan into Baller. He inhale it and hold it and now it was time to blow it out to his crew. They drove down to Baller's crack house. Baller was like, "Damn!" because the trap was rollin' and he didn't see his crew out there getting that cheddar. Baller kiss Dee Dee on the cheek, got out the car. Dee Dee pulled off. Cuddie and his crew was throwing up their hands yelling, "What's up, Nigga?! Glad you can make it home, Nigga!"

Baller spoke back, but he was like, "Damn! What the fuck have Hezzy done to this 'hood?" He walk up the driveway still in shock, step on the porch, knock on the door.

Ten & Pete was sitting in the living room drinking and smoking on blunts, talkin' about a plan to infiltrate the Killahoe Posse.

Knock, knock, knock.

Ten got up to answer the door.

Ten: "Who is it?"

Baller: "It's me, Baller."

Ten opened the door.

Ten: "Oh, shi-ittttt!"

Pete: "What dat?"

Ten: "Yo--guess who back!"

Pete jumped to see who was at the door. Ten unlocked the bar door to let Baller in . Baller step in. Pete and Ten rush hm with a big ass hug. Their spirits lifted when they saw Baller.

Pete: "Man, I can't believe my ninja home!"

Ten: "Man, how did you do it?"

Baller: "Patience, my Ninja, patience. Yo, the 'hood is rollin' and that nigga Cuddie them out there doing it. They spoke to a nigga, too. What the hell have Hezzy done to make them niggas switch up like that?"

Pete: "The game, man, the game."

Baller: "Where that ninja Hezzy at, anyway?"

Ten: "Come on. He upstairs messing with his dreams."

Baller: "You mean he got his stereo equipment?"

Ten: "Hell, yeah, and he know how to work that shit, too."

Baller: "Oh yeah?"

Pete: "Come on. Let's go fuck with him."

On the way upstairs, Baller: "So what you ninjas been doing?"

Ten: "Shit, me and Pete been out to Jazzy Bell's place planning out the lick on the Killahoe's. We going to set them niggas up. If our adversaries fall for it, man, it's going to be beautiful."

They got upstairs and couldn't see because of the thick clouds of weed smoke. All they heard was music, but as they got closer, Baller could see two bodies with their faces turned toward the stereo equipment. Hezzy was puffin' on a blunt. They were listenin' to Casino and Joker Too, member's in Cuddie's clique. Hezzy felt that they had talent to be a big rap star. They made a underground cut called "Make Some Noise".

Baller called out Hezzy's name but he couldn't hear because of the earphone, but the guy next to him didn't have on earphones. He turned around and was like, "Damn! My ninja!" and Baller looked and saw that they other guy was Eazy. They both gave each other a big ass hug, both with tears in their eyes. Pete and Ten smilin', sayin', "Yeah, we stick together."

Hezzy was deep into the music with his back turned, not knowing what's going on behind him. For a minute Baller and Eazy just stood in front of each other, talking about

"Damn, it just feel good to be at home all together." And they both know that Hezzy have been putting in work. He switch the 'hood around and had Eazy in a safe place to kick it and even made it where the clique is makin' money when it just look like they're just chilling. This family got plans for all those that go against code. Baller sat in the seat next to Hezzy. Hezzy just jamming, smokin' on a blunt. He turned to pass the blunt and saw that it was Baller. He snatched the headset from his ears and jump up out his seat and look around and saw everyone smiling, saying, "Yeah, Nigga! Yeah, Nigga! Yeah, Nigga! We together once again! Hezzy shit yeah!" Baller and Hezzy laugh, cry, hug--there was nothing but love floating through the room. They all walked back downstairs into the living room, smokin' big dank, drinkin' on cognac, and talkin' about big bank.

Baller: "Yo, y'all ninjas didn't see that shit on the news?"

Ten: "Naw, but we saw Jade on the news."

Hezzy: "Yeah, she was right behind that lawyer cat, she put work on that fool this past week."

Baller: "Oh, yeah--what was the score?"

Eazy: "A fat $18 million."

Baller: "Damn!"

Hezzy: "We all chop it up yesterday."

See, the Corporation work like this--if one crew hit a nice lick or just a lick, all five of the captains get together to chop up the cash. The captains then take the flow to their crew and chop it up between them. If the captain is not present, then the lieutenant make the pick up. And if he can't make it, that's when one of the soldiers come and handle business.

Pete: "Yo, Diamond's clique be-bout that big bank."

Eazy: "Shi-ittt! Nigga, we all do."

Baller: "Yeah, I know."

Ten: "But look, you gots to look how long them 'ho's stay down for the lick. The longer they wait, the bigger the pay."

Eazy: "Now y'all niggas can't forget about my crew. On them fight parties we bring in 2...4...5...6 million a party. And it's going to be more this upcoming fight with Iron Mike Tyson vs The Real Deal Holyfield. Man, she got so many licks she might have to use the whole Corporation on this one. She's going to have bitches boxin' at the party just like in Nikki. Oh, yeah--and that Mona Lisa got married to that fool Fidel Cartel and that fool had his wife killed, too, and Mona Lisa is sitting on a gold mine, but she going to break the bank when it time to make that move."

Baller leaned back in his chair, laughing, talking about "Damn, Chicago is going to have some 'ho's boxing at the party."

Eazy: "Hell, yeah--and the winner is getting $5 thousand."

Baller: "What?! Five thousand?! You mean to tell me she's going to let some bitch come in and win the price it cost to get into the party back?"

Eazy: "Hell, naw, because Sky is going to be there knocking 'ho's out. We rackin' up on fight night big time, you understand me? No mercy, baby."

Baller: "So what's up with Sky's clique?"

Pete: "Shi-ittt. Me and Ten was kickin' it with Greed and them niggas raking in some paper. They got that pimp shit down. Sugar Wolf & MJG brings in the 'ho's, schooling them how to sell dope & pussy then turn them 'ho's over to Sky. She give them bitches that lady-like skill. She run the stable. She got a big ass house keeping 96 'ho's in line and all them 'ho's bring in bank. Greed set the niggas up in the club. You know how niggas be wantin' to date them 'ho's. Look here, none of them 'ho's date for free. Maybe for a fee, 8 to 10 gees a date, and you know how niggas like to flex at the club. MJG & Sugar Wolf done hit up over 461 niggas in just four years. Them niggas be havin' cocaine in the back of the ride, 4 and 5 keys in the trunk with about $100G. Greed say at the club all the bitches & niggas call sky 'Queen Bitch, Lady of Power'. All them bitches in the club roll blow for her right now in the club except for that 'ho' Dove from the jury.

"She's doing something for that nigga Oz Escobar and that nigga got them two fools who be ridin' with him."

Baller: "Yeah, I know their face, but what's them niggas names? Ten, you was outside by the car that day them niggas came over. What's their names?"

Ten: "Oh--Cotton and Blood."

Baller: "Yeah. Damn sho' is, now. What were you saying, Pete?"

Pete: "Dat nigga Greed said them niggas shot up the club about a month ago over some silly shit."

Baller: "Yeah, yeah. Them niggas act just like Tray & Deuce. So what's up with the biggest mama clique?"

Pete: "Who--Jazzy Bell?"

Baller: "Yeah."

Pete: "Shi-itt, you ain't know. Getting paid. Okay, now you know. Big Mike & Jim Kelly was down with that $18 million lick last week."

Baller: "Naw, I didn't know that."

Pete: "Well, if you be cool, I'm gonna tell you. Now they got the money, but with the help of me & Hezzy's li'l faithful lambs Jewel & FeFe. But check this out. Jazzy Bell's clique rolls all the dope each crew brings in, but her crew get one percent on each dollar. Like if our crew brings in one or two keys from a lick and the family split it out, it's still like that. It just that her crew get paid that one percent for rollin' it. And guess what--them six tons is just about gone."

Baller: "Say what?!!"

Hezzy: "It's true, my ninja, and ain't nobody complaining. The family money is on stack. But see, that four percent we put into that 4444 plan Milk still owes us."

Baller: "Damn right. Have he said anything about it?"

Pete: "Well, Jade talk with him and she said he was depending on this white chick."

Baller: "White chick?"

Pete: "Yeah, but she's dead now. She was the wife of the white dude with the $18 million."

Hezzy: "So how dat sound, man?"

Baller: "Damn, it sound good, man. It seem like I been gone for so long and y'all done so much in li'l time. I'm impressed. But, Hezzy, what in the hell you do to Cuddie and his crew?"

Hezzy: "Well, I talk with him, telling him there's money out here to make. Ain't no sense in us beefin' when we're on the same street, doin' the same thing. I showed him what I had and told him I can keep him on, I gave him a good price he couldn't refuse. I gave him my word that no more beef between us and he gave me his word and you know my balls is my word. See, when you put a nigga like that on and getting him to make big money he would bend over backward for you and if you keep him makin' money he would kill for you. Now, you show me a nigga that wouldn't kill for his investment. I'm his investment; we're his crew's investment. These niggas don't know Milk and Milk don't know them. Milk is looking for his dope in all the wrong places because if he rolled through here with that shit, what we gonna do?"

Ten: "Rat-tat-tat-tat."

Hezzy: "Damn right."

Baller: "Damn, look like the Corporation don't need me no more."

Eazy put his arms around Baller and said, "Come on, bruh, you know we need you. You see, we haven't killed Milk yet and that's the main hit. And after we do him, we can retire with stars and stripes sitting out on a beach for about four years."

Hezzy and the boys telling Baller, "Yeah, we need you, bruh, so you still down with us?"

Baller got up and put his arms around his crew with a smile on his face and said, "And you know this man."

Baller: "But, yo, I need something to wear in the club tonight. My slick potna Flamingo said it's going to be on at Club Nikki tonight."

Pete: "Baller, you know me and Hezzy stay in them malls. We got much fly gear upstairs."

Baller: "Okay, I'll do that. Let's all of us kick it at the club tonight."

Eazy: "Sho' 'nuff."

Baller: "Sho' 'nuff."

Then there was a knock at the door. Ten got up and walked to the door.

Ten: "Who is it?"

Oz Escobar: "Oz Escobar."

Ten turned to the boys and said, "It's that nigga Oz from the Jury."

Baller: "Yo, let him in."

Ten: "Yo, but Eazy."

Eazy: "Let him in."

Ten opened the door. Oz Escobar fell in the house, suckin' on a fat ass Cuban cigar like a titty, holding a black leather brief case.

Oz Escobar: "What's up, fellows? You know what I'm here for, so show me some love."

Baller: "Naw, we don't know what you're here for. Tell

me."

Oz: "Baller, I love your show. I seen it on the news today. That's why I came over. To see if you had some work cocaine yeyo."

Baller: "What make you think I got some coke?"

Oz: "'Cause you the man and all these other fools out on the street got that blow up dope. I ain't with that shit--I need the truth, the real, and you know real niggas go to real niggas to get real shit. It might as well be the drought season for me if I have to mess with that blow up come back shit."

Oz looked over at Eazy and said, "Why you lookin' at me like that, Fly-guy?"

Eazy: "Fuck you, nigga," and Eazy leaned back in his chair still eyeing Oz Escobar down.

Oz: "Yo, Baller, what's up with your boy? What you with Luchi or Drama huh Duke?"

Eazy then step to Oz and got face to face with him, pointing two fingers to his heart telling Oz Escobar, "This here is straight drama, little ol' asp. Oz step back two feet.

Oz: "Yo, look, Player. I came here by myself to do business because I trust you cats."

Baller: "You know in this game you trust no one. My man Eazy just don't like nobody coming on his turf acting all hostile."

Oz: "Hostile?"

Baller: "Yeah, hostile, man. Last time you came in here you was all cool and shit. That's why we let you in. But now you actin' like we did something wrong to you. Look, drama don't make duckets."

Hezzy went in the back room and came back out. Oz got a li'l nervous. Hezzy handed Oz a pound of weed.

Hezzy: "Here you go my li'l Africa asp."

Oz Escobar didn't know what the word meant, but he

accepted the pounds of weed. Because it was all they said they had. He was like, "Give me four more pounds. I need some good grass any old way. Yo, how much a pound?"

Pete: "A gee apiece."

Oz: "Bet. Let's get it over with."

Hezzy went in the back and came back out with the four pounds.

Oz: "You mean to tell me you players don't know anyone with blow? Here you go--five gees. Yo, I need a bag to put this shit in."

Baller took the bag with the $85G in it and poured the money out on the living room table, handed the bag to Hezzy, and Hezzy handed Baller the five gees then gave Oz the bag to put the five pounds of weed in.

Hezzy: "Hey, I might can help you, asp. Let me call my friend Jazzy Bell. She always know who got it and who don't."

Hezzy got on the phone to give Jazzy Bell a call.

Ring...ring...ring.

Jazzy Bell: "Hello."

Hezzy: "What up, big mama? Oh, what's up the biggest, ha ha."

Jazzy Bell: "What's up, baby boy?"

Hezzy: "Yo, you got something?"

Jazzy Bell: "Yeah, what's up?"

Hezzy: "You don't, but you know who got it 'cause I got a buddy of mine over here who wants to buy. How many keys you want, buddy?"

Oz: "About twenty."

Hezzy: "He want about twenty of them thangs."

Jazzy Bell: "Do I know him?"

Hezzy: "Naw, you don't know him, I don't think. His name is Oz Escobar. He cool."

Jazzy Bell: "Let me talk to him, Hezzy."

Hezzy: "Yo, asp, she want to talk to you."

Oz got on the phone.

Oz: "Hello."

Jazzy Bell: "Hey, Oz."

Oz: "Hey."

Jazzy Bell: "Now you want twenty, right?"

Oz: "Right."

Jazzy Bell: "Now, I can get you one today, but tomorrow I can get you nineteen more from a friend I know just down the street if that's cool with you."

Oz: "Yo. It sound lovely."

Jazzy Bell: "I'm located out in Decatur, Georgia. Now tell Hezzy to give you the address. Now, I sell my keys for $22,500 and the man down the street sell for $25G. That's cool with you, Boo?"

Oz: "I can swing it."

Oz hung up the phone. Hezzy gave him the address and things.

Oz: "Hey, I thank you, player, for that."

Baller: "You stay cool. Sorry about the misunderstanding."

As Oz Escobar was walking out the door he had a smirk on his face like Bobo Sausage Head. Oz got in his ride and dip out to Jazzy Bell's crib.

Baller: "Man, y'all niggas know what y'all just did?"

Pete: "Yeah."

Baller: "He's going to go back and tell that nigga Milk that Jazzy Bell got blow and he's going to know that we hit him up."

Pete: "That's the general idea. See, if Milk do think that, that mean the Jury is his first crew in New York and his second here. And far as him thinking that Jazzy Bell got dope,

Fuck him! After that nigga killed Brown Sugar and after that nigga disrespect our brother Eazy, naw--Fuck that nigga! Fuck that nigga!!"

Eazy: "It's war time, Baller baby, this is our move."

Ten: "See, it's like this, Baller. Oz Escobar is just going to tell Milk that he just purchased one key from Jazzy Bell and he knows we can get our hands on one key he ain't going to sweat dat, but what he is going to sweat is that the Killahoe Posse is selling 19 with no problem. They jack, brag and talk down on the next player name. See them stupid ass niggas Baby Face, Dillinger, Jesse James, and Billy Bad Ass broke into Jazzy Bell's crib and took $60G of counterfeit money and 19 synthetic fake ass keys. She was settin' them niggas up and right to this day them niggas still sittin' on all that shit. Them fake keys going to Oz Escobar and he going to be mad and, knowin' Dillinger and his boys, they're going to try to pay Oz back with the counterfeit money and Oz Escobar, he going to be mad.:

Baller: "Oh, that is beautiful. Killing two birds with one stone."

Pete: "Oh, but it better..."

Click, click...Boom! Boom! Click, click...Boom! Boom! Boom!

Baller and the boys got down on the floor. Ten ran to the back to grab them thangs. Someone was bustin' at the house.

Rat-tat-tat-tat Boom! Boom! Boom! Click, click...Rat-tat-tat-tat-tat-tat-tat-tat. Click, click...Boom! Boom!I

Ten passed the boys them thangs and they headed out the door. There was a car burning rubber, fish tailing down the street and Cuddie and his boys was bustin' shots at the car. Baller and the boys went bustin' shots at the car also. Somehow the car made it out the 'hood, but the car was riddled with bullet holes.

Hezzy: "Damn, my nigga!"

Baller's crew and Cuddie's crew was in the street together, all holdin' their gats in their hand, workin' together. Last time that happened they were bustin' at each other.

Hezzy: "Damn, my nigga! Y'all's bullets flyin' all over at our house."

Cuddie: "No, them niggas was bustin' at y'all's house. We saw that and we retaliated on them busters. We ain't having no nigga coming down here with that disrespect. When they shoot at y'all they shootin' at us."

Hezzy: "Yo, how did them niggas look, my nigga?"

Cuddie: "Okay, one of them niggas had a small curl 'fro and one had braids in his hair with a raccoon hat on like Daniel Boone and one had a low cut fade and one of the niggas had on a black beanie with a white logo on it saying the click. I know 'cause I try to knock his head off his body. It was four of them niggas."

Hezzy looked at Baller and said, "Cotton, Blood, and Tray and Deuce."

Baller: "Hell, yeah. Yo, Cuddie, you did good, man. Yo, y'all niggas get ready. I'm leavin' you niggas with a key later on. It going to be on consignment. Can you niggas handle dat?"

Cuddie: "Yeah, for how much?"

Baller: "For you, 17.5."

Cuddie: "17.5--shit yeah!"

Baller: "But I need you to do one little thing for me."

Cuddie: "What's dat?"

Baller: "Clean up this broken glass out the street."

Cuddie: "Bet. Yo, Joker, where dat nigga Dope Fiend Leroy?"

Joker: "He down in that car getting his blast on."

Cuddie: "How you know?"

Joker: "'Cause I just had sold dat fool a rock."

Casino: "Yo--Five-0."

Everybody dip back into the house. Someone from up the street or down the street heard the gunshots and called the cops. They just rolled up and didn't see nobody and they rolled back down and didn't see anyone. It's like this in every 'hood. When the cops come a drug dealer get the hell on. But the geek monsters, the fiends, they don't give a fuck. When the cops rolled back down the street, they saw Dope Fiend Leroy hitting on his straight shooter. They stopped to see what the fuck was going on.

Cop: "Hey, you--get out of the car with your hands up!"

Fiend: "I ain't got nothing, Mr. Officer."

Cop: "Who was shooting? We got a call that shots was fired."

Fiend: "Man, them was firecrackers. If it would have been gunshots I would have been shootin' too, 'cause I'm the mayor down here."

Cop: "So you mean to tell me you got a gun on you?"

Fiend: "Got it right here."

Dope Fiend pulled out his shooter. The cops drawed down on him as he reached for his straight shooter.

Fiend: "Gott Damn, it ain't loaded. I just hit it."

He held his straight shooter up to the cops. The cops looked at each other and took Dope Fiend Leroy's shooter and broke it by throwing it to the ground, breaking it all to pieces, and the cops got in their squad car and left. Dope Fiend Leroy walk up the street and everybody wanted to know what the cops was talking about. Cuddie then gave Dope Fiend Leroy a boulder for his shoulder.

When Baller's crew entered the house, Ten put the guns up then Baller was like, "Hezzy, you were right there. That was a smart move to put the Powder Rangers on our team.

Yo, they still fuckin' with that raw?"

Hezzy: "Yeah, a little bit, but not as much as they used to. See, I told them if we come together we can make a lot of money. Even now we're going to make more. Shi-ittt, they like it; I love it."

Eazy: "That's damn sho' was a good move, Hezzy."

Pete: "Yeah, man, you used your head then, baby boy."

Ten: "My ninja always use his head." Coming from the back room from putting the guns up.

The phone started to ring. Ring...ring... Hezzy picked up the phone.

Hezzy: "Hello."

Flamingo: "Hello. Let me talk with Baller, baby boy."

Hezzy: "What's up, Flamingo?"

Flamingo: "You, Player."

Hezzy: "Yo, Baller, phone."

Baller picked up the phone.

Baller: "What's up?"

Flamingo: "Yo, I heard all that shooting around there and then I seen a car pass here riding fast with holes in it."

Baller: "Yeah, just some fools tripping. Yo, it's still on at the club tonight, right?"

Flamingo: "Oh yeah. That's why I called. What time you coming to pick a nigga up?"

Baller: "Give me three hours."

Flamingo: "What time is it now?"

Baller: "It's about 6:41 p.m. Yo, we fallin' in the club with the crew tonight. That's cool."

Flamingo: "Damn right. I'll be ready. Later."

Baller: "Later." And Baller hung up the phone. As soon as Baller hung up the phone it rang again. Baller picked it right back up.

Baller: "What's up?"

Jazzy Bell: "Hello, who is this? Baller?"

Baller: "Yeah."

Jazzy Bell: "I just called to say Oz Escobar came by."

Baller: "You all right?"

Jazzy Bell: "Oh yeah. We did business and I turned him on to Dillinger. They set up a date for tomorrow."

Baller: "Yeah, that slick little asp's boys just paid us a visit."

Jazzy Bell: "Y'all okay?"

Baller: "Yeah, we fine. So y'all just be on the lookout."

Jazzy Bell: "Oh, I got all my brothers with me. I could just feel that snake vibe coming off him. We ready if anything jump off and it's good to hear from you. I knew you was coming home. Prison ain't no place for a black man."

Baller: "Yeah, I know. You take it easy, Jazzy, and it was good to hear from you, too."

Jazzy Bell: "Oh, Baller, tell Ten & Pete I will see them tomorrow."

Baller: "Sure thing." And they hung up the phone.

Ten: "Who was that?"

Baller: "Jazzy Bell. She told me to tell you she will see you tomorrow.. And she also said our little Africa asp adversary is going to bite his own apple tomorrow."

Hezzy: "Ha! That nigga must think he's dealin' with a Eve. He just don't know how Jazzy Bell was the most crucial female in the Holy Bible."

Pete: "Sho' 'nuff?"

Hezzy: "Sho' 'nuff. It's in the Bible."

Eazy: "Yo. Let's start getting ready to get our club on.

They all agreed and went upstairs to get fly.

9:30 Tuesday night. All the ninjas got cleaned up and was looking fly, all ready to get their club on

Eazy: "Yo, Baller, what we ridin' in?"

Baller: "Shi-itt, let's all ride in the van."

Hezzy: "Hell, yeah."

Pete: "Oh, shit. We're going to fall in that mother fucker like the mob."

Eazy: "Sho' yo right and Hezzy, bring those mix tapes you put the hook up on," as they were getting ready to leave.

Baller: "Hezzy, how much dope we got in the back?"

Hezzy: "About a half of a ton broke down in keys."

Baller: "Go get me one so I can leave it with Cuddie."

Hezzy: "Yeah."

Baller: "Pete, you driving."

Pete: "Bet. Ten, throw me them keys."

Ten: "Okay. Let me turn these security cameras on."

Hezzy: "Yo, I'm ready."

Eazy: "Let's do it."

Baller: "Y'all ninja ready?"

Ten: "Yeah, that's it. Here you go, Pete."

Pete: "Let's ride," while walking out the door.

Baller: "Yo, y'all ninjas strap, right?"

Everybody: "Hell, yeah!"

Eazy: "American Express, Baby!"

They went in the back yard and got in their whoridin' van which looked ragged on the outside but plush like a mother-fucker on the inside. Soon as they got in the van Ten, Baller and Hezzy went to rolling blunts big as Chick-O-Sticks. Eazy was in the front seat playing with an ounce of raw powder getting his scar-face on.

Pete drove out of the driveway and pulled over to Cuddie's crack house and blowed the horn. Cuddie came out to the van. Baller slid the door open on the van. Cuddie couldn't see nothing but gold teeth, smoke, and fire from the tips of the blunts.

Baller: "Here you go, my nigga."

Cuddie: "This it?"

Baller: "Yeah, a key. 36 ounces."

Cuddie: "Okay, my nigga, I'll have your money. Where ya'll niggas headed?"

Baller: "Going to get on some 'ho's. Wanna ride?"

Cuddie: "Naw, my nigga, I got work to do. Our first key...shi-i-ittt--money over bitches. Maybe next time."

Baller: "Okay, my nigga. Keep it money."

Eazy: "Yo, Hezzy, pass me that tape."

Hezzy passed Eazy the tape. Baller slid the door closed and Pete pulled off and went around the curb to pick up Flamingo. Eazy put the tape in and the first song that came on was Rapper Ball with E-40, Too Short & K-CI off E-40 The Hall of Game CD. They got around the curb and pulled in Flamingo's driveway and Pete hit the horn pimp-like. Flamingo came out singin' "Pimpin' ain't e-z, you got to keep them 'ho's from talking back." Flamingo went over to the driver's side to see who was driving. Pete was jammin' to the music.

Pete: "Stick yourself Pretty Tony."

Flamingo: "What's up nigga? Who dat sittin' next to you?"

Pete leaned back. Eazy leaned up and gave Flamingo that player gangster look.

Flamingo: "Where that nigga Baller at?"

Baller: "In the back, Nigga."

Flamingo went to the side door. Baller slid the door open. Flamingo stepped in and was like, "Damn! Y'all niggas already ballin'. Who got that raw?"

Ten: "Smoke choke fool!"

Flamingo: "Yo, what's the dealio, Ten, Hezzy and Baller Baby?"

Baller: "Yo, Eazy got that raw up front. Yo, choke one

fool!"

Flamingo: "Yo, I'll toke one later on. Let me get my nose dirty first. What's up, Eazy?"

Eazy: "What's up playboy? Here you go; this shit is pure now."

Flamingo: "How you feel?"

Eazy: "Right now, shi-ittt, I'm high as giraffe pussy."

All the fellows in the back busted out laughing and Pete pulled out of the driveway and headed for the club.

They arrived at the club and sat in the van for about four minutes finishin' up on their blunts and Ten, Baller, Flamingo, and Pete took a li'l toot before going in the club.

Eazy: "Yo, y'all ninjas coming in the back door with a ninja?"

Everybody: "Hell, yeah!"

Eazy: "Yo, Flamingo, go to the door and give Fat Albert at the door this hundred dollar bill and tell him there're five of us coming in the back."

Flamingo: "Shitt! I want to go in the back way, too."

Eazy: "For what, you got a strap?"

Flamingo pulled us his shirt and said, "Hell, yeah."

Eazy: "Okay. Tell him it's six of us and tell him we coming in one minute apart."

Flamingo: "Okay."

Flamingo got out and did just that and he came back to the van and said that Fat Albert said give him four minutes. They gave each other dap and walked in the club one by one and in ten minutes they were all in the club kickin' it like big players.

The club was thick with players. Players like Sky, Greed, Crow, Nickel and Dime and lots of tricks and players and lots and lots of ladies. And over half of the fine ass women who were there worked for the Corporation. Even Dove from the Jury clique was workin' that night walkin' the floor spyin' on Sky & Greed. She couldn't figure them out. She was puzzled. You can be lookin' at them with a sharp eye all together, but you will still see missing pieces. The Corporation made Atlanta, Georgia the way it is today. It's half New York and half California mixed with every state in the south and I mean that shit. See, the Corporation have people on their team who people in the game wouldn't even expect.

Everybody was having a good time; some watching the lady boxers, some watching the dancers. Some niggas in the club so high they're just tryin' to come down and some niggas putting their mack hand down trying' to come up.

Eazy went to the bar and bought Hennessy & coke and a round for the crew and then they all spread out in the club. Pete and Hezzy was getting their shine on fucking with the ladies. Ten went over in the corner kickin' it with Greed to see what was happening in the club so far. Ten and Greed stay on niggas at the club. See, if you go to a club just one time to analyze the people you will find there's a whole lots of niggas walking around here asleep trying to be something they just dream about being. Some niggas make it happen in the club and some niggas find their self in the middle of a bad dream where they can't wake up and the music be so loud and they still be asleep.

Flamingo was kickin' it with Nickel and Dime talkin' about pimpin'.

Flamingo: "What's up pimping?"

Nickel & Dime:"What's up, Flamingo?"

Flamingo:"Pimpin' player breakin' these 'ho's and these sucker for love ass niggas."

Nickel: "Tell me about it pimpin'."

Flamingo: "You know how they do. Lay up & pay up.

My bitch asked me the other day, she say, 'Baby, I done brought you in enough money to retire on. How long you going to be pimpin' me?' I say, 'Bitch, I'm in it for the long term; I ain't going to be through with your ass until you wear out a thousand pairs of shoes and when Channel 2 stops doing the news. You there, me pimpin.'"

Dime: "I hear you pimpin' speak on it."

Flamingo: "You know these niggas want to be like me so bad they want to fuck a bitch or just get with the bitch because they heard the bitch been dealin' with me. Just last year I just had to see how many niggas was on my dick. I went out and got a ragged ass 'ho' off the street on rock and smelling bad."

Nickel and Dime was laughing and stomping their feet.

Dime: "Gott damn pimping. She was smelling bad!"

Flamingo: "Yeah. Check me out now. I got that bitch, cleaned her up. Put her on some of the flyest shit. Got her hair fixed and put that bitch on my arm and kick it at some of the baddest clubs. Gave that bitch twenty dollars and told her just to shake that ass li'l bit and buy herself one drink and drink it slow. And I left that bitch in the club with no way of getting in contact with me.

That bitch found me, I was sitting on the porch drinkin' lemonade, sniffin' raw. That bitch walk up to me, gave me everything I spent on her and throwed me a gee and said, 'Thank you, Mr. Flamingo, for turning me on. Cause of you a bitch got a second chance. See my car? It wasn't hard to find you cause so many talk down on your name. I told them I'll trick for them to get to you, but I will just bless you not hurt you. Look, I got to go. My Boo, King Goldie, waitin' on me. He takin' me to Florida.' And the bitch send me money all the time through U.P.S. Now, what's your pimping like?"

Dime: "Shitt, Nigga, just today a bitch came at me with a sad story. She say she don't got my money because she went to her uncle's funeral today."

Flamingo: "What you do pimpin'?"

Dime: "Player, I slapped that bitch out ouf her heels and told that bitch, 'Bitch! You could have sold some pussy at the funeral home' and that's when I introduced that 'ho' to these lime green gators and in a few hours that bitch came back with my money and bowed down to pimping. A bitch get out there for me. Where that nigga Baller?"

Flamingo: "There he goes, over there, kickin' it with Crow."

Nickel: "Why Baller be kickin' it with that nigga?"

Flamingo: "Oh, they go way back. That nigga save Baller's life before. You 'member when Baller got shot about ten years ago at Club Sugar Daddy? That nigga Crow got him to a doctor in time to save his life."

Nickel: "Damn, I knew that nigga was cool."

Dime: "Hell yeah."

Baller and Crow was over at the bar having a deep conversation about the game.

Crow: "So what's been going on inside that master mind of yours?"

Baller: "Shittt...money, money, money and more money. I been diggin' in that powerful book."

Crow: "Which one? Hypnotizing Game - Who Cross You by Earnest Bennett?"

Baller: "Yo, that one too, but I'm talkin' about the Holy Bible."

Crow: "Nigga, what kind of game did you get from the Holy Bible?"

Baller: "I know this much. We got to bind the strong man before we enter his house and spoil his goods. Mark 3:27.

This the year for us to show all the doubters. All the big boys in the game, we knockin' them off their feet this year. Now you with me?"

Crow: "100%."

Baller: "Now the first thing we need to do is to get that nigga who's puttin' you on, King Goldie."

Crow: "I been thinking about that. Now is a good time for it. I just can't put it together. You know, two heads are better than one."

Baller: "Shi-itt. Here I go, Nigga. Tell me what you got so far."

Crow: "Well, right now that nigga lyin' on his death bed dyin' from some kind of disease."

Baller: "What is it? AIDS or cancer?"

Crow: "Yo, I don't know, but he's callin' in all his soldiers at his house. He's going to label one of us to take his place to be King of the Street."

Baller: "How many soldiers are going to be at the house?"

Crow: "There's about 50 of us, and Uncle Luke, his boss man down in Florida, comin' up with Big Dope and His Boyz. So in all there's going to be 55 niggas packed in this one big ass house with two big ass dogs guardin' King Goldie's door. Uncle Luke wants to see for his self who's going to be his next boy in Atlanta, Georgia. Now you see why I couldn't put shit together. So many niggas."

Baller: "We can handle it."

Crow: "How dat?"

Baller looked around the club and looked Crow in his eyes and said, "We put them masks on.

Crow: "Nigga, that's two niggas against 55 niggas and two big ass dogs."

Baller: "Now, Crow, you know once we put them masks on we're no ordinary ass niggas. It's like this, once any nigga put any type of mask over their face it's on. No pity, no mercy, no feelin', no heart...see, the mask give you that feelin' that you can do what the fuck you wanna do and that is to get away with murder."

Crow: "It's going to be a massacre."

Baller: "I know, but what is now said is going to have to be done. You with me?"

Crow: "Hell yeah. What's the plan?"

Baller: "We will talk about it a week from the score. Now let's get our club on."

Eazy was over in the VIP havin' big fun. There were a few niggas in the VIP, but in order for them to stay in the VIP and just chill, they had to buy Eazy drinks and bring a 'ho' in to dance for him. Man, Eazy had over ten drinks and twenty bitches. They were all showing him love because if they didn't he was going to clown on that ass in the VIP blunts raw powder and lap dances with the dick out getting pussy. The club was on pack half through the night. The Corporation and their folks who put in work to make the Corporation what it is today filled the VIP room.

While all that was going on, Tray, Duece, Cotton and Blood was on their way to the club loading up guns, sniffin' raw powder and smoking on geek blunts with more coke rolled inside than weed. They were headed out to the club to get revenge on Eazy for stickin' the blood out of Milk. Milk and Oz Escobar was at Milk's Al Capone suite speaking on game and chopping up money. Tray, Duece, Cotton and Blood pulled into the club parking lot high and out of their minds.

Deuce: "Yo, y'all niggas listen up. I'm going in here to get that nigga. I'm going to call him out and if he get out of line I'm going to have to wallow. If I don't come out in five minutes, you niggas come in, guns blazing. And yo! Y'all niggas save me some of that raw."

Cotton: "Shi-it, Nigga, we got a whole key, right?"

Deuce: "Just like I said, save me some of dat raw."

Deuce got out of the car, walked up to the door, and gave Fat Albert five bucks to enter the club. Tray, Cotton, and Blood had the music low, smoking and sniffing like it was going out of style. They had their guns between their legs and their eyes on the door of the club. Deuce walked in the club with his mug on mean, walkin' around lookin' for Eazy. He looked over in the VIP section and saw Eazy sippin' on his drink, standin' behind a female while she danced for him. Duece walked over to the VIP.

Deuce: "Yo, Eazy."

Eazy turned from the girl and looked at Deuce and saw that he was at the club to start some shit so he turned back to the girl dancer.

Deuce: "Yo, punk ass nigga! Don't you turn your back on me!"

Eazy turned back and said, "Fuck you, Nigga!"

Deuce rushed Eazy and that's when the fight broke out. They wallowed from the VIP to the middle of the club floor. Deuce tried to jack up Eazy, Eazy kneed him in the face and threw him over a table. Deuce jumped up and toward Eazy. That's when Eazy pulled out his gun and fired two shots, popping Deuce in the chest and face, giving Deuce the pumpkin head. Eazy ran out the front door tryin' to make it to the Van. Tray, Cotton, and Blood saw Eazy as he came out of the Club.

Tray: "There that nigga go! Come on!"

Tray and the boys jumped out of the car, busting caps at Eazy and Eazy was returning fire back. Rat-tat-tat-tat....Boom! Boom! Boom!...Click-click-click...Rat-tat-rat-tat-tat.

No one was hit, but cars were riddled with bullets. Glass filled the parking lot. Eazy ran to the back of the club. Tray and the boys entered the club bustin' caps. Baller and the boys was bustin' caps at them. Rat-tat-tat...click-click...Boom! Rat-tat-rat-tat...Boom! Click...Boom! Glass breakin', big timers runnin', bitches hidin', yelling and screaming. Everybody was running for their life. Click-click...Boom! Boom! Rat-tat-tat-tat...click.

There was four minutes of gunplay. Baller and his boys ran out the back way, and everybody else was doing the same. Fat Albert was on the phone, calling the police, telling them there was a big fight going on and now there's gun fire. "We need help!"

The police operator called in to dispatch "Code 27, Code 27. Big fight and gunplay at Club Nikki. Need officers. Need officers on the scene."

When the gunplay stopped and the smoke cleared, Duece was laying on the club floor dying. Tray got down on his knees to aid his brother. Baller and the boys got to the van and there was Eazy, with gun in hand, breathless. Pete opened up the van doors and they all got in. Pete was burning rubber tryin' to make it out of the parking lot. Cotton and Blood heard the tires burnin'. They ran out the door bustin' shots at the van. Baller opened up the side door. Eazy was bustin' shots out the front window and Baller, Hezzy, Ten, and Flamingo was bustin' shots out of the side door while getting away.

Cotton and Blood looked up and saw a line of police cars headed toward the club. They ran back in to get Tray.

Cotton: "Yo, Tray, the cops are coming. Man, let's go!"

Tray: "Man, they shot my brother. I can't leave him like this. He's dying, man!"

Blood: "Man, if we don't get out of here we're going to be

dead or in jail. Let's go, man! Them police ain't going to be playing when they get here."

Cotton: "Yo, man, he's right. Deuce will make it. The ambulance will be here soon."

Tray heard the siren getting closer and closer. He looked at his brother and looked up at Cotton and Blood, grabbed his gun, and they headed out the door. When they ran out the door, the cops was pullin' into the parking lot. Tray, Cotton, and Blood opened fire on the cops, causing them to lose control of their car. The cops crashed into each other and jumped out and got in position and fired back. Tray made it to the car. Cotton and Blood and the cops went back and forth with gun fire. Rat-tat-tat-tat-tat...Boom! Boom! Click-click-click-click...rat-tat-tat-tat...Boom!   Click-click...Rat-tat-tat.

Tray pulled up on the side of Cotton and Blood.

Tray: "Yo! Get the fuck in the car!"

Cotton and Blood got in the car still bustin' shots at the cops while getting away. Tray busted through the gate of the club and they headed out to Milk's Al Capone suite. When the ambulance arrived on the scene, two cops was hit and inside there were three dead, seven wounded, and over $100,000 in damages. Deuce was still alive. He was the most injured; a helicopter flew him to Piedmont Hospital. There he was on life support. Tray didn't know where his brother was until a few days later.

Baller and his crew was heading back to the club once they grabbed some more artillery back at his crack house. They got all the guns they needed and Pete drove back to the club and only 200 yards away from the club Pete and the boys could see police headlights surrounding the club. It looked like over 100 cop cars. Pete turned the van right back around and they headed to the house. They all had calmed down.

Ten went in the back and brought out a key of coke and a pound of weed. The boys put in a few gangster flicks, busted the coke and weed open and got mellow. It almost slipped Hezzy's mind. Hezzy reached into his work desk and pulled out the letter Brown Sugar wrote to Baller before she died.

Hezzy: "Yo, Baller."

Baller: "Yeah, baby boy?"

Hezzy: "I got a letter for you. It's from Sugar."

All the boys looked at Baller. Baller told Flamingo to pass him that raw. He took a toot and a sip of his drink and opened up the letter. For that nigga, Hezzy, he was still rolling them fat ass blunts because he don't snort blow. He just cooks it and sells it.

Baller read the letter and he was full of grief. He put the letter down and his eyes were full with tears.

Eazy: "Everything all right, baby?"

Baller: "Man, I just feel like if I was here I could have saved her."

Eazy: "It wasn't your fault, man."

Hezzy, puffin' on a blunt, telling the boys: "See, that nigga Milk, he kill one of our cats, so we kill all of his dogs. Y'all niggas with me?"

The boys: "Hell, yeah!"

Ten: "Yo, after this job tomorrow with Jazzy Bell. What time is it?"

Hezzy: "3:00 in the morning."

Ten: "Okay. While today is tomorrow, we're going to put an end to that nigga Milk and I mean that shit. Yo, but I got to get some sleep."

Baller felt a lot better because he shared his feelings, let it all out. That's what you got to do because if you don't the pressure you hold in is stronger on the inside and if you don't let it out you just might hurt yourself or someone else who you never ever meant to hurt.

It was early in the morning. Ten woke up while all the rest of the boyz was sleeping. Ten turned on the TV set to watch the news and there it was all over the news, the shooting at the club. Ten woke up Pete, telling him it was time to put in work. Pete stood up yawning and trying to talk at the same time.

Pete: "Shittt...what time is it?"

Ten: "It's early."

Pete: "Man, I'm still sleepy."

Ten: "Nigga, we got work to do. That shit what happened at the club was just on the news."

Pete: "What was they talkin' about?"

Ten: "They was just talkin' about what had happened. They didn't say no names, but they did say the Deuce is still living. They got him over at Piedmont Hospital. He's in critical condition, so he's in intensive care. They say he was falling in and out of a coma."

Pete: "So what's the dealio on that?"

Ten: "Shittt...Baller is going to take care of that."

Pete and Ten got ready, but before leaving, Ten woke Baller and told him the news on Deuce. Pete woke Flamingo, asking him did he need a ride home. Flamingo got up and stretched out, yawning.

Flamingo: "Yeah, let's do it."

They walked out the door and got in one of four cars that was parked in the back yard. They chose the '72 Chevrolet Impala. They dropped off Flamingo and made their way out to Jazzy Bell's house. When they arrived, Jazzy Bell had breakfast on the table, ready for all of her little brothers. They knocked at the door. Jazzy Bell welcomed them in.

Pete: "It smells good in here. What's cookin'?"

Jazzy Bell: "Go see."

Pete hurried to the kitchen.

Ten gave Jazzy Bell a big ass hug.

Jazzy Bell: "It's good to see you, Ten."

Ten: "You, too, Jazzy."

Jazzy Bell: "Come, let's eat. Food for thoughts."

Sitting at the table eating was Greed, Fly-Mar, Jim Kelly, and Big Mike. They were chowing down on some hot pancakes and sausage, cheese eggs, bacon, and apple juice.

Jim Kelly: "What's up, brothers?"

Big Mike: "Y'all niggas have a seat and feed your brain."

Greed: "Man, Jazzy Bell cook the shit out of this breakfast. Y'all sit down. You know a hungry man can't think."

Pete and Ten sat down and Jazzy Bell served them.

Jazzy Bell: "Ten, so what happened at the club last night?"

Ten: "Oh, you seen the news."

Jazzy Bell: "Mmm hm."

Ten: "That nigga Milk sent his boys to do a man's job. Deuce came in the club poppin' shit to Eazy. Eazy took it to that ass, busting him in the chest and face. Then Cotton, Tray, and Blood fell in the club bustin' shots, so we retaliated like a good soldier would. Man, y'all niggas should have been there. The club was packed, too. The Corporation had it crunk."

Fly-Mar: "Yo, that shit sound like it was on crunk, but check it out--we going to need some help on fight night because there's so many houses to hit. We need two crews in fours. MJG showed me how to pick a safe. I got that shit down pack. We practiced six hours a day for 30 days on some of the best safes they make. Man, this lick, it's going to be big chunks of money, jewelry, we already got keys made to their houses and cars. It's going to gravy on fight night.

Chicago is going to tape the fight so after the lick, shi-id, we all can kick back at her crib, chop up the flow, get high, and watch the fight."

Jazzy Bell: "That's all good, but we got to do this lick first and it's about that time."

Jim Kelly: "Yo, Jazzy Bell, how much flow you think them niggas got up in that crib."

Jazzy Bell: "I don't know and don't care. This is retaliation on them niggas for breakin' in my house tryin' to see what we got up in here."

Greed walked to the living room with a set of binoculars, looking out the window, keeping an eye on the Killahoe place. Jazzy Bell went to the back and got the video tape. Ten, Pete, Big Mike and Jim Kelly was putting on their soulja rags because Oz Escobar was to arrive at 12:00 and the time was 11:50.

Ten minutes later Oz Escobar arrived on the scene. Jazzy Bell knew that this lick took perfect timing. Oz Escobar stepped out of his white, 1995 600s Mercedes Benz sedan with suitcase in hand. Jazzy Bell gave Jim Kelly the video tape while her and Greed sat in the car watching and waiting for Oz Escobar to leave with the package. Greed stayed in contact with the boys by walkie-talkie. Greed used his binoculars to see who came to the door and trying to see who was all in the house. Escobar knocked on the door. Jesse James came to the door.

Jesse James: "Yo, Dillinger, it's Escobar."

Dillinger: "Well, let him in."

Oz Escobar walked in.

Dillinger: "What's up Escobar?"

Escobar: "Players, let's get down to business."

Dillinger: "Yeah, right here. Meet the boys. This here is Jesse James, Billy Bad Ass, and this right here is Baby Face, and we are the Killahoe Posse."

Billy Bad Ass went in the back to get the 19 synthetic keys.

Dillinger: "You're going to love this coke. I've been sitting on this for awhile."

Oz: "Oh yeah?"

Dillinger: "Yeah."

Oz: "Now if the coke you give me is the shit I'll be back to buy more. Can you say '50 keys'?"

Dillinger: "Can you say 'Hell yeah'."

Billy Bad Ass came out of the back with the coke. Oz Escobar busted open a key and tasted the coke. It gave him a freeze by numbing his tongue. Oz leaned his head side to side and looked at Dillinger before he could speak.

Dillinger: "Ain't it the true?"

Oz Escobar: "It's tasteful, but I got to take it to the lab and cook it and see how it comes back."

Dillinger: "Oh, it's going to bubble for sho'."

Oz Escobar: "Here's your money. It's all there."

Dillinger gave Baby Face the money and told him to count it.

Dillinger: "You see, boys, what you get when you have patience?"

They all agreed.

Oz Escobar: "Yo, I buy big coke all the time. How come I never heard of you boys?"

Dillinger: "They jealous, man. We run this shit out here in the Decatur, Player. The Killahoe is the ghetto mafia, baby, the only competition we got is that fat ass bitch Jazzy Bell and her crew and they can't stand us."

Oz: "But wait--she turned me on to you."

Dillinger: "Yeah, I know. She just want you to come back to her when she get something so she had to turn you on to me. Just watch. But you coming back to me, right?"

Oz: "Yeah, but Jazzy Bell told me that you and your posse was cool like that."

Dillinger: "That bitch said that?"

Oz: "Oh, yeah."

Dillinger: "Well, she's cool sometimes. But, yo, if you need anything else come to us. We do it all--jack stack roll fold chill & kill by any means necessary."

Oz Escobar: "Bet dat up, Player. Yo, I got to go."

Oz got his dope and left. Dillinger sent Baby Face, Jesse James, and Billy Bad Ass to follow Oz Escobar and learn his whereabouts. But Jazzy Bell and Greed was on their tail. Ten, Pete, Big Mike, Jim Kelly, and Fly-Mar stayed in position until Greed called in and gave them the location on Oz Escobar. Jesse James, Billy Bad Ass, and Baby Face had the location on Oz Escobar, but on their way back to their house they ran into three lovely ladies--Mia, Queen Blac, and Mary Jane. The Killahoe Posse stop at the store and kicked it with the girls for about an hour.

And half an hour later, Oz Escobar had found out the dope was fake synthetic bull shit. Oz Escobar got Cotton, Tray, and Blood to ride with him to set that nigga Dillinger straight. Greed gave the boys a call tellin' them that Oz Escobar and his boys were on the way, so send the tape. Fly-Mar walked down to the Killahoe Posse's crack house and knocked on the door.

Dillinger: "Who is it?"

Fly-Mar: "It's me, Fly-Mar from up the street."

Dillinger came to the door with his gun in hand.

Dillinger: "Yeah, what's up?"

Fly-Mar: "Yo, I just got this new Master P Bout It Bout it movie and I just figured y'all niggas might want to check out. Shittt, y'all niggas cool with us. I come in peace."

Dillinger: "Yeah, okay. Oh, I know y'all niggas cool. Yo,

and tell Jazzy Bell that I like what she did for me. We needed that shit and yo, if someone wants something and we don't have shit, I'll come to y'all."

Fly-Mar: Right. Yo, Master P act his ass off in the movie."

Dillinger: "What's it about?"

Fly-Mar: "Oh, it's about this dirty ass cop put him on and set him up so he broke into that niggas house and stole all his coke."

Dillinger: "Sho' 'nuff?"

Fly-Mar: "Sho' 'nuff."

Dillinger: "Oh, I got to check it out. I'll send the tape back when we finish watching it."

Fly-Mar: "Later."

Dillinger poured him a drink, sniffed a li'l powder, and popped the video tape in. But what he saw wasn't Master P breakin' in the dirty cop's house takin' dope, it was him and his boys breakin' in Jazzy Bell's house taking her dope and money. He watched the tape for about a minute and jumped up and ran to the door and when he did that he was snatched for a kidnap.

Oz Escobar and the boys took him from the house and tortured him. Jim Kelly, Ten, Pete, Big Mike, and Fly-Mar went into the Killahoe's house and ransacked the house, getting everything they had in the house, and they had lots of shit from guns to dope and money. Greed called in on the walkie-talkie, talkin' with Fly-Mar, tellin' him do not touch the money with the green rubber bands, it's the counterfeit money and do not forget the video tape.

Fly-Mar: "Okay."

They did everything that was planned and they got the hell out of the house. By that time the girls had brushed off Baby Face, Billy Bad Ass, and Jesse James, so they was on their way home. When they got there, they saw that the house was fucked up. Right then they thought that that fool Oz and some of his boys came back and took Dillinger. They went lookin' for more guns, but they was gone. They only had their hand pistols on them. They thought about going back just with their hand pistols, but then the phone rang.

Baby Face: "Hello."

Oz Escobar: "By now you know I got your boy. I want my money or this nigga gets it."

Baby Face: "Fuck you. I'll get you your money...come and get it!"

Oz Escobar: "Look, I just want my money. I don't want to kill your boy. The dope you gave me was fake synthetic bull shit."

Baby Face: "Calm down. What you mean?"

Oz Escobar: "Just what I said, Nigga, fake. Now you niggas get me my money and I will forget about this big matter."

Baby Face: "Man, that dope was pure."

Oz: "Yeah, pure bull shit. You got four hours."

Baby Face slammed the phone down.

Baby Face: "Damn! Fuck! That nigga Oz Escobar holdin' Dillinger hostage, talkin' about the dope was fake synthetic bull shit."

Jesse James: "What we do now?"

Baby Face: "I don't know."

Billy Bad Ass: "I know."

Jesse James: "What?"

Billy Bad Ass: "We go to war. Let's go get Dillinger."

Jesse James: "Man, that's suicide."

Baby Face: "Wait, Jesse. Bad Ass is right. This here is a test. Yeah, the test of all tests."

Billy picked Dillinger's gun off the floor and said, "Let's

go get our nigga. If it was one of us, he would do it for us. See, if we go and retaliate on them niggas ass right now, they ain't going to be ready. Now, if y'all niggas ain't with it, I'll go by my damn self!"

Baby Face: "Let's do it."

Jesse James: "Hell, yeah, let's go."

Jazzy Bell and her crew was in the living room, chillin', choppin' up cash and dope. Them niggas had so much dope and money in that house it would have been another year before they touched Jazzy Bell's dope. They just sold Escobar the 19 keys because Jazzy Bell had it wrapped so well and it weighed in just right.

Milk and his old family, the Jury, surrounded Dillinger. They had him tied down to a chair, butt ass naked, burning him with blunts and beating him with a pipe. They was coming down hard on him. Dillinger was confused at first, he thought he was just getting robbed. And then he thought it was retaliation from breakin' in Jazzy Bell's crib. But they kept hitting and hitting and hitting and hitting him.

Oz Escobar: "Nigga, I want my fuckin' money or dope. Why you sell me that synthetic bull shit?"

Cotton took the duct tape from his mouth. Dillinger was smothered in blood and the pipe they beat him with made him speak with a slur.

Dillinger: "I-I-I got m-m-money a-a-at the house. If if you say th-the dope w-w-w-was fake, I-I-I believe you ca-ca-cause I ja-ja-jack f-f-for it. I-I-I didn't ch-ch-check it, b-b-but I got m-m-money at th-th-the house."

Dove looked up at Milk because they heard a car slam on the brakes outside the door.

Milk: "Yo, one of y'all go check that out."

While Blood went to see what was going on outside the door, Escobar was still asking Dillinger questions.

Escobar: "So you got more than just my money and dope at your house."

Dillinger sneered at Oz and spit blood in his face and said, "Fu-fu-fuck you."

Escobar fell back cursing. That's when Blood opened up the door and stepped outside. But when he opened up the door, Billy Bad Ass, Jesse James and Baby Face was coming in with guns blazing, popping Blood in the chest four times. He fell to the floor and died. As they entered the house they stepped on his body. Milk and his crew skee-skurt into different rooms once they heard the shooting.

Dillinger: "I'm here, I'm in here."

It's funny how your voice can change when you are in trouble or when you are about to be saved. Billy Bad Ass, Jesse James, and Baby Face made it to the room with Dillinger and untied him.

Dillinger: "I knew you niggas would come. Them bitch ass niggas ran in different rooms so let's split up and, yo, y'all niggas be careful."

Dillinger and his boys went through the house, but the house was like a maze with trap doors. The Killahoes was in and out of doors but nothing. Milk had his house fixed up just like Scar Face Al Capone's. Dillinger, Baby Face, Billy Bad Ass, and Jesse James all bumped into each other in one room. They were like, "I don't see them."

And that's when Milk and his boys came out trap doors bustin' shots. The Killahoe Posse fired back. Rat-tat-tat-tat-tat... ...click-click...Boom! Boom! Rat-tat-tat-tat...click-click...rat-tat-tat-tat...Boom! Boom! Boom! Click-click...Boom! Boom! Boom! Five minutes of gunplay, and when the smoke cleared, Dillinger was picking Baby Face up off the floor, takin' him out the door. Billy Bad Ass had Jesse James in his arms.

As they got outside, headin' to the car, Dillinger got the keys from Baby Face's pocket. Unlocking the door, putting his dogs in the car. Dillinger put Baby Face in the car and Billy Bad Ass was putting Jesse James in the car and that's when Cotton came to the door with a pump shotgun busting Billy Bad Ass in the back. Bad Ass fell in the car. Dillinger turned around busting shots, hitting Cotton in the shoulder blade, causing him to drop his gun. Dillinger then got in the car, crunk it, and pulled off, burnin' rubber back to his crack house.

Milk was hit in the hand. Tray was all right, so was Dove. Escobar was hit in the arm. Billy Bad Ass was hit bad. So was Jesse James and Baby Face. Dillinger got them back at the house. Dillinger picked up each of his boys and walked them to the house and sat them down on the couch and chair and started looking for his stash of money, coke, and guns. All he saw was the $60G. He got it and sat in the living room.

But when he got back in the living room, all his home boys had died. Dillinger fell on the couch in between Jesse James and Billy Bad Ass and shed tears. He looked over at Baby Face and shook his head, looking up at God. Then it hit him. He reached at the VCR and saw that the tape was gone. He was like, yeah, that bitch Jazzy Bell set me up.

He grabbed the money, his car keys, and gun and headed for the door. When going out to the car, Oz Escobar came flyin' around the curb with Tray hanging out the window with a Mac 11. Lettin' off rounds at Dillinger. Dillinger got in the car and drove off, but Oz Escobar was right on his ass. Tray shot out his car tires, causing him to wreck and he hit a tree. Dillinger was hurt.

Tray got out of the car with the Mac 11. Dillinger was still alive with the car motor in his lap. Tray put the Mac 11 over in the car and shot Dillinger over 75 times and reached into the back seat and got the $60G of counterfeit money and walked back to the car winking his eye at Cotton. Cotton then got out of the car with a Coke bottle bomb, lit it up, and threw it in the back seat of the Dillinger car. As they pulled off the car blew up. Boom!

They then drove to the hospital because Tray wanted to see his brother. As they were driving out to the hospital, Greed and Jazzy Bell was on their ass. As they got to the hospital, Jazzy Bell called Chicago telling her it's on. Then Jazzy Bell and Greed headed back home. Tray, Escobar, and Cotton headed to Deuce's room. When they walked in, Tray fell to the floor in tears 'cause the bullet that hit Deuce in the face had swollen his head big as a 30 pound pumpkin. Cotton and Escobar helped Tray up. Tray was talking to his brother, telling him how sorry he was for not being by his side at the time of the shooting. Deuce didn't move, he just looked at Tray with tears rolling down his face. They sat and sat and sat.

Escobar: "Yo, I'm hungrier than a mother fucker."

Cotton: "You too?"

Tray: "Yeah, let's go get something to eat."

Tray told his brother Deuce he would be right back, he was going to get something to eat and get him a gift from the gift shop. Tray, Cotton and Escobar went down to the cafeteria to eat. And after they ate they went into the gift shop and they all got Deuce something. Cotton got a hundred dollars worth of flowers, Escobar got him a hundred dollars worth of get well balloons, and Tray bought 200 dollars worth of get well soon cards. They was all laughing, saying that Deuce is going to trip when he sees all the stuff they have for him.

They walked into the room.

Tray: "Look what we got you man."

Cotton: "Oh, you're gonna love this."

Oz Escobar looked and saw that Deuce wasn't breathing and ran out of the room.

Oz Escobar: "Yo! Yo! I need a nurse down here!"

Tray: "What's up, Oz?"

Oz: "He ain't breathing no more, man. Yo! Can somebody help us down here?!"

Tray looked and saw that his brother wasn't breathing. He just looked with a frown on his face.

Two nurses rushed in and made Tray, Escobar and Cotton leave the room. Ten minutes later a nurse came and told Tray that someone came in the room and silenced the alarm on the EKG monitor and shot an air bubble in his vein.

Nurse: "I'm sorry, but there's nothing we can do."

Cotton: "What the fuck you mean?! You telling me just anybody can walk in this hospital and kill our brother?! Bitch! Fuck you!"

Oz: "Yo, chill, Cotton."

Tray reached into his pocket and gave the nurse a knot of money and gave her an address telling her to ship the body to New York. And they left the hospital with hate in their hearts.

Jazzy Bell's crew had taken over 150 keys, 21 guns, and over $3 million in cash from the Killahoe Posse crack house. The lick was a success. Everyone who was a part of the lick, Jazzy Bell prayed for them. Talking to God was Jazzy Bell's thing.

Three weeks later in Atlanta, Georgia, yes, it was the Olympic City. Man, when the Olympics came to our town it was the most exciting thing that could ever happen in your state. Baller, Hezzy, Pete, and Ten walked up the street, went under the bridge at the Lakewood train station and walked to the main street to see the person running with the torch.

Everyone was standing on the sidewalk cheering the runner on. And after the running was over, the runner ran the torch into the Olympic Stadium. There he passed the torch to "The Greatest", Muhammed Ali, and he lit the big torch on the opening of the ceremonies. Everyone in the Olympic Stadium went wild when he lit the torch. And then The Greatest held up his power fist to the people just like John Carlos and Tommy Smith at the 1968 Summer Olympics in Mexico City.

I think that the state of Georgia owed that to The Champ because in the 1970s Ali came to town and beat up on the world's first white hope. Black people welcomed Ali but white folks was like "Get out of our town, nigga." But Ali stood his ground and spoke his mind and that's what made him the greatest.

Security, security, security. The state of Georgia had security out the fucking ass. Cops and cameras on every block, surveillance all around Centennial Park. From block to block, the FBI had the city on lock. The Olympic Games was doing well--maybe a li'l too well, cause crime was down. Niggas stay in the 'hood, away from that shit. Centennial Park had a concert for white folks and they had a good time but the next day it was on all the news that a black performer was going to perform at Centennial Park, so that was a key sign to let black people know that it was okay for them to come down to the park and have a good time. But that night there was more black down at that park than any color and the world knows if black people find a spot to come and have a good time at they're going to tell a friend. So the next day there were going to be more blacks and white people knew it so that night while everyone was at the park enjoying their self, Boom! an explosion rocks Centennial Park.

Now, maybe dogs, or police, or gunfire at a place like that, black people will still show up. But a bomb, black people stay away from shit like that and they did. People running, yelling, and screaming. But when the smoke cleared, one black was killed, a black with power, a judge, a black woman judge. Now, if you think like me, you will say, "How could that happen with surveillance cameras on every block?" It was said before the Olympics came to town that cameras was watching the whole downtown. Now, before the explosion, there was a call that came from a nearby pay phone minutes before the explosion.

The ambulances and paramedics were on the scene so fast it was like they knew. I was sitting back, smoking a blunt, watching the news, saying to myself, they knew. See, the bombing at Centennial Park was a conspiracy, a wag the dog. There were too many cops and FBI men for anything to happen. Things were just going too smoothly, but the TV ratings were down, so the FBI, the state of Georgia, and the federal government all got together and caused the explosion to happen. So that's who cross you--your own government.

Then the FBI got on the news and blamed someone who had nothing to do with the bombing. TV ratings jumped to the ceiling and then the whole world was watching the Olympic Games. Now, you know and I know if there were cameras on every block, wouldn't it have seen the pay phone suspect? They didn't say anything about the cameras no more; they just blamed a man and showed his face on the news every minute on the minute, dragging his name and face through the mud. But then at the end they made him a hero saying that he was trying to let someone know that there was a suspicious backpack under a bench.

Now, he was a security guard. Wasn't he supposed to

check it out? It was a set up, a wag the dog. Every state does what the next state does but in a different way. Copy cats, that's what it is. They do it just for the TV ratings. The TV is power, the FBI is power, the government is power.

Look, bringing a person down and bringing that person out of something as bad as blowing up some shit, that's God's work. God is the only one who I believe in. The FBI lies, the government lies, but God tells the truth. God makes this world go around. But the FBI and the government try to make you believe they're running shit. That's why you got white power groups, black power groups, cause they know that the government and the FBI is the most crooked group on the planet.

Now at the Olympics, there were some great blacks that made a name for their self. Like boxers Lawrence Clay-bey, David Reed, and Floyd Mayweather. And in Track & Field, Michael Johnson, Gail Devers and Gwen Torrence. And in gymnastics, Dominique Dawes, and in Tennis, Malivai Washington. The USA got away with all the golds; Russia was on their ass--they were in second. Germany and China were running neck and neck; so were France and Australia.

But the Olympics were a hit in Atlanta, Georgia, holding over 600,000 and had only one big problem and that was the bomb shit. Niggas stayed in their 'hoods and made money because the cops had their hands full, but when the Olympic games were over, the cops rushed the back and front crack streets and the FBI was in town macking the city. More bombs hit places like a gay night club and an abortion clinic and they say there is no suspect, but they know who's doing it. It's just to have people glued to the tube.

A week later detective Ren Shockley was on his job getting close to the killer. He asked any of the cops, have they seen anything or anybody suspicious on the night of Miss

Bout It's murder? One blue jean cop stepped up named Officer Tucci.

Tucci: "Yes, I saw a man that goes by the name Corn Bread covered in blood in College Park."

Ren Shockley: "What's his M.O.?"

Tucci: "Well, he is a smoker and a roller. I bought crack from him and tried to go back and find him. By the time I got back he was gone. But he hangs out on 34th and Broadway."

Ren Shockley: "Okay, I will check it out. You've been a big help."

It's been a month and a half and Corn Bread still hasn't gotten paid his money from Billy Lawrence and he was mad about it so he went looking for Billy. He found him at a local bar.

Corn Bread: "Hey, Billy. Why you been ducking and dodging me? I want my money. Yo!"

It wasn't that Billy Lawrence was dodging him because he didn't have the money. It was just that Bread Bout it hadn't paid him, either

Billy: "Hey, Corn Bread, my man. What's up?"

Corn Bread: "My money, yo!"

Billy: "It's comin', just give me until tomorrow, I'll have your money. But look, how did you find me?"

Corn Bread: "Shitt--it wasn't hard. It was at first. I took a life for you! And you owe me. If you don't have my money, I know something and the shit is going to hit the fan. Now let me hold something. I want to get fucked up and get a li'l head."

Billy: "What, you need a twenty?"

Corn Bread: "Hell, naw. I said I want to get fucked up, not just high. And I want to catch me a li'l super freak so I can get my Jimmy waxed, so I need about a hundred."

Billy: "I got eighty bucks. What's up?"

Corn Bread: "I'll take it, but you know what--you're a cheap mother fucker."

Billy: "I know, and that makes $9,900 I owe you now."

Corn Bread: "Mm hmm."

Corn Bread left. He went back to the 'hood to get his high on. He went to Spoon to get his rocks.

Corn Bread: "Yo, Spoon, let me get four."

Spoon: "Okay, I got 'em fat to my nigga. Yeah, and there was a clean cut white boy came through here lookin' for you, talkin' about 'I need five twenties'."

Corn Bread: "Damn! Did you catch him?"

Spoon: "Hell, naw! He look like Five-0 to me. Everybody else crowded around his car trying to catch him."

Corn Bread: "Who caught him?"

Spoon: "I think Super Star, he already spent $200 within 30 minutes. That honky is the police."

Corn Bread: "Naw, he ain't no police. That's my buddy. He spend money like that. Look, just give me eight of them. I know my buddy is coming back. I'm going to double this right here."

Spoon: "Okay, go 'head, my nigga."

Corn Bread got his rocks, pulled out his shooter, and got a blast from the past. While he was hittin' his shooter, Spoon yelled out to Corn Bread, "There goes your buddy!" Corn Bread looked and saw the clean cut white boy coming around the curb and everybody rushed his car except Spoon. Corn Bread ran and jumped on the hood of the white boy's car yellin', "Here I go, Buddy! Here I go, your Buddy Corn Bread."

The clean cut white boy looked up and said, "There's my buddy right there."

Corn Bread got off the hood and got in the car and told the

white boy to pull off because the dealers was still crowding the car, trying to get that sell.

White Boy: "Where you been, buddy? I been lookin' for you."

Corn Bread: "I been around. How many you want, buddy?"

White Boy: "Well, I have already spent $200. What you got, buddy? Shit, I'll get all you got because I know you."

Corn Bread: "Well, I got 7 twenties right here, and I'm smoking on one. Want a hit?"

White Boy: "Naw, not right now. I'm gettin' this right here for a friend, but if he like it I'm coming back to get $500 worth from you, buddy, so be out here."

Corn Bread: "Oh, I'll be out here. You see I got on a red shirt."

They drove back around to the trap. The white boy dropped Corn off. He got out of the car smiling, smoking on a rock, doing the Bankhead Bounce, talkin' about "That's my buddy, y'all. He gonna come to me every time. Now who's going to give me twenty rocks for the one-forty or sell me an eight ball for the one-thirty-five? Shit, he coming back to me. Now who's gonna ride?"

Super Star: "I got you. Give me the money."

Corn Bread took the eight ball, chopped it up, and waited on that white boy with twenty five rocks in his possession, tryin' to come up. Corn Bread waited and waited in the trap for the clean cut white boy, Officer Tucci.

So Corn Bread got tired of waiting. He got with Geek 'Ho, a female friend. They went into an empty house. Corn Bread got him some head and cock for a few rocks. They stayed in the empty house for a good li'l while. Corn Bread had only eight rocks left, and that's when he got upset with Geek 'Ho. He started cursin' and yellin'. She was cryin' and yellin' back.

Corn Bread: "Hell, naw, bitch. Look what you made me do! I done smoke up all my shit fuckin' with you!"

Geek 'Ho: "Wait a minute, mother fucker! You don't got to yell at me, baby! I didn't make you do shit you didn't want to do. You called me over, nigga!"

Corn Bread: "Shut the fuck up, bitch! 'Fore I kick your fuckin' ass!"

Geek 'Ho didn't say a word, she just started pushin' up her stim inside her shooter and that's when Corn Bread went off on Geek 'Ho, beatin' and kickin' her while she was down. She fought back, but Corn Bread won the battle. She just laid down on the ground yellin' and screamin'. Corn Bread just walked around the empty house with his fist clenched tight.

Corn Bread: "Bitch!! You don't fuck with me! I'm Corn Bread, you heard me?!!"

Geek 'Ho: "I'm sorry! I'm sorry! Please don't hit me no more. I'll suck your dick! For the free! Just leave me be. I'm sorry."

Spoon walked on the side of the house to take a leak. He looked through the broken window and saw Geek 'Ho suckin' on Corn Bread's dick. He just shook his head. After he finished takin' a leak he walked out into the street and yelled out.

Spoon: "Yo, Corn Bread! Here come your honky!"

Corn Bread came runnin' out of the empty house zipping up his pants.

Corn Bread: "Where he at? Where he at?! Where he at, yo?"

Spoon: "Ha, ha. I was just fuckin' with you. I saw you in there gettin' to it."

Corn Bread: "Don't play with me like that no more, yo."

Spoon: "Fuck you, Nigga, I said I was just jokin'. What, you want to make something out of it?"

See, in the ghetto, a fiend will act a ass on you if you don't stand your ground. In the ghetto, I seen shit like this. Dealers beat Geek Monsters over the head with pipes, baseball bats, and with forty bottles. Sometimes a dealer go as far as shootin' a fiend just because they were tryin' to take some shit. A drug dealer ain't going to let shit go when his boys are around. Because I use to be the same way, hard as project bricks.

The key to being a successful drug dealer is to have control and get in and get out, 'cause some geek monsters get bold if they can't get that blast. You got some that will pull up in a car and ask for two or three and give you one dollar and pull off. Some geek monsters won't give you shit--they will just pull off with your rocks. And you got some drug dealers that will bust shots at the car, causing it to wreck, and then go up to the car and beat the fiend's ass and take their shit back.

When I was rolling, a fiend pulled off with my rocks and I reached over into the car tryin' to stop the car from rollin' off. Man, that fiend scratched me all in my mouth causing my gums to bleed. I let that fiend have them rocks. I got lucky. I got a friend who had a li'l brother who was trying to stop a fiend from pulling off with his rocks. The fiend dragged him six blocks killing him. The fiend ran over his head and broke both of his legs all just for three rocks. Young people, it ain't worth it--let them have it. You will see them again; they might stay gone for awhile, but they will come back. Like that shit what happened in Menace 2 Society when O-Dog shot that geek monster talking about suckin' his dick for a rock; that shit was real! Dope and money, man, a nasty attitude come with that shit.

Corn Bread: "Ha, ha! Here come my buddy for real, nigga!"

Spoon: "Fuck you, nigga."

Corn bread went running to the car telling everybody to get out of the way, "he's lookin' for me, he's lookin' for me! Here I go, buddy, here I go!" Corn Bread ran to the car window.

Officer Tucci: "Get in, buddy."

Corn Bread got into the car doing the Bankhead Bounce, talkin' about "give me the money, buddy, so I can hook you up." The clean cut white boy Officer Tucci handcuffed Corn Bread to the steering wheel and jumped out of his car with his gun in hand tellin' everyone to freeze. All the drug dealers looked at each other like "what the fuck?" And that's when about 20 cars of policemen came from the left and the right with Detective Ren Shockley in front. And that's when all the drug dealers took off running. Everybody got away except for Corn Bread. Detective Ren Shockley took Corn Bread and put him into his car, and asked him.

Ren Shockley: "Are you Corn Bread, son?"

Corn Bread: "Hell, naw. My name is Johnnie Walker."

Ren Shockley looked around to see if there was anyone in the street that could identify Corn Bread. He saw Geek 'Ho coming out of the empty house.

Ren Shockley: "Hey, you there. Come here."

Geek 'Ho walked over to the car.

Geek 'Ho: "You talkin' to me? I ain't got no rocks. They beat me up and took my rocks."

Ren Shockley: "Who took your rocks?"

Geek 'Ho: "These bad ass drug dealers around here."

Ren Shockley: "Miss, do you know this man right here?"

Geek 'Ho looked over in the car and saw Corn Bread.

Corn Bread was like "Hey, Geek 'Ho, tell Mr. Man my

name is Johnnie Walker."

Geek 'Ho: "Hell naw! You Corn Bread, fool! Officer... Officer this is Corn Bread and he's the one who took my rocks. He got them in his right pocket and they are in some green bags."

Ren Shockley: "Miss, is you sure this man right here Corn Bread that took your rocks?"

Geek 'Ho: "I'm sure, and you can call me Geek 'Ho. I'm the Queen Bitch around here and he got my rocks in his pocket. Can I get them?"

Ren Shockley: "Go right ahead."

Geek 'Ho was goin' in Corn Bread's pocket. Corn Bread was crying and yelling into Geek 'Ho's ear while she was going into his pocket.

Corn Bread: "I'm sorry! I'm sorry! I'm sorry! I'm sorry, oh lord, I'm sorry. Forgive me, Boo!"

Geek 'Ho got the rocks and told Ren Shockley, "Thank you," and twisted her ass on down the street. Ren Shockley put his hand up and said, "Let's go, boys. We got him."

Detective Ren Shockley took Corn Bread on down to the police station into the dark room with one light and one chair. Ren Shockley and Officer Tucci stayed on Corn Bread pressuring him to confess about the murder of Ms. Bout It.

Ren Shockley: "Okay, Corn Bread. We got you on selling crack cocaine to an undercover officer, lying to an officer, and with the murder of Ms. Bout It."

Corn Bread: "Shittt! You got me fucked up, Mr. Man. I ain't killed nobody."

Ren Shockley: "Oh, we know you did it. You were just high. You didn't mean to do it--she made you do it by blow-ing your high."

Corn Bread: "Hell, yeah, that bitch blew my high!"

Ren Shockley and everybody knows if you blow Corn

Bread's high he will kill you right.

Corn Bread: "Hell, yeah, I told that bitch."

Ren Shockley: "What did you tell her?"

Corn Bread: "Who? What, man? I ain't did nothing. Could I get a cigarette?" Corn Bread then scratched his head.

Officer Tucci: "We'll give you a rock if you tell us who put you up to killin' Ms. Bout It. 'Cause you know you did it. Hell, even we know you did it 'cause we seen you and after you killed her you had blood on your hands. We followed you. You went to the 'hood to get high and you took a bath to get the blood off your hand, right buddy? We got high together, remember buddy?"

Corn Bread started to break.

Corn Bread: "You're right, buddy. Could I get a blast right now?"

Officer Tucci: "Yeah, if you tell us who put you up to killin' Ms. Bout It. Look, I got your shooter and ten fat ass rocks right here."

Corn Bread: "Sho' 'nuff?"

Officer Tucci: "Sho' 'nuff. Got them right here. This here is some of Super Star's dope."

Corn Bread: "Damn, you know Super Star?"

Officer Tucci: "Corn Bread, look. We know everything."

Corn Bread: "But if I tell, that will make me a snitch."

Officer Tucci: "Look, we don't want you to snitch; we want you to vouch for us."

Corn Bread: "Vouch?"

Officer Tucci: "See, we go get a few pictures. You pick one out of the bunch. We go pick him up, bring you into the room, and you say 'I vouch that this person gave me the order to kill Ms. Bout It' and you walk right back out of the room and you go. Now that don't sound like no snitching to me, do it to you, Mr. Shockley?"

Ren Shockley: "Oh, no. That's vouching."

Corn Bread: "Well, it sound like snitching to me. I'll do it all because that nigga didn't pay me my money."

Ren Shockley: "Who didn't pay you your money, son?"

Corn Bread: "That nigga Billy Lawrence. He's the one who came to me talking about 'kill this woman and I will pay you good'." Corn Bread took a deep breath and said, "Could I get me a blast now? If that cheap ass nigga just would have paid me. Boy, I tell you." Corn Bread put his head down. Officer Tucci gave Corn Bread his shooter and a rock. Corn Bread got hyped then, and crunk up the Bankhead Bounce.

Ren Shockley went to go and run a check on Billy Lawrence. Corn Bread fixed up his shooter and got him a blast.

Corn Bread: "Want a hit, buddy?"

Officer Tucci: "No, thanks."

Corn Bread: "You know, you fooled the shit out of me and it's hard to pull one over on me. You got a hell of a job smoking rocks to bust a nigga. Shittt--I should have been a cop a long time ago. Tell me this: How is it that you can smoke rock and then when someone asks you 'do you want a hit' you say 'no, thanks'? Man, I ain't never turned down a hit. I always got my blast on."

Officer Tucci: "Believe me, it ain't easy. Sometimes I have my setbacks, crying to my wife in bed because the crack be calling me. Sometimes I wake up in a cold sweat, and sometimes I just say 'fuck that shit' and beat it."

Ren Shockley walked into the room and walked right back out to go get some air spray to spray the room. He came back into the room, sprayed it, and sat Billy Lawrence's photo in Corn Bread's lap. Corn Bread look at the picture and said, "Yes, I vouch this him. This him!"

Ren Shockley left the room and put out an A.P.B. on Billy Lawrence. They put Corn Bread in a one man cell. There he sat. And the search was on.

The next day, Billy Lawrence was at Diamonds & Pearls sitting in the VIP with Bread Bout It talking about his money. But Bread was giving Billy the run-around.

Billy: "Man, I need my money."

Bread: "I heard you the first four times."

Billy: "Yeah, so you got my money? I need my money tonight. I got bills. I even came out of my pocket to pay that fool Corn Bread. With my money, man."

Bread: "That fool killed her just a hundred yards away from the house. Right in front of the kids."

Billy: "I know it was fucked up, but that bitch provoked him. I got on his ass about it, too. I didn't want to pay him, but the man did his job. Anything for you, baby. Now, can I get paid?"

Bread: "Give me a week so I can collect the insurance money."

Billy stood up and knocked the table, causing the drinks to spill on Bread.

Billy: "What! Man, I don't want to hear that shit! Nigga, don't you know I will tear this club up and burn it all the way down? Now, you going to get me money tonight! I'm going to go home and get my shit and come back. And if you don't have my money, that's your ass."

And Billy walked out of the club mad as hell. Bread just watched him leave and snapped his fingers to get someone to clean up the mess and fix him another drink.

On the way home, Billy was thinking about going back to the club and killing Bread Bout It. But when Billy got home there were 50 cars full of police blocking the street and surrounding his house. Billy drove into the road block, right up to Detective Ren Shockley.

Billy: "What seems to be the problem, Officer?"

Ren Shockley: "License and insurance, sir."

Billy handed over his license and insurance card. Ren Shockley looked at them and saw that this was his man.

Ren Shockley: "Could you step out of the car please, sir?"

Billy: "For what? What's wrong, Officer?"

Another officer stepped up and saw that Billy was giving Ren Shockley a small problem.

The Officer: "Could you please get out of the car, sir."

Billy: "Look here, yo, last time a nigga got out of a car he had to be carried off. I ain't gettin' out..."

Before he could get out another word, the officer grabbed him out through the window and put it on his ass. The officer then handcuffed Billy and handed him over to Ren Shockley. Mr. Shockley put Billy into his car and threw up his hands and told his boys, "Okay, we got him."

A few of the detectives came out of Billy Lawrence's house with gats and dope and the pump shot gun that was used to kill Ms. Bout It. Down at headquarters in the dark room with one light and one chair, Billy sat looking around waiting for someone to cut the lights on and to tell him what's going on.

Detective Ren Shockley and Officer Tucci were in Corn Bread's room putting one and two together. They were in Corn Bread's cell with the pump shotgun he used to kill Ms. Bout it with.

Corn Bread: "What's up, doc?"

Ren Shockley: "Corn Bread. Corn Bread, look what we found at your friend Billy's house, and he says that it's yours."

Corn Bread: "He's lyin'. Yo, that's his gun, you found it at his house."

Officer Tucci: "But he says it's your gun and after you killed her you told him to put the gun away for you."

Corn Bread: "Yo, I will tell him to his face that's his shotgun!"

Officer Tucci: "So are you ready to vouch for us?"

Corn Bread: "Let's do it."

Ren Shockley and Officer Tucci rushed Corn Bread down to the dark room door. Billy looked up. Corn Bread looked in.

Corn Bread: "That's that nigga. I vouch that shit. That's that nigga."

Officer Tucci and Detective Shockley rushed Corn Bread back to his cell. Because they'd heard all they needed to break Billy Lawrence.

Detective Ren Shockley and Officer Tucci walked into the dark room. They stood over Billy Lawrence breaking him down.

Officer Tucci: "Well, well, well, look what we got here. Bad Ass Billy Boy, you know that's your ass, right? Yeah, Corn Bread told us all about it. So I got to break the news-- you should have paid him. Now, you can play dumb and act like you don't know what I'm talking about and that's when it's going to get harder on you. Do you know how much time you get for killing a white woman in the state of Georgia? 50 to 100 years. Now, that's a lot of time for a young black man like you."

Ren Shockley: "Be a good boy and feed us, Billy. We're hungry. Put us something on the table. See, right now you're shuffling the cards. You put the cards on the table. I pick them up and make the deal."

Billy wasn't no fool. He knew with a deal he could play both ends against the middle.

Billy: "Look here, Mr. Man, what are you going to deal

me once I place the cards on the table?"

Ren Shockley: "Three years is a short time. We can put you in protective custody and we can send you through school so you can make something out of yourself."

Billy: "All that sounds good, yo. But put it in writing, and once you do that it's all good."

Detective Ren Shockley did just that. Then they set the tape recorder in front of Billy, and that's when he spilled his beans. He told Detective Ren Shockley and Officer Tucci that Bread Bout It had him to find someone to kill his wife so he could collect the insurance money and that he got Corn Bread to do the job for him. And that's when Billy dropped his head, sayin' "Why, why, why?"

Officer Tucci: "You should have paid Corn Bread."

Billy: "Shittt--I didn't get paid shit, neither."

Ren Shockley: "Billy Boy, you did good."

Officer Tucci: "Should I put out an A.P.B.?"

Ren Shockley: "Naw, I know where he's at. Just take Billy Boy to his cell and let's go get our man."

Riding out to Bread Bout It's house.

Detective Ren Shockley: "You know, Officer Tucci, you helped me out a lot on this case. If it wasn't for you I'd still be trying to put 1, 2 and 3 together. After this case I will recommend to Chief Beverly Harvard to make you a detective. Would you like that?"

Officer Tucci: "Very much, sir."

They pulled into Bread Bout It's driveway. Bread had company; it was the kids' grandparents. Ren Shockley knocked on the door. The grandfather came to the door.

Granddad: "May I help you, sir?"

Ren Shockley: "Yes, you can. I'm Detective Ren Shockley and this is my partner, Officer Tucci. I met you down at the station. Sir, I'm here with an arrest warrant for Mr. Bread

Bout It."

Granddad: "For what?"

Ren Shockley: "For the murder of Ms. Bout It."

Granddad: "Come on in."

Ren Shockley threw his badge into Bread Bout It's face and read him his rights. Officer Tucci placed handcuffs on him and headed for the door. The kids started crying and yelling "Don't take my Dad! Don't take my Dad!" The grandparents calmed the kids down. And Detective Ren Shockley drove Bread Bout It back downtown to headquarters and placed him into the dark room with one light and one chair.

Detective Ren Shockley and Officer Tucci questioned and questioned Bread Bout It for hours about his wife's murder. He didn't break down. All he kept saying was that he did not kill his wife 'cause he was out of town and that he loved his wife more than life itself. But all that didn't matter, 'cause Billy Lawrence had turned State on him saying that Bread Bout It gave the order to have his wife killed.

Bread Bout It was charged with conspiracy, murder, racketeering, and money laundering. The federal government gave Bread Bout It a 20 year sentence to serve in a federal prison. Billy Lawrence had gotten a sweet ass deal--his time was on the low low. Corn Bread got life plus 15 years.

They closed down all three of Bread Bout It's clubs: Club Dominique, Club Dion, and Diamonds & Pearls. And when all three of the clubs closed down, a funny thing happened. Atlanta let two of the best players go on their teams. Dominique Wilkins of the Atlanta Hawks and Dion Sanders played for the Atlanta Braves and Falcons.

They really let them go because it was a club named after them that was owned by a white man who did wrong by killing his wife. These two players was the best at the game-

-Superstars. And let me tell you, they sold tickets! They sold lots of tickets. The stadium and the auditorium stayed packed when these All Stars played the game. Atlanta was wrong for letting these two key players go. I think it was a conspiracy.

FATAL CONFLICT

Baller had a few of the boyz coming over to talk about the upcoming lick that he's been scoping. It was the bank job that li'l Dee Dee blowed into his ear. Baller had everything planned out just like he liked it. Now it was for him to put his soldiers together for this lick. He got Hezzy, Pete, Ten, Panama Black, and Flamingo to help him pull it off.

It was an hour before the meeting, but before they came over Baller was upstairs talkin' with Hezzy about the letter that Brown Sugar wrote to him.

Hezzy: "What's going on, Soulja?"

Baller: "Man, I'm just going over this letter Brown Sugar wrote to me."

Hezzy: "Oh yeah? What's up?"

Baller: "She said if anything was to happen to her, look after her li'l sister 'cause she has a li'l baby and she want me to be the godfather."

Hezzy: "Oh yeah?"

Baller: "Hell, yeah. And she said at her sister's apartment in the bathroom ceiling is where she put her ton of coke, and six million in cash is up in the ceiling, also."

Hezzy: "What cha gonna do, Playboy?"

Baller: "Shittt--I'm goin' to take care of my responsibility."

Hezzy: "And what's that?"

Baller: "Goin' into that apartment and getting what's owed to me then get Sugar's li'l sister and buy her a big ass house and furnish the whole damn house with some of the best furniture that money can buy."

Hezzy: "Oh, man, that's nice; but how in the hell are you going to get the shit out of the apartment? There's always someone home in the project."

Baller: "You damn sho' right. I'll just go over there tomorrow and lay some bread on them. Tell them to go shopping, you know, and get something nice for her and the baby and anybody else who might be there and when they leave - boom! - me and you go through the back window, get the money and the coke and come on back home and get ready for the lick this Friday. Simple as that."

Hezzy: "Nigga, you be workin'."

Baller: "Shittt--I got it from you."

Hezzy: "Yeah, I know."

They both laughed. By that time, Ten yelled upstairs tellin' Baller and Hezzy "It's time--the boys are here."

Baller: "We're on our way down."

All of the ninjas gathered into the living room. Baller laid out all the plan, puttin' his soldiers in position.

Baller: "Okay, it's going to be like this. We're going in two cars. Ten, Hezzy, and Pete, you'll take the station wagon and me, Flamingo, and Panama Black will take Flamingo's old beat up Cadillac."

Everybody busted out laughing when Baller mentioned Flamingo's old pimped out beat up Cadillac.

Flamingo: "Shittt--I don't see why y'all niggas laughin'. Shittt--pimpin' had them 'ho's, man, I use to ride that bitch. When them 'ho's see that Cadillac come around that curb, they straightened up and bring that money to pimpin'. After this here lick I'm going to see if you niggas still going to be laughing."

Baller: "We just fuckin' with you, man."

Flamingo: "I know. I'm just having fun, but I am going to fix that bitch up so when li'l pimpin' get bigger he can have something to ride."

Baller: "Okay, it's like this. We hit the bank at 2:58 p.m. Friday. The bank will be holding two million in cash. We got 90 seconds to get all the money and at 3:00 p.m. there will be an armored car pulling up to come pick up the money with five more million in the back of the armored car. We're going to hit that, too. Okay, Flamingo and Panama Black, I want you two to run in the bank to tell everybody to freeze and get 'em up. We're right behind you, so don't look back. I will spray the cameras. Pete, you and Hezzy go into the back vault and just start filling up your bags with money. Ten, me and you will get the money in the front and be checkin' it for dye packs.

"Now, we have to do that in 90 seconds flat. Because when that armored car pulls up and the guard step out of the armored car I will rush him back into the armored car and take his gun and the and the driver's gun and then bust up the radio and tell the guard in the back to open up the back so you two, Hezzy and Pete, will go in the back and take the guard's gun away.

"Ten will then get the station wagon and drive it to the back of the armored car. Pete and Hezzy, I want you to throw every bag you see back there into the station wagon. I will then take the two guards into the bank. Flamingo, I want you to go and get the Cadillac and drive it to the front of the bank and pick up me and Panama Black with the money from inside the bank.

"By that time Pete and Hezzy should be through unloading the armored car. They will close the guard inside the armored car and we split. And the time should be 3:05 p.m. It's a seven minute job that pays seven million an hour. Now the timing's got to be perfect because the cops will fall on the scene in exactly eight minutes so we got to be moving coming out of that parking lot.

"We drive down Highway 166 where there will be an old ragged ass Suburban. We will get out of the cars and load all the money into the Suburban and ride. We get off at the Sylvan Road exit. We hit that back street next to BlockBuster Video, come on around past the train station, turn that right, and we home. We chop up the money, snort some blow, smoke some choke ass weed and that's it.

"Any questions?"

Panama Black: "I got one."

Baller: "Go ahead."

Panama Black: "How come we just don't all ride out to the bank in the Suburban and do the job and then we head out to the highway and jump into both cars and head back out to the house?"

Baller: "Good question. See, if we drive the Suburban and come out of that bank or armored car a minute off schedule, the cops are going to be coming with guns blazing, bustin' just at the Suburban 'cause we're headed that way. But see, in two cars, we can split up, giving the cops no sense in direction. See, if the cops bust shots at me, you and Flamingo, Pete, Hezzy and Ten will have our back by busting shots at them, and the same thing goes for Pete, Hezzy and Ten, if the cops are busting shots at them we bust shots at the cops and we can also hide behind our car picking off the cops one by one. Ten went and got us some more gats and some new gats. Tell them, Ten."

Ten: "Yeah, I got some more high-powered weapons. I

got us some more MAC-11s, MAC-10s, Uzis, AK-47s. But for us this Friday we going to fall in the bank with our bullet proof vests on and holding in our hand is going to be some whopper choppers."

Flamingo: "What kind of gun is that?"

Ten: "Nigga, a mother fuckin' AR-15, know what I mean?"

Baller: "Now, is there any more questions?"

Hezzy: "Shittt--I was but not no more since we got them whopper chopper cop stopper it's on."

Pete: "Where is this bank located at now?"

Baller: "In the Greenbriar Mall parking lot. Is there any more questions? If not, we meet back here on Thursday night. We go over the plans one more time. Then we eat together, sleep together, get up and eat once more together and we do this job together. An that's the kind of spirit that will keep us together. Now, let's get high."

Hezzy: "Hey, hey. Hold up before we pop the top on this here Carlos Rossi. I just want to know one thing. Ten, where in the hell did you get those AR-15s, 'cause I been looking for them too."

Ten: "Shittt-they wasn't hard to find. I got this friend that work up the street. He's in the army and he stay on base."

Hezzy: "You talkin' about up at Fort McPherson?"

Ten: "Yeah, I pay him money to get me guns at Red Dragon Gun Shop out of town. Nigga, I even got a few more grenades. Now bust that key of coke over there, Flamingo, and let's get raw dog."

Flamingo: "'Nuff said. It's already busted open."

Hezzy: "Yo, Pete, put that movie 'Friday' in and let's trip and choke."

They all got high and trip off the movies until the next day. When the next day came, Baller woke up. It was 1:00

p.m. He got his self together to go see Brown Sugar's li'l sister, Neva. Ten and Pete was still asleep. Hezzy was upstairs messing with his stereo equipment.

Baller went upstairs to tell Hezzy he wants Hezzy to ride with him. Baller tapped Hezzy on the shoulder. Hezzy turned and took off the headset.

Hezzy: "What, Playboy? Damn! You lookin' fresh. Where you headed?"

Baller: "Yo, I'm going over to Sugar's li'l sister's apartment and break the news that I'm the godfather. And as soon as I get there I'm going to play with the kid a li'l bit then I'm going to ask for some water, pour a li'l on my leg to make it seem like the kid pissed on me. Then I will go to the rest room to play it off, and then I will check out the stash. If it's there I'm going to give them some money and tell them to go out and buy the kid something nice. And when they leave the apartment, me and you going in."

Hezzy: "When?"

Baller: "Today, if they will fall for it."

Hezzy: "Is you ready now?"

Baller: "Yeah."

Hezzy: "Let's dip, and do the damn thang."

Hezzy turned off his stereo equipment and they left out the door, drivin' out to the apartment. When they arrive at the scene it's 2:05 p.m. Sitting in the car.

Baller: "Yo, it's only going to take me 15 minutes to do this, so chill until I come back out."

Baller got out of the car, walked up the driveway, and started looking around the house, checking out the apartment to see if they were any front ways to get into the apartment besides the door. Hezzy was just chillin' out in the car, playin' one of his mix tapes, listenin' to Jake the Flake, "The Street Is All I Know".

Baller knocks on the door. Abbie came to the door.

Abbie: "May I help you?"

Baller: "Hey, what's up? I was a close friend of Sugar and she told me if anything was to happen to her she would like for me to come by every now and then and look out for here li'l sister and the baby."

Abbie shook her head, then dropped it. She looked back up with tears in her eyes.

Abbie: "I'm glad to see that you care, but you're too late."

Baller: "What do you mean?"

Abbie: "I think you need to come in and sit down."

Baller came in to the apartment and all of a sudden he felt something move through his body that brought sweat from his body. Baller started feeling funny.

Baller: "What's up? What's wrong?"

Abbie: "Well, like I said, you're too late."

Baller: "What do you mean?"

Abbie: "The baby died yesterday."

Baller: "What happened?"

Abbie: "It wasn't Neva's fault." Abbie couldn't get it out, she just started to cry.

Abbie: "It...it wasn't...we had the house clean...oh, lord, help me."

Baller: "What? What?"

Isra came downstairs to see what was wrong with her sister.

Isra: "Girl, it's going to be all right. Who is you?"

Baller: "I'm a friend of Sugar's. She told me to look out for her li'l sister if something was to happen to her. My name is Baller."

Isra: "Hi. My name is Isra." Isra took the pain of the baby's death more better than anyone.

Isra: "Well, have my sister told you?"

Baller: "She try."

Isra: "Well, the baby died yesterday. She choked on a cockroach."

Baller: "What happened?"

Isra: "She was playin' in the floor. Somehow she got the cockroach, swallowed it and suffocated. Neva took damn good care of that baby. She kept her lookin' pretty. Sugar used to get on us about cleanin' the house, but the house was clean the day she died. It...it just don't matter how good you clean these damn project houses. You look here, you look there, a roach, a roach, a roach...I'm just sick of this rats and roaches infested ghetto. You know what? I think it was a sign from God. I believe he is tryin' to tell us something."

Baller: "Is there anything that I can do to help?"

Isra: "Yeah, if you can help us out of this ghetto."

Baller: "Anything for Sugar's folks. Will you please excuse me? I would like to use the rest room."

Isra: "Sure. Upstairs to the right."

Baller walked upstairs to the rest room. He closed the door and took a look into the mirror. Baller closed his eyes and took a deep breath and opened up his eyes and seen Brown Sugar's reflection in the mirror. He closed his eyes again and opened them; this time he saw Brown Sugar holding the baby. He dropped his head into the sink and ran cold water over his face and looked. Sugar and the baby was gone. Baller saying to himself, Man, I'm trippin'.

Baller looked up at the ceiling door. He stood on top of the toilet, and opening up the small door stuck his hand up there and pulled out a knot of money. He looked at the money and saw Brown Sugar holding the baby, saying to him to do the right thing. Baller stuck the money back up in the ceiling and rushed back down stairs and asked Isra when is the funeral?

Isra: "Friday at 1:30 p.m. Why?"

Baller: "Cause I want to help."

Baller pulled out a thousand dollars and gave it to Isra and said, "I will do more next time. I'll see y'all." And Baller walked out the door and walked to the car and got in.

Hezzy: "What's up, Ninja? You were in there a long time. What's the word?"

Baller: "Yo, pull off, I'll tell you on the way back to the house."

Hezzy pulled off.

Hezzy: "So what's up?"

Baller: "You ain't going to believe it."

Hezzy: "What?"

Baller: "Man, when I walked into that house I felt something go through me. The shit made me feel cold and then I got hot. Sugar's Aunt Isra told me that I was too late because the baby died yesterday."

Hezzy: "What--died?"

Baller: "Yeah, man, died."

Hezzy: "How?"

Baller: "Just be cool, I'm going to tell you. She was playin' in the floor and messed around and swallowed a cockroach."

Hezzy: "Damn, that's fucked up, that's fucked. So what's up with the money and the coke?"

Baller: "It's there, but, yo, this is where it get's crazy. I walked into the rest room, right? Looked into the mirror and saw Brown Sugar."

Hezzy: "What?! Man, you trippin."

Baller: "Naw, man, this shit was real. I closed my eyes again and looked, and I saw Sugar this time, but she was holdin' the baby."

Hezzy: "The dead baby?"

Baller: "I guess that was the baby. So I shook my head

and put some cold water on my face and looked and she was gone. And that's when I looked into the ceiling, felt the money, got the money, and when I looked, at that moment I saw Sugar holding the baby over in the corner telling me to do the right thing."

Hezzy: "Got damn! Baller, man, you serious?"

Baller: "Hell, yeah, Nigga! I got no reason to lie to you baby boy. I love you Nigga. So check it out. I put the money back and went back downstairs and gave Isra a thousand dollars and told them I will do what Brown Sugar told me to do."

Hezzy: "So when are we going to get the money?"

Baller: "Okay, the funeral is Friday at 1:30 p.m. We get back at their apartment at 1:20 p.m. We go in and get the money and coke and get back to our house, meet the boyz and pull off the bank job."

Hezzy: "Yo, that's two licks in one day."

Baller: "I know. I did it before. Can you?"

Hezzy: "Fo' sho'."

Two days later. July 24, 1996. Thursday night. All the ninjas sat in the living room going over the plans once more.

Baller: "Yo, Flamingo. What's your job?"

Flamingo: "Me and Panama Black run off into the bank first and draw down on everybody makin' them get 'em up and come to the front corner of the bank and lay it down."

Baller: "Check. Hezzy, what's your job?"

Hezzy: "Me and Pete will go straight to the vault and clean it out."

Baller: "Check. Ten, what's your job?"

Ten: "Me and you will spray the cameras and then get all the money out of the front drawers and we check the money for dye packs."

Baller: "Check. Now, like I said, we got 90 seconds to pull

that off. Tell me why, Pete."

Pete: "Because there will be an armored car pullin' up in 30 seconds, which then the time will be 3:00 p.m. and inside the armored car will be five million in cash and it's me and Hezzy's job to unload and reload the money. But we do that after you rush the guard back into the armored car."

Baller: "Check. Okay, Panama Black, what are you going to be doing?"

Panama Black: "Me and Flamingo will be on the inside of the bank holdin' down the money and the people inside the bank."

Baller: "Check. Ten, what's up?"

Ten: "Okay. After you bring the guards from the armored car in the front corner of the bank, I will go and get the station wagon and pull it to the back of the armored car so Pete and Hezzy can load and unload the armored car by filling the station wagon up with all the cash in the back."

Baller: "Check. Okay. Anybody else knows what's next?"

Flamingo: "Yeah. I leave Panama Black and Baller inside the bank to go get the Cadillac and drive back to the front of the bank to pick up Baller and Panama Black with the money because by that time Pete and Hezzy should be through with unloading the armored car."

Baller: "Check. Okay, everybody. What the time should be..."

Everybody: "3:05 p.m.!"

Baller: "Yeah, yeah, that's it, that's it. Now look, we're going to ride on stolen tags and we're going to strip off the manufacture's ID number and the decal, cause they can trace that shit back to the owner. And the owner will give us up."

There was a knock at the door. Ten got up and went to the door.

Ten: "Who is it?"

Eazy: "It's me, Eazy."

Ten opened up the door.

Ten: "What's up, gangster?"

Eazy: "You, my ninja one love."

Ten: "One love."

Eazy: "One love everybody. Everybody one love. Damn! Look like y'all ninjas ready for war."

Baller: "Matter of fact, we is. We got a bank job tomorrow."

Eazy: "What's the take?"

Baller: "Seven mill."

Eazy: "Damn! I wish I could get down on this one but, man, we got licks on top of licks, not next month but the month after, and Chicago sent me over to tell you ninjas she is going to need y'all's help on fight night."

Baller: "Tell her it's on."

Eazy: "Oh yeah. On fight night it's Chicago's birthday."

Hezzy: "Sho' 'nuff."

Eazy: "Yeah, on September 13. And she told me to tell y'all niggas just coming by to help her on these licks is good 'nuff for her." Eazy rubbed his hand through Hezzy's 'fro and said, "Y'all ninjas be safe," and left.

Hezzy: "Damn, I just thought about it."

Baller: "What's that baby boy?"

Hezzy: "Oh, my Aunt Helen's birthday's next week. I just got to get her something nice 'cause she raised a nigga."

Baller: "What happened to your folks?"

Hezzy: "Well, my mom left me when I was five years old. My aunt told me she didn't want to leave me and my brother, it was just that my dad used to beat the shit out of her. He would kick her ass for no reason at all. And he fucked up her head mentally. Everywhere she would go he would make it bad for her. My aunt told me she couldn't eat the way she wanted, she couldn't sleep. My dad drove her crazy. So one day she took me and my brother over to our aunt's house while she went to work. But she knew my dad would be there every time she come to pick us up. And he would start some shit. So that day my mom tricked his ass, and me and my brother, too. She never came back.

"I would sometimes ask my Dad why did Mama leave us. He would say shit like 'The bitch was no good. She left me when I was down on my luck. Your Mama was no good, you hear me?' And I would still say, 'But that's my Mama, Daddy.' And he would say, 'Boy! You don't have a mother.' Then I would say, 'But I still want to see her.' Man, my dad would get mad as hell at me. He used to whip my ass when I talked about my mom. But my Aunt Helen used to tell me I had a sweet mother, it was just my dad. She said he stayed drunk and everytime he got drunk he would kick her ass.

"I see him on the street sometimes. I speak because he speaks, but I don't really want to speak to his dirty ass. He acts like he loves me, but he hates my black ass 'cause I look just like my mother and that shit burns him up."

Ten: "I feel you. Yo, my punk ass dad the same way. Man, that mother fucker didn't raise me but he stayed all in my business. When I was li'l, he would come around and say some stupid shit like 'I know you and your sister don't love me and when I get old y'all ain't going to take care of me. Y'all going to try to put me in a old folks home.' He be tryin' to make us feel sorry for his stupid ass. Me and my sister will just look at him like he's crazy.

"Yeah, but like I was sayin', one of my baby's mama's right, this bitch is dumb as hell. My fuck ass daddy goes over to her house and act like he there to be a granddaddy for my child when he wasn't a dad for me. She don't see it's a act, but she lovin' that shit 'cause he givin' that bitch all my business. And then he payin' her for some pussy every month, tellin' her it's for the baby. He even gave the bitch my Social Security number so she can take out Child Support on a nigga! Every time I see that bitch ass nigga my eyes hurt. I don't give a fuck! if that nigga die cause he is a dirty ass nigga. He will hurt his own kids for a piece of pussy and that's cold."

Flamingo: "Shittt, I ain't never met my father. But I ask my mom about him. She would just say 'Your dad was a player, son. He just got to have all the womens.' That old nigga broke my mother's heart. She said he left before I was born."

Pete: "Well, I had both of my parents. But my dad wasn't there for me. And the only reason why he was there is because my mother hated being alone. He would go out every night and get with another woman. And my mom would know this shit. My uncle would come over and teach me shit like how to be a man. I love my uncle; fuck my daddy."

Panama Black: "Shittt--I grew up without a dad and a half of a mother, in a house with ten brothers and sisters. My mom kick it with my li'l sister's father for awhile. He work, but he also smoke rocks on the side. He fuck around and turned my mom onto the rock. And then he left her with ten kids to raise. Now it's like this: I got three brothers in jail, one dead, and all my li'l hot ass sisters have had babies and their baby's daddies is nowhere to be found. If it wasn't for that nigga Baller I would probably be dead or in jail. Ever since I got with this man right here I got money, I got a new family, and I got love. And there's nothing in this world that I wouldn't do for this crew right here."

Baller: "I feel you. But fuck my punk ass daddy, too. My

grandmother raised me. Yo, Pete, when are we going to put some food on? I'm hungrier than a mother fucker. I know y'all niggas hungry too."

Pete: "Yeah, yeah. Tonight we gonna eat some T-bone steaks and baked potatoes with a salad. Now, Hezzy, put on some music. Put that WC & The Maad Circle on Ain't a Damn Thang Changed. Play that song for them ninjas. There's a song on there called 'Fuck my Daddy'. The after that pump that 'Dear Mama' by 2pac on that Me Against the World."

Baller: "Pete, I see you know a lot about that music now."

Pete: "Yeah, Hezzy turned me on to that real underground shit."

Hezzy: "But, yeah, Ninja, you showed me how to cook in the Job Corps. 'Member that in Morganfield, Kentucky in the Sticks Dorm 1553 at Earl C. Clemens."

They all sat and ate and slept and got ready for the next day. Morning came. Hezzy and Baller got up that morning and went to the Waffle House to get everyone some breakfast.

Hezzy: "What do you want to eat."

Baller: "It don't matter."

Waitress: "Could I help you, sir?"

Hezzy: "Yeah, let me get six orders of waffles with sausage grits and cheese eggs to go."

Waitress: "You say you want six waffles with sausage grits and cheese eggs to go."

Hezzy: "Yeah."

Waitress: "It will be right up."

Baller and Hezzy sat and waited on the food.

Baller: "Damn, I got this feeling it's going to be a long day."

Hezzy: "Why you say that?"

Baller: "I just feel it."

Hezzy: "I know one thang. We going to be paid. I know that much 'cause I believe in God."

Baller: "Yeah, but can you handle Him when He's hard?"

Hezzy just sat and thought about that.

Hezzy: "Yo, Baller, look at that nigga over there with that fuck up 'fro. Look like Jermaine Dupri."

Baller: "Damn sho' do. Ha, ha."

Hezzy: "Now this is a 'fro."

Waitress: "Your food is ready, sir."

Hezzy got up and paid for the food and they left. Back at the house, time 11:30 a.m.

Baller: "Yo, yo, y'all ninjas got some breakfast. Let's eat. Pete, say grace."

Pete said the grace and they all ate. Time 12:39 p.m.

Baller: "Yo, baby boy, it's about that time."

Hezzy: "Yeah, I know, let's do it."

Baller: "Yo, y'all ninjas just chill until we get back."

Hezzy and Baller stuck a sign on the side of the van which said BellSouth and on the inside of the van they got dressed as phone men. Drivin' out to the apartment, Baller's pager goes off. Baller check the number. It was Crow. Baller called back on his cellular phone.

Crow: "Hello."

Baller: "What's up?"

Crow: "Yo, there's been a change of plans."

Baller: "What do you mean?"

Crow: "The lick on King Goldie."

Baller: "What, it's still on for next week, right?"

Crow: "Naw, my nigga, it's tonight."

Baller: "Hell, naw, nigga, not tonight. What's up?"

Crow: "That nigga King Goldie is dyin' and Uncle Luke is making it his business to come tonight. He will arrive in town at 7:30 p.m. and he is bringing tons and tons of coke with him and in King Goldie's house, that's where he's got his whole stash of coke and cash."

Baller: "Okay, so what's the dealio?"

Crow: "I want you to come to the house at 8:00 p.m., kick in the door, and just start shooting niggas from the front and I will take care of the back, man. There's going to be over $25 million in cash in that house."

Baller: "It sounds good to me. I'm with it."

Crow: "Okay, later."

Baller: "Later."

And they hung up the phone.

Baller: "I just knew it was going to be a long day."

Hezzy: "What's up?"

Baller: "Just another lick for the night."

Hezzy: "Damn, nigga, that's three in one day. You think you can handle three?"

Baller: "I'm going to try."

Pulling up in the project dressed as phone men they got out of the van and checked the front and the back. It was all clear. Hezzy kicked in the back door. Him and Baller rushed into the house. Hezzy closed the door behind them. Hezzy checked the house; Baller went straight to the rest room.

Hezzy: "The house is clear."

Baller: "Open up your bag."

Hezzy held open the BellSouth bag and Baller filled it with money and told Hezzy to take the money to the van.

Baller filled the other two bags up with the ton of coke. Baller fixed everything back like it was and headed for the van. But when he got downstairs he saw Hezzy just sitting there on the couch in shock.

Baller: "Hezzy, what the hell's wrong with you? Why

haven't you taken the money to the van?"

Hezzy just sat in silence. Baller grabbed Hezzy by the hand and took him to the van. They went out the same way they came in. Baller drove.

Baller: "What's wrong with you? Seen a ghost?"

Hezzy: "Hell yeah!"

Baller: "What did you see?"

Hezzy: "Dog, you ain't going to believe it."

Baller: "What?"

Hezzy: "Dog, I was coming down the stairs with the money. I saw Brown Sugar. She stopped me and said to tell you to do the right thang."

Baller: "See! See! You believe now, right?"

Hezzy: "Yeah..."

Arriving back at home. Time 2:00 p.m. They removed the sign from the van and went into the house.

Flamingo: "Where y'all been? It's almost that time."

Baller: "We had a small job to do."

Panama Black: "Damn! Dress like the phone man?"

Baller: "Hell, yeah. Next time it might be a mailman or a pizza man. Anything to get the job done. All right y'all ninjas, get strap & gear up. It is about that time."

Baller and Hezzy took the money and coke and put it up and got ready and then it was time. They hooked up the video camera inside the house before they left. They got out to the bank at 2:55 p.m., three minutes early, so they cased the bank and scoped the parking lot. It was all clear. They all ran into the bank.

Flamingo and Panama Black: "All y'all mother fuckers get 'em up and get you ass to the front! And lay it down!"

Ten and Baller sprayed the cameras and hit up the front registers and they checked for dye packs. Pete and Hezzy was in the vault cleaning it out. They came back in the front.

Time: 85 seconds. 5 seconds later the armored car pulls up, two in the front and one in the back.

The guard in the front on the right hand side started to get out of the armored car. Baller rushed out of the bank with his AR-15 aimed at the guard telling him to get back in the armored car. The guard turned and Baller put the gun into the guard's back. The driver was froze with his hands up. Baller got into the armored car and took both of their guns and gave the driver orders to tell the drivers in the back to "open up the door with his hands up or I will kill you both." The driver told the guard that while Baller smashed the radio by kicking it to pieces.

The guard in the back thought about it for a second. And then he opened up the back door. Hezzy and Pete rushed to the back of the armored car with their guns first. Ten ran and got the station wagon. Baller rushed the two guards into the bank. Pete took the gun from the guard and made him lay down in the back of the armored car. Pete put the gun into his front pocket. Ten pulled the station wagon to the back of the armored car and Hezzy and Pete was filling it up with cash. Time: 3:02 p.m.

Ten: "How many more bags we got left?"

Pete: "Five more, yo."

Ten threw up five fingers. Flamingo came out of the bank and got into his Cadillac and drove it to the front of the bank. Baller and Panama Black came out of the bank with the money. Pete was on the last money bag. Pete reached for the money bag and when he threw it to Ten the armored guard grabbed the gun from Pete's pocket and shot him in the Gluteus Maximus. Pete fell out of the armored car and on top of the station wagon. The guard also hit Hezzy in the back but the bullet proof vest saved him from a gun shot.

Hezzy jumped out of the armored car and him and Ten

cocked back their AR-15 and gave the guard his last dances. The sound of the gunfire rang out all over the parking lot. Hezzy helped Pete into the station wagon. The mall security guards rushed to the scene. Ten went busting shots on the security jeeps causing the guard to jump out running to the mall to avoid any gun shots. All of a sudden two cop cars was pulling up on the scene. It was a shoot out. Ten, Hezzy, Baller and Panama Black, they all started bustin' on the cops. The cops tried busting back, but the cops 9mm and bullet proof vest was no match for the players with the AR-15s. They tore holes in the cops vests and chests, leaving them dead on the side of their car. Baller and the boyz all jumped into their rides and headed for Highway 166.

Pete: "Drive this bitch, man drive! Don't let me die, Hezzy."

Hezzy: "I won't."

As they got on the highway, three more cop cars was on their tail giving chase with Flamingo in front and Ten right behind. They zigzagged their way through traffic. They drove past their getaway ride. There was no way of stopping. Pete still yelling, "Save me!"

Hezzy just started bustin' shots on the highway at the passing cars causing a wreck to happen. And it did--a seven car crash on the highway and ten people hurt. They made it off the highway and to the house. Ten and Flamingo covered the cars in the back yard. Baller already had phoned Dr. Fox to come over to see about Pete. They entered the back way of the house and got Pete on the couch. Pete: "Don't let me die. Man, this shit burns."

Baller: "Stay cool, the doctor is on his way. Ten, I want you and Flamingo to do away with both the cars at nightfall."

Ten: "Check."

Twenty minutes later Dr. Fox arrived to remove the bullet from Pete's gluteus. The boyz sat and sat and waited. Hezzy helped out the doctor with Pete until he was patched up. Baller gave the doctor a big chunk of money.

The boyz: "Thanks, doc."

Dr. Fox: "Okay. You boys take it easy. Pete will be okay, he just need to stay off his feet for a few days and he will be just fine." And the doc left.

Ten put up all the guns and bullet proof vests. Baller laid out the 7 mill across the table. Hezzy went upstairs to get a pound of chokin' ass weed and a key of raw. They smoked and choked and snorted blow and chopped up flow. Time: 4:16 p.m.

Baller just helped chop up the cash. He didn't get high cause he got one more wild lick for tonight. Like I said, bein' sober is the way to be when it come down to business. Time 7:15 p.m.

Baller went upstairs to get ready. He grabbed his bullet proof vest and a few weapons and a couple of hand grenades. He came back downstairs and told the boyz that he will see them later. Pete was laying on the couch in pain, chokin' on a blunt, telling Baller to be careful. All the boyz was telling Baller to go and come on back so we all can get fucked up together. Hezzy walked Baller to the door.

Hezzy: "Can you handle it?"

Baller: "I got to go, but it's gonna be all good. If I don't come back, you know what to do."

Hezzy: "I'm not going to worry. I know you're coming back."

Baller: "Yeah. Yo, but I got to be going. You take it slow baby boy." And Baller left heading out to King Goldie's house. At King Goldie's house everyone was having a good time. All of the soldier's was at their best that night trying to build their rank. Crow just kept it real. Uncle Luke was going from one soldier to another, checkin them out to see do they fit the profiles that he's lookin' for. It's more style, attitude, and guts is what Uncle Luke is lookin' for to run his billion dollar a year operation. King Goldie as laying in his death bed dying with the AIDS virus. He was seeing each one of his soldiers one by one, telling them what he expected of them when he was gone. Time 7:55 p.m.

Baller pulled outside of King Goldie's big ass house. The house was as big as the house on Fresh Prince of Bel-Air. Matter of fact, it looked just like the house. Baller saw all of the cars in the yard. He took a look at his self in the mirror as if he was just looking one more time. He put on his mask and when he did that lightning struck and the clouds turned purple. At that time, Crow walked into the room to have his talk with King Goldie. Time 7:58 p.m.

King Goldie is speaking with a sick voice.

King Goldie: "Crow, my boy, you're the best (cough). I want you to run my army. You remind me of me; you know how to go out and get money. (Cough-cough-cough.) It's just that I was girl crazy. I just love myself some pussy...but look what it did to me. It's killing me. Fuck it--I'm already dead. This virus got me fucked up. (He coughs long and hard.) I like your style. You don't give a fuck about a bitch." Time 8:00 p.m.

Boom! A loud explosion blew open the front door. King Goldie raised up from the bed. The loud explosion from the grenades shook him. When Crow heard the explosion he pulled his mask away from under his shirt and put it on and lightning struck once more. But it was more louder--it was like the door to Hell had just opened up. Hommie the Clown grabbed the pillow from the bed and slammed King Goldie down to the bed and took the pillow and placed it over King Goldie's face, suffocating him to death.

Hommie the Clown then walked to the doorway with gun in hand. Everybody was getting up off the floor. The front doorway was full of smoke. The grenade killed ten soldiers. A few of King Goldie's men headed for the door. But before they could get to the door, in walked Michael Myers coming through the door, letting off rounds from his MAC-10. Rat-tat-tat-tat-tat-tat-tat-tat...and killed ten more soldiers, leaving 35 more soldiers for Michael Myers and Hommie and that's when the gunplay jumped off. Uncle Luke and his klan started letting off rounds. Rat-tat-tat-tat-tat....Pop-pop-pop-pop-pop-pop. And King Goldie's soldiers started busting caps. Click-click-Boom! Boom! Rat-tat-tat-tat-tat. Hommie the Clown came from the back, bustin' shots on Uncle Luke and his klan and King Goldie's soldiers. Rat-tat-tat-tat-tat. Click-click-Boom! Boom! Pop-pop-pop-pop-pop-pop-pop-pop-pop. Rat-tat-tat-tat-tat. Click-click-Boom! Boom! Click-click-Boom! Boom! Duckin' and dodgin' bullets flying and niggas dying. Ratah-tatah-ratah-tatah-ratah-tatah-Boom! The gunfire was tearing the house to pieces. Everyone started reloading around about the same time. Michael Myers pulled out another grenade and threw it into the crowd of soldiers, blowing them up. One of the soldiers flew across the room into a door and into another room where King Goldie kept his two big ass dogs (two Rottweilers).

The two big ass Rottweilers came running out of the room. One dog jump up on Hommie the Clown. Hommie was fighting with the dog, choking the dog by the neck, stopping the dog from biting him and the other dog jump up on Uncle Luke, biting on his arm, pulling him all over the room. That's when Uncle Luke's boyz all put big bullet holes into the dog, killing him instantly. That's when

Michael Myers became Agility with a MAC-10 in one hand and a MAC-11 in the other, busting shots, killing Uncle Luke and his Klan. There were only a few of King Goldie's men left. They went busting shots on Micahel Myers but the body armor protected his body from the flying bullets that was coming his way. He turned and started letting loose shots on the flesh body.

Hommie the Clown was still strugglin' with the big ass dog. Michael Myers pulled out his baby chop ax and walked over to Hommie the Clown and the big ass dog and he held the ax up high and chopped the big ass dog in half. Hommie the Clown stood up still holding the dog by the head. The dog head was still growling and his legs, ass, and tail was on the floor wriggling. Hommie the Clown looked the dog eye to eye until the growling stopped and when it stopped the dog's body stopped squirming. See, dying is all in the mind. Kill the head and the body will die.

Hommie the Clown threw the dog head to the floor and picked up his gun. Him and Michael Myers walked around the whole house shooting each soldier that lay on the floor in the head and chest, checking to see if there was anyone just laying on the floor playing dead. A twenty minute shootout. They ransacked the whole house. They came out of the house with a million in jewelry, $25 million in cash, and 350 keys of pure, uncut dope.

After they loaded the van with the jewelry, money, and coke, they went back into the house to chop up the bodies and put them in a pile and set fires to the flesh and the house. The fled the scene, leaving behind a burning house with 55 lost souls. When I saw the scene it kind of reminded me about a dream I had about Hell. On the news they talked about it for weeks. They said you could smell the flesh burning from miles and miles away. When the drug dealers, pimps, players, pushers, bangers, and down ass bitches saw and heard the news on how the murders occurred, they knew that it was the most dangerous, the most talked about, vicious, wicked, violent killers in the game. Michael Myers and Hommie the Clown. It was once said as a joke but now it's true. They say that Michael Myers and Hommie the Clown had more people in their trunk than Coolio had in his video Fantastic Voyage.

Two weeks later, August 4, 1996, the Corporation met up at Milk's Al Capone suite. Everyone except Eazy. But Milk and Tray had it like if he would have came, no hard feelings.

Milk: "Look, the misunderstanding is all in the past. It was just that six tons of coke would make any man act up on his family. Now, I know you're here for your money from the 4444 investment plan."

Tray went into the back room and Milk explained why he just all of a sudden had a change of heart. Tray came back into the room dragging five big bags of money with $16 million in cash for each crew, $4 million apiece for each soldier. They all each invested $500,000 a year which was $40 million in four years. From this 4444 plan, Milk came on in and Doubled the $40 million and made it $80 million. The family was shocked.

Baller: "Damn, playboy, you're beautiful."

Milk threw both of his hands in the air and told the family how you luv that.

Baller: "Like I said, you're beautiful, baby."

Milk: "How that jail thang go?"

Baller: "Ohhh, man, they tried to break me down--but that's the past. Here I go, baby. What's up with you?"

Milk: "Come. Let's go talk."

Milk telling the family to party, have fun. Coke and weed was all laid out on the round table. As soon as Milk said that they went bustin' open pounds of weed and keys of raw, pure, uncut cocaine, getting high and mellow. Tray was friendly with everyone. Milk and Baller walked out to the Terrace that overlooked the swimming pool.

Milk: "You know, Baller, some crew out there did hit me up for six tons of coke I had for the family," looking into Baller's eyes.

Baller: "Yeah, my crew told me about that dat there. They thought you were pulling some slick shit."

Milk: "What do you think, Baller?"

Baller: "You know, this here is a wicked game we play that has rules that change every 4 seconds, 4 minutes, 4 hours, and 4 days. This game make you do and say some crazy things sometimes."

Milk: "I know. I got the battle wounds to prove it."

Milk showed Baller his stab wounds right next to his bullet wounds.

Baller: "I know you're a soldier. So what is it between you and Eazy?"

Milk: "There is no beef, like I said. It was just a misunderstanding. That's over. The past. I just want to make some big money before this year pass on by. We can take this game to another city and build. How you luv dat?"

Baller: "I can luv that."

While Milk and Baller was on the outside wrapping each other up with game, Chicago was on the inside placing bugs. Wire taps. Greed was gettin Tray coked out, fillin' his head with that real talk, keeping him off balance.

Now, this is one thang that every player should know. While Baller was having a deep private conversation with Milk, just for their ears to hear, he had his cellular phone on with Eazy on the other side of the line listenin' in on their conversation and Milk didn't know. But Milk is so true to this game he was doing the same thing. He had Oz Escobar on the other end of his line. Two true soldiers standin' in each other's faces, going at it with hellagame. Tellin' each other they're down for each other, but both are just waitin' for one to slip so they can do the stabbin' in the back. This game is just like how I explained: to make it you got to have straight gopher game underground like a mother fucker. See, niggas play all on top of your surface and try to get under your skin. That's why you got to stay strong and focused at all times.

Or it's like this, Brother and Sister. You got some folks that will come over to your house and ask to use the phone to call up your enemy, talk for a li'l bit, then hang the phone halfway up and have you to talk about your personal business while the person on the line listens in, makin' plans to destroy your dreams. No lie--I'm tellin' you what's real. Money truly is the root of all evil.

Milk and Baller walked back into the living room where the Corporation was havin' a good time. Shi-i-id...you would too if you'd just received your retirement money from selling dope and then you got to snort, drink, and choke on some fire ass weed and not have to spend one cent. Now that's the street American Dream.

Milk: "Now tell me how y'all luv that."

They all said they luv dat.

Chicago: "Milk, with this money we can live like folks. Now all we need is some work (dope).

Milk: "Don't worry; I have 50 keys apiece for each crew. So tonight or tomorrow you can get your grind on."

They all came at Milk thankin' him for the money and dope (work).

Chicago: "Milk, would you like to come to my fight party?:

Milk: "Why, sure I do."

Those were the words Milk wanted t hear because Milk had big plans set up; that's why he came on in with the money from the 4444 plan and some work (dope) to set it off. Milk, Tray, and The Jury had big plans before they leave Atlanta, Georgia. But the Corporation knows that with six tons of coke gone, Milk wasn't gonna take that shit laying down. So they set up and planned some shit also. At Chicago's fight party it was going to be the element of surprises.

They all kick it for about another hour at Milk's Al Capone Suite, left, and jumped right back on their post.

Five weeks later with days away from Fight Night, Chicago was so excited. But she wasn't the only one--The Corporation and the whole world was because this was going to be the fight of the century. The Real Deal Holyfield vs. Iron Mike Tyson. Chicago had the house set up so sweet with a boxing ring, coke, choke weed and food everywhere. The homes the crews hit a few months back with all the high tech equipment and top notch safes and electric eyes everywhere. The Corporation did their homework and studied hard for this one.

During drought time Chicago's customers were the only big timers screaming "I got white girl for sale." It was set up like that. Chicago had to move her ton of coke and make her some money and make her customers rich and happy. And when they come to the fight party--bragging, mingling, fucking and getting high--The Corporation will be off in their house taking them for what they got.

Chicago broke the souljas down in three groups. Crew one was Fly-Mar, Pee Wee Loc, Greed, and Big Mike. The Second crew was Baller, Jim Kelly, MJG, and Eazy. The third crew was Sugar Wolf, Hezzy, Pete, and Ten.

While the souljas was at the house drawing up plots and plans on fight night, all the divas went shopping out at Lenox Mall and Phipps Plaza, and I must say these womens were lookin' ragooey super saucy! You know woo!!! The first building they hit was Victoria's Secret. From there on it was Macy's, Neiman Marcus, Saks Fifth Avenue, Parisian, and Lord & Taylor. The divas have good taste in clothes from Donna Karan, Fendi, Jil Sander, Gucci, and Gianni Versace. They kept it raw.

This coming event was special to the girls because after this lick there would be just one more lick to pull off. And that was Big Six the Untouchable. And after Big Six they can retire from this Crucial Game and live like folks. Because they expect to hit up Big Six for 50 million or maybe more, because Big Six have more money than anyone in this Book. Now, he don't have more money than everybody put together, but he got big money. Yo, but it's like this--if you know how to go out and get money then you deserve the finest things in life. Now, you got some niggas that just sit on their ass and just down talk on the next man because he or she got big paper. You know, fat stacks, been poor, got rich and don't give a shit about what people say. Because what people say ain't always right. Believe that.

A day later...ding ding...Fight Night. Just like I said before, Chicago had the Ring surrounded with all types of food, fire ass choke weed, cognac, and some of the best pure cocaine that ever hit these city streets. And pussy! Man, the pussy!! It was everywhere you looked--93 females. Every bitch that turned a trick, suck a dick, and broke her back to make a stack for the Corporation was there, except Mia, Mary Jane, and Queen Black. They were at one of Jade's safe houses with a million dollars of counterfeit and keys and keys of synthetic dope. Jade's house is where the souljas switch the real for the fake and take it to Chicago's.

With the fight being an hour away, all of the ladies was getting ready and in position while the souljas was in the front middle room discussing Baller type tactics. Chicago came out into the front middle room dressed in Donna Karan, looking woo, woo, woo. She gave the souljas the addresses and the keys to her customers' houses and cars. An hour later the party was packed. Crews two and three were already gone putting in work. Crew one had laid back out of sight until everyone was inside the party stuck on high. And when they were, crew one (Fly-Mar, Pee Wee Loc, Greed, and Big Mike) broke into their cars and they came up with 60 to 92 keys of coke and 6 to 8 million in cash. 13 out of 50 was ridin' dirty, tryin' to protect their investment from the night creepers. So the souljas took what they had to the safe house and got right back on the job. Crew one had 15 houses to hit, crews two and three had 16 apiece.

Back at the fight party it was jumping off the hinges.

Milk: "Chicago, I must say you and the girls are looking stunning."

Chicago: "Why, thank you, Milk. You lookin' good yourself."

Milk: "So how you feeling?"

Chicago: "I feel great. I'm just happy that everyone is having a good time mingling, drinkin', smokin', snortin' and fuckin'. Ha ha."

Milk: "That's right. So when is it going to be me and you?"

Chicago: "Milk, you are a player. I don't need no player, I need a man."

Milk: "I am a man, Baby."

Chicago: "Yeah, a player man."

Milk: "Ha ha. I should have chose you over your sister

because you are truly the best in this high life living."

Chicago: "Diamond says she's the best."

Milk: "Oh, yeah, she is at what she do."

Chicago: "Well, why not choose her?"

Milk: "Hmm. Diamond is wild. You know, too aggressive. She don't want to use my ideas, she got her own."

Chicago: "We all do."

Milk: "Yeah, I know it. So what's next on the menu?"

Chicago: "Just look out on the floor at all the rich tricks and busters. Look right there--that's Flaming, a pimp player hustler. He makes his money off ugly 'ho's. He sends them bitches off in the clubs lookin' and smellin' good. And when them 'ho's come out the club they're either pregnant or paid. That fool got loot. And you see those two cats with him? That's Nickel and Dime. They're always trying to make a dollar out of fifteen cent. They earn their money the old fashioned way.

Milk: "How dat, inherit?"

Chicago: "Naw...jackin', robbin; sellin' dope, and pimpin'."

Milk. "Oh, the American way."

Chicago: "That's right."

Milk: "Who that big timer with Diamond?"

Chicago: "Where?"

Milk: "Right there, by the TV set."

Chicago: "That's the Untouchable Big Six, Diamond's soon to be husband."

Milk: "Is he rich?"

Chicago: "Can't tell you."

Milk: "Well, have she touch him yet?"

Chicago: "Didn't you hear me say 'Untouchable'? He's good, Milk. I call him pussy foot."

Milk: "Why?"

Chicago: "Because he move quickly and carefully, like a cat."

Milk: "What's he into?"

Chicago: "Real estate. Lots of land, baby. He get paid off the living and the dead. He got more money than anyone in this whole party. I'm sure glad you're here, Milk. Maybe you can figure something out."

Milk: "No doubt. How much cheese we talkin' about?"

Chicago: "About 5 or 6 billion."

Milk: "Does he have a crew?"

Chicago: "I suppose so. I seen his crew one time, and they are some spooky lookin' brothers."

Milk: "What do you mean?"

Chicago: "I mean they look like voodoo soldiers."

Milk: "I don't believe in the supernatural voodoo stuff, Li'l Mama. Just leave him to me, I got him."

Chicago: "Okay. And when you go over there, tell Diamond I would like to see her."

Milk took a sip of his drink and headed toward Big Six and Diamond. Chicago winked her eye at the boys, Flamingo, Nickel, and Dime. Big Six and Diamond was watching the fight.

Milk: "What's up, Diamond?"

Diamond gave Milk a big hug.

Diamond: "Hey Milk, how you doing?"

Milk: "Just fine, and you?"

Diamond: "Feeling good. Milk, this is my Boo, Big Six. Big Six, Milk."

They both spoke to each other.

Milk: "Oh, Chicago would like to see you."

Diamond: "Okay. You boyz just chill. I'll be back, Boo. And it's good to see you Milk. You are a sight for sore eyes. Really."

Diamond stepped off while Nickel and Dime stepped in around the tube. Small bets circulated around the room until the main event.

I know thousands of homeowners feel safer by converting to the Brinks Home Security System. It's true, Brinks is number one when it comes to protecting your home and stopping burglars cold in their tracks. But a true burglar don't give a fuck. If they want the money and valuables that lay in your home, they're coming in and they really don't give a fuck if you are home. A burglar have some of the most boldness nerves on this planet. But a dopeman burglar got bigger nerves but they study the timing and they also do their homework on breakin' the code system every year. A true burglar grows with the times. Better security system, better burglar. And that's the bottom line on that note.

The first crew had no problem with none of the 15 houses they had except this last house on the left. Pee Wee Loc popped the code on the outside. They all entered the house, avoiding all electric eye beams. Pee Wee Loc and Big Mike checked the three bedrooms while Fly-Mar and Greed checked the rest of the house. Greed and Fly-Mar came up with a large quantity of cocaine and expensive paintings. Pee Wee Loc and Big Mike searched Baby Bear's room and came up with nothing. Mama Bear's room, nothing. By this time, Fly-Mar and Greed took what they had out to the car. Pee Wee Loc and Big Mike entered Papa Bear's room. Pee Wee Loc shook his head because he thought he saw something shoot past his eye. They searched the room, and inside the master bedroom was a floor safe. Loc took out his tools and started to operate. Big Mike had the flashlight. As soon as Pee Wee Loc bent over to go to work, a big ass attack cat jumped in his face, causing pain. Before Big Mike could look, there was another big ass that attacked him on the arm.

They were both yelling, "IIIII!!!! Get it off me!! Get it off me!!" It's true in Atlanta some people got attack dogs, but in Atlanta there is a place where you can train your cat to attack.

Fly-Mar looked at Greed. Greed and Fly-Mar dropped what they were doing when they heard the yelling and screaming. They burst into the house gun first. When they entered the master bedroom, Pee Wee Loc and Big Mike were struggling with the two big attack cats. Greed and Fly-mar had their guns pointed, but they couldn't shoot. Loc was jumping all over the room trying to pull the cat from his face. The cat was just clawing him in the face, trying to bite him in the neck. Big Mike was trying to pull the cat from his arm, but he couldn't. The cat had his nails and teeth deep into his arm. They tore the room up, knocking over lamps, breaking the bedroom mirror, knocking the TV to the floor and destroying the phone.

Greed and Fly-Mar grabbed Big Mike by the arm. Fly-Mar took his gat to pistol whip the cat. Mum...mum...mum...mum...mum...mum. The cat eased off a li'l bit. And that's when Big Mike snatched the cat from his arm. Big Mike then took the cat by the head and tail and snatched the cat in half. Big Mike yelling "IIII!!!!", blood and guts all over him. He then ran to Pee Wee Loc and punched the cat in the back, causing Loc to fly across the room onto the bed. The punch caused the cat to get drunk and the cat let go of Loc. Big Mike then grabbed the cat by the tail and started spinning the cat around and around and then slammed the cat into the wall head first, killing him by breaking every bone in his body.

Big Mike was breathing hard with both fists balled up, looking at the blood run all down his arm and body. Loc was laying across the bed in pain. Greed cooled Big Mike down.

Fly-Mar ran into the bathroom and got some towels, ran cold water over the towels, and came to the aid of his comrades. Fly-Mar took one of the towels to stop Loc's bleeding wounds. Greed took the other towel and wrapped Big Mike's arm.

With Loc still in pain, he still popped the safe. The safe contained millions of stacks of cash and expensive jewelry. They filled their bags and started to leave. As they got to the front door, they saw flashing lights outside. Fly-Mar and Greed had rushed the house so fast without workin' the code, unknowing they've set off the silent alarm, and outside was the police, The souljas got down out of sight and cocked one in the chamber. The cop got out of his squad car with gun in hand, headed toward the house. But he looked to his right and saw that the Hummer door was open on the souljas' ride, so he put his gun up and pulled out his flashlight, lookin' inside the Hummer. When he looked inside the Hummer, he saw keys of cocaine. He started to call it in, but by that time Big Mike eased out of the house and tackled the police to the ground. The cop reached for his gun, but Big Mike was so hyped he jumped up an snatched the cop off the ground so fast and held him over his head and sent him flying through the air head first into the window of his squad car.

The souljas came out of the house with the money and jewels. Greed looked and saw a video camera inside the cop car so he removed the tape and they fled the scene, headed for the stash spot to make the switch, the real for the fake. Greed told the ladies Mia, Queen, and Mary Jane to look after Pee Wee Loc and Big Mike while they go and take the fake to the fight party. They changed cars and clothes and dip.

Second crew had no problem. They were breaking the

Brinks code alarm and cracking the safes so fast, going in and out of houses in approximately under five minutes flat, taking money, coke and jewelry. Now, what I'm saying is that each crew is fast, it's just this crew is a li'l quicker. MJG cracks the Brinks code alarm and pops the safes while Eazy, Baller, and Jim Kelly ransack the whole house, getting everything except the bag of Doritos. Crew two got to the safe house (stash spot) to change cars, clothes, money, and dope so they could jump back at Chicago's fight party and play the game how it goes. But when they walked into the house they had a fit when they saw Pee Wee Loc and Big Mike.

Baller: "Got Damn!! What the hell happened Mr. Loc and Big Baby?"

Big Mike: "We got attacked."

Eazy: "By what?"

Loc: "By two fuckin' big ass attack cats."

Jim Kelly: "Damn, Loc, you okay?"

Loc: "Yeah, a li'l bit. I need to clean these wounds a li'l better and get a few stitches. Shi-i-id...then we'll be back ready for war."

Baller: "Yo, fuck that. I'm calling Dr. Fox. He'll hook you ninjas up."

MJG: "Y'all watchin' the fight, right?"

Big Mike: "Yeah, when we all get to Chicago's place."

MJG: "Naw, I need y'all to watch it now. Mia, come in here, baby. Order the fight."

Mia: "Okay."

MJG: "And when Holyfield and Tyson start to fight, page Milk. And when he calls back, tell him you want to be with him, then get his location. Check?"

Mia: "Check."

Jim Kelly: "Yo, Mia, Queen Black, and Mary Jane, y'all li'l

mamas take care of our dogs until the doc get here."

Mary Jane: "Is the party crunk?"

Baller: "Girl, you know all Chicago's parties be jumping out the roof."

Queen Black: "So, Baller baby, is we gonna party and trick a li'l bit?"

Baller: "Yeah, we're gonna all get together when the fight is over with."

Mary Jane: "When it's over with, a bitch want to get her groove on, what's crackin'?"

Baller: "Look here, li'l ol' girl, Milk is at the party and he knows y'all. See, we don't want to spook him. And if he see y'all li'l mamas, he's going to know that the Corporation got y'all on the clock stickin' and trickin'."

Queen Black: "True. So what a bitch to do?"

Baller: "Just chill, baby, until Sugar Wolf, Hezzy, Pete and Ten (third crew) get here. Then, when they come, they gonna take our money and dope, the first crew's money and dope, and their money and dope, pack y'all and the money and dope in the Hummer, and bring y'all and the money and dope to the house. There we're gonna sniff raw, choke on weed, and get a little freakish.

Mia: "Sounds good to me."

Baller: "I know. But before we do all that we gots to chop up the flow and weigh up the white sand."

Baller and the souljas got changed, grabbed the fake money and dope, and left. Dr. Fox came and did his job patching up the souljas and he headed out to the fight party also. Man, I'm telling you, everyone wanted to see this fight.

Back at the fight party, Fly-Mar and Greed had already made it to the party. They were all kickin' it over by the big screen kickin' game with Big Six, Milk, Flamingo, Nickel, and Dime. While Chicago was going in and out of the rooms checkin' on the money and dope, Milk saw Fly-Mar and Greed go into the rooms with the Big Bags. Milk was kickin' it with everybody, but he had his eyes on Chicago at all times.

By this time the second crew arrived at the party. Eazy and Jim Kelly took the fake money and dope into the same room Chicago was in and out of. Baller and MJG walked over to the fellows. They spoke and they all spoke back. Third crew had finished up on their last house and was on their way to the stash spot. All of a sudden, "Whoop Whoop"...the sound of the police. Everyone cocked a bullet into the chamber. Pete pulled the Hummer over. Two cops jumped out of their squad car with their guns drawn.

Sugar Wolf: "Oh, shit."

Ten: "Fuck 'em. Let's kill 'em."

Hezzy: "Pete, you with it?"

Pete: "Let's do it."

The cops got on each side of the Hummer. Before the cops could step to the front window, Ten and Sugar Wolf opened fire on the cops. Hezzy and Pete jumped out of the Hummer and finished the cops off, killing 'em dead. Hezzy ran to the squad car and took the video tape from the car and they left, headed to the stash spot (safe house).

While back at the fight party it was one fight away from the main event. But right now everyone had their attention turned to the boxing ring. Sky was knockin' 'em out of the box, and so was this one big husky woman named Big Juicy. Her and Sky was 3-0, so it boiled down to them gettin' it on to see who would be the king of the ring in the street fights. Big Juicy was brought in by one of Chicago's customers that heard that it was going to be a house fight exhibition.

Big Juicy, she was a bad bitch in the ring, giving 'ho's that second round knock out in her three fights. All of the bets was placed on her by the customers, but the Corporation took all bets on Sky. Sky was knocking out her opponents in the first round. But the crowd went with Big Juicy because of looks--big and ugly--and not with Sky because she was tuff and pretty. Sky was lookin' good, too. You heard me. She had on a red and white tight Main Event outfit with her long silky black hair pulled back in a ponytail. Jazzy Bell was the fight announcer.

Jazzy Bell: "Ladies and Gentlemen, let's get ready to rumble!!! In this corner is Big Juicy."

Everyone cheered.

Jazzy Bell: "And in this corner, Sky."

That's when the whole Corporation jump on crunk. Jazzy Bell called both fighters to the middle of the ring.

Jazzy Bell: "Okay, I want a good fight. Big Juicy, are you ready? Sky, are you ready? Okay, let's get it on."

Ding! (The sound of the bell.) They both went at it...left...right...left...right...left. Big Juicy came in with a wild right, left. Sky ducked, danced, and came in with two quick jabs. Big Juicy shook off the jabs and came in with a strong right, causing Sky to stumble across the ring. The bet got heavy on Big Juicy. Big Juicy came quick at Sky, strong with the one-two punch, knockin' Sky to the floor. Jazzy Bell with the count.

Jazzy Bell: "One...two...three...four..."

Sky looked over at Chicago and winked her eye and jumped up on the four count. Big Juicy started to take control of the fight. She came at Sky swinging wild, trying her best to knock Sky out. But with Sky bobbing and weaving, air was all Big Juicy got. Sky came in with a strong jab; a quick body shot, and a left-right combination knocked Big Juicy out. Jazzy Bell came in with the count.

Jazzy   Bell:

"One...two...three...four...five...six...seven...eight...nine...ten...
You're out!!!"

And once again the Corporation jump on crunk. Jazzy
Bell grabbed Sky by her hand to announce her the winner.

Jazzy Bell: "And the winner is..."

Boom! The door was kicked open by the Red Dogs (the
robbing crew). "Freeze, everybody! Get 'em off, get 'em up,
and lay it down! This is a jack!"

You've seen it before, either on TV or real life. One of the
customers got mad and went off.

The Customer: "Naw, man, fuck this shit! Chicago, I
thought you paid these fruity ass pigs off."

Chicago: "Shhh...hush. These are not cops."

The Customer: "What?!"

That's when Milk pulled out his nine millimeter and shot
the customer point blank range in the head, killing him
dead. Then that's when the rest of the Red Dogs pulled up
their ski masks and it was Tray, Dove, Cotton, Escobar, and
Happy--the Jury. The Jury patted everyone down and made
them get butt naked. Everyone threw their clothes into the
middle of the floor. Milk was giving out orders.

Milk: "Dove, go to the bedroom and bring back two bed
sheets, one to wrap the clothes and the other for the dope and
money."

Milk , Cotton, and Tray had their guns drawn on everyone. Happy and Escobar ransacked each room, coming out
with millions and pounds of cash and coke. Dove laid out
the two sheets. Happy and Escobar put the cash and coke
into the sheet and wrapped it up. Dove then got with Cotton
and Tray and stayed drawn down on everyone, while Milk,
Happy, and Escobar took everyone's clothes, jewelry, and
weapons and packed it into the other sheet. Everyone just
looked and stayed silent as Milk and the Jury started to leave.

Milk: "Warriors! Let's posse up. Time to roll. Ladies and gentlemen, this have been a wonderful night for me. I have never took so much from so many at one time. This is a blessing, and may God bless you.

Chicago: "Milk, why?"

Milk: "You don't get it, do you? You just don't get it."

Chicago: "No, I don't."

Milk: "The Benjamins, Baby, the Benjamins."

And the Jury left. Everyone was getting off the floor, mad and shit.

Customer One: "Man, I don't believe this shit. I paid good money to have a good time and this shit happens again. Hell, naw!"

Customer Two: "Yo, this shit is the second time for me, too. I want my money back."

Everyone started to act.

Chicago: "Calm down, everyone. I expected some similar shit like this to happen. But not exactly like this. Just calm down; give me four minutes."

By this time, third crew arrived. They entered the back way. Chicago went to the back to meet third crew and family--Sugar Wolf, Hezzy, Ten, Pete, Mr. Loc, Big Mike, Mia, Mary Jane, Queen Black. From there they took the real money and dope to Room J. Chicago asked Big Mike and Mr. Loc was they okay. They replied "yeah". Chicago told Mary Jane to go to the kitchen and bring her a sauce pan and a platter. While Mary Jane was doing that, she told Hezzy to bust open a key of coke and a pound of choke weed. She went into the closet and grabbed stacks of pajamas. She put on a pair. She told the souljas to come out of their clothes and to get into a pair of pajamas. Mary Jane came back to the room and she also came out of her clothes. They all grabbed a stack of pajamas and headed to the front room.

Hezzy had the platter full of choke weed and Chicago had the sauce pan filled up with raw powder. She turned her fight party into a pajama fight party, the first ever in the world. The pajamas were "One size fits all". Hezzy spread choke weed all over the table. Chicago did the same with the raw coke.

Everyone was happy again except Big Six. He was furious. He sipped his drink, sniffed a li'l raw, and puffed on a blunt with Diamond, but he was still upset.

Diamond: "What's wrong, Boo? It was just material stuff, we can get that li'l bit back with the snap of a finger."

Big Six: "Baby, it's just I ain't never got jack like that. I...I got to go."

Diamond: "Boo, don't go."

Big Six: "Boo, I gots to go and let them niggas know you just can't do that shit to me. I ain't no grasshopper or a Sugar Baby ass nigga! Now let me go. Where is my keys?"

Diamond yelled over to Chicago, "Keys!" Chicago came over with the keys.

Chicago: "What's the matter?"

Diamond: "Nothing. It's just my Boo gots to go. Make him stay, Chi."

Chicago: "Stay, Big Six, for Diamond's sake."

Big Six: "Chicago, I had a nice time, but I gots to let them Sugar Babies know it ain't no punks where I'm from. Now, you got my keys?"

Chicago: "Right here."

Big Six: "Thank you. Diamond, you have a way home?"

Diamond: "I'm going to stay with my sister tonight. See you tomorrow."

Big Six: "Okay."

And Big Six stormed out of the house. Chicago gave Flamingo, Nickel, and Dime the eye. They left out the door following Big Six to see what was up on his whereabouts. Everyone was having a good time smoking on blunts, sniffin' lines, and watching the Tyson and Holyfield fight. Even Dr. Fox was blowing on some stinky green, getting mellow.

Hezzy: "Yo, Baller, did that nigga Milk take the bait?"

Baller: "Oh, hell yeah. The Jury fell in here lookin' like the Red Dogs (Drug Enforcement Agency)."

Hezzy: "I wonder where did they get those uniforms?"

Jim Kelly: "From the police department; they had bitch ass Happy with them."

Sugar Wolf: "Fat nappy neck."

MJG: "Yeah, man."

Ten: "What type of guns them niggas represented?"

Baller: "Oh, they had some shit. Some motherfuckin' H-K mp-5's with the infrared scope."

Ten: "Oh, shit, them niggas came to kill something."

Fly-Mar: "They did. Milk shot a customer in the head for acting a donkey. Me and Greed got the body up and the girls cleaned up the blood."

Greed: "Let's go get this tag fag."

Eazy: "Fuck, yeah! Let's get out of these pajamas, put back on our souljas' rags, and let's go get this nigga and his crew."

MJG: "Yeah, and he's gonna be ready just like when the Killahoe Posse tried to strike."

Pete: "Fuck 'em, let's do it!"

All of the souljas jumped out of their pajamas and got back into their souljas' rags. Pee Wee Loc and Big Mike chilled out in the relax room and watched the fight while the souljas got ready for war. Baller told Dr. Fox he would see him when he got back for his pay cut.

Dr. Fox: "I'll be here."

Baller: All right. Ninjas, let's dip."

Ten was carrying all the artillery in a big soulja bag.

Hezzy: "Yo, Ten, what type of guns we playing with tonight?"

Ten: "Oh, we going to fall out in that nigga shit with these A-K 47s with 100 round drums and 10 Hawaii coconuts (10 hand grenades) and body armor to protect our necks. It's all about survival, and if you know like I know, only the strong will survive and the weak get beat."

An hour later the Corporation arrived on the scene. But Milk and the Jury was ready for anything. They were all sitting back, watching the fight, chopping up the loot, sniffing raw choking weed with their hands on the trigger, ready to blast if someone come with that fuck shit while unknowing that the Corporation was making their move on the outside.

MJG had took the cable wire from the front of the Hummer and hooked the cable wire hook to the burglar bar door of the Al Capone Suite and put the Hummer in reverse and snatched the door off the hinges. The Jury heard the ruckus and scattered out in the maze out house. Fly-Mar, Greed, Baller, Pete, and Ten each grabbed an A-K 47 with the 100 round drums. Sugar Wolf, Hezzy, MJG, Jim Kelly, and Eazy grabbed two coconuts each. Fly-Mar ran up to the house and kicked in the door. The souljas ran in blasting. Rat-tat-tat tat...Rat-tat-tat-tat...Rat-tat-tat-tat...Rat-tat-tat-tat...Rat-tat-tat-tat...But nothing. Baller ordered everyone outside. The Corporation wasn't falling for the tricks. Baller smelled it was a set-up. So they eased out of the grand house. That's when the grenadiers, Sugar Wolf, Hezzy, MJG, Jim Kelly, and Eazy pulled the pins and threw the coconuts into the house. Boom! Boom! Boom! Boom! Boom! Boom! Boom! Boom! A few of the Jury clique tried to make it out of the house on fire, bustin' shots. Rat-tat-tat-tat...Boom! Boom! But as they were coming out, the

Corporation souljas was chopping 'em down one by one. Rat-tat-tat tat-tat-tat-tat-tat-tat-tat. As they were falling and rolling down the stairs, the flames were smothered out. Four bodies came out of the burning house. Hezzy walked up to the house to identify the bodies. He came back to the Hummer and told the souljas "I don't see Happy and Milk." The house was still burning and blowing up. Baller squinted his eyes as the flame got higher and said, "Man, you know how the captain like to go down with his ship. Fuck that nigga, he's dead. If not, I will personally take care of it myself. Let's bounce." And they all got into the Hummer and bounced off the scene like Flubber, heading back to the fight, which was over when they arrived.

As soon as the souljas stepped into the house, Big Mike spoke.

Big Mike: "My ninjas. It was beautiful, baby. Holyfield shock the world."

The Souljas: "What, what, what? What round?"

Big Mike: "In the eleventh."

Fly-Mar: "Naw, I still don't believe."

Chicago licking her thumb, counting greenbacks, running the money through the money machine.

Baller: "What's up, Baby? What's the score?"

Chicago: "Well, right now so far we got 225 keys of pure uncut, and in revenues so far we've counted 76 million in just this half of the stacks. We'll be finished counting up in a few. Oh yeah--Dr. Fox had to go. He said it was an emergency. His wife paged him 911 and he stormed right out of here. So what's up with the Jury and Milk."

Baller: "Evaporated."

Chicago: "Huh, someone should told that fool you do bad shit and bad shit comes back. That's what I found out growing up as a kid."

Baller: "Oh that's why you so ruthless."

Chicago: "Naw...you're the reason."

Baller: "Ha ha. But look, you say Dr. Fox's code was 911?"

Chicago: "Yeah."

Baller: "Did he look worried?"

Chicago: "Yes, he had the same look you have on your face right now."

Baller: "Damn, I got to go, Baby. Something's wrong." Baller told everyone to hold everything down until he got back.

Hezzy: "Yo, Ninja, you want me to roll with you?"

Baller: "Naw, I got it, Baby Boy."

As Baller was headed out the door, Flamingo, Nickel and Dime was coming in.

Flamingo: "Yo, Baby, we got to talk."

Baller: "It will have to wait."

Flamingo: "But..."

Baller: "Tell the family later." And Baller rushed out the door, headed for Dr. Fox's house,.

On the way there he called Crow from his cell phone. Ring...ring...

Crow: "Hello."

Baller: "What's up, Ninja? I need you tonight."

Crow: "Where you at?"

Baller: "I'm on my way to see the Fox. Meet me at his house."

Crow: "What's wrong?"

Baller: "He got the page 911 from his wife. And he told me that's the code when something is wrong. Real wrong. So, you with me?"

Crow: "Hell, yeah, Nigga."

Baller: "And, yo, bring some ammo."

Crow: "Bet. Should I bring my mask, too?"

Baller: "Hell, naw, Nigga. We not trying to kill everybody. Just the ones we need to kill."

Crow: "Okay, see you in a minute." And they hung up the phone.

But when Dr. Fox walked into his house, Happy grabbed him and took him into the living room where his wife and kids was tied up and was being held hostage by Milk. When Dr. Fox looked at Milk's horrid face and body it caused great fear. He just dropped his head because he knew that his family was horrified by this badly burned man that was in their house yelling loudly and making demands.

Milk: "Hi. I'm Milk and you can fuckin' see that Milk doesn't do the body no fuckin' good!"

Dr. Fox: "What do you want me to do?"

Milk: "Take one good got damn guess!! It ought to not be that fuckin' hard."

Dr. Fox: "Will you please just take the gun away from my family?"

Milk put down the pump shotgun.

Milk: "Let him go, Happy. He's going to act right, I can tell. Now Doc, can you help me?"

Dr. Fox: "What...what do you want me to do?"

Milk: "A face off, Doc! A fuckin' face off! Now stop fuckin' playin' with me."

Dr. Fox: "A face off?"

Milk: "Yeah! A new identity. Now what's up? Don't tell me you can't do it, because I been all over this house, I seen your tools down in the basement."

Dr. Fox: "Who do you want to be? Who do you want to look like?"

Milk: "Damn sho' not like the Darkman. Make me look like a rapper, Doc."

Dr. Fox: "What rapper?"

Milk: "Fix me up like Snoop Dogg Dog."

Dr. Fox: "Snoop Dogg Dog."

Milk: "Right. Right. Right, you know...Biaaaatch!!!!"

Happy laughed a li'l as he walked around Dr. Fox's family with a pump shotgun.

Milk: "Naw, wait Doc. How 'bout hooking me up like Master P so when I return I can make 'em say 'Uhh!'. Shi-i-i-d...I got the golds, all I need is the skin and it's on, uhh!"

Dr. Fox: "Do you have a picture of this person?"

Milk: "Hell naw. Do it look like I have a fuckin' picture? You ain't got no Source, Murder Dog, XXL, Vibe or Rap Pages hip hop magazine around here?"

Dr. Fox: "No, I don't. I can do it, I just need the picture."

Milk started getting upset.

Milk: "What type of magazine do you have around here?"

Dr. Fox: "I have an 'Inc.' magazine."

Milk: "What's dat?"

Dr. Fox: "It's a magazine for growing companies."

Milk: "Fuck, naw, white boy magazine. What else you got?"

Dr. Fox: "I have a few 'Emerge' magazines."

Milk: "Emerge?"

Dr. Fox: "Yes. It's a Black America's new magazine."

Milk: "What type of pictures this magazine hold?"

Dr. Fox: "Well, from Dick Gregory to Jesse Jackson."

Milk: "Jesse Jackson...man, you must be crazy. You gonna have to do better than that, Doc. Hell, naw, come on."

Happy: "Wait, Milk. Rev. Jesse Jackson is a powerful leader in politics. You can get lots of shit done with his face. Like run for President. Shi-i-id my Nigga Milk. Jesse Jackson for President."

Milk: "You dreaming. Ain't no nigga voting these days."

Happy: "You crazy. It's more nigga voting than it ever was. Anyway, the year 2000 is the year of the black man, right, Doc?"

Dr. Fox looked at Happy and said, "Yeah, right."

Milk: "Okay, let's do it."

Dr. Fox: "You know that this operation could take weeks to heal."

Milk: "I wouldn't give a damn if it took a year. You gonna help me. And if you don't, my friend Happy here is gonna kill your family. You heard me."

Dr. Fox: "I hear you."

Milk: "That's good, because Happy have killed for me before and he don't mind doing it again."

Dr. Fox: "I understand."

They all headed toward the basement. Dr. Fox's pager goes off. Beep...beep...beep. He checks it. Code 164. He looks back at his wife and kids and smiles.

Milk: "What you smiling for?"

Dr. Fox: "Oh, nothing."

Milk: "Give me that pager." Milk smashed the black button and saw code 164 and looked up at Dr. Fox and said, "Baller".

Dr. Fox reached and dived toward his wife and kids. Before Happy and Milk could make a move, Crow and Baller kicked in the door and got in a killing position, making Milk and Happy drop their weapons.

Baller: "Surprise, surprise, surprise."

Milk: "My friend Baller. Look what someone did to me, Friend. Look at me! Just look at me!" Milk looked like Cropsy in the movie The Burning.

Crow closed the door behind them and took several steps toward Milk and Happy but stayed out of reach.

Baller: "Oh I'm sorry. Did I do that?"

Milk: "But why? We're friends, not enemies."

Baller: "With friends like you, who needs enemies? You come in here and threaten my friend and his family. You robbed Chicago's party. And every day of your life you try to set us up. But somehow God helps us out. Now you're telling me we're friends? Fuck, naw, you're a monster...a dead monster."

Milk had tears running down his burned face.

Milk: "You can't kill me, we're family."

Baller: "Someone should have told you family can sometimes be your worst enemy."

Milk: "But I started you out in this big money game."

Baller: "Damn, Buddy, you must not have game."

Milk: "I got game, I got game. Look, listen. You called me Buddy. So you can't kill me, Buddy, friend. Ha ha. Look, look, Baller, I got ten million in cash in the trunk of Happy's squad car. It's the boss man. You can have it. Just don't kill me."

Baller: "What! You playin' games with me. Trying to give me back our own money."

Milk: "No, no...that money got burned up along with the cocaine. This is money I stashed way back."

Baller: "Okay, I'll take this money. You're all right by me."

Milk: "So we okay?"

Baller: "Yeah, we okay."

Milk: "So you know you can't kill me once you take the money, Buddy."

Baller: "Yeah, I know it."

Milk: "That's my Buddy."

Baller: "Crow, blast that piece of shit."

Crow stepped up to Milk. Pop...pop. Point blank range to the face. Milk fell to the floor and his soul floated from his body and went straight down into the ground floor. Happy tried to stay cool, but the sweat came running down his face. It showed his weakness.

Happy: "I tried telling him."

Baller: "What you try telling him?"

Happy: "I told him what you do in the night will someday come to light."

Baller: "You told him that?"

Happy: "I sure did."

Baller: "What else you tell him?"

Happy: "I told him 'you are a unpredictable killer and that you will kill any man that will try to baller block your dreams from reaching the top, anytime and anywhere'."

Baller: "You told him that?"

Happy: "I sure did."

Dr. Fox's wife was fixing the house back up.

Baller: "Happy, I thought you was the good cop."

Happy: "I am the good cop. Just let me fix everything up."

Baller: "Just like you fix up everything else. You been sneaking around here for years killing off people, you fat bumpy neck sonuvabitch!!"

Crow took Happy's handcuffs and handcuffed him.

Crow: "What are we gonna do with him?"

Baller: "I got an idea. The real problem is this body. With the cops ridin' it's going to be hard to dump somewhere."

Dr. Fox: "Leave that up to me, Baller: Help me take Milk's body down to the basement."

Baller didn't know what to expect.

Baller: "What's up, Doc?"

Dr. Fox: "Just sit the body down. And here, y'all put on these rubber gloves, goggles, and this leather apron to protect yourself."

Crow: "From what, Doc?"

Dr. Fox: "This here is nitric acid and this shit will destroy anything it touches. First I run some water in this container and pour about two bottles of nitric acid into the container and start stirring it up. Okay, now I need you two to place him in the container easily. And I stir a li'l bit and a li'l bit...and he's gone! Evaporated. The acid ate the meat off of his bones in seconds and ate his bones in minutes."

And that was the end of Milk, a vicious drug dealer. Baller thanked Dr. Fox and Dr. Fox thanked him right back.

Baller: "You're a bad mother. What else you know how to do?"

Dr. Fox: "Well, I know how to blow stuff like buildings and cars. I use to be in the Marine Corps where they use to call me the Demolition Man."

Baller: "It's 50 gees owed to you, right?"

Dr. Fox: "Right."

Baller: "Make it 100 gees."

Dr. Fox: "Okay."

Baller and Crow took Happy and headed out the door.

Baller: "I'll see you tomorrow, Doc."

Dr. Fox: "Later."

Baller left his ride behind and got into the cop squad car. Crow got in his ride and they left. An hour later they arrived back at Chicago's place. Baller and Crow stepped in the house. Baller threw his hands in the air and said, "What's up, I'm back."

Hezzy: "Who that you got with you?"

Baller: "Everybody, y'all know my ninja Crow."

Everyone: "What's up Crow?"

Crow: "What's up?"

Crow walked in the crowd with the rest of the ninjas while Baller went straight to Chicago to check on tonight's figures.

Baller: "What's the score?"

Chicago: "Baby, a 169 million 350 thousand 264 dollars. The best lick ever."

Baller: "Wait--it ain't over."

Chicago: "What you talkin' about?"

Baller: "Yo, Crow, bring me that suitcase."

Crow brought over the suitcase. Baller popped it open--10 million in cash. Everyone was like, "What?!"

Hezzy: "Where did that come from?"

Baller: "Compliments from our friends Happy and Milk, who are no longer on this earth."

The whole Corporation made a big chunk of money that night.

Baller: "A-yo, Flamingo, what's that you, Nickel, and Dime had to tell me that was so important?"

Everybody in the house: "Ohhh, Shit."

Baller: "Ohhh shit what?"

Flamingo: "It's some real crazy shit, man."

Baller: "Shi-i-i-id. I live for crazy shit. So what's up ninja?"

Everyone was getting comfortable, waiting to hear what Flamingo got to say. Some was drinking, some choking on fire weed, and some sniffing lines. Jazzy Bell was just kicked back reclining on the stacks of money, listening.

Flamingo: "Okay. Right after Milk and the Jury pulled that Red Dog move, Big Six was mad, so he stormed out the door. That's when Chicago had me, Nickel, and Dime follow him and we did. Man, this motherfucker drove straight into a graveyard."

Baller: "A graveyard?"

Nickel: "Hell, yeah."

Flamingo: "So me and Nickel and Dime waited until this

fool came out of the cemetery. So we waited for about, let me see...pimpin how long did we wait?"

Dime: "About six minutes, to be exact."

Flamingo: "So six minutes later this black hearse pulls out of the driveway of the graveyard. Now it's dark as fuck, 1:00 a.m. in the morning. And I ain't never seen a funeral going on at night. Matter of fact, I ain't never seen a hearse ride at night. So we check it out. We follow this hearse. Man, this nigga rode all night until he seen these cops getting ready to close shop on a road block. It was about four cops; they pulled the hearse over to the side of the cops and their cars and roll down their window. Oh, pimpin, hear me now, I thought they were gonna shoot. Look here pimpin, four niggas jump out the hearse dressed like Kung Fu Samurai Cinema flying through the air. Before the cops could reach for their weapons, these Kung Fu Executioners pull out a sword, a scimitar, a short sickle, and the last one had a long ass scythe. Hear me now, pimpin, they chop up them cops something terrible. And when they finish chopping up the bodies, man they flew back into the hearse with their weapons and didn't get cut. Big Six got out of the hearse and got the two video tapes out of the cops squad cars, but before that fool got back into the hearse, he looked around like he knew someone was watching him. So I fucked around and hit the car lights. That's when Big Six gave chase. He put the hearse in reverse and was driving backward tryin' to catch a pimp. "

Everyone was deep into the story when they saw Baller paying attention.

Flamingo: "I was driving my pimpin ass off. Tell 'em, Dime."

Dime: "Hell, yeah, pimpin was doing about 90 in a 25 zone. But that hearse was on our ass until it tried to turn around. And when the hearse spun around, that's when pimpin' lost that fool. We drove back into the cut across from the graveyard. 10 minutes later, here they come, going back into the graveyard and stayed in that motherfucker and didn't come back out."

Flamingo: "I'm telling you, pimpin, them niggas sleep with the dead. I looked at pimp one and two and said 'Fuck this shit' and we came on back here."

Baller: "I believe you, pimpin."

Hezzy: "That's where that nigga got that money. That sonuvabitch, sleeping on the grave."

Baller: "Hell yeah. Flamingo, you just got to excuse the family. They just got scared when you mentioned grave-yard."

Everybody started saying, "Who, not me! I wasn't scared. It was just a wild ass story."

Chicago: "Well, Diamond baby, now it's all on you. So what you gonna do?"

Diamond: "It in the makin'. He goes to funerals twice a week and leaves me the house."

MJG: "Is there a safe in the house?"

Diamond: "Yes, there it. There's one in the master bed-room. And I ain't never been or seen anything go in it."

Baller: "We need to get in that safe while he's at a funer-al."

Diamond: "That's easy. When he's away on business I can let a few of the ninjas in and Boom! pick the safe, run some names and start going in and out of the graves in the grave-yard digging for loot."

Everybody was like, "Yeah, that's beautiful." But Baller wasn't.

Baller: "That sounds good, but there's a flaw."

Diamond: "What? He trusts me."

Baller: "Yeah, I know it. That mean he love you, right?"

Diamond: "Right, conditionally."

Baller: "Well, if he love you he will have someone to watch you while he's away."

Diamond: "So, what's up?"

Baller: "You just make a copy of the key and give us the Brinks code to the house. Give it to Sugar Wolf or MJG or Fly-Mar. Those three will go into the house while you and Big Six is at the funeral."

Diamond: "Me at the funeral?"

Baller: "Yes, you. Sugar Wolf, MJG, and Fly-Mar, you three will peep the safe and take pictures of the needed documents."

Diamond: "So are we going to kill him?"

Baller: "Naw, baby, he got too much money for us to kill him. Now Diamond, you should know we kill 'em off when their broke because a dead man can still spend money."

They all partied a few more hours and chopped the cash, and just before dawn the captain and lieutenant got their crew's share of the money. And they all got back on their post.

When morning came it was on all the News. First it was Evander Holyfield upset WBA heavyweight champion Mike Tyson. It was the talk of the world. And so was the news of eight murdered Atlanta police officers; one of the officers was badly, brutally beaten and was thrown through his squad car window, killing him. Two of the officers was killed in a routine traffic stop. And that's not all...four officers were cleaning up the pieces when they were attacked. Their bodies mutilated; yes, mutilated. Heads and arms and legs, decapitated, and another officer was found dead in the trunk of his squad car. He died from multiple gun shot wounds to the face and body. The GBI is doing a full investigation to find these cop killers.

THIS IS FOR MY LOVE

(DEAD MAN'S MONEY)
THIS IS FOR MY LOVE

A week later the Corporation got straight to it going after Big Six. Diamond went to both funerals. The first funeral the ninjas went into Big Six's house and took pictures inside the whole house and got the important names off the ledgers inside the safe. Inside the safe was VHS tapes and ledgers. The ninjas stayed inside the house 96 seconds flat, and after that they jump right back on post waiting to hear from Diamond. Diamond will come back to the family and tell them that the first funeral lasted about six hours. The second funeral, the ninjas timed it. There it was six hours on the dot. Next week, third funeral, the ninjas went back into the house and grab a few VHS tapes and ledgers and headed back to the safe house (Jade's hideaway) to discuss hardcore tactics on stealin' money from a dead man's grave.

Back at the house,

Hezzy: "Where they at? Shit, they should have been back."

Mona Lisa: "Have patience, they'll be here."

Jade: "I just don't see how Diamond do it."

Chicago: "Do what?"

Jade: "Going to those funerals. I hate 'em."

Mona Lisa: "Girl, have you ever been to one?"

Jade: "No! And I don't want to go to one."

Mona Lisa: "We'll all have to go to one some day. "

Jade: "Yeah, I know that."

Mona Lisa: "Chicago, what about you?"

Chicago: "I've been to a few, but no more. And the reason why I don't no more, is because I just feel sorry for the dead. People be off in the funeral ALL FAKE. You got some people who just go to funerals to see other people's reaction and pay no attention to the dead. But then they be the main one's actin' a ass. And that's FAKE to me. You suppose to show your respect and bless the dead."

Raven: "Girl, I know what you mean. Those are the type that steal from their loved one's, fight 'em and cursing 'em-- just straight up disrespect. And when they gone--oooh Lord! They act a ass, cryin', yellin', fallin' out...just havin' a fit in church. Makin' it seems like the ones that did for their loved ones didn't do shit. Because they be so quiet. But when the funeral is over they let it out at home in their own li'l way."

Sky: "That's true. I seen as a li'l girl coming up family fighting over who get what. And 'they love me the most. I did this, I did that, so I should get the house. You just sat on your ass doing nothing.'"

Precious: "I know that's right. I know this one dude who use to talk down to his father real bad. But right now he got the nerves to be living in one of his houses. One day his father got sick and was about to die. You know, that fool didn't go see his father. He just snooped around his father's house looking for the will, wishing that his father would die."

Chicago: "Did he die?"

Precious: "Naw, he's a tuff old man. Still kickin'. He don't take no shit off his sorry ass kids."

Jazzy: "That's messed up. I know this one girl, she just show out on her drunk mother all the time. Sometimes she will fight her mother, draggin' her into the house, callin' her all types of names like 'drunk bitch', stankin' 'ho'.' Her mom use to just say, 'You're gonna miss my old drunk butt one of these day.' I mean, her mom is a good lady. She is so sweet to her daughter; every time she would get paid she would get her a li'l bit out to get drunk with and give her daughter some and tell her to keep the rest for her until she ask for it the next day. And girl, she will mess up her mother's money and then call her all types of names saying 'You should have kept it yourself.'"

Chicago: "Who is this girl"

Jazzy: "You might know her. Her name is Karma."

Chicago: "Naw, I don't know her, but she's going to Hell for that.

Greed: "Shi-i-id; my brother was the same way. He use to come in the house all drunk and high on dope and would curse out my aunt bad, callin' her bitches and 'ho's--and then would have the nerve to ask her for some money. She would be all scared then and give him money. I be like, 'Man, this gots to stop.' But she would just tell me if I like it, you love it. And I never ever said nothing else about it till now. Right till this day she love that fool more than she love me. Right till this day his grown stankin' ass still living off her, smoking rocks and stealing from her on the down low."

Hezzy: "Now that's fucked up."

Greed: "Tell me 'bout it. I tried to buy her a house she wouldn't accept."

Hezzy: "Yo, Precious, whatever happen to your pretty

388   HYPNOTIZING GAME

388   HYPNOTIZING GAME

fine ass red-bone cousin Peppermint with that sorry pussy."

Precious: "You tell me. You was fuckin' her. She don't come around the way no more until there death in the family."

Hezzy: "What's up with that?"

Precious: "You know my aunt raise her when her parents didn't wanna have shit to do with her. She wasn't always pretty, she was a pitiful lookin' girl. Hair stayed nappy; it was coming out on the side. She looked like Mr. T. Our aunt taught me and her how to be a women."

Chicago: "So she don't go by and see your aunt sometimes."

Precious: "Oh no, she act like she's all that now. She walk right pass my aunt's house and gossip about people for hours. Outta those hours she don't even look her way until there's death in the family, and that's cold."

Jade: "Naw, that's a dirty bitch."

Jazzy Bell: "And you know it."

There was a knock at the door. Knock-knock-knock.

Ten: "Who is it?"

Fly-Mar: "It's us. Open the door."

Ten opened the door.

Fly-Mar: "What's up? What's up? We got work to do."

Sugar Wolf: "Hezzy, how much time we got?"

Hezzy: "We got three hours to go over the tapes and ledgers."

MJG quickly popped in the VHS tape--and there it was, the police killin'. Half watched the tapes; the other half went over the ledgers. Before Baller could get good into the ledgers...

Pete: "Yo, Baller, I think you need to see this."

Baller looked up and seen the worse on the television. Big Six Kung Fu Zombies flying in the air chopping up the police. The Corporation was in shock seein' the dead killin' off the flesh with vengeance.

Jim Kelly: "Man, look at 'em fly."

Pete: "Look at the tools they're workin' with."

Ten: "Damn, just like Flamingo explained."

Big Mike: "Damn, it's gonna be a bitch getting off in that grave yard and pulling a 211."

Greed: "Damn sho' look that way."

Eazy: "Just listen at y'all niggas soundin' like cowards. This here is the test, the test of all tests. I never ever heard none of y'all say no shit like you saying now. Man, we're the Corporation. Do or die, one of us fall, we let the bullets fly! Baby, you know once we stop testing ourself we get slow and this is not the time to be slow. This is not the time. Let's take it to the grave Baby!"

Baller: "You're right from the cradle to the grave! I'm all in!"

Eazy and Baller looked at the rest of the family.

Pete: "I'm in."

Hezzy: "Me too."

Ten: "Me three."

Sky: "I'm in."

MJG: "I'm in."

Sugar Wolf: "Me too."

Jade: "I'm in."

Mona Lisa: "Me too."

Greed: "I'm in."

Jazzy: "I'm in it like Earnest Bennett."

Big Mike: "I'm in."

Jim Kelly: "Me too."

Flymar: "And you know this."

Chicago: "I'm down."

Pee Wee Loc: "I wouldn't miss this for the world."

Precious: "I'm in."

Raven: "Let's do it."

Hezzy: "We got an hour and a half left, so let's get to it."

They got right to it, breakin' down the ledgers.

Li'l Loc: "What all this mean? Black Caesar, Tommy Gibbs - 10 million; Mr. Cardoza - 10 million; Joe - 10 million; Bucktown, Duke - 10 million; Aretha - 10 million; Roy - 10 million; Super Fly, Priest - 10 million; Eddie - 10 million; Scatter - 10 million."

Chicago: "Super Fly is a movie starring Ron O'Neal as priest."

Hezzy: "Damn sho' is. Let me see that list."

Loc handed Hezzy this list.

Hezzy: "Well Gott damn. I know this."

Baller: "What you know, Baby Boy?"

Hezzy: "This list and this list and this list. Okay, Black Caesar's starring Fred Williamson as Tommy Gibbs and Mr. Cardoza is the one who gave Tommy Gibbs his start in the game and Joe was his best friend who fucked his old lady and then she set him up. Yeah, yeah, this nigga Big Six is a master mind."

Chicago: "Why you say that?"

Hezzy: "He use black movies characters names to bury the money under. I bet you...I bet that's what he do."

Jim Kelly: "Naw, Hezzy, man you crazy."

Hezzy: "Oh no I'm not. Jade: "Didn't you say that Diamond said that Big Six watch a lotta TV?"

Jade: "She damn sho' did."

Baller: "What all this, Baby Boy?"

Hezzy: "It means that someone who constantly watches a lotta TV shows or movies will sometimes admire the good guy or bad guy style and most of the time they will carry out that image."

Sky: "Ha ha ha. Hezzy, you wild."

Hezzy: "Okay, do anyone remember the movie Scream?"

Mona Lisa: "Yes, I do."

Hezzy: "Good, explain."

Mona Lisa: "Well, it was a good movie. It was about these crazy two boys who loved scary movies, so this one kid killed his father's girlfriend because she took him away from his family then somehow the killer started dating the girl who's mother he killed. Then he started killing off her friends and said that he was gonna blame it on the movies. They might have named over a hundred scary movies in that movie."

Hezzy: "You see, movies. Movies and books fucks with people's heads."

Baller: "I love ya Baby Boy. It make sense to me."

Fly Mar: "So all we got to do is look for these names on the tombstones and the money's there."

Hezzy: "That's right."

MJG: "Hezzy, how much time we got?"

Hezzy: "An hour and a half."

Jazzy Bell: "How is it that you know so much about these old blaxploitation movies?"

Hezzy: "I'm a Pisces, and all Pisces hobbies are money, music, movies. Every week me and Pete kick it out at the mall and pick up some CDs, clothes and a couple of black movies. I got all these movies at the house, don't I, Pete?"

Pete: "Yeah."

Baller: "Sho' 'nuff? So what's up with Bucktown?"

Hezzy: "That's the movie starring Fred Williamson as Duke; Pam Grier as Aretha. Duke old lady; Tony King as T.J. T.J. turn on Duke trying to get into Aretha's panties. But see, that nigga Tony King started in Hell up in Harlem with Fred Williamson as Zach Tommy Gibbs Enforcer. He turn on him in that movie too. He always played the tuff bad guy."

Baller: "So we got these movies at the house, right?"

Hezzy: "Right. Every black movie that's on these ledgers I got at the house. Like the Mack, Goldie - 10 million; Slim - 10 million; Pretty Tony - 10 million; and Mack Truck Turner, Gator - 10 million; Blue - 10 million; Frenchic - 10 million."

The Corporation got crackin' on making copies of the ledgers and putting everything back in place where it belonged. And got right back at the safe house. An hour later Diamond arrived at the house giving the info on Big Six's billion dollars a year operation. When Diamond fell in the house the girls came to her with hugs and kisses. The souljas saluted her.

Chicago: "So what's up, girl?"

Diamond: "Girl, y'all ain't gonna believe it."

Sky: "Try us."

Diamond: "All right. Let's all sit." Everyone gathered around to hear what Diamond had to say.

Diamond: "As we were leaving the funeral field riding out to the house, girl! he asked me to be his huckleberry."

Chicago: "Girl, what you say?"

Diamond: "I said yes! yes! yes!"

Eazy: "Oooh, shit, Diamond jumpin' the broom."

Everyone was happy for Diamond, congratulating her.

Mona Lisa: "Girl, married life is great."

Sugar Wolf kissed Diamond on the cheek and gave her a blessing and said, "I just hope this married life don't effect your devilish diva street performance, because you always consider yourself the best at this game."

Diamond: "I still am, and once I get married next week I'm gonna get better. But naw, I'll pass the torch to Chicago. She's the baddest bitch."

Chicago: "Thanks girl. Now let's get down to business."

Baller: "So, Diamond, how do he work?"

Diamond: "He's cunning. Every week he goes down to the hospital morgue and picks out two dead bodies, people that have no family and friends. He then takes the bodies from the morgue to his mortuary. There he fix 'em up nice so they will look good for the few family and friends they do have. Now at this first funeral I didn't notice anything, but the second funeral I did; just like the first time, the preacher preach over the body and bless it. After that he order everyone out to their ride. As they carry the body out to the hearse, I notice it was a different coffin they were carrying."

Jazzy: "What was the difference?"

Diamond: "See, the first coffin had gold handlebars. But when the coffin came out the church it had silver bars. So we get to the grave site. There the preacher bless the dead to rest in peace until eternity. So when the funeral is over, the florist van will always pull over to our ride and ask Big Six which name would it be today on the tombstone at this grave site. Okay now, on the first tombstone it was Jesse Lee. Second one was Colonel Gram. And just today it was Father Time. That's when I say to myself, Damn, those names sound familiar. That's when he ask me to marry him. And that's when he pull out this 7.75 carat Cartier gold diamond ring."

Everyone went "Daaammmnnnn!!!"

Mona Lisa: "That's beautiful."

Raven: "That's you, that's you Fa Shiggy."

Diamond: "Thank y'all. But wait--as soon as I step in the house it came to me."

Jade: "What girl?"

Diamond: "Those names. Big Daddy Kane was Father Time in this movie we watch together last week. I just can't think of the movie right now. But Big Daddy Kane was about that money."

Hezzy: "Posse was the name of that movie."

Diamond: "Yeah, that's it, that's it."

Hezzy: "Big Daddy Kane was Father Time, Billy Zane was Colonel Gram, and Mario Van Peebles was Jesse Lee. Now that was a good black western movie."

Diamond: "It damn sho' was, Hezzy. Six liked those three characters."

Hezzy: "Now what I tell y'all? He pick the ones he like in the movie, good or bad, and put 'em down on what he love best, and that's his dead man's money."

Jazzy Bell: "Do y'all watch a lotta movies?"

Diamond: "Girl, yeah, too many."

Baller: "But do y'all watch lots of old black movies?"

Diamond: "Yes, yes, we enjoy the hell outta those."

Chicago: "Name some of the old black movies."

Diamond: "Let me see, Foxy Brown, The Mack, Hell up in Harlem, Superfly, Car Wash, Mack Truck Turner..."

Sky: "Wait a minute. Name some of the characters he liked in Truck Turner."

Diamond: "He liked Gator, Blue and this one girl name Frenchic, a pretty black girl look just like you, Raven."

Sky: "Hezzy, check that copy."

Hezzy check the copy of the ledger and there it was like before, Gator, Blue, and Frenchic. Hezzy looked up at the family and said, "Bingo--it's real."

Mona Lisa: "Name some more movies."

Diamond: "Slaughter, Slaughter Big Rip Off, Black Caesar, Bucktown, One Down Two to Go, Three the Hard Way, Which Way is Up, Black Belt Jones, Boss Nigga, Peaty Wheat Straw the Devil's Son-In-Law, J. D. Revenge, Bingo Long Traveling All Stars & Motor Kings, the Human Tornado, Dolemite...it's so many."

Precious: "So, Diamond, when is the wedding?"

Diamond: "Next week, September 24, 1996. And after the wedding we're going outta town and coming back in town September 29, 1996. By then the job should be done, one hundred more million in our corner."

Big Mike: "Where y'all honeymooner's kickin' it at?"

Diamond: "Paris, Big Baby."

Jade: "Ooohh, the City of Love."

Diamond: "It's gonna be a top of the line small wedding. Just family and friends. And I need my sisters to help me out on this one."

The girls all had tears in their eyes.

Chicago: "Girl, you know we'll be there for you."

Diamond: "I know."

The ninjas had a week of planning. The divas got with Diamond and helped plan out the wedding. Diamond picked out her own wedding dress--which was designed by Donna Karran. While the Divas picked out the flowers, cake and chapel. The prices on this wedding estimated at $500,000 days later.

The day of the wedding the Corporation was there along with Family and Friends. Big Six's father was his best man. Chicago, Jade, Jazzy Bell, Mona Lisa, Precious, Sky, and Raven was the flower girls. Raven's little boy was the ring carrier and her little girl sprinkled rose petals all over the floor before Diamond's father walked her down the aisle giving away her hand in marriage. Hezzy played the song "Here Comes the Bride" on the piano.

Preacher: "Dearly beloved, we are gathered here on this wonderful day to wed two of God's children as one in Holy Matrimony. Big Six, do you take Diamond to be your lawful wedded wife, to hold, to love, to cherish until eternity?"

Big Six: "I do."

Preacher: "Diamond, do you take Big Six to be your lawful wedded husband, to hold, to love, to cherish till death do you part?"

Diamond: "I do."

Preacher: "The ring please."

Big Six slid the ring onto Diamond's finger.

Preacher: "By the power vested in me I now pronounce you man and wife. You may kiss the bride."

Big Six pull up her veil and kiss the bride. Tears came to some eyes. Diamond threw the bouquet into the air and her and Big Six went running out the door to the limo while everyone threw rice. Sky caught the flowers. She smell 'em and just smile. All the divas went, "Ooohhh!!!" then they all smile. Later on everyone kick it at the reception having a good time. Love was in the air. Diamond was really in love and Big Six really love her. They all stayed a few hours until Big and Diamond's plane was ready. They took Big Six's helicopter from the reception to his own private jet. The divas all headed over to Chicago's place to just chill out for the rest of the night and they were all talking about how happy Diamond really was.

Chicago: "Diamond in love; I can see it in her eyes."

Precious: "Me too."

Sky: "I'm really happy for her."

Jade: "Me too. But in love with a trick? Naw, that ain't right. It can't be happening--not with Diamond anyway."

Raven: "I think it real. You know how Diamond get, talkin' about slowing down."

Jazzy Bell: "It's real. I felt love in the air."

Mona Lisa: "It could happen; love have a funny way of sneaking up on you."

Chicago: "You girls want something to drink?"

Precious: "Yeah, hook up with Potion Number 9."

Chicago: "What about you Jazzy?"

Jazzy: "I'll take a lemonade."

Chicago: "Okay, coming up."

Jazzy: "What type of movies you have around here?"

Chicago quickly brought the drinks back.

Chicago: "What you say?"

Jazzy: "What type of movies do you have around here?"

Chicago: "I got Waitin' to Exhale in the VCR right now. I was gonna watch it, but this has been a busy week."

Raven: "Ooohh, let's watch it."

Chicago turned on the set and hit Play on the VCR and they all cuddled up under each other as they movie played on. Chicago came right out and said, "You know what--I miss Sugar, I really do." And as a tear rolled down her face Jazzy Bell was there to wipe it away and said, "We all do."

As the movie played on, the ninjas all kick it over at Baller's place discussin' MOB type tactics. Time--10:01 p.m. and 27 hours away from the last lick of their life.

Baller: "All right, ninjas, it's like this: It's our money that's layin' out in that grave yard and we're gonna get it. Now it may sound simple and plain, but this may be the hardest lick yet. Maybe because it's our last one. Now it's do or die. You could get paid or killed on this just like the rest of 'em. We're going off in that grave yard with no mercy, killing off them spooky lookin' fuckers!"

Jim Kelly: "But Baller, how do you kill something that's already dead?"

Baller: "We're going in with the Lord on our side. Tell 'em, Hezzy."

Hezzy: "That's right. AK-47s and water guns laced with Holy Water."

Sugar Wolf: "Say what!? Water guns against them crazy flyin' through the air ass zombies? Ha! Give me a AK-47.

Man, that crazy...water gun."

Greed: "Where are you gonna get some Holy Water?"

Hezzy: "Down at the church, at Reverend Do Wrong."

Sugar Wolf: "Oh, Lord, now I know we're in trouble."

Baller: "Be cool, Wolf. This Holy Water is a sure thing. It works in the movies."

Sugar Wolf: "Yeah, the movies. This is our life, Baller, not no fuckin' movies!"

Baller: "Okay, we're going off in the grave yard as a two man team. Each team is responsible for their weapons, flashlight, duffel bag, and shovel. Okay now, choose your weapons and who you want to roll with you in the Valley of Darkness."

Eazy: "Give me a water gun and I want Fly Mar to roll with me."

Fly Mar: "Yeah, give me a water gun, too."

Jim Kelly: "I'm rollin' with Li'l Loc, and give me an AK-47."

Loc: "Give me a AK-47 too."

Greed: "I want Baller to roll with me, and I'll take a water gun."

Baller: "Me too."

Big Mike: "I'm gonna roll with Ten, and give me a AK-47 with some extra clips."

Baller: "Our AK-47s comes with extra clips."

Ten: "That sound sweet. I'm rollin' the same way. What's up, Wolf? What's up Wolf?"

Sugar Wolf: "Give me a AK-47 also with extra clips. And for my backup, I got MJG with me. What's up, Dogg? Choose your weapon."

MJG: "Dogg, I gotta go with the super soaker."

Sugar Wolf: "Man, I don't believe you pimpin."

MJG: "It's the dead, Wolf. Those AK-47s ain't gonna do

shit but make 'em mad. Holy Water tear dat ass up every time against the dead."

Hezzy: "Now that's my man."

Sugar Wolf: "Man, y'all niggas crazy. Hezzy and you know that Reverend Do Wrong used to be a big pimp."

Hezzy: "Yeah, use to be." Hezzy looked at Pete and said, "It's me and you, Baby. Ha ha."

Pete: "Choose your weapon."

Hezzy: "Shittt, a water gun, fool. What about you?"

Pete: "Nigga, I watch movies, too. Ha ha ha--I got to have one of those super soaker jokers."

Hezzy: "Fa shiggy. Look, I'm going down to K-Mart tomorrow and get our super soakers and then head over to Reverend Do Wrong."

Sugar: "Could I roll with you?"

Hezzy: "Sure. You just wanna see have he mended his ways."

Sugar: "That's right. I don't want y'all going in the grave yard with just plain water."

Baller: "Okay, it's ten million in each grave. One will dig while the other will stand guard lookin' out. Now I have the name of the graves in this Swisher box. Now, who wanna pick first?"

Li'l Loc: "I'll pick first for me and Kelly." Loc reach into the Swisher box and came out with The Mack, Goldie and Pretty Tony.

Fly Mar reach into the box and came out with Mack Truck Turner, Blue and Gator. Big Mike reach into the box and came out with Superfly, Priest and Scatter. Hezzy reached into the box and came out with Bingo Long, Esquire Joe and Charlie Snow. Baller reached into the box and came out with Peaty Wheat Staw, Skillet and Leroy. MJG reach into the box and came out with Slaughter Big Rip Off, High

Life and Slaughter.

Baller: "All we gotta do now is wait and meditate. Come 3:00 in the mornin" the next day after we're gonna be 120 million dollars richer. Now is you with me?!"

Everybody: "Hell yeah!!"

Baller: "So we're gonna ball a li'l bit. You know might Joe Young style and after this lick we're gonna King Kong ball till we fall. Hezzy, put some music on. Pete, pop in a movie. Ten, go get them two cases of beer in the refrigerator. Somebody roll something so we can smoke something."

Li'l Loc: "I got it. Where the weed?"

Baller: "I got it."

Ten came back with the beer. Hezzy put some music on (song) "Retaliation" by the BGs on the Chopper City CD. Pete put a movie in, Surviving the Game by Ice-T, and Baller came back with a pound of weed. He threw Loc the pound. Loc bust opening the pound of weed, rollin' 'em, lightin' 'em, puffin' 'em, and passin' 'em. When the ninjas got a li'l high they decided to pop some shit.

Ten: "Yo, after this here lick I'm gonna get me a Hogg."

Sugar Wolf: "Wooo--what type of Cadillac?"

Ten: "Naw, naw, Wolf. A Hogg is a Harley Davidson motorcycle."

Sugar Wolf: "Nigga, a Hogg is a Cadillac."

Ten: "Nigga, a Harley too."

Sugar Wolf: "Shi-i-id."

Ten: "On the forreala, my nigga."

Fly Mar: "It's true that they're both call Hoggs."

Big Mike: "Why you wanna Hogg and not a fly ass Yamaha, Kawasaki, or a Suzuki? The girls go crazy over them type of bikes."

Ten: "'Cause when the police see a black man ridin' 'em he right off think that's a dope boy. And anyway a Hogg is a American classic, that can ride a road."

Hezzy: "Man, in the 'hood girls go crazy over them Yamaha, Kawasaki, and Suzuki."

Ten: "Because they're flashy. Anyway, I'm doing this for me, fuck them 'ho's. I bet you niggas ain't never heard about a nigga riding cross country city to city on them type of bikes or you ain't never seen a nigga with a tattoo that say Yamaha, Kawasaki, or Suzuki, have you? Hell naw. 'Cause they ain't shit. But see, the real big boys ride a Harley Davidson 'cause they ride that road like it ain't nothing. Right now it's somebody out there getting a Harley tattoo 'cause they love their Hogg more than they car. But see, a dope boy love his car more than his bike."

Baller: "You damn sho' right about that. Now that's something to think about."

Sugar Wolf: "Hezzy, what time are we going to see Reverend Do Wrong?"

Hezzy: "Early noon."

Sugar Wolf: "Bet. Yo, put The Mack on."

Pete: "Yeah, I was watching it the other day. But something came up so I pop it outta the VCR and did what I had to do."

Pete pop in The Mack and push "play."

Pete: "Yo. This is the part where Goldie just walk off from the crooked cops. They wanted him to run so they could pop a cap in him. Goldie just walk off to church. But Slim (Richard Pryor) went off.

"Yo, but check out what this preacher is saying. The preacher as he walk down the road, he look back at his old home town. He didn't know where he was going, what he was doing, but he was going into a world of trouble, a world of misunderstanding, a world of dole, a world of whores, a world of hypocrites, a world of gamblin', a world of dope smokers, a world of prostitution. He was going into a mean world, but he didn't know where he was going. It's so many of us today doing the same thing to ourselves because we don't know what we doing, you understand. If we will just stop and think about ourselves sometimes, everything will be all right, you understand me? We gonna go jump off the Bay Bridge worried about this, man, worried about that, man. Because we don't know who we are, we don't know where we going and we don't know what we're here for, you understand me? Yeah. Good God ah mighty. Oh look at this boy with his big money, oh he's on the drug table now. He shootin' his dice. But he ain't got sense a nuff to know his money ain't gonna last doing all these wrong thangs. Doing these worldly thangs. Gambling and drinking, it's an end to these things. One of these days, one of these hours, it's gonna run out. But one of these days you gonna have to make up your mind. Then change your ways.

"I can see this young man, oh good God I can see this young man as he made up in his mind to start back home. His money done run out. His friends walk off and left him. His buddies walk off an left him. His girlfriend's quit him. He lost all he had. He had got down on his clothes, his hair had got bad. He said, 'Look at me, just look at me. Here I am, a young man, had a good home and had a good father and had a good mother. But here I am, done turn from rags to riches out here in this mean world. Don't know where I'm going or where I'm coming from. I believe I'll go back home.'

"And that when the congregation jump on crunk. And the preacher kept preaching, 'I-I-I believe I'll go back home. I don't know about you but I'm gonna go back home. I-I-I believe I'll go back home. Yes, yes, yes.'

The young man wanna go back home. Goldie just sat and

thought about what the preacher use to say when he was a young man. He look up at God, smile, and just thought about it. But Goldie didn't go home right then. He went to the player ball."

Baller: "Damn, that was some real shit that preacher spittin'."

MJG: "Sho' was."

Sugar Wolf: "You think that was a real preacher they use to play that part."

Pete: "Hell yeah, it was too real. And besides that it's real pimps in this movie."

Hezzy: "The Mack was a real movie based on true characters."

Eazy: "You can't fake that pimp shit. If you do, a bitch will let you know. They watch old black movies back to back until they all fall asleep as the movies play on." Big Six and Diamond was on their way to Paris, the City of Love, on the plane.

Diamond: "I love you, my Baby Boo."

Big Six: "I love you, too," and they kissed as the plane flew over the dark blue clouds.

Noon the next day. Hezzy and Sugar Wolf first picked up the super soaker from K-Mart and headed out to see the infamous Reverend Do Wrong.

Sugar Wolf: "Say Hezzy, you really think the Reverend Do Wrong has mended his way?"

Hezzy: "Most definitely."

Sugar Wolf: "So you think he can turn wine into blood and water into holy water."

Hezzy: "I didn't say all that. But I do know if a man have a strong belief in God all things are possible."

Sugar Wolf: "But a pimp, playa, hustla."

Hezzy: "I don't care if he was a drug dealer, killer, if God put his hands deep into your life you gonna change, 'cause God is a bad, bad man. But you know what, Wolf? It's funny how God take the worst one to be his Holy Souljas."

Sugar Wolf: "Yeah, right."

Hezzy: "Fa shiggy, my nigga. Check it out, if God wanted to pick somebody perfect, why would he make a person like Malcolm X shine like a star? He wasn't perfect."

Sugar Wolf: "Malcolm X."

Hezzy: "Hell yeah, man he would send shock wave through thousands and thousands of people when he speak. God pick him for a reason."

Sugar Wolf: "Yeah, but Dr. Martin Luther King made thousands and thousands of black and white people cry and tremble when he spoke. He had a tremulous voice and he was perfect."

Hezzy: "He damn sho' was. But that's just what's I'm saying. God is good and they both spoke about the Lord all the time. See, Wolf, when you keep God in your heart He will give you a overflow."

Sugar Wolf: "A overflow."

Hezzy: "Yeah. God will give you so many blessing you wouldn't know how to receive all of them. Just...just good thangs happening to you. People just wanna do things for you because they see that shine the Lord has put on ya. The Lord is good all the time. We're here."

Sugar Wolf: "This is the church."

Hezzy: "Yeah, big ain't it? Just wait until you step inside. It's Vaaainglooorrrious. And it is protected by the G--the O--and the D, piiimmmpiiinnn'."

Reverend Do Wrong's church seat over 16,400 people. His TV show Praise the Lord is shown all over the world. People come from miles away to hear his words. Hezzy and Sugar Wolf walked into the church.

Sugar Wolf: "Oh my Lord. It's Heaven."

Hezzy: "Ha ha ha. Almost. Come on, there the deacon."

The Deacon: "May I help you young men?"

Hezzy: "We're here to see Reverend Do Wrong."

The Deacon: "You're here to join the church."

Sugar Wolf: "No sir. This sure is a nice church. How much y'all bring in a service?"

The Deacon: "Son, money is not the issue. We save souls and heal hearts."

Hezzy: "You will have to excuse my brother, Deacon. But we're here to see Reverend Do Wrong about some Holy Water."

The Deacon: "Yes, yes. Holy Water. He's in the back."

Hezzy: "Could we go see him?"

The Deacon: "Yes."

Hezzy: "Thanks, Deacon. Come on Wolf."

As they started toward the back the deacon stop 'em and held out his hand. Hezzy went into his pocket and pull out 20 dollars and put it in the deacon's hand. The deacon look away. Hezzy look at Wolf and shook his head. Wolf went into his pocket and came out with a Big Face Frankenstein (a hundred dollar bill) and put it in the deacon's hand.

The Deacon: "Right this way, my sons."

Hezzy: "I see why this is the biggest church on the block."

Sugar Wolf: "I told ya so."

The Deacon: "Wait right here. The Reverend has been busy all day." The deacon went into the back where Reverend Do Wrong was. When the deacon walk in, Reverend Do Wrong was smokin' on a blunt gettin' a blow job with four more womens laying around.

The Deacon: "Excuse, Reverend, you got company."

Reverend Do Wrong: "What is smell like?"

The Deacon: "It smell like long bread."

Reverend Do Wrong ease the lady off him, put out the blunt, sprayed the room, lit a perfume stick, then told the deacon to show them in. And the deacon did that.

The Deacon: "The Reverend will see you now."

Hezzy: "Thanks."

Sugar Wolf: "I want my change when I come back out."

The deacon just walked off with a smirk on his face.

Reverend Do Wrong: "How y'all doing, how y'all doing? Welcome to the Church of Life. I'm the Reverend Do Wrong. How could I help ya, Hezzy?"

Hezzy: "I see you still remember me."

Reverend Do Wrong: "How could I forget you? We was in the same jail cell in the Rodney King riot and you kept my cigarette lighter. Man, that day I had a trunk full of shit, I mean stuff, in my Cadillac."

Hezzy: "Yeah, boy. It was about 50 of us in one cell. But you know what? You was one of the first to get out."

Reverend Do Wrong: "Yes, my bitch came--I mean my sister came--and got me out."

Hezzy: "I see you're surrounded by angels."

Reverend Do Wrong: "Yes, yes."

Sugar Wolf: "Man, you're a pimp. I know you. Back in the days they use to call you 'Stack-A-Lee' the pimp. You killed your wife and her lover. You caught them in bed and you killed them."

Hezzy: "Wolf, be cool. Chill out."

Reverend Do Wrong: "Naw, naw. It's okay. I'm not ashamed of my pass. See, the pass made me what I am today. See, God told me in order for me to see where I'm at I need to see where I'm going. So can you see me? Can you see the shine? It doesn't matter how you try to block prodigal son, you can't stop the shine. Now I help people. I feed Christ into their life. Yes, yes, I was a bad man but God spoke to me and I listen. You can be the baddest S.O.B. out in the street or jail, but when God speak to you, you better listen and answer back 'cause if you don't He will take his hands off you and make you feel His wrath! Ohh, Lord, He's a bad brother. Ezekiel 25:17, 'And I will execute great vengeance upon them with furious rebukes; and they shall know that I am the Lord, when I shall lay my vengeance upon them'."

Hezzy: "I believe, I believe."

Sugar Wolf: "I'm sorry if I disrespect you. I'm sorry, Reverend Do Wrong."

Reverend Do Wrong: "I'm sorry for ya."

Reverend Do Wrong look at Hezzy and they both bust out laughing. "Ha ha ha."

Reverend Do Wrong: "Loosen up, young nigga."

Reverend Do Wrong giving Hezzy dap.

Reverend Do Wrong: "What's up Baby Boy? It's been a long time."

Hezzy: "Yes, it has."

Reverend Do Wrong: "So what brings you to my establishment?"

Hezzy: "Holy Water. I need some Holy Water."

Reverend Do Wrong: "Yes, yes, I got you."

Reverend Do Wrong grab the half blunt and told Sugar Wolf to fire it up.

Sugar Wolf: "I knew you was cool. I'm Sugar Wolf."

Hezzy and Reverend Do Wrong hug and kiss each other on the cheek. Sugar Wolf was still trying to shake off the confused look he had on his face.

Hezzy: "Loosen up, Wolf. That's just the Reverend's way of seeing if you all right."

Reverend Do Wrong: "'I sorry if I disrespect you.' Ha ha ha."

Sugar Wolf: "You got me."

Reverend Do Wrong: "Come, let's talk."

They walked around the church before going to the basement.

Reverend Do Wrong: "So what you need Holy Water for?"

Hezzy: "To fight the living dead."

Reverend Do Wrong: "Is it about paper?"

Hezzy: "Yes, it is. Big paper."

Reverend Do Wrong: "I heard that. I got some of the best Holy Water on the block."

They enter in the basement. Hezzy and Sugar Wolf was in shock as they look around the basement and saw pounds and pounds of weed and cocaine, gallons of Holy Water everywhere, and shelves filled with all types of automatic weapons.

Hezzy: "You've been grindin'. What's up with all this?"

Reverend Do Wrong: "This is from young mens who wanted off the streets. They come to me searching for God 'cause the street ain't safe no more. So they bring their evil to me. I take it and flip it on the under, the right way. Building a bigger church. I feed God into the young men's lives, gliding 'em down the righteous path. That ends at the cross road.

Hezzy: "The cross road."

Reverend Do Wrong: "Yes, yes, the cross road. See, we all wear the cross; without the cross there is no cross road. Those that don't wear the cross wear the mark of the beast the wicked road to Hell where you slave and shovel coal day and night without a cold glass of ice water. Jesus carried the cross. Jesus died on the cross for our sin."

Hezzy and Sugar Wolf kicked it all day with Reverend Do Wrong, smokin' and choppin' up holy game, speakin' religiously before leaving. Hezzy and Wolf left with four

five-gallon jugs filled with Holy Water and some holy game.
Ridin' out...

Sugar Wolf: "Man, that Do Wrong is a fool with it."

Hezzy: "I know. That's my dirt dogg."

Sugar Wolf: "I heard that. Me too, right."

Hezzy: "And you know it."

Sugar Wolf: "The game as sho' 'nuff change."

Hezzy: "Like how?"

Sugar Wolf: "Well, it still the same by puttin' a bitch on
the track and she coming back with chesse, that ain't never
gonna change. Look at me, I having been balling all my life
bitches use to dogg me."

Hezzy: "Nigga, please."

Sugar Wolf: "No lie, Baby Boy, but I learn from that shit.
Let me tell how these niggas and bitches is today. Niggas
and bitches running around here with that Chucky love.

Hezzy: "Chucky love."

Sugar Wolf: "Yeah, Chucky love. That stab you in the
back love. That friend to the end love. Chucky is the one
who tell you 'I'm your friend to the end' then he kills you
with a knife. Ha ha ha."

Hezzy: "Yeah, that's right."

Sugar Wolf: "Now this is how some of the games be
played. I had a girl who was down with me, a good girl, so
I thought. Now you got some niggas that come around your
way to see what you're clockin' and some will see what you
got in your stable. Chucky will take you out clubbin' and to
parties, keepin' you away from your money and woman.
While on the other hand, his playa potna got his eyes on your
money and your woman, catching your woman at the store,
and with his eye on you when you're not lookin'. Now
Chucky love got game and so do his playa potna, shooting
game to your woman the right way. After a day or a few

days playa potna diggin' off in that pussy doggy style. It's then. Chucky love then introduce you to his playa potna. Then the playa potna take you out ballin', keepin' you away from the money and your woman. While you out ballin', Chucky callin' your house, ask for you when he know you ain't home, building a phone relationship with your gal. Next thang you know, he's fucking her. She giving Chucky love the pussy for the 411 on you. Believe me, he's gonna give up information on ya, and fuck your women, and fuck 'er good, too. Now you think you got friends and she think she playing them. That's when the set up sit in. They kill ya or rob ya, or maybe get you incarceration 25 years to life. When that shit happen, both of them niggas be in your house at the same time throwing a tag team party on that pussy, fuckin' her ass, pussy & head on camcorder froggy style."

Hezzy: "Wooo, now, ha ha ha. Gott damn, sho' 'nuff."

Sugar Wolf: "Fa shiggidy, Baby Boy, Chucky love."

Hezzy: "So every nigga that say he's down for you and the 'hood, ain't for you and your 'hood. It's Chucky love."

Sugar Wolf: "Fa shiggy, that's just some of the trick niggas be playing, giving you that slutty pussy so they can get your house pussy and once they're in your house money gone."

Hezzy: "So how did you get set up?"

Sugar Wolf: "Well, back in season I was fuckin' this chick Chucky love had sent my way. I laid game and dick on her before she could game and fuck me and I wore a condom 'cause you got some players in the game that will send you a bitch with that poison in her blood just because he's jealous. Anyway, a week went by, so I got with my main girl. Chucky love had her head all fuck. She set me up by puttin' dope under the passenger seat when I told her I had business. But she knew I was lying because Chucky love turn on me again. So I went to go get my new chick. I pick her up, we got about 2 miles away from her house then Boom! cops everywhere."

Hezzy: "Damn. That's fucked up--how did you come outta it?"

Sugar Wolf: "The game. It's the game. I ran down on the chick, paid off, she took the blame for the 'cain. They lock her up, I got her a lawyer and they gave her 4 years of probation. It was first charge, Baby Boy. And right to this day, she's still down like Moesha (you know, Brandy)."

Hezzy: "Who?"

Sugar Wolf: "Mia, Nigga."

Hezzy: "Oh yeah, I always knew Mia was a boss bitch. So whatever happen to the bitch and Chucky?"

Sugar Wolf: "Think about it."

Hezzy: "'Nuff said."

Sugar Wolf: "Pimpin' ain't easy now."

Hezzy: "I know, it's hard work for a player too, now. It's just a playa like to play 'ho's for sex, money, and games. A player get that money and pay his bills. When a player get paid he put his fuck face on. A player don't fuck for free, 'cause bitches are quick to put a label on a nigga if he's pussy crazy. A player will get his bitch to fuck other nigga with Big Paper just to see if he's pussy crazy and if he is Kaboom! that's dat ass. A nigga who put pussy over money is weak. A bitch will take a trick, suck 'em, fuck 'em and absorbs his energy and game like a sponge and pass it on to the player building his game and destroying the trick. Imagine when enervating a trick or player game and energy, they could easily be boobytrapped.

Sugar Wolf: "You got good potential to be a pimp, Baby Boy."

Hezzy: "So that mean we both got enough game to be

pimps, playas, and hustlas."

Sugar Wolf gave Hezzy dap and said "Sho' ya right" as they pull into the driveway. The souljas was on the inside going over the plan set for 3:00 in the morning. Ten and Baller came out the back side door to help with the super soakers and 4 five-gallons of Holy Water.

Ten: "Yo, what kept y'all so long?"

Sugar Wolf: "Fooling around with Do Wrong kickin' the bo bo."

Hezzy: "What time is it?"

Baller: "4:16 p.m."

Hezzy: "What's wrong, playboy?"

Baller: "Why say that?"

Hezzy: "It look like you got something on your mind."

Baller: "I got a letter today."

Hezzy: "What kind of letter? Child support?"

Baller: "Hell naw. Here, check it out."

Hezzy open up the letter and read it. "I know what you did last summer."

Hezzy: "What the fuck is this shit?"

Baller: "I don't know, but someone playing games."

Hezzy: "You talk with the souljas about it yet?"

Baller: "Yeah, same thang. They know nothing."

As Baller and Hezzy stepped in the room with the souljas, Pete was like: "Yo, Baller hip you to that shit?"

Hezzy was like, "Yeah, we gonna handle it."

Pete: "You damn right."

Baller made an announcement.

Baller: "Souljas, listen up. I'm bringing Flamingo, Nickel and Dime in on this one. They know the way and we need someone that could drive us in and get us out in case something goes wrong. Any question?"

They all agreed that bringing along the three will make a

big difference in the Valley of Darkness. Half the souljas filled the super soakers with the Holy Water and the other half loaded up the AK-47s with the tape up 50 rounds banana clips. An hour later, Flamingo, Nickel and Dime arrived. Baller told everybody before they ride they will pray and meditate and they did for six hours straight. Time 12:30 a.m.

Just minutes after they came outta meditating the phone rang. Big Mike pick it up. "Hello." It was Jazzy Bell. "Hey Big Baby, what's up? What's happening?"

Big Mike: "Nothing much, just getting ready for war. What up with you?"

Jazzy: "Oh we all just chillin'. I went by the house today."

Big Mike: "By yourself?"

Jazzy: "Naw, I had a few of the girls with me."

Big Mike: "Everything okay?"

Jazzy Bell: "Yeah. I just got this strange letter out the mailbox today."

Big Mike: "What it say? 'I know what you did last summer'?"

Jazzy Bell: "Big Baby..."

Big Mike: "What?"

Jazzy Bell: "Exactly that's what it say. How you know?"

Big Mike: "'Cause Baller got one today."

Jazzy Bell: "Let me speak with him."

Big Mike: "Baller."

Baller: "Yeah?"

Big Mike: "Phone."

Baller: "Hello?"

Jazzy Bell: "What's up?"

Baller: "What's happening?"

Jazzy: "I heard you got a letter today."

Baller: "Yeah, some fool playin' games."

Jazzy: "I got a letter today also."

Baller: "Yeah?"

Jazzy Bell: "Yeah. And Mona Lisa's house was broken into and ransack."

Baller: "Say what?"

Jazzy: "Yeah. Her neighbors say that a strange unmarked blue Pontiac 6000 was park in her driveway."

Baller: "Did they get the tag?"

Jazzy Bell: "Naw. What time y'all pullin' out to the grave site?"

Baller: "3:00 in the morning."

Jazzy Bell: "Didn't you know anytime before 12:30 a.m. the good spirits plays. Anytime after 12:30 a.m. the evils plays."

Baller: "Naw, I didn't know that."

Jazzy Bell: "Baron Samdi is the leader of the dead. He teach the dead after midnight how to channel their anger against the living who betray them in the flesh. He teach 'em how to fight and how to mess with the living by showing their self on the streets or in a dream."

Baller: "Why so much hate?"

Jazzy Bell: "'Cause, the living ain't right. You got some people that will bury their loved one and that's it. They don't even visit them no more. Years go by and so-call home boys don't even come by to drop off a flower or nothing. But niggas always claim they're real. If niggas die twice it would be a lotta more home boys killin' home boys because niggas ain't real. The dead get lonely too, and when that happens Baron Samdi, King of the Dead, steps in an' comfort them with understanding and knowledge. You hear me?"

Baller: "I hear you, but we got some shit for that ass."

Jazzy: "I'm sure y'all do. I'll pray for y'all."

Baller: "Later."

Jazzy Bell: "Bye," and they hung up the phone.

Baller look at the souljas and said, "It about that time." The souljas jump into their soulja rags and taped their flashlight around the middle of their barrels for sight and they all pack into the van on mission to get paid, listening to the song "Do or Die" by La Royce off his Wake the Dead CD. An hour later Flamingo pulled in the graveyard driveway.

Greed: "It's foggier than a mothefucka out there."

Hezzy: "Let's go and get this dead man's money."

Baller: "Flamingo, Nickel, and Dime, what's your duty?"

Nickel: "If we hear any type of funny noise we come blasting and skeeting."

Nickel and Dime had AK-47s and Flamingo a super soaker.

Flamingo: "Don't worry, we're coming gunning."

Baller: "I like that. Let's go souljas."

As soon as the souljas step on the soil lightning struck and all the souljas duck down and look up at the dark purple skies (a sign of evil). A hundred yards onto the graveyard the dead started to wake. As dead started raising from the soil, each team soulja got back to back, eyes buck, heart beating fast, weapon ready to blast. All of a sudden two zombies flew over a tombstone with sickles in their hand. Grrrr! Grrrrrrrr! Baller and Greed aimed and started squirting Holy Water. Skeeee---Skeeee. B-LAAAM! B-LAAAM!

"It works!" Greed said as the zombies exploded as old bones and a green gooey sticky sperm-like substance flew from their bodies.

Baller: "What the fuck?!"

Zombies pack the land and air, flyin' across the souljas, tryin' to kill 'em with all types of weapons from sickles, sabers, swords, scythes, scimitars and chainsaws. Grrrrr Grrrrr!Grrrrr!Grrrrr! Jim Kelly and Li'l Loc speaking with

their AKs. Rat-tat-tat-tat-tat-tat. Rat-tat-tat-tat-tat-tat-tat.
The AK-47s flipped the zombies 20 to 30 feet away but they
jump   right   back   up   and   kept   coming.
Grrrrr!Grrrrr!Grrrrr!Grrrrr!   Eazy and Fly Mar Skeee
Skeee Skeee Skeee B-LAAAM! B-LAAAM! B-LAAAM!
B-LAAAM!   Grrrrr! Grrrrr!Grrrrr!Grrrrr! Grrrrr! Skeee
Skeee B-LAAAM! B-LAAAM!   Rat-tat-tat-tat-tat-tat.
Skeee Skeee B-LAAAM! B-LAAAM!

One zombie knock Sugar Wolf into a tombstone. Sugar
Wolf's weapon fell from his hand. The zombie got on top of
Sugar Wolf with a stiletto in his hand, but before he could
stab Sugar Wolf, MJG put it on him. Skeee B-LAAAM!

Sugar Wolf: "Thanks, potna."

Big Mike and Ten constantly busting shots. Rat-tat-tat-
tat...click...click...Rat-tat-tat-tat-tat-tat-tat...Rat-tat-tat.
Flamingo, Nickel, and Dime heard the noise and came like
a tornado riding through the graveyard, knocking over
tombstones. Nickel and Dime hangin' out the van letting off
shots. Rat-tat-tat-tat. Flipping 'em. Rat-tat-tat-tat. Flipping
'em. Rat-tat-tat-tat. Flipping 'em. Flamingo spun the van
around and jump out with Nickel and Dime skeeting. Skeee
Skeee Skeee B-LAAAM! B-LAAAM! B-LAAAM!

Flamingo: "Y'all niggas come on!!!"

The souljas warring. Rat-tat-tat-tat. Flipping 'em. Rat-
tat-tat-tat. Flipping 'em. Skeee Skeee Skeee B-LAAAM! B-
LAAAM! B-LAAAM! The souljas was deep into battle
avoiding swords, sickles, and chainsaws. As the souljas ran
to the van, more zombies came outta the gound throwing
spears. When all the souljas jump into the van and lock the
doors, the zombies crowded the van, sockin' it, rockin' it,
tryin' to get in. Flamingo crunk the van, pullin' off wildly
trying to escape death. Flamingo straighten up the van,
bustin' out the gates of Hell, shaking the devil off. The soul-

jas rode back to the house in silence.

An hour later, back at the house, jumpin' outta the sticky soulja rags, cleaning their selves, having a heavy conversation. 5:00 in the morning, chokin' on a pound of skunk weed and sniffing on some raw girly girl.

Eazy: "Snok, snok...we need to go back...snok, snok...and get our money, man."

Fly Mar: "Snok, snok...I'm with ya, Dogg."

Sugar Wolf: "Y'all niggas crazy!"

Flamingo: "Snok, snok...damn sho' right."

Hezzy, coming out the back, drying out his 'fro.

Hezzy: "What ya niggas talkin' about?"

Pete: "Snok, snok...going back. Back, Baby Boy."

Hezzy: "Shi-i-i-id, y'all niggas crazy."

Baller: "Here you go, Baby Boy."

Hezzy got the blunt from Baller as he pour up a glass of Crown Royal.

MJG: "Baller, what you think?"

Eazy: "Be for real, now."

Baller: "On the for real, I was scare up."

Hezzy: "Me too."

Fly Mar: "Snok, snok...me too."

Eazy: "Snok...that shit fuck me up too."

Big Mike: "Me too."

Jim Kelly: "I ain't going back."

Li'l Loc, sitting back with his drink in one hand, a blunt in the other with girl on his noise bouncing to the music feeling good.

Li'l Loc: "Hezzy, who's that right there?"

Hezzy: "That's the Dayton family."

Li'l Loc: "That mother fucka fire right there, what's the name of that song?"

Hezzy: "My Posse is Dayton Avenue."

Li'l Loc: "Make me a tape of that, all right?"

Hezzy: "All right."

Li'l Loc: "Oh, oh fuck going back. Nigga ghost busters can't even get off in that bitch."

Greed: "I was scared also."

Sugar Wolf: "I ain't going back."

MJG: "I'm with ya."

Flamingo, Nickel, and Dime was like, "Hell, yeah! But it's on y'all."

The souljas was really wore out. They all fell asleep at six and woke up at 12:00 p.m. and got back on their post with a feeling of relief. Baller and the crew got up and started cleaning the house, talkin' about the lick. Pete say, "Baby Boy, you was scared, huh?"

Hezzy: "Hell, yeah! You was too, Nigga. I never seen a fat nigga run so fast, jumping over tombstones and shit." Baller and Ten laughing.

Pete: "Shi-i-i-d! Y'all niggas was moving like Carl Lewis too now, slow ya roll on me, we're all scared."

There was a knock at the door. Knock-knock-knock.

Ten: "Who is it?"

"It's me, Cuddie."

Ten opened the door. Cuddie step in.

Cuddie: "What's up, what's up y'all?"

Everybody: "What's up, Cuddie?"

Cuddie: "I was just bringin' over the money. It's payday. And I'll take some work if you got it." (Some cocaine.)

Hezzy took the money.

Cuddie: "It's all there, count it."

Baller: "No need."

Ten went into the back and came back with two keys.

Ten: "Here ya go, two birdies."

Cuddie: "Oh Hell yeah, what a beautiful thang."

Hezzy: "Nothing but the best for a friend."

Baller: "Yo Cuddie, you seen Dope Fiend Leroy (the mayor) around?"

Cuddie: "Yeah, that nigga out there actin' foolish looking for some work."

Baller: "Yeah, tell that nigga I got some work for him.

Cuddie: "I'll do it. What's up?"

Baller: "Naw, this is a job for the mayor."

Hezzy: "Cuddie, you just got some work."

Cuddie: "Man, y'all niggas pay good."

Baller: "Say we pay good, huh?"

Cuddie: "Hell yeah!"

Baller: "Ha ha, naw but this job is for The Mayor, not a player. When you see him tell 'em I want him to clean the van in and out."

Cuddie: "Okay, I'll tell 'im."

Baller: "Yo, you got some hard hard left over there?"

Cuddie: "Yeah, a few ounce, halves, and a couple of quarters."

Baller: "Let me get a quarter of that hard hard. We'll straighten out later on."

Cuddie: "All right. I told ya, y'all niggas pay good. I'll get one of my li'l potna to bring that over. Y'all niggas take it easy."

Everybody: "All right, Cuddie."

Hezzy be start out there, Cuddie walkin' out the door saying all the time.

Ten: "That nigga be workin'. Pete he's down for his scratch."

Hezzy: "Can I pick 'em."

Baller: "You can pick 'em, but he got two keys now, let's see what he do."

Knock-knock-knock.

Ten: "Who is it?"

"Joker and The Mayor."

Ten openin' up the door.

Joker: "Here you go, this the quarter y'all ask for."

Ten: "All right."

And Joker left. The Mayor stepped in, dancing and singing.

The Mayor: "I need a bag dope, need a bag dope. What's up, what's up? They wanna be like Baller, a shot caller, but they can't 'cause they're too smaller, huh what huh what."

The souljas laugh.

Ten: "Yo Dope Fiend Leroy, we got a job for ya."

The Mayor: "That's why I brought tools...and call me The Mayor, I ain't no dope fiend, geek monster, or clucker. I'm a smoker. And a smoker work for a hit, they don't steal. But a geek monster, dope fiend, and a clucker don't work, don't eat, don't sleep, just geek geek geek and they don't wash their ass! Nigga, I eat, sleep, and wash my ass, you can't even tell I smoke."

Baller: "Nigga, shi-i-i-d."

The Mayor: "You just saying that shit 'cause I weigh about a buck-o-five."

Baller: "You damn right. I want you to clean the van real good inside and out.

The Mayor: "I got it. I'm gonna customize that mother fucka! When you see it it's gonna gleam, baby. And when you get in that botch you gonna be able to shine and recline and them hater ain't gonna like that, ya heard?"

Pete: "Here go the keys. Do ya thang."

The Mayor got the keys, ready to work, but before he left out the door he said, "Could I get a li'l hit?"

Hezzy: "Not till I see that shine."

The Mayor walk out the door, bouncing and singing.

The Mayor: "Boy in the 'hood are alway hard, come talkin' that trash and they'll pull your card."

The souljas went right back to cleaning the house. 30 minutes later a knock at the door. Knock-knock-knock.

Ten: "Who is it?"

"It's me, Razor Sharp."

Ten: "Oh shittt."

Hezzy: "What up?"

Ten: "It's Baller shit-starting-ass-cousin. What y'all want me to do?"

Baller: "Open the door."

Ten open the door. Razor stepped in and spoke. "What's up y'all cousin?" Baller gave his cousin a big hug and kiss on both cheeks.

Baller: "What's happening, cuz?"

Razor: "Nothing much, just chilling. What y'all niggas smoking on? Let's smoke one."

Pete: "We outta smoke."

Razor: "I know y'all big ballers got something around here to smoke."

Hezzy: "We're out, sho' 'nuff, who got that fire?"

Razor: "I know where it at. Let's ride."

Baller: "Where it at, cuz?"

Razor: "Offa Broadway. It's smoking too. Come ride with me, cuz. Y'all boyz actin' funny like a nigga's broke or something. I know y'all niggas got some smoke around here."

Baller: "All right. I'll be back; y'all ninjas hold it down."

Razor: "Yeah, hold it down. We're gonna get high today."

Ten: "What ya gonna bring back, a pound?"

Pete: "That nigga ain't got that type of bank."

Razor: "Yeah, a pound."

The ninjas laugh. Razor went into his pocket and pull out

a knot money and said, "Y'all nigga ain't the only one got bank."

Hezzy: "Oh shit!"

Razor: "That's right, oh shit! Y'all niggas just get ready to smoke. Let's go, cuz."

Razor and Baller left out the door. Before they got into the car, Baller ask Razor, "Who car is this, cuz?"

Razor: "Oh this is a geek monster car. He let me hold it for today for three rocks."

Baller: "This mother fucka is sho' 'nuff junky."

Razor: "I know, but this bitch ride good" and they dip.

Riding out to the spot.

Razor: "Cuz, to me it seem like you love them niggas more than me."

Baller: "They're my dirt dogg."

Razor: "But I'm you blood, right?"

Baller: "Right."

Razor: "And blood is thicker than water."

Baller: "But mudd is thicker than blood."

Razor: "What cha mean?"

Baller: "See, cuz, a dirt dogg can stand the rain. See, when it rain on a dirt dogg, a dirt dogg will still put in work! It don't matter if he's hurt, muddy, or bloody, he's gonna do that job then show that love. Hey, but I love you. You know that, right?"

Razor: "Yeah, I know."

Baller: "How much farther we got to go?"

Razor: "Just a little bit more farther."

Baller: "I'm ready to smoke one now."

Razor: "Just be cool and hand me one of those tapes on the floor. Let's listen to some music."

Baller grabbed a tape off the floor and stuck it into the tape deck. Razor started singing with the song. "I never let a 'hoooo pimp meeee."

Baller: "That shit jamming, cuz. Who dat?"

Razor: "That's Short Dogg! Gettin' it Album Number Ten, Baby. He say this his last album and he's gonna start full time pimpin' now. That shit was bound to happen."

Baller: "That nigga ain't gonna leave the rap game, he too fire!"

Razor: "I'm tellin' you, cuz, he say it on the album."

Baller: "Other rappers ain't gonna let him. They gonna pay him good money to be on their album and Short Dogg gonna tear it up. Other rapper gonna hear it and be like, 'Hey, I thought he quit the rap game. Hey Short Dogg, rap on my album, man.' Short gonna be like 'Fuck, I can't stay away'."

Razor: "On know, cuz, 10 albums."

Baller: "Yeah, but money talk."

Razor: "We're here, cuz, soon as I bust this left turn."

Razor turn down the street and it was ten cars of police ahead of them. Baller look back and it was more cars rushin' from the back. Baller look at Razor. Razor drop his head and look back up, tellin' Baller, "I'm sorry. I love you, cuz."

Razor jump out the car running. Before Baller could jump out the car the cops was all over him with their guns drawn. Baller put his hands up on the car, and over walk Chief Detective Ren Shockley. He look at Baller with a smirk on his face. He took out a picture of Baller, look at the picture, look at Baller, look at his boys and said, "This him, boys. We got him." Cops searched the car and came up with 3 guns, 2 pounds of weed and 18 ounces of crack cocaine.

Detective Ren Shockley took Baller down to headquarters in the room with one light and one chair.

Ren Shockley: "Big Baller, Big Baller, you know you done

fuck up, don't ya."

Baller: "I was set up."

Ren Shockley: "I know. I set you up."

Baller: "Say what?"

Ren Shockley: "I set you up."

Baller: "Whatever you tryin' to do ain't gonna prosper 'cause the Lord is gonna see me outta it."

Ren Shockley: "Naw, I'm gonna help you out of it. Besides, you really must don't know what you're being charged with, son."

Baller: "What?!"

Ren Shockley: "First of all, you're an escaped convict with multiple charges and on top of that 3 hot guns, 2 pounds of weed, and 18 ounces which was supposed to have been 4 pounds of weed and 36 ounces. Your roguish ass cousin got me out the other half. You lookin' at 99 years boy, but all that can disappear if you join the team."

Baller: "What team?"

Ren Shockley: "Our team."

Baller: "Man, I don't wanna be no fuckin' cop!"

Ren Shockley: "Just shut up and listen. When you killed Milk that put you in his position, you're next in line for a miracle. The boss wants to see you."

Baller: "Who's the boss?"

Ren Shockley: "Kellogg Nickatina, the lawyer, the supplier, and the cleaner. He wants you and your crew to work for him, just like when Milk was living. It will be no different than before, except the price will be lower and you will be dealing directly with the man."

Baller: "Yeah, man, get outta my face talking crazy. You selling false dreams, it ain't such a man call Kellogg Nickatina. Wake me up when it's over. Ha ha ha."

Ren Shockley started showing emotions.

Ren Shockley: "You saying I'm talking crazy, huh! You saying you don't wanna get back in the street, huh! You say it ain't such a man name Kellogg Nickatina, huh! Well what's love, you sitting in jail for another mother fucka, huh! What's love you help this mother fucka get on his feet, gave him a place to sleep, huh! What's love you even killed somebody for this fool, huh! And he stab you in the back, huh! What's love with 99 years over your head. What's love, Nigga! What's love!

"Now if I'm crazy look me in my eyes and tell me I'm crazy! Look at me! Look at me! You can't, huh, you can't 'cause I'm tellin' the truth!"

Baller drop his head and for 30 seconds he thought about the good times him and his cousin had.

Ren Shockley: "Now you gonna join the team or take your chances with the 99?"

Baller raised his head and said, "I'll take my chances with the 99."

Ren Shockley: "Okay, Mr. Badd Ass. Just remember, Kellogg Nickatina has the judges and everybody else on his payroll."

Baller: "Yeah, I know one somebody he don't have on his payroll."

Ren Shockley: "Yeah, who?"

Baller: "Why my cousin turn on me, anyway?"

Ren Shockley: "'Cause he wanted to be like you and you never gave him any credit. We caught him trying to sell a half a block of cocaine to an undercover officer. We caught him with the drugs and a hot pistol with the serial numbers filed off. I told him he was looking at 99 years of federal time. That's when he buckles like a li'l bitch, tellin' me what I wanted to hear."

Baller: "And what was that?"

Ren Shockley: "I got you, Babe...I got you, Babe...I got you, Babe. You remember that song by Sonny & Cher?"

Baller: "Naw, I'm into rap."

Ren Shockley: "I hate rap. Come on, I'm taking you to your cell."

Baller: "I need to make a phone call."

Ren Shockley: "Not today, Boy! Get in that cell. No phone, no warning, no join, no family...you know too much. You must join or your friends die without warning."

Baller yelling out the cell as Ren Shockley walk off: "You fuck with my friends, I'll kill ya!"

Ren Shockley walk on off laughing.

Meanwhile, back at the house, the souljas was complimenting The Mayor on a job well done with the van.

Hezzy: "You got down."

The Mayor: "Thanks. Now can I have my medicine."

Ten: "Here ya go."

The Mayor: "Oh, this that shit! I like this dope, it don't clog up your shooter. I can hit this shit, sit it down for a li'l bit, then hit it again and again off one rock. This some good dope."

Pete: "Go head on, you just saying that 'cause you got a fat ass quarter."

The Mayor: "Naw, Dogg, fa real. I wouldn't lie."

Hezzy: "'Cause that's some shit a clucker or a geek monster will do, right?"

The Mayor: "Right, a geek monster and a clucker will tell you your shit is good and go buy dope from another dealer. If your dope ain't good to me I'm gonna tell you. Aaa, I gotta go, gettin' the zone. Ya'll niggas keep it jiggy." And The Mayor went on his way, dancing and singing, "I don't really wanna shoot this fool blast on that ass pop 187, I don't really wanna shoot this fool blast on that ass pop 187."

Ten: "That nigga dope fiend is a fool. Yo, I got an idea."

Pete: "What's up?"

Ten: "Let's ball, let's get Fly and kick it out at the mall. Do a li'l shopping, get something to eat, go get my Hogg, spend about 50 thou and it's all on me."

Hezzy: "Fa shiggy."

Ten: "Fa shiggidy. We can jump in the Hum-V, go ball at the mall, then go get my Hogg."

Pete: "It sound good to me. I know this li'l spot where we could eat. They got steaks bigger than elephant ears."

Hezzy: "Damn, elephant ears."

Pete: "Fa shiggy."

Ten: "So is it on? I gotta get me a bike. Y'all niggas know how cars are to me! Jainky as fuck. So what's up?"

Hezzy: "Let's do it."

The playas got dressed. Riding out on the highway in their hummer, blowin' big smoke, chokin' on blunts, heading out to the mall. They hit the mall and everyone was jockin' them like they were superstars, I guess 'cause they were ballin' outta control. They spent about 20 thousand out at the Lenox Square Mall buying fresh gear, CDs and tapes, eating on lobsters, crabs, potatoes with steaks. An hour later they left Lenox Mall on their way to the motorcycle shop Bumpin' Master P break 'em off something burning one. Ten pass the blunt back to Hezzy, asking him which song do he like on Master P Ice Cream CD.

Hezzy: "I like that last one my ghetto heroes."

Pete: "I like this one."

Ten: "I like that playa from around the way. That shit is nice and smooth."

Pete: "Yo, playas, we got company."

Ten look into his rearview.

Ten: "I see 'em. Hezzy, pass us the point prover."

Hezzy slid Ten and Pete their gun. They each cock one in their chamber.

Hezzy: "What type of car is it?"

Ten: "A blue Pontiac 6000. Look like a unmark Police car."

Hezzy took a quick look back and said, "Pete, don't that look like Reebok old ride?"

Pete: "Yeah, it do."

Hezzy: "Fuck 'em. If they come with that fuck shit we blastin'. Pete, speed up."

Pete step harder on the gas, losing 'em. The Pontiac 6000 caught up with the Hummer on Marietta Street. That's when Pete turned in the motorcycles parking lot. The Pontiac 6000 drove on by, giving the Hummer a suspicious look.

The players walk into the motorcycle shop. Ten was excited.

Ten: "What's up, what's up? Can I get some help?"

The motorcycle shop owner came out the back. "Hi fellow. I'm Norwood Jones. May I help you?"

Ten: "Yeah, man, I wanna take a look at some of your Hoggs."

Norwood: "A Harley, huh?"

Ten: "Yeah."

Norwood: "I would have suspected playas like you to ask for a Yamaha, Suzuki, or Kawasaki or something."

Ten: "Well we ain't your average playas."

Norwood: "I can tell, only the real ride Harleys."

Ten: "That's right."

Norwood: "Right this way. Here you go."

Ten: "Oh shit! I want this one. Ring it up. What y'all niggas think?"

Hezzy: "It's a beautiful thang."

Pete: "It's you, Baby."

Hezzy: "A man, he said he want this one. Go get the paper work ready!"

Norwood: "Well he said he wanted this one and he haven't even look at the price tag. This Hogg cost 27,750 dollars."

Ten: "Yes, and I want it."

Hezzy unzipped the green Polo bag. Ten stuck his hands into the bag, pull out two big chunks of money, stuck it in Norwood's face and said, "It's 30 gees right here. Will that cover the taxes?"

Norwood scratch his head and said, "Sure, let's take this up front. What's your name?"

Ten: "I'm Ten, this Pete. What's up? And that's Hezzy. What's happening?"

Norwood: "Nothing much. Hey, I'm sorry about doubting ya on the price, you know, like I said, I don't get guys like you coming in here asking for a Harley. What, you guys rappers or something?"

Hezzy: "Yeah."

Norwood: "What's the name of your group?"

Hezzy: "We're the Hot Boys."

Norwood: "The Hot Boys. I like that. Well, y'all, this is my wife Serina. She's gonna count it while we sip on a li'l something. Come, let's go in the back. I got some Tequila right here with the worm at the bottom. Who want some?"

Pete: "I gotta drive."

Ten: "Me too."

Hezzy: "I'm smokin'."

Norwood: "What you got some chronic?"

The playas chuckle.

Hezzy: "Yeah, man, I got some chronic."

Norwood: "Shit, man, fire it up."

Hezzy already had one rolled. He lit it, puff it, and pass it on to Norwood. He took two tokes and started coughing hard.

Pete: "That's that 747. How ya feel?"

Norwood: "Like I'm flying."

Norwood pass the blunt to Pete, running to the back side door gasping for air.

At the door (he coughs two times): "Hey Ten, what type ride y'all riding?"

Ten went walking toward Norwood saying, "We riding in a Hum-V Baby."

Norwood: "You better come take a look at this. Someone snoopin' around it."

Ten: "What!"

Ten rush out the door. Hezzy and Pete was right behind him.

Ten: "What the fuck you niggas think y'all doing!?"

The three men turn with their guns in hand before Ten could pull out his chitty chitty bang bang. The 3 men open fire--Bang Bang Bang Bang Bang Bang Bang. Ten was hit in the chest and arm. He fell to the ground. Hezzy and Pete came out bustin' shots-- Bang Bang Bang Bang click...click...click. Bang Bang Bang Bang click...click. Bang Bang Bang Bang Bang Bang Bang click...click...click. 3 minutes into the gunplay, Norwood came out the door with a M-16. Rat-tat-tat-tat. Rat-tat-tat-tat. Bang Bang Bang Bang click...click...click Bang Bang Bang Rat-tat-tat-tat. One of the 3 men yell out, "We're cops!!! We're cops!!!" But Hezzy, Pete, and Norwood the motorcycle shop owner kept bustin's shots. That's when the blue jean cops retreated from the scene when more bullets began to swarm. But before leaving they took a few bullets with them. One was hit in the leg, one in the stomach, and the other one got hit in the wrist.

Hezzy ran to Ten as he lay on the ground in blood.

Hezzy: "Oh shit! Shit! Shit! Ten, talk to me, Baby!!!"

Norwood's wife Serina came outside sayin' she got the make and tag of the car, a Pontiac 6000, and help is on the way.

Hezzy: "Don't die on me, man."

Pete stood over Hezzy in silence as Hezzy held Ten in his arms. Hezzy then pulled up Ten's shirt and saw that Ten wore his vest.

Hezzy: "Thank the Lord you wore your vest."

The blood was coming from Ten's arm. Ten was knocked out when he hit the ground and the bullets left serious chest pains. Ten opened his eyes.

Pete and Hezzy: "That's my nigga. You gonna make it. You gonna make it."

Seconds later the Pontiac 6000 crash into a nearby TCBY Ice Cream Shop 100 yards away. The driver was hurt bad. That's when the other two cops jump out the car and then pulled out their badge that was on a chain hanging around their neck inside of their sweatshirts yellin' for help. "We're cops! We're cops!" Minutes later sirens pierced the air. More cops and the paramedics was on the way.

Ten came to. Norwood took the fellows weapons for their safety. The souljas gave 'em up with no question asked. Minutes later cops, yellow tape, and reporters filled the street like wild fire. But when the smoke cleared, Ten, Hezzy, and Pete was at home on the phone talkin' with Jazzy Bell, Sky, and Chicago on the three way, watching the news. First on 5 News Chief Detective Ren Shockley got on TV and lied about what the witnesses told him what really happen.

Ren Shockley: "My officers followed the suspects to the motorcycle shop because of reasonable suspicion. They suspected the Hummer was stolen. When my officer checked it out, three armed men came out shooting at the officers. That's when my officers quickly drew their guns in response to the deadly situation."

Hezzy: "Y'all hear that shit! That nigga lying. The cops blast on us first."

Jazzy Bell: "Hezzy, where is Baller?"

Hezzy: "I don't know. He should have been back. He left with his cousin to get some weed. We ain't seen him since morning."

The News: "But witnesses say that the officers didn't identify themselves as policemen until after the fact. Store owner Norwood Jone and his mechanic Buck Forest said they thought that the motorcycle shop was being robbed so they came out blasting. They say if they would have knew, it was cops they were shooting at they wouldn't have let off one round. Norwood Jones also said that he didn't see a badge. Numerous other witnesses to the shooting also say that none of the officers wore identification. Employees at the TCBY Ice Cream Shop were surprised to learn that the injured men were police officers. They say if they would have known they were police officers they wouldn't have hesitated to help...'I'm certain I didn't see a badge.'"

More witnesses came saying the same thing.

Hezzy: "Damn right them fucks didn't look like cops."

Jazzy Bell: "Do you think it was a hit, Hezzy?"

Hezzy: "Naw, it wasn't a hit because the shit was sloppy. Me and the souljas getting up first thing in the morning lookin' for Baller if he don't call or come in."

Sky: "Keep us informed, and stay safe."

Chicago: "I'll look into this dirty cops situation."

Jazzy Bell: "Hezzy, I want you and the souljas to come over tomorrow so we can draw up some type of game plan on letterman."

Hezzy: "Bet."

And they all hung up the phone going crazy thinking about Baller throughout the night.

The next morning Chicago call Hezzy asking "has Baller made it in?"

Hezzy: "Hell naw."

Chicago: "Turn your TV on the news."

Hezzy: "What channel?"

Chicago: "Channel 5."

Hezzy turn on the news.

The News: "Just hours, a judge ordered an arrest warrant on the three officers, Crockett, Tubbs and Hurricane Smith. The judge said that the three police officers violated the rights of four people, one of whom was wounded. The police officers are charged with assault on four civilians, armed robbery, home invasion, and extortion scam. The GBI is doing a full investigation to clear the matter, because this incident has a lot of unanswered questions."

Hezzy: "Oh hell yeah! It's a beautiful thing, crooked bastards!

Chicago: "That is beautiful. So what time are you guys heading around Jazzy Bell's way?"

Hezzy: "This afternoon, after checking the local hot spots, where Baller sometimes kicks it."

Chicago: "Well, call me when y'all get over to Jazzy Bell's."

Hezzy: "I'll do dat." And they hung up the phones.

The souljas quickly got dress and dip. The search was on. Meanwhile, Baller was in his cell doing push ups when Ren Shockley came to his cell. Ren Shockley stood and watched him for a minute and said, "You can be doing come ups if you were out on the streets. Get cha mind right."

Baller: "My mind is right."

Ren Shockley told the guard to "take five, I got it." The guard walked off.

Ren Shockley: "You heard the news."

Baller: "Yeah, three more of your pussy ass cop friends are arrested, while my souljas roamin' the streets. It ain't nothing you can do to me and the family now. The feds are in town."

Ren Shockley: "Is that what you think? Is that what you really think?"

Baller: "Yeah."

Ren Shockley: "Kellogg Nickatina is gonna do the job his self, so keep your ears to the street."

Baller: "There you go with your imaginary friend. Kellogg Nickatina is a myth."

Ren Shockley: "You know after he do your family he's coming for you."

Baller: "I'll be waiting. I'll be waiting."

Ren Shockley walk off and Baller continue doing pushups. Baller called the guard to his cell when Ren Shockley got out of sound. Baller told the guard that he will give him 500 dollars to make a phone call for him. And the guard did it. But his souljas wasn't there. Baller then gave the guard Chicago's number and said, "Make it a gee." The guard told Baller, "Later on."

Hezzy and the souljas search and search while Jazzy Bell crew stack chips selling big ass break down dimes, rocks, and keys of raw uncut powder. They had lines longer than Kroger's grocery store on food stamp day. Before Fly Mar could clear the line, one more customer drove up in a green 1996 Lexus SC400 Spt Cpe SC dress in black leather with black loc's. The customer walk up to Fly Mar and ask for 5 thousand dollars in break downs.

Fly Mar: "I like that leather trench coat. Where did you

get it?"

The Customer: "I got it out at Southlake Mall, at Wilson's."

Fly Mar: "What's your name, potna?"

"It's Kellogg Nickatina, a friend of the game."

Fly Mar: "Okay Nickatina, wait right here."

Fly Mar went and came back with the rocks. When he reach out his hand to give Kellogg Nickatina the rocks, Nickatina grab Fly Mar by the hand tightly, pulling him toward him, then came out with his pistol shooting Fly Mar point blank range in the chest four times. Buck buck buck buck. That's when Jim Kelly, Big Mike, and Jazzy Bell went breaking windows, letting off shots pop-pop-pop-pop-pop...rat-tat-tat-tat-tat-tat-tat...Bang!   Bang! Bang!...click...click...click. Nickatina took off running toward his car. He crunk it up with his remote start key ring. The crew was certain they were hitting Kellogg Nickatina with bullets. But the bullets didn't faze Nickatina 'cause he was bulletproof and so was his car.

The crew ran outside to aid Fly Mar. He had chest pains, but he was all right because he was bulletproof also. Big Mike lifted Fly Mar into the house. Jim Kelly pick the drugs off the ground. Jazzy Bell took care of Fly Mar until Dr. Fox arrived.

Jazzy Bell: "Did he say who he was?"

With his chest still in pain, he spoke slowly. "Kellogg...Kellogg Nickatina."

Jim Kelly: "Who?"

Fly Mar: "Nickatina."

Dr. Fox: "He said Kellogg Nickatina, but it couldn't be. He died years and years ago."

Minutes later Hezzy and the souljas drove up, got out, and started picking empty shells off the ground. Big Mike met 'em at the door with his AK-47 in hand.

Ten: "Say, Big Baby, why the gun? Y'all been warring too?"

Big Mike: "Hell yeah. Y'all niggas come on in."

Pete: "What's going on?"

When the souljas enter the house they all spoke to each other.

Jim Kelly: "Yeah, man, some nigga name Nickatina came through here boldly like. Like he was some kind of super hero or something try to kill a nigga."

Jazzy Bell: "We better warn the family. Did y'all have any luck with Baller?"

Hezzy: "None."

Jazzy got on the phone giving Sky the news on what's going on. Meanwhile, Chicago was at home on the couch in her special made Ally McBeal pajamas reading How Stella Got Her Groove Back, a book by Terry McMillans. Then it was a knock at the door. Knock-knock-knock. She look out the window and saw a UPS truck outside her door. The phone started to ring. She look at the phone then the door, the phone, the door, the phone, the door.

Chicago: "Who is it?"

"It's UPS. Got a package here for a Miss Chicago."

Chicago: "Who it's from?" Chicago looking through the peep but couldn't see because of the package.

"It's from Dolce & Gabbana from Baller to Chicago."

With the phone still ringing, Chicago put the chain link lock across the door and crack it and saw that it was UPS. She told the UPS man to hold up while she answer the phone, but before she could close the door the distinguished UPS man who was really Kellogg Nickatina burst into the door. Chicago started to run. Nickatina let off three shots-- Buck Buck Buck--hitting Chicago in the back. She fell through the glass living room table. She was covered in glass and blood.

Kellogg walk over the broken glass and blood and pick the phone up off the floor.

Jazzy Bell on the other end: "Hello? Hello? Hello?"

Kellogg Nickatina: "You're too late."

He then laid the phone on top of Chicago and walk out the door. Everyone left Jazzy Bell place and rush over to Chicago's house. When they arrived at Chicago's house she was lying up on the couch in pain.

Chicago: "What kept y'all so long? Come help me, Doc, can't you see I'm bleeding?"

Dr. Fox got on his job.

Jazzy Bell: "What happen?"

The souljas search the house with gun in hand ready to blast on sight.

Chicago: "It was some bastard busted in here trying to kill me. He shot me three times in the back. Thank God for my bulletproof Ally McBeal pajamas."

Jazzy Bell: "Yes, thank God."

Dr. Fox patched up the few cuts Chicago suffered from the fall on the glass table.

Dr. Fox: "What did he look like?"

Chicago: "He's black, about 5' 11", 190 pounds, small 'fro. He look like Hezzy a li'l bit."

Fly Mar: "That's him! That's Kellogg Nickatina!"

Jazzy Bell got on the phone callin' Sky, telling her to get in touch with everyone and meet up over at Jade's safe house. Sky got on the phone giving the family the 411. The souljas help clean up the blood and broken glass while Chicago got ready. Baller was in his cell thinking of master plan that will kill three birds with one Love Jones. Baller call the guard to his cell.

The Guard: "What's up, man?"

Baller: "I need for you to make that call for me now, bro'."

The Guard: "I said later on."

Baller: "It's later on now, bro'."

The Guard: "All right. That's a gee you owe me."

Baller: "I got cha bro'."

The guard left to make the call. A minute later the guard came back with the same thing "I got no answer."

Baller: "Shit, shit, shit!"

His family had already left headed over to Jade's safe house. Just about when everyone got there they were talking about Kellogg Nickatina. Minutes later, Eazy and Pee Wee Loc walk in.

Hezzy: "Where y'all niggas been?"

Eazy: "Me and Li'l Loc had got with some li'l young stanks chicken head 'ho's, we kick it at the Omni Hotel, playboy style."

Hezzy: "Did you know Baller missing?"

Eazy: "Yeah. Went lookin' around for him, but did you know Cuddie dead?"

Hezzy: "What?"

Eazy: "Yeah, we stop by Flamingo. He told us about what happen to y'all with the police. The police have declared war on all the big ballers and local dealers. The cops are snatching up all their snitches, 'ho's and Donnie Brasco's and getting them to snitch out the bigger niggas."

Hezzy: "So what happen to Cuddie?"

Eazy: "Flamingo said that Cuddie crew sent him on a bogus mission for some gold Dayton rims."

Hezzy: "So you think that Cuddie crew had one or two Donnie Brasco's in his click?"

Eazy: "Had to. Flamingo said that when Cuddie li'l brother started screaming retaliation, the Powder Rangers wasn't even with it. And that's not like the Powder Rangers, 'cause when Cuddie screamed 'let's go get 'em' the Rangers was with it. You know that. Flamingo said the nigga car they were trying to steal was up all night waiting on Cuddie. Cuddie was in the nigga's car trying to pop the steering wheel collar. The Rangers was in the other ride waitin' for Cuddie. That's when the nigga who car it was came outside dumping bullets inside his car yelling, 'Die Nigga! Die!' and the Powder Rangers didn't let off one shot. They pull off leaving Cuddie to die."

Hezzy: "Damn! Local busta's."

Ten: "That's fuck up."

Li'l Loc: "So what's going on here?"

Jazzy: "Our crew was hit and the same fool that hit us tried to off Chicago."

Eazy and Loc: "You all right?"

Chicago: "I'm fine. We need to find Baller."

Precious: "Who did this?"

Fly Mar: "Some nigga name Kellogg Nickatina. Dr. Fox says he's a bogy."

Everyone look at Dr. Fox.

Chicago: "Doc, who is this Kellogg Nickatina?"

Dr. Fox: "He's evil. The evil of evil. When he was young he watch his crack fiend mother die. She was being raped by a other crack fiend. After the crack fiend took the sex, he started choking the life outta her. That's when Kellogg Nickatina took a broken bottle and cut the crack fiend across the neck, killing him. He die on top of his mother. A vicious drug dealer from the 'hood took him in and trained him like a Viking. The vicious drug dealer also put Nickatina in Law School so he will be street smart and book smart. In Law School he had dirt on everyone and right to this day he still do. He took his street smart and book smart to another level with lawyers, judges, and public defenders in his pocket he couldn't be stopped. He killed his guardian (the vicious drug dealer) and turn a billion dollars a year cocaine business into a zillion dollars a year operation serving the world. Kellogg Nickatina supposedly have died, but nobody really knows and no one ever seen him twice. An' if they did it's their life, 'cause with him it's your money or your life."

Mona Lisa: "So what we gonna do now?"

Hezzy: "I'll tell you what we gonna do. We go out and find Baller and eat that Nickatina for breakfast. Half of the souljas stay here in case Kellogg Nickatina come here and the other half will be on the hunt. Now, who's riding with me?"

Pete: "I'm riding, Dogg."

Eazy: "Me too."

Li'l Loc: "Me three."

Greed: "Let's go get 'em, Doggs!"

Big Mike, Sugar wolf, MJG, Jim Kelly, Ten, and Fly Mar watch over the divas while the rest of the souljas went to go pull off that 24 hour hoo-ride.

A day later Diamond and Big Six came back from their honeymoon. They were the most happiest couple in the world right now. When they got home it was sex, sex, sex and more sex. Just like in Paris while laying in bed Diamond look over at Big Six and said, "I think I'm pregnant," and when she said that it brought tears to Big Six's eyes. He took Diamond into his arms and embraced her telling her he love her even more and it would be a honor for him to be the father of her child. Diamond and Big Six's love was more, nothing fancy, just more. They hold each other for hours until they hear a noise.

They jump up. Big Six grab his gun. As they search the house, Diamond went to the window and guess what she saw? Naw, you wrong. It wasn't Elvis. It was 24 dozen of roses red, yellow, pink, and white. When seeing the roses, her eyes got bright, butterflies filled her belly.

Diamond: "Ooohh, look Honey Boo, flowers."

Big Six came and look as the florist TransWorld Delivery van pulls off. Big Six tuck his pistol in his trousers. They walk outside smelling and gathering the roses into the house.

Big Six: "Who they're from?"

Diamond took a card from one of the dozen of roses, open it, read it, and look up at Big Six and said, "Kellogg Nickatina."

Big Six reach at the card and said, "Kellogg Nickatina, who's that?"

That's when Kellogg Nickatina drove the FTD van straight through the front door. KABOOM!! Big Six push Diamond out of the way. Kellogg Nickatina jump out the van with gun in hand. Big Six reach into his trousers and him and Nickatina was face to face, toe to toe, gun to gun, dumping and pumping bullets at each other until both guns was empty. Bulletproof Nickatina watch as the body drop. Big Six hit the floor lookin' at Diamond. Just about out of his last breath he told Diamond that he love her.

Kellogg Nickatina gave Diamond a sidelong glance and slowly step into the van, back out the house, then left. Diamond held Big Six and grieve over his death hours before calling the Corporation. When the family left Jade's house to see about Diamond they were suprised that she was home so early. They didn't call the police until they all got there because the cops are not to be trusted. After the coroner pick up the body, they all left, headed out to another one of Jade's safe houses. The next day the Corporation was thinkin' what to do next. While Baller sat in his cell thinking.

An hour later Ren Shockley came to Baller cell.

Ren Shockley: "Hey boy, have ya got cha mind right?"

Baller: "Yeah, yeah, I got it right, Boss. You win. I'll join, I'll join the team, Boss."

Ren Shockley: "Now that's what I wanna hear. But for some reason I just don't think you got cha mind right."

Baller: "It's right, Boss, it's right. Just don't hurt my family."

Ren Shockley: "He wants to see you now. He'll be here at 4:16 p.m. tellin' you what's real."

Baller: "So can I make a call now, Boss?"

Ren Shockley: "Yeah. I'll tell the guard to let you use it."

Baller: "Thanks, Boss."

And Ren Shockley left. The guard let Baller use the phone. Baller call everywhere--no answer. Then he call over to Dr. Fox house and he wasn't there. But his wife gave Baller the number to where he was. Baller call the house and Mona Lisa pick up the phone.

Mona Lisa: "Hello."

Baller: "Thank God! Hello. What's up? Who's this?"

Mona Lisa started yellin' "It's Baller! It's Baller!" Everyone ran to the phone.

Mona Lisa: "What's up Baller? Where you at?"

Baller: "Lock down, Baby."

Mona Lisa: "He say he's lock down."

Hezzy: "Ask him what happen."

Mona Lisa: "Hezzy said what happen?"

"Tell 'em my cousin set me up."

Mona Lisa: "He say his cousin set him up."

Ten: "What I tell you about that nigga."

Hezzy: "Let me talk with him."

She hand Hezzy the phone.

Hezzy: "One love playboy."

Baller: "One love Baby Boy."

Hezzy: "What's going on, man?"

Baller: "The cops are declaring war."

Hezzy: "I know, but why?"

Baller: "Money shortage. And that Chief Detective Ren Shockley been pressuring me to join some team that's ran by some bogy name Kellogg Nickatina. I play Cool Hand Luke on his ass so they would let me use the phone. So what's been going on?"

Hezzy: "Baller, that nigga Kellogg Nickatina is real. He try to kill Fly Mar, Chicago, and Diamond. He miss her but he killed Big Six."

Baller: "Damn. That's sad to hear."

Hezzy: "Yeah, and guess what."

Baller: "What?"

Hezzy: "Cuddie dead."

Baller: "Yeah, I heard about that, and them pussy ass nigga left him alone."

Hezzy: "How you hear that?"

Baller: "Shi-i-id, you know nigga hear shit in here before it hit the street."

Hezzy: "What you want us to do 'bout that 'ho' blooded nigga Razor? Just say it and it's done."

Baller: "Be cool, Baby Boy. I got something cooking. You all right?"

Hezzy: "Yeah, man, just worried about ya. Shi-i-i-id, we all was worried."

Baller: "I feel ya, Baby Boy. Let me talk with Chicago."

Hezzy put Chicago on the phone.

Chicago: "Hello."

Baller: "You all right?"

Chicago: "Oh yeah."

Baller: "It's time. Code Six. I can't say what I want, this phone may be funny. Code Six. Ace in the Crack, you got it?"

Chicago: "I got it."

Baller: "Now let me talk with Dr. Fox."

Chicago: "Doc--phone."

Dr. Fox: "Hey now."

Baller: "What's up, Doc?"

Dr. Fox: "You had us all worried."

Baller: "Yeah, Code Six, Doc. Now this Kellogg Nickatina supposed to come see me at 4:16 p.m. running down what he want it to be. Now, how long would it take you to dress up like the Demolition Man?"

Dr. Fox: "An hour."

Baller: "Good."

The guard came over tellin' Baller, "Hey, don't forget that gee you owe me, and time's up."

Baller: "Bring some money. I got a score to settle. Tell the family I'll be home soon. Later."

Dr. Fox: "Later."

They hung up the phone and Baller went to his cell. Time 2:16 p.m. Dr. Fox started cookin' up plastic 34 while Chicago got in touch with the Corporation Ace in the Crack. 2 hours later a slow motion moment walking down the clear hallway to Baller cell came Kellogg Nickatina in his all black leather fit. When Kellogg Nickatina step to Baller cell, Baller stood up. Kellogg Nickatina open up the cell door and step in. They look at each other for about a minute before speaking.

Baller: "So you're Kellogg Nickatina."

Kellogg Nickatina: "Yeah, and you're the infamous Baller."

Baller: "All the time. So what you want, man?"

Kellogg Nickatina: "First of all, I don't want nothing. You owe me. When you killed Milk you choke my money.

Milk left this world owing me 10 million dollars and since he didn't pay me my money 'cause you took him out, you owe his debt to me. Double, 20 million dollars, now. If that's too much let me know, 'cause I hate to kill you."

Baller: "That's cool, that's cool. But one thing."

Kellogg: "What's that?"

"I want to fix my cousin for setting me up."

Kellogg Nickatina: "You talkin' about Razor?"

Baller: "Yeah, how you know?"

Kellogg Nickatina: "Shi-i-i-id, I'm God. I like Razor with his dirty sorry ass. You know, a sorry ass nigga make a good dirty ass back stabbin' hating ass nigga."

Baller: "Yeah, I know. I want him right here."

Kellogg Nickatina got out his cell phone and called up Ren Shockley, tellin' him to pick up Razor and put a case over his head, a felony, and to call when it's done.

Kellogg Nickatina: "Anything else?"

Baller: "Naw. I just want to get out when he's going in, so let's just wait on that call."

They waited. Meanwhile, Ren Shockly went to go get Razor, riding out with Officer Tucci.

Ren Shockley: "Tucci, I'm gonna run it to ya straight. I take money from drug dealers. Big money from big dealers."

Officer Tucci: "Why you tellin' me this?"

Ren Shockley: "'Cause I want you to get down with me. You can be my lieutenant. My next in command. Look, these dealers got money to burn. Have you ever took money?"

Officer Tucci: "Oh no, that's wrong, right?"

Ren Shockley: "It's wrong when you get caught. Just think, cops get paid 16 to 23 thousand a year. That's nothing! Chump change. You get with these big dealers like me and you can be making TRUMP change. You FEEL me?"

Officer Tucci: "I got you."

Ren Shockley: "Yeah, that's what I wanna hear, so you down."

Officer Tucci: "I'm with it. So where we're headed?"

Ren Shockley: "I got to pick up my li'l Donnie Brasco, lock him down for awhile before he get himself killed. See, we're gonna sit back and let smaller dealers get bigger. The more bigger they are, the more street soldiers they recruit. We then free our Donnie Brasco's from prison, giving them an alibi. They then hang around the bigger dealer set until he's recruited. The Donnie Brasco's then bring us the info we need to bring down the bigger dealer or to get paid off by the bigger dealer. Now is you with me?"

Officer Tucci: "I got you."

Minutes later they pull up at the spot where Razor was hiding out. When Ren Shockley and Officer Tucci walk in the house, Razor was smokin' on a woo joint (a coke joint) with his finger on the trigger. Razor was suffering from paranoia.

Ren Shockley: "Give me the gun, son, give me the gun."

Razor slowly gave Ren Shockley the pistol. Ren Shockley hug Razor around his neck and told him that he gotta go to jail.

Razor: "No! No! Hell naw!"

Ren Shockley: "Wait! Wait! Just cool down now! Your cousin Baller is getting out of jail and he's mad at you for setting him up."

Razor: "But you told me to."

Ren Shockley: "Yes, yes. That's why I'm helping you, getting you off the streets."

Razor: "Okay, okay."

Razor took off and jumped out the window trying to get

away, but the fall slowed him down. He was hurt.

Ren Shockley: "What's wrong with you, fool? Didn't I tell you I'm helping you?"

Razor: "Yeah, man, it's just I don't know what to think no more. I'm sorry."

Ren Shockley: "I'm sorry for ya. Now let's go."

They left, headed toward jail. Ren Shockley call Kellogg Nickatina tellin' him that they have their man and that they are bringing him in.

Kellogg Nickatina: "They have him and he will be in soon."

Baller: "Yeah, I like that. So when I'm going to be free from all charges?"

Kellogg Nickatina: "You're already free, you been free."

Baller: "What about all those other charges on there?"

Kellogg Nickatina: "That was somebody else, not you. We just wag the dog and pay off some folks. There is no charges. You're free."

Baller: "All because of you, right?"

Kellogg Nickatina: "Yes."

Baller: "Well Gott damn the man."

Officer Tucci: "Could you pull over in one of those alleys? I got to take a leak."

Ren Shockley: "It's a restaurant about a half mile away."

Officer Tucci: "I have to use it bad, like right now."

Ren Shockley pull over in an alley. Officer Tucci got out and drain his thang. He got back in the car.

Ren Shockley: "You feel better now?"

Officer Tucci look at Ren Shockley and said, "I got you, babe...I got you, babe...I got you, babe."

Ren Shockley gave Officer Tucci a strange look. That when Officer Tucci dump eight bullets into Ren Shockley's body. Bang-bang-bang-bang-bang-bang-bang-bang. Then he looked back at Razor and said, "You killed my partner."

Razor: "Naw I didn't, naw I didn't, naw I didn't."

Officer Tucci got out the car and open up the back doo
telling Razor to run. "Run, Fool! Get somewhere!" Razo
wasn't nobody's fool.

Razor: "I killed your partner. Take me in. I killed you
partner."

Officer Tucci: "That's good. Now let's go."

Officer Tucci shut the door and called it in and took
Razor's ass to jail with the charges Baller had. Kellogg
Nickatina told Baller that he had to go and gave the guard
permission to let Baller go when his ride come. Anothe
slow motion moment as Kellogg Nickatina walk down the
hallway. Dr. Fox walk pass him without looking in his
direction. Dr. Fox got to Baller cell and they showed each
other love.

Dr. Fox: "Was that him?"

Baller: "Yeah."

Dr. Fox: "So the myth is true."

Baller: "Hell, yeah. Is everything in place?"

Dr. Fox: "As soon as he starts it up."

Before Dr. Fox could say more, KABOOM!!! Dr. Fo
look at Baller and said, "Bingo." Baller just started laughing
as him and Dr. Fox made their way out the cell. Dr. Fo
paid the guard. When Dr. Fox and Baller walk out the jail
house Officer Tucci was bringing Razor in. Baller look a
Razor and started singing to Razor, "I never let a hoooo
pimp meeee."

As Razor went to jail, Baller and Dr. Fox watch Kellogg
Nickatina and his Lexus go up in smoke and they left.

Months later the Corporation and everyone who is affili-
ated with the Corporation was at Chicago's Christmas ball
kicking it like huge playas. Diamond was still a li'l sadden,

but she'll get over it. Besides, she inherited everything Big Six own (billions) somewhere in Georgia. Jade bought some land six times bigger than the world's largest golf course and she got the family to invest in it. They all put billions together and invested in a 10 billion dollar amusement park, bigger and better than Six Flags with four Five Star hotels with a casino in each one. It was the Corporation's idea to turn Georgia into Baby Vegas. It's gonna take four years to build, so in the year 2000 Atlanta is gonna sho' 'nuff be crunk.

Hezzy's openin' up one of the biggest record stores in Atlanta, Cry Now Laugh Later, and it has some of the best underground goups in Rap and R&B. It was just like old times. The Corporation has always exchanged gifts on Christmas Day when things are going well.

When everyone has received their gifts they started back mingling (having fun). Baller and Hezzy walked out on the terrace having a drink talking.

Baller: "Well, Baby Boy, look like we did it."

Hezzy: "We did do it. We can do anything in this world we wanna do now."

Baller: "Shi-i-i-id, we been doin' that. Ha ha ha ha." They both laugh.

Hezzy: "What you got right there?"

Baller: "It a gift someone in the family had for me."

Hezzy: "Well damn, it sho' ain't from me. I got you a shoe box full of hundred dollar bills with the Big Faces."

Baller: "Damn, Baby Boy, I got you the same thang."

Hezzy: "You know we always thought alike."

Baller: "That's what blood brother do."

Baller open the gift laughing, sayin' "oh shit!"

Hezzy: "What you got?"

Baller: "Somebody done got me a Lexus."

Baller hand hezzy the Lexus key while he opened the

Christmas card.

Hezzy: "Who it's from?! What it say?!"

Baller and Hezzy smiling in suspense. Baller open the card and just look at Hezzy.

Hezzy: "What it say?!"

Baller with a surprised look on his face.

Baller: "It say, I still know. I still know what you did last summer. I'll be back."

Right then Baller knew that troubled times lay ahead.

Game Over...

...For Now.

The Ten Crack Commandments

1. Never let anyone know how much loot you got because your niggas around you will scheme and plot.

2. Never let anyone know your next move. Now days you got Baller Blocking Niggas (Haters) they can counter on it and beat you to your own plan.

3. Trust no one.
   Your Brother
   Your Sister
   Your Dad
   And Your Mom will set that ass up if the price is right.

4. Never get high off your own supply. I don't care if it is weed, crack, that girl (powder), that boy (heroin) or what thats hustling backwards.

5. Never give credit. A geek monster don't give a fuck about you, just that next high.

6. Never sell where you lay your head. There's no better way to incriminate yourself.

7. Keep family and business separate. Because family can sometimes be your worst enemy.

8. Never pack your stash on your person. There gotta be a safer place. Fuck over your girl house, get you a soulja they will die for your shit.

9. If you're not being arrested, never be seen communicating with the po po's (the police). Every nigga that do crime will turn on you.

10. Consignment. Giving your niggas some work (cocaine) so they can come up and get their shine on-after they pay you.

   Kids, just say no to drugs, this means you too!!!

DRUGS ARE BAD IN EVERY WAY.

Coming Soon From
Georgia Gorilla Publishing...

Wages of Sin (Time'z Up)
The Writer
King of the Slam
The © Files (Ghetto Poetry)
Wig Spliters & One Time (Hot Boyz & Crooked Cops)

Also Watch for the Soon to be Released Soundtrack for
Hypnotizing Game

Numbers to be call if you need help

Rape Crisis Center
(404)616-4861 (Grady Hospital)

Missing Children Information
Clearing House (888)356-4774

Georgia Help Line
(800)338-6745

Drug Helpline
(800)DrugHelp (378-4435)

Battered Women's Shelter
(770)969-6423 (Fulton County)

Battered Woman Domestic
Violence Hotline
(800)33-HAVEN (42836)

Chid Abuse & Neglect Reports
(404)699-4399 (Fulton County)